KRISTIN JACQUES

a Draught of Ash and Wine

CITY OWL
PRESS

A DRAUGHT OF ASH AND WINE
Midnight Guardians, Book 2

CITY OWL PRESS
www.cityowlpress.com

Illustrations by Yorugami. Cover Design by MiblArt. All stock photos licensed appropriately.

Edited by Danielle DeVor.

For information on subsidiary rights, please contact the publisher at info@cityowlpress.com.

Print Edition ISBN: 978-1-64898-285-9

Digital Edition ISBN: 978-1-64898-286-6

Printed in the United States of America

To dad.
It can be so scary supporting creative paths.
I am so very grateful for every moment you chose to lift me up.

PRAISE FOR THE WORKS OF KRISTIN JACQUES

"Jacques has a talent for pacing that feels effortless, and moves the story along with snappy dialogue, adorable flirting, and winning found-family relationships. This delightful romp, *A Bargain of Blood and Gold*, is sure to appeal to fans of Cat Sebastian and Gail Carriger."
— *Publisher's Weekly*

"Jacques does a wondrous job crafting a world rich with creatures lurking among the shadows... If you love vampires, detective work, mysterious creatures, and a little romance this book, *A Bargain of Blood and Gold*, is for you! I can't wait for the next one!"
— *Jessica Julien, YA Fantasy Author*

"In a moment when words are greatly needed, I am at a loss to properly articulate the captivating read, *Marrow Charm*, was for me. The author writes fluently and effortlessly bringing scenes and characters to life in your mind."
— *Permanently Booked*

"I fell in love with the characters within the first few pages of *Ragnarok Unwound*, and the story had me hooked by the end of chapter one. This is one of those books where I didn't want to finish it because I didn't want it to be over."
— *The Paper Valley*

"*Zombies vs Aliens* is a fabulous mix of rollicking romp through zombie-land, action, and adventure that is pure entertainment."
— *Leigh W. Stuart, Contemporary Romance Author*

CHAPTER ONE

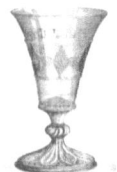

JOHNATHAN NEWMAN WAS ABOUT TO BURST OUT OF HIS SKIN.

This was a literal problem for him now. As he sat, muscles wound tighter than a coiled spring, he feared for the safety of the sleeping passengers around him. Heat surged through his veins, searching for release, for a hint of weakness. He grasped for a mental anchor, focusing on the uneven clank of the train over the tracks. The car swayed and bumped along, the regular irregularity of the movement lulling the exhausted passengers around him into a fitful slumber. The motion did little to quell the uneasiness knotted between Johnathan's shoulders, his forced calm fleeing from the internal reach of fire.

His knees jogged up in down in a rabbit rapid rhythm, matching the tap of his fingertips along the hard edges of his seat. Shallow breaths fanned the air, a shimmer of heat escaping from his parted lips that sent a jolt of alarm down his spine. Taking a deep breath would be worse, akin to an assault of his new sharper senses. He fought hard to ignore the varied scents clogging the air, vicious as a hornet swarm stinging his nose. Where the hell was Vic?

Had he really expected to get a handle on his new condition in a matter of days? Johnathan was a fool. The thought made him wince, fingers tightening briefly on the edge of his seat until the wood whined in his grip. 'Condition' made it sound far less life altering than the truth. He peered out the window, trying to evade the direction of his thoughts. Outside the half-shuttered window, the train slithered through the surrounding forest like some great metal serpent, drenched in the shades of night. The vibration of the tracks shivered up through the soles of his boots. Cress Haven and the possibility of his former life catching up to them were now separated by time and distance. Vic's boundless charm kept most unwanted attention off them, and when that failed, a touch of vampiric glamour made their departure far smoother than Johnathan could have hoped.

But being surrounded by a train full of people for hours pulled at him. A reaction, Johnathan was loathe to admit, that he should have expected from a lifetime of chasing monsters driven by innate appetites.

Though, if pressed, Johnathan wasn't sure what he hungered for. Flames were the crux of his waking thoughts, burning through his dreams. He didn't know why the fire licked at the underside of his skin with increasing urgency.

What he did know, with each slow, crawling mile, was he had left his humanity far behind.

The path of his thoughts wove inward, caving to his newest obsession: scrutinizing the differences. The gloves on his hands chafed against too sensitive skin, too hot and sweat slick, the press of his thicker, sharper nails strained against the leather at the tip of each finger. He couldn't call them claws, not yet. Giving voice to the term, even in the privacy of his mind, made it too real. If he stared at his gloved hands long enough, he suspected steam would escape through the seams.

Worse were the glasses, the heavy, wide frames butted against the bones of his eye socket, creating a tunneled view, while the lenses further muted colors. They didn't affect the clarity of his vision, but they obscured a discomfiting amount of his peripheral view. He didn't dare take them off.

His gaze flicked to the artificial darkness framing his world, worrying at it the same way his tongue touched the new fine edges of his teeth. Too many changes, too much sharpness and heat. A betrayal of his body that he dwelled on in those quiet moments when his only company was the tangled mess of his thoughts. A preoccupation that distracted from the knot of frustration, hurt, and rage of that night.

Stop. Johnathan inhaled a sharp breath through his nose before he could stop himself. The sharp tang of greasy hot metal surrounded him, threaded with sweat, body odor, stale syrupy sweet perfume, pungent tobacco smoke, hints of boiled mutton, meal flour, and a dozen other scraps he couldn't identify. A condensed wallop of scents, strong enough to make his head spin. The sense of smell was the biggest change, one he hadn't adjusted to in any capacity. There was no time to adjust. Johnathan didn't want to adjust. *He shouldn't be here. A wolf among sheep. A monster. He should have died.*

Johnathan fought to rein that thought in. He'd made his choice, limited as it was. Easier to ignore the unwelcome thoughts when he had a distraction. Unfortunately, his favorite distraction currently argued with the porter about their current accommodations.

Despite Johnathan's intention to avoid complications, Vic noticed his unease, suggesting they sequester themselves in one of the compartments of the sleeper car. An accommodation Johnathan stubbornly argued unnecessary, but Vic merely raised a brow until the back of Johnathan's neck grew hot. The private luxury of a sleeper compartment had been above his means in his former life, but that wasn't what sent a flush to the roots of his hair. He could practically hear Vic's smooth voice whispering in his ear. *Come now, Johnathan, we can think of something to occupy ourselves.* Their destination was hours away and while the idea of sharing a sleeper car with Vic was thrilling, it added another layer to his anxiety.

It wasn't that Johnathan didn't want to be alone with Vic in close quarters because he did, very much, but the heat clawing inside him soured the mood. He silently begged for Vic's return, clenching his jaw hard enough that his pulse throbbed inside his head. This went beyond his limited grasp of his new state, an intangible sense that had gained on him since Vic left him alone.

A feeling Johnathan couldn't voice, though it curdled in his stomach, akin to dread. It crawled between the knot in his shoulder blades, twining around that vise of nervous energy inside him, a constricting coil incensing his panic. Johnathan jerked around, staring into the faces of the sleeping passengers, searching for the source yet unable to pinpoint it. Frustration pricked at him.

The door to the passenger car slid open, and for a moment, at the sight of that smug, far too charming grin, the dread and anxiety vanished. Vic flowed down the aisle, moving across their shifting conveyance with a dancer's grace. Even through the dark lenses of Johnathan's glasses, Vic remained vibrant. The deep auburn red tint of his hair was threaded with moonlit bronze, loose from its usual queue to curl around his angular face. Mischief shone in his bright silver-grey eyes, snaring Johnathan's full attention. It wasn't until Vic's long fingers curled over the top of his seat that Johnathan remembered to breathe again. The now intrinsic scent of Vic washed over him, dominating the tangle of other scents surrounding him. A wild scent of deep dark woods, threaded with hints of citrus and gentle wildflowers that was a balm to Johnathan's taut nerves. The overwhelming desire to bury his face in the crook of Vic's neck and let the rest of the world melt away rocked him.

"I've emerged victorious," said Vic, tilting his head. "Of a sort. Come, let us celebrate the fruits of my labor."

"Of a sort? You were gone nearly an hour," said Johnathan, his tone piqued. Fifty-two minutes to be exact. Far longer than he'd expected. Johnathan raised his brows, refusing to let his companion see the depth of his relief. Vic's smile consistently threw him off balance. He didn't think he would ever regain his equilibrium around the other man.

"Took a fair bit more negotiating than anticipated, but I think it will be worth the effort," said Vic.

Johnathan's lips twitched. "Couldn't you compel your way in?"

"Johnathan, how scandalous." Vic pressed a hand to his chest in mock indignation. "It so happens the sleeping car is full up and rather than compel some unfortunate soul out of their well-earned rest, I sought out a suitable substitution." His leaned down, his spicy scent wrapping around Johnathan as Vic reached for his hands. "A little nook for just you and me."

Johnathan's pulse spiked and with Vic's fingers circling his wrists; it was clear by the man's knowing grin he noticed. The anxious heat, however, remained persistent, intruding on Johnathan's more amorous thoughts. Vic's good humor dimmed, a crease marring the smooth skin between his brows when he noticed Johnathan's demeanor.

"Come on, John, let's get you out of here." Vic's thumb smoothed over the back of his gloved hands, shifting his grip to lace their fingers together.

A tug got Johnathan up from his seat, his thoughts tumbling together where unease clashed with desire. There hadn't been time for privacy since their flight from Cress Haven, their train bound journey punctuated by absent touches and longing glances that made him equal parts flustered and nervous. Was it only two days ago he'd courted death and damnation? Barely confirmed his burgeoning feelings for Vic before his world shattered.

Johnathan still hadn't processed he was here, alive, and while he'd established a fair level of trust with Vic through their shared trials, he couldn't ignore the dismaying gaps in his knowledge regarding his companion. An unequal knowledge, where Vic possessed most of Johnathan's secrets after their encounter with the Morrigan. He hadn't lived long enough to accumulate many. Vic had lived through centuries.

At the rear of the car, the same niggling sensation distracted him. Johnathan stopped short and glanced over his shoulder. A final futile search, his senses clipped by the infernal goggles. He shook it off, letting Vic lead him into the gap between cars, the rushing wind a welcome relief on his heated face. Following Vic through another car half full of dozing passengers, the mire of Johnathan's thoughts continued to tangle in on itself. He was a ball of anxious energy by the time Vic guided him through the sleeper car to the far rear of the train, holding the door open for Johnathan with a flourish.

Their suitable substitution was the luggage car. The luggage was stacked in tall, tight columns against the walls to make room for a thin mattress, hopefully a spare from the sleeping car, covered in clean sheets.

"How quaint," said Johnathan, attempting to keep his tone neutral though a note of disappointment must have slipped through. He couldn't miss an experience he never had. The luggage car was probably a safer space for him to be if his tenuous control snapped.

"So quick to judge. Get a feel for it first," said Vic. Johnathan bit down on the grin that teased his mouth and ducked through the door.

The floor around the mattress was swept and laid with sprigs of fresh herbs. Johnathan took a cautious whiff, surprised by the earthy scent of fresh sage that overpowered everything else without blowing out his olfactory senses.

"Where did you get fresh sage?" Johnathan took a deep breath, relishing the herbaceous air. The constant press of fire beneath the skin slackened.

"A gentleman's agreement between myself and a compliant tradesman," said Vic with a secretive grin.

"How did you know it would help?" Johnathan turned to face him, unable to glance at him sideways due to the limiting goggles.

"You forget, my dear Johnathan, you aren't the only one with heightened senses," said Vic. He tugged Johnathan down onto the mattress. "Not as grand as a sleeping compartment, but I think we'll make do."

"More than adequate," said Johnathan, his throat gone dry. The mattress pad sank under his weight, betraying the hard wood beneath. Johnathan crawled across it and sat on the far side to remove his shoes, embarrassed he forgot to do so before clambering over the clean sheets. Immediately, he tugged his laces into a gordian knot. Johnathan clenched his teeth, resisting the urge to rip apart his only pair of boots. He reached deep into his exhausted well of patience to untangle them. Vic ceased his frantic hands with a touch, flicking the knots apart to slide off Johnathan's boots which he carelessly tossed to the end of the mattress.

"Now that we're alone, let's have these off," said Vic, his voice a touch deeper, roughened by his evident desire. A shiver of anticipation rolled through Johnathan's chest, shifting to confusion when Vic reached for his face. Vic gently tugged the glasses off, tucking them into Johnathan's coat pocket.

"There," Vic murmured. "Much better."

"Oh." Johnathan blushed. Color and light rushed back in, a physical release accumulating to exposure. The world was no longer shuttered, and it was filled with Vic. That knowledge crashed into Johnathan and he surged forward, his gloved hands threading through Vic's hair as he sought lips he knew were soft and full.

He could be bold when it came to kisses, confident he possessed enough skill to keep Vic on his toes. Johnathan swallowed Vic's surprise, tasting the seam of his mouth. Vic opened for him. Johnathan accepted the invitation, tentatively exploring until his tongue flicked one of Vic's fangs. A groan poured into his mouth. Vic wrested control, peeling off Johnathan's coat and pushing him down onto the mattress. Vic's long fingers stroked up Johnathan's side, sliding under his shirt to skim a cool touch over his overheated skin.

Johnathan sucked in a breath, his muscles flexing in anticipation. Were they doing this? They were really doing this. Was he ready for this? What was *this?* "I've—I've never done this before." A flush flared up his neck, across his cheeks, rankled by his inexperience.

Vic's brow cocked up. "Done what exactly?" His fingers continued their upward path, lifting Johnathan's shirt. "Hmmmm?" He shifted, straddling Johnathan's legs. Bending down, Vic pressed his lips to Johnathan's throat while a free hand traced the muscles of his stomach in an agonizing downward progression.

"What—" Johnathan wheezed, cut off when Vic licked along his pulse point. "What I assume we are doing?" he managed, embarrassed by the high note in his voice. Vic's hand slid further down, its destination unmistakable. Johnathan didn't realize he held his breath until that hand paused at his waist, his breath leaving him in a rush when Vic's fingers splayed over his belly.

"Oh, what are we doing then?" Vic's tongue gave a lick up the side of his neck, a teasing lilt in his voice.

"This?" Johnathan bit back a noise when Vic deftly unfastened his pants. Another pause that made him want to yell.

"Say the words, John," said Vic. His hand crept lower.

"Intimate relations," Johnathan bit out, straining to keep still. Vic snorted, and dropped his head to Johnathan's shoulders, attempting to muffle his lost composure. His hand moved away to brace on the mattress as he threw back his head for a full-throated laugh.

"Damn cock-tease." Johnathan flopped back down with a huff,

throwing an arm over his face to cover his pronounced blush. Vic pinched his chin.

"No, don't look away," said Vic. Johnathan peeked out from under his arm. Vic's merry grin eased some of his embarrassment. "I'm sorry, John. I didn't mean to laugh, but you are just—" He bit his lip, giving a glimpse of fang while his gaze slid over Johnathan like a physical caress. Not so long ago, the sight of teeth would have made him nervous, and they still did, for an entirely different reason. "We'll work on your pillow talk. Though that blush does terrible things to my self-control."

The words made him blush harder. He wasn't the former monk in this relationship, though he might as well be compared to Vic's history of conquests. Nor had his companion let the austerity of his surroundings deter him from relations while human. "I'm sorry."

"Don't you dare apologize," said Vic, sitting up, his hands on Johnathan's chest. His expression turned thoughtful. "I haven't enjoyed myself this much in ages."

Johnathan frowned at him. This sentiment he didn't understand. The man left behind his home and dearest friend for a bond newly formed and barely understood between them, one Johnathan clung to with disconcerting ferocity. "You're on the run because of me."

"That's half the fun." Vic's eyes were silvered in the dim space of the luggage car; the forest choked moonlight cast striated shadows across the ceiling. Johnathan stared up at him. This new form also still adjusted to Vic. Johnathan could see far better in the dark, akin to the night creatures he'd been trained to hunt. To his new vision, Vic's pale skin held a barely perceptible pearly luminescence, an otherworldly hue he never noticed while he still human. Tangled strands of auburn hair haloed Vic's face, evidence of Johnathan's touch. The sight sent heat pooling southward. Delighted wonder lit Vic's expression.

"Your eyes are glowing," said Vic.

The words were a bucket of icy water, dampening his ardor so fast Johnathan cringed away from him.

"John?" Vic grabbed his shoulders. "Oh god, John, what is it?"

Hide, that's what he wanted to do. He wanted to curl into a ball, bury his face in the bedding. The reminder of his inhumanity thrummed beneath his skin, the lick of flame that soured the pleasant sensations Vic caused only moments ago. The urge to hide was so strong he turned on his side, dislodging Vic from his position, but he didn't cover his face. He simply couldn't, torn between his desire and his shame to be seen, his expression stricken.

"John, please talk to me?" Vic pleaded. "You were right here with me. Where did you go?"

Johnathan swallowed hard, his clothes suddenly too tight, the fabric straining between his hunched shoulders. His hands closed into fists, the tips of his *claws* pricking through the leather. Unease flushed through him. "I'm sorry," he rasped, trying to give voice to his discomfort. "I just —I'm not—"

Not human anymore. The words stuck in his throat. How could he say something like to Vic, who hadn't been human in centuries? Except, Johnathan's rather violent transition was fresh, one he'd far from acclimated to, or the grim bloody future it entailed. A future they hadn't discussed. Nor had they discussed the perils of their present, including the possibility of their pursuit. Johnathan had no idea how deep Dr. Evans' machinations within the Society ran. They might have avoided direct contact with his former comrades, but that didn't mean they weren't being hunted. It was a matter of not if but when the Society caught up to him.

The biggest unspoken question was *how* Johnathan remained on the earthen plane. There was now a creature lurking inside him, one that posed a growing threat he gauged by the heat raging inside him. His body may be human for now, but how long would that last? The demon who created him had returned to the Nether, possibly dead, though Johnathan very much doubted that was the case. If the creature broke free, there was only one method he knew to return to human form and the truth made his stomach roll.

"Johnathan, look at me."

He turned, need overshadowing his shame. Vic kneeled over him, far closer than he expected.

"You're still you," said Vic, cupping his jaw. He brushed his lips over Johnathan's brow.

"How can you be so sure?" Johnathan caught his wrist, craving the contact though his doubts continued to spiral. "We haven't known each other that long."

Vic pursed his lips. "Are you no longer Johnathan Newman, annoyingly stubborn Prospective of the Society?"

"Ex-Prospective," muttered Johnathan. "I'd doubt they'd take me back now."

Vic tugged out of his hold, dropping his hands to his thighs. "Would you want them to?" He stared at Johnathan with an unreadable expression.

"God, no," said Johnathan, with more vehemence than he intended. His final encounter with his former mentor churned a deep well of guilt and rage, not something he wanted to explore in current company. The Society would either kill him, or Dr. Evans' remaining subordinates would attempt to subdue him again, a shuddersome fate. He sat up with a sigh, scrubbing his face. "I've ruined your amorous intentions, haven't I?"

That distant expression disappeared in a leer. Vic leaned forward, a gleam in his eye. "You most certainly have not."

The train jolted, the squeal of metal sliding along metal a painful stab in Johnathan's sensitive ears. Gritting his teeth, he clasped the sides of his head. The violent rocking nearly toppled Vic, who braced himself on the floor, an incredulous look on his face when the train came to grinding stop.

"That might put a damper on my amorous intentions," said Vic.

Johnathan wanted to answer him, but the sense of dread he'd left behind in the passenger car smothered him. "Do you smell that?" A sharp, acrid scent swamped his senses. Johnathan sneezed, the scent coating the inside of his mouth until he gagged.

"Smell what?" Vic frowned, nostrils flaring as he sniffed the air. "I don't smell anything, aside from a few humans in desperate need of a bath."

Johnathan barely heard him, muscles pulled taut. The heat doubled in his chest, sizzling through his veins. He exhaled, a faint curl of smoke rising from his mouth. "Something's here."

Vic's jaw tightened. "Can you describe what you're sensing, John?"

The question grounded him, somewhat. Johnathan tried to internally map the terrible dread. "I don't know," he admitted, uncertain the sensation was quantifiable. He lifted his nose, forcing himself to reach through the pleasant cover of sage. Old sweat, cooling metal, coal smoke, perfume, tobacco smoke, a faint influx of smells the human Johnathan never picked up on. Trying to solve a puzzle with a tool he'd never used before, he plucked away the layers he recognized until one gave him pause. "I smell gun powder."

The perplexed expression on Vic's face now mirrored his own. "There are a lot of persons who carry a gun for many reasons." Vic rolled his lower lip, a telling fidget. "It would be best if you stay here. I'm going to scout the train." Vic rolled away from him, giving Johnathan a pointed look before he donned his shoes and left.

A simple request, to stay put, and one he loathed to follow. Johnathan's knees began to bounce once more, unable to keep still beneath his mounting worries and suspicions. Their train had stopped two or three times to onboard passengers, only one of those stops long enough and close enough to his former home base in Boston for possible pursuit.

The Society couldn't have caught their trail that fast. Could they? Dr. Evans' entire team was demolished in that clearing. Except...Johnathan knew how the Society operated, or at least he thought he did. Whatever plan his former mentor had in play, it wouldn't be confined to the unfortunate souls who accompanied him to Cress Haven. Not with that many Agents present. It would normally take weeks to mobilize a full response, but what if there were more waiting for action, in case things went wrong? What if his entire chapter house was aware of Dr. Evans' plan? Embittered by the idea, Johnathan stood up and paced the strip of cleared floor beside the mattress, pondering his life and the keen sense of isolation that remained. Aside from Dr. Evans, his ties to his fellow Prospectives were, generously said, superficial. His life in the Society hadn't been a pleasant one, but now Johnathan was adrift, a newborn monster without a purpose, with Vic providing his only tether to the world.

Vic hadn't ordered him to stay, yet Johnathan automatically listened. Vic wasn't a superior officer or an Agent who out ranked him. Johnathan sneered at himself, disgusted by his blind Prospective's obedience, and yanked open the door. He poked his head into the proceeding passenger car. There was no sign of Vic, the car eerily silent. Closing the door, he stifled the urge to continue pacing like a caged wolf since there was scant room for such an activity. He had to trust Vic, who was more than capable of looking after himself. Shutting his eyes, he sought to center himself.

Don't dwell on the fact his single tie to this Earthen plane was currently scouring the train for danger without back up. Johnathan swore, quickly yanked on his coat, and shoved his boots on his feet. It was possible, he was now convinced, the Society followed Johnathan and Vic on the train from Boston, possibly even from Cress Haven. They might have waited until the train was isolated by the imposing wilderness, far from any farmland or town, before they struck. After Evans' manipulation of Cress Haven's unfortunate residents, he doubted a train full of sleeping, innocent passengers would give them pause to enact violence.

Johnathan stumbled into the attached passenger car, struggling to finish tying his laces. Vic's citrus and musk scent lingered, beckoning him to follow. At the last second, he remembered the glasses in his pocket. Muffling any of his senses at present seemed a poor choice, but the last thing he needed was some unsuspecting passenger panicking at his fiery gaze. He shoved them back on his face, concentrating on the pull of Vic's scent. The hint of gun powder was stronger now. Johnathan's pace sped up, his muscles going lax and loose with a hunter's intent, steps silent while his hands dangled free, ready for ambush.

His leather gloves creaked with each flex of his fingers. The sounds made him flinch, too loud, too close. Rolling his shoulders, he reached through the jittery bundle of nerves currently pulsing in his chest for the calm mind of his training. Why was it so difficult to summon that side of him now?

Johnathan stopped inside the sleeper car and leaned against the wall. He wouldn't be useful to Vic like this. Sorting his incensed thoughts, he tried to reclaim a rational foothold. *Could* Dr. Evans' men be responsible for this? Unlikely, the effort to organize pursuit so quickly after the devastating blow to their resources and manpower was further crippled by the power gap of Dr. Evans' death. This could be a large wild animal or a herd of stubborn deer clogging the tracks, something else equally ridiculous. And yet....

Dread continued to clench his nerves.

Foolish not to listen to an insistent warning, no matter his mastery of the sense. Johnathan pushed off the wall, trying not to be obvious as he scented the air like an untrained bloodhound. No one poked their heads out of the sleeper cabins. He slid open the door between cars, met by the thick, sticky scent of pine and moldering vegetation. The train had stopped in a heavily forested area, the trees so close they reached out to grasp at the roof with green needle thin fingers. Out among the trunks, he caught shots of movement through his tunneled vision, nocturnal animals going about their business, ignoring the invasion of human progress in their realm. A heavy wind buffeted him. Johnathan braced himself against the handrails while it ruffled his hair, bearing another flood of scents. There it was again. Gun powder, and another acrid smell he couldn't place, strong enough to sting. Where was it coming from? Perhaps a marshal and company on board? It wasn't beyond the realm of possibility. What worried him was Vic's scent came from the same direction. He pushed his way into the next car. There were more passengers in this one but most of them ignored his entrance, stubbornly trying to reclaim their rest or grumbling about the sudden stop.

Stalking past them, his steps slowed the closer he came to the end of the car. That awful scent was overpowering, made his eyes water. *What was it?* Had something died? Death and decay were familiar smells, but perhaps they registered differently to his new senses. His hands shook when he reached to open the door to the next car. What was wrong with him?

A hand came down on his shoulder. Years of training kicked in before the rest of his mind caught up. Johnathan seized the wrist above that hand, shoving his hip back. The focal point of gravity shifted, pulling the figure over his shoulder in a throw he had practiced until his muscles ached. Vic hit the ground with a huff, a mix of irritation and bemusement on his face. Mortification froze him in place, the shocked murmurs of the other passengers ringing in his ears. They hadn't noticed Johnathan until now. Impossible to ignore an oaf tossing around his traveling companion.

"I believe I told you to stay put," said Vic, not even winded.

"It was more of a suggestion," said Johnathan, "which I determined to be a daft suggestion."

"That's fair," replied Vic. His voice remained even, his reaction skewing toward amusement when he nodded at Johnathan's fixed grip on his wrist. "Plan on letting me off the ground? Or do you prefer me in this position?"

Johnathan was certain the back of his neck would burst into flames. "Sorry," he muttered. He released Vic's wrist and stepped away, realized he left Vic sprawled on the floor without assistance, and stepped forward again to offer him a hand up.

"That's sweet, John, but you are standing on my coat, and I rather like this one." Vic's grin turned into a full leer. "Though I see you weren't very thorough in your dressing." His voice was murmur for Johnathan alone, his appraising gaze drifting upward. Johnathan glanced down to discover he'd forgotten Vic unfastening his pants earlier. His blush crested up through the back of his head, flushing through the curve of his ears while Johnathan attempted to subtly right his clothes.

"You can stop with that look now," Johnathan snapped.

"But I enjoy this side of you so very much," said Vic. "Not to mention the view—"

Dread slid an invisible blade against Johnathan's spine, stripping his civilized veneer. A snarl ripped from his throat, a sound so vicious and inhuman several of the passengers screamed and scrambled away from him. Johnathan ignored them, his entire focus on the dread, now a physical thing to his senses that moved toward him. Vic rolled to his feet in a seamless movement, crouching beside Johnathan without touching him.

"What is it?"

Johnathan couldn't answer at first, there were no words. He tracked the dread approaching them, unable to describe in his own thoughts how he did so. An instinct he couldn't ignore, though it baffled the remnants of his rational self. In his mind's eye, the dread was a shadow, threaded in gold, heralded by a soft chiming sound. His skin crawled at the innocuous sound, carrying the scent of gun powder and violence. Ill intent whispered in his thoughts, riling the creature inside him until Johnathan feared he would transform right then and there.

"I don't know," Johnathan bit out, his voice an octave lower than usual. The muscles of his jaw locked. A tight knot of heat thrummed in his gut. He tried to reign it in, wholly aware he had no idea how to do so. Fear bit down on him, winching his muscles in place. Not a fear of the unseen, unmeasurable dread, but of himself and what he would do to the innocents in the car should the beast break through his skin. "Get them out of here. Please." The words were ragged, reflecting his internal struggle.

Vic didn't stop to question him. He spun to the other passengers, and while Johnathan couldn't see his face, he could feel the soothing effect of Vic's voice, laced with a vampire's compulsion. "Everyone, out of concern for your safety, I must ask you to rise and file out in an orderly fashion to the next car."

If Johnathan wasn't concentrating so hard on keeping control, he wouldn't have been able to hide his shock. A vampire could compel so many humans at once? They *were* compelled, leaving the car in a parade of shuffling feet without question or protest, though he doubted any would fight the suggestion to get away from him. There would be time for marvel and wonder about Vic's vampiric abilities later. Survival came first.

A tinkling sound filled the air, the soft chime of silver bells vibrating through his bones. Johnathan's head snapped up. It was no longer in front of him, but behind them. Two people had appeared in the car, their entrance announced by the dread clouding around them in a palpable haze. Tension buzzed through Johnathan. One of the two strangers had masked their movements.

Masking ratcheted the element of danger. The Society coveted those techniques that bordered on magic, requiring extensive training of the mind and body for a student to master. When dealing with so many inhuman threats, one couldn't ignore such a useful tool. Those who managed to learn were swiftly promoted through the rank and file, sent on the deadliest of missions. Masking took years to master, and most hunters never achieved it. Johnathan stared at their foe, surprised by their youthful appearance. The man's clean shaven face maintained a hint of youthful softness, possibly younger than Johnathan, dressed more in line with a clerk than a Hunter. The only softness the stranger possessed. He was shorter than Vic's humble height by a few inches, but stocky. The Society uniform he wore hugged his muscular frame, neat and crisp without single wrinkle. Close cropped dark hair slicked back against his skull. A pair of spectacles framed dark, black eyes, lit from within by cold rage.

His female companion was a waif, her pale wispy hair drifting around her face in a cloud. An unfamiliar crimson uniform fitted snug against her tall, willowy physique. As Johnathan had never seen her apparel on a Society Agent, his unease escalated. His gaze flickered to the strange instrument strung between her hands, a series of strings and chimes rippling in her steady grip. The source of the chiming....and the dread. Johnathan couldn't look away.

"It seems our target is not alone, Sister Wilhem," said the man.

Sister Wilhem tilted her head, her features obscured by strands of ash blonde hair, except for her pale eyes, a clouded milk white. She regarded them, her expression serene. "A regrettable development."

"Shall I destroy this creature then?" The man stepped forward, cracking his knuckles. "Or take them both for study?"

Vic tensed beside him. Johnathan frowned at the two Agents. Their terminology bothered him, not for the obvious disdain in their tone, but their indeterminate target. The man didn't move, his hateful gaze snapped to Jonathan. Violence emanated from him, a throbbing pulse that baited reciprocation.

The instrument in Sister Wilhem's hands emitted a cascading chime. Hunger tightened her features. The sound scraped under his skin. Johnathan froze at the unsettling sensation racing through his system.

"No, Luthor. Don't kill him," she said. Her gaze remained fixed on them, pinning Johnathan in place when Luthor stepped forward. The sense of dread tipped over a ledge.

An animalistic sound rose from Johnathan's chest, one he thought impossible for a human throat. The threat was too much, too close, and Johnathan didn't know if he could protect Vic from the pair. He shifted forward a step, blatantly placing himself between Vic and the obvious threat.

"What are you doing?" Vic hissed behind him, grabbing his wrist. Johnathan didn't budge, his gaze fixed on the other male.

Luthor paused, regarding Johnathan with cold calculation.

Sister Wilhem hummed. "Interesting. Take them both down."

Vic tensed. "I believe that is our cue to depart," he drawled. "Good day, my lady, sir." He gave a hard tug on Johnathan's wrist, taking a step back toward the door. Luthor struck.

The Agent moved with a serpent's swiftness, whipping a blade in their direction so fast Johnathan couldn't guess its destination until Vic plucked it out of the air a few inches from his face.

"Young man, that was rather rude," he scolded, wagging the blade at Luthor. "You should really...watch..." Vic's gaze widened, his words trailing off. His hand shook. The blade dropped from his slack grip.

Johnathan wrapped an arm around Vic's waist and kicked the door open behind them. He tossed Vic over his shoulder, turning away from the pair to make their escape. A trio of blades buried themselves in his exposed back. Johnathan grunted, vaulting over the rail to hit the ground running. Luthor tracked their progress. Another blade whizzed by, burying itself in a tree trunk. Johnathan dove into the arms of the surrounding forest, but the Agent didn't press the attack.

Soon, the presence of the Agents and the dread they carried waned to nothing. Johnathan knew, sure as the sun rose, the hunt had just begun.

CHAPTER TWO

ENSCONCED BY THE THICK PRESS OF TREES, JOHNATHAN RAN WITHOUT a destination, seeding a trail of loops and false leads in his panic driven flight. Vic dangled over his shoulder, a dead weight due to the toxin on Luthor's blade. He should have been faster, should have caught the blade, protected by his immunity. A successful intervention would have only staved off one trick from the mysterious duo; he knew in his heart flight was the correct call.

Johnathan forced a brutal pace, thigh muscles burning when the trees began to blur together. He knew how the Society's Hunters tracked their targets and his false paths and red herrings should have been enough to buy them a lead. The problem was the two unknown players they fled on the train. What he really needed was a body of water to obscure their trail. The roar of a river called to him, a distant promise. Johnathan pushed forward, his speed nowhere near Vic's, but he could feel the differences between his former and new self. There would be time to be unsettled by those changes later. The riverbank loomed up, sudden and fast, giving Johnathan a split second to tighten his grip around Vic's legs and launch off the crumbling shore.

Johnathan sucked in a lungful of air, the dark churning surface of the water rushing up to meet them. They landed in icy water that knocked the beast back in its proverbial cage. Its rapid retreat left him gasping, consequently gulping a lungful of frigid water. The water performed a dual service, rinsing the toxin from Vic's skin. He recovered quickly, regaining enough motion to roll off Johnathan's shoulder while the latter thrashed toward the surface. Johnathan came up sputtering, glancing around wild eyed until he found Vic, treading water beside him.

"That could have gone better," said Vic. "But nobody died." His grin was all teeth, lengthened canines prominent in the moonlight glimmering off the water's surface. The shadows framed the hollows of Vic's face. A reminder Johnathan wasn't the only one still recovering from their last encounter with Evans. Yet Vic managed that impressive show of mental strength on the train.

"I didn't know you could do that, compel that many people at once," said Johnathan, a thread of awe creeping into his voice. Waiting for his body to adjust to the cold was a special sort of agony, sapping his energy.

Vic shrugged in the water. "There's a lot you don't know about me, stud."

Johnathan wrinkled his nose. "Oh please, no, that is not a pet name I want attributed to me."

"John, that merely suggests you do want a pet name," said Vic. "What about darling dearest?"

"No," Johnathan snapped.

"My trollop?"

"If I could drown you, I would," said Johnathan. He tuned out the next 'pet name' Vic tossed at him, observing their surroundings. Once again, he found himself surrounded by wilds, the press of trunks closer than the forest he'd run through in Maine, chased by nightmares. The trees made his hackles raise.

"Are you even listening, my cherish?"

Difficult though it was, treading water through the heady rush of the river, Johnathan managed the proper glower that term of endearment deserved.

Vic chuckled, his expression sobering. "Did you recognize them, John?"

Worrying his lower lip, Johnathan shook his head. "Not in the slightest." The Boston chapter of the Society was sizable, but without question, Johnathan knew the full roster of his former comrades on sight. It wasn't a quirk, but part of a Prospective's training to memorize the faces of those in their chapter house to prevent any undue violence toward one another in the field. "I'm not sure the woman was a member of the Society."

The man certainly was, his use of toxins and masking earmarks of upper echelon Society training, but the woman's startling red uniform was something he hadn't encountered before. He swore he could still hear the chiming instrument she carried, a faint echo ringing through his ears. Johnathan shook his head, attempting to dislodge the phantom sound.

"We should keep moving," he said.

Vic spat out a mouthful of water. "Should we stay in the river?"

"No, the river's carried us enough to break our trail." Remaining might be a wiser strategy. Johnathan didn't think he could stand the freezing water much longer. The cold crept into his joints, creating a surprisingly sharp ache. He'd managed to lose the goggle-like glasses when he submerged; an inconvenience, much as he hated them, because they concealed his peculiar eyes.

"Thank god, I loathe swimming," Vic muttered, powering through the current in deep smooth strokes for the shore. Johnathan was slower to follow, his limbs sluggish to obey, heavier than sacks of bricks when he finally crawled onto the muddy bank.

Vic tugged at the sleeve of his overcoat in disgust. "Ruined." He grimaced, wringing water out of the sodden fabric. His fastidiousness almost made Johnathan smile from his position, shivering on all fours, when liquid fire ignited through his veins.

Johnathan hissed, gloved fingers digging into the ground while he burned from the inside out. His vision blanked, neck muscles straining. The heat spread through him, banishing the icy chill of the river with a vengeance. His legs abruptly gave out. Johnathan caught himself on his elbows before his face kissed the mud. The wave of heat finished its progression, receding back to his core. His vision refocused to find Vic kneeling in front of him, hands hovering as if he wasn't sure whether he should touch Johnathan or not. Thankfully, whatever strange episode had seized him, he hadn't transformed.

"Still me," Johnathan rasped.

Vic's worry remained. "That was…interesting."

Johnathan frowned up at him, shifting back onto his legs to kneel in the mud. Attempting to wipe the mud off his leather gloves onto his already filthy trousers resulted in a smeared mess. "How so?"

"You were literally steaming," said Vic, lifting a brow. "I wager Hellhounds do not enjoy the cold."

The words made his shoulders tense. He hadn't allowed himself to so much as think the term. Still, steaming? He assessed himself. Vic continued to drip water. Johnathan's clothing was now unpleasantly damp, whatever warmth he'd summoned rapidly draining off in the chill night air. The cold mud beneath him continued to sap at his strength, an unwelcome confirmation of Vic's theory.

"I reckon you're right," said Johnathan, his voice faint.

"You look exhausted," said Vic. And he was. Sleep had evaded Johnathan since his transition. Given the opportunity, he could sleep for a week, though they didn't have the luxury. Going still, he listened for a faint chiming that couldn't possibly be there.

"We need to keep moving," he murmured.

"That's the second time you've said that." Vic's expressive brows drew down. He swept an arm at the surrounding trees, flinging drops of muddy river water onto the grass. "Do you realize how much distance you've put between us and the train? You ran for miles, John." Vic sighed, a note of distress in his expression. "I'm not sure I could find the train again if I tried, never mind those idiots finding us."

Johnathan shook his head, uncertain why Vic's logic did nothing to assure him. "I don't think they're tracking us by the usual means." And they were being tracked. Johnathan scrubbed his face, uncaring if left more streaks of mud behind. It was an effort to keep his eyes open if not for the urgent inner alarm begging him to flee. "We need more miles between us."

Vic swore. "You can barely stand."

Johnathan waved him off. "I'll keep up."

"Or I take a turn carrying you," said Vic, turning to offer his back. "Hop up, my dove."

"Toss off, Vic," Johnathan grumbled, staggering to his feet. He shook himself to regain the feeling in his limbs.

"Now you're just being stubborn," said Vic. He sighed at Johnathan's mulish expression. "Really John, you look right haggard. Would it be so awful if I swept you off your feet for a while?"

It wouldn't be the first time. The notion he needed to be carried irritated him, though he'd be damned if he could figure out why. "I'm sorry. It's not awful, it's just—" He paused, struggling to put his feelings into words. "I can't protect you like that." The words fell flat from his mouth, lame to his ears. Vic's gaze widened, clearly finding the statement as absurd as Johnathan did.

"Protect me?" Vic's brows knotted. "My dear John, I'm not sure you could protect me from a belligerent possum at present. You are weaving on your feet. Besides," said Vic, stepping in to press his forehead against Johnathan's, cupping his cool fingers over the back of his companion's head. "You already did protect me tonight."

He gave Johnathan's nape a gentle squeeze. "We protect each other, remember? In this together."

"Come Hell or high water," breathed Johnathan.

Vic's lips quirked up. "Quite accurate in our case." He took the opportunity to wring a few drops of cold water from his sodden sleeve down Johnathan's neck.

"Ack!" Johnathan jumped away from him, arms failing while the trickle of droplets slid down his back.

"There's a bit of your energy back," said Vic.

"Vile wretch," Johnathan said through his teeth. He shook out his limbs in a gesture he realized midway through was too reminiscent of a dog, rocking to a stop.

Vic clicked his tongue against his teeth. "Now, now, I thought we were past name calling, my dew drop—"

"Absolutely not that one," sputtered Johnathan.

"But you are the one who stressed the need for more distance between us and our unknown pursuant. I suggest we make use of your burst of energy."

Johnathan nodded in silent agreement, resuming his previous punishing pace through the thickest clusters of trees. Vic followed without complaint, until Johnathan stumbled for the third time. Not giving him another chance to protest, he shoved Johnathan onto his back. The position wasn't much more dignified than being carried in the man's arms, and while Johnathan disliked being a burden once again, it was clear Vic wouldn't allow him to run himself to the ground.

Once he had the recalcitrant Johnathan on his back, Vic flew through the forest, boots barely touching the ground. Travel by train had nothing on vampires. Awareness sizzled through Johnathan; the fluid shift of Vic's legs, his gait even and strong despite carrying the additional weight. As the miles slid along, Johnathan tucked his head against Vic's shoulder, silently calling himself an idiot. Why hadn't he simply let Vic carry him? Instead, he'd pushed harder, further exhausting himself. Even now, the drive to be at Vic's side, guarding him, remained a stinging shame.

The reasoning connected in his thoughts. Of course, Evans told him Hellhounds were servants by nature. Did he really wish to serve Vic? The idea made his throat tight. They knew so little of the bargain they struck to keep him on this plane. What if—

"John, it's almost dawn. We should stop. At least to figure out a plan and to rest," said Vic. There was the slightest strain in the man's voice, the only giveaway his endless stamina flagged.

Johnathan peeked over Vic's shoulder, scanning their surroundings. They were still deep in the forest, without a relief to the endless tree trunks. Not ideal conditions, but better some cover than stranded in an open field. There was an overgrowth of low trees nearby, the curved hollow a natural shelter. He hesitated only a moment, remembering the last time he was deep in a forest.

He cleared his throat. "Are there any fairies out this way?"

Vic chuckled. "Possibly, but they'll stay well away from us." That's right, the Other had no love for vampires, and they wanted nothing to do with Johnathan's kind.

"Let's tuck in there for a few hours then," said Johnathan,

attempting to slide off Vic's back. His mutinous legs wobbled but held until he made it to the shelter, where he collapsed in a graceless heap.

Vic didn't join him immediately, staring off into the surrounding forest. His long fingers flexed against his thighs, a distant expression on his face.

"What's wrong?"

The distance receded, shifting to a wan smile. "Nothing. We could both use a rest." Vic joined him on the ground, shoring up against Johnathan's warmth. His clothes were still damp despite their lengthy flight and cold. Johnathan pulled Vic into the circle of his arms, the restless need finally subsiding.

"You really are a walking oven," said Vic, leaning his head into Johnathan's shoulder with a delighted sigh. "My backside was toasty warm the whole run here."

Johnathan huffed. Though their temporary shelter was a far cry from the alluring comfort of a mattress, he was satisfied, holding Vic in his arms. He closed his eyes, willing sleep to come, the weight of exhaustion sucking at his consciousness.

The relief of true slumber continued to dance beyond his reach. He let his head fall back with a soft thud against a thin tree trunk. The quiet of night allowed other worries to creep in. Grateful he held Vic in his arms, he wondered and feared how their missing companion fared. Alyse was the most vulnerable member of their trio, though Vic insisted she could take care of herself. Rocky start aside, Johnathan did care about the woman, wishing he possessed the same faith Vic had for her capability.

"Do you think Alyse is safe?"

There was a long pause; he was certain Vic had fallen asleep when his companion let out a breath. "My god, man, aren't you tired?"

"Yes. Do you think the Society will go after her?" He worried how much information Dr. Evans passed on about his companions before his demise.

"She'll run circles around them. Trust me, John, without two idiots to worry over, she'll be safe," Vic murmured.

An unsatisfactory explanation, though Johnathan believed him. "How did you and Alyse meet?"

"John," Vic griped. "Rest!"

"Lull me to sleep with your riveting conversation," said Johnathan.

"I can't decide if that was charming or insulting." Vic chuckled. Resigned to a longer conversation, he tapped his fingers against the forearm wrapped around his chest.

"You know, I had no idea how to ingratiate myself to the people of Cress Haven when I got there. I could charm my way into any party or gathering in Europe, but the sensibilities here are different. People were more guarded, wary of outsiders. More so in those roughshod pioneer towns; the smaller community, the lower the trust."

"Why even pick a place like Cress Haven?" Johnathan hadn't meant to interrupt. It was a detail he'd wondered about often since his revelation about Vic. Vampires generally kept to cities or larger settlements, not only to conceal their feeding habits but to disguise their peculiarities. Small communities were a difficult challenge for the vampire trying to blend, and though Vic's feeding habits were far from the norm, there was other peculiarities to set him apart.

Vic was silent for another long pause. Johnathan worried he'd breached an old wound. "I wanted something that was mine," said Vic, his voice soft. "A home, a place of my own making, by my choice. A community I didn't have to compel my way into but welcomed me as one of their own. I wouldn't have that without Alyse."

A home and companion he'd left without hesitation. Johnathan's hold tightened. Vic patted his arm. "Enough of that. The town still exists, and she is alive thanks to you." He tilted his head, glancing through the interwoven branches overhead at the hues of dawn creeping across the sky. "Maybe someday we'll make it back there."

We. Johnathan buried his face in Vic's neck, giving in to the urge to breathe in the man's scent, deep into his lungs. "Alyse?" He murmured her name, swathed in citrus and musk.

"She approached me, of course," said Vic. "It was at a midwinter gathering, the whole town turned out to celebrate the passage of another year. She sashayed over to me in her home spun skirts, threaded her arm through mine, stole my beer, and whispered in my ear she knew what I was."

"Sounds like her," said Johnathan with a chuckle.

Vic echoed his laugh. "Exactly like her. Here was this brazen young woman, not only unmarried but the pastor's daughter. When she made it clear she had no intention to out me to her fellow parishioners, I was intrigued."

"How did she recognize you were a vampire?" Johnathan hadn't spotted Vic for what he was until it was far too late, to his good fortune. Ignorance allowed him to see the man as something other than his enemy.

"She watched me, pieced it together during the first few weeks after my arrival," said Vic.

"Least it took her weeks," Johnathan grumbled. He could sense Vic's amusement.

"I've had a lot of practice blending. More than most," said Vic. "I like being around people. Being in the thick of humanity. To be seen and be known. To not be the wolf lurking at the edges of the night."

Johnathan frowned. "Is that why you don't feed from the vein?"

"Among other reasons," Vic murmured. "Our connection ingratiated me to the others. She talked to everyone, kept tabs on them. If someone was sick or injured, she knew about it and she took care of them all. Astonishing when she hated most of them."

The statement startled a laugh out of Johnathan. "Why would she hate them?"

"Her intelligence set her apart. And she was trapped there. There were expectations to be the obedient pastor's daughter, to marry a man of her father's choosing. To be docile and demure." Vic smoothed a hand down Johnathan's arm. "My arrival excited her because she finally had someone she could connect with, someone different."

"You wish she'd come with us," said Johnathan. He wished she had too.

"Of course." Vic swallowed "I don't understand why she didn't." There was a tinge of sadness in his tone. Her decision baffled Johnathan. He regretted leaving her so trapped and stifled. Would she truly be safe when the Society would come sniffing around, searching for Dr. Evans? They should have waited for her. They couldn't go back for her, at least not yet.

"She'll be okay, John," said Vic. "Better without our presence making her a target or distracting her."

There was little he could do aside from worry, a useless emotion he had more than enough of these days. "Without the train, how difficult will it be to reach our mysterious destination?"

"Very smooth topical transition, John," teased Vic. "Our destination isn't a mystery. We still need to get to further inland."

Not a mystery, though Vic hadn't clarified any details regarding the matter. Johnathan rolled his eyes; they'd passed into New York some time ago, though he had no idea where they were geographically other than woods. If Vic wanted to be cagey about their ultimate destination, he wouldn't press him too hard. "Not by way of the city, I presume?"

"Perhaps. We are off the beaten track, but it shouldn't be too difficult to find a new means of transportation," said Vic, not quite answering the question. "Now, as much as I enjoy our scintillating conversation, both of us should rest while we can."

An effective stop to Johnathan's stream of questions, though he'd made scant headway into his companion's history. It wasn't that Vic held himself back, necessarily or intentionally avoided personal conversation, but Johnathan wondered if they would ever reach the same open vulnerability they shared after their disastrous encounter with the fairies. He itched to ask more questions, biting them back when Vic's body relaxed in his arms, the tension draining from his body in sleep. The sun had fully risen by then, painting Vic's pale skin in dappled shadows. In the daylight, the shadows under Vic's eyes were more pronounced, twin bruised hollows, and Johnathan wondered if he'd managed to feed since they boarded the train. He would have to insist Vic do so before they went much further, except...except they'd left those supplies with the rest of their luggage back on the train.

Johnathan quietly swore, unwilling to wake Vic, though he wanted to shake the man. Why hadn't he said anything? Of course, Johnathan answered his own question immediately. Why would he bother? They couldn't retrieve their bags, nor could they do much else but move forward. Perhaps Vic was intending to restock his unusual equipment once they hit a city, where such items might be easier to come by. It bothered Johnathan he kept the loss to himself.

There was no use, continuing to dwell on the cyclical nature of his thoughts. Johnathan tried to relax, aiming for an internal stillness so the elusive phantom of sleep would visit him again. No matter how long he floated in that muted state, sleep never came. Johnathan wondered if it ever would.

CHAPTER THREE

THE SHADOWS STRETCHED INTO THE LATE AFTERNOON WHEN VIC stirred in his arms. Johnathan unwrapped his hold, noting the angles of Vic's face were more prominent than before. Sleep provided little in the way of nourishment for a vampire, though the hungrier they were, the more their bodies craved it, reserving what energy they could, where they could. The fact he'd hadn't noticed his companion was slowly starving filled Johnathan with searing, raw shame. Vic groaned and stretched his arms above his head before he noticed Johnathan's stare.

His gaze widened, flitting over Johnathan's features. "Goodness, did you sleep at all?"

Johnathan snorted. "No. Do I look as bad as you do?"

"Not exactly," said Vic. "Wait, what do you mean?" His hands rose to his face, touching the corner of his eyes, revealing the state of his hands. Deep purplish blue bruised the underside of his fingernails.

"You should feed before we go." Johnathan scrutinized him for his reaction.

Vic's mouth drew into a thin line. "I assure you, I'll be fine."

Damn the man! "I know you left your valise on the train," said Johnathan, unable to completely hide the anger in his tone.

"I did indeed, which is why I keep a spare set of instruments on my person," said Vic without missing a beat. He patted his chest, hinting at a concealed pocket. The rebuttal was smooth, and Johnathan wanted to believe him, yet doubt remained.

"Did you happen to save some blood as well? I could leave if you'd prefer—"

"Leave it, John!" Vic braced his hands on his knees, irritation lacing his words with the sharpness of a whip. He exhaled, glancing at the sinking sun overhead. "Aren't you the one who insisted we're being pursued? We should have left hours ago."

Johnathan shrugged. "You needed the rest."

Vic stared at him. "There it is again. Look me in the eye."

The request puzzled him, but Johnathan acquiesced. He startled when Vic gripped his chin, his cool fingertips gently scraping through his unshaven growth, thumb tracing the length of his jaw.

"Your pupils keep dilating and retracting," Vic murmured. "What's wrong?" His touch made Johnathan forget his frustrations with the man. Heat began a lazy dance, low in his belly.

"I'm not sure," he breathed. The moment deepened. Vic's face drew closer when the faintest chiming sound reached his ears. "Damn."

"Have an epiphany, my tender blossom?" Vic grinned.

"I did," said Johnathan. He stood, pulling Vic to his feet. Though he hadn't slept, his body seemed to have regained some energy while resting. "It's them, the Agents from the train."

Vic blanched. "That's impossible. It should have taken them days to catch our trail."

"Why the devil are they so persistent?" Johnathan tipped his head, straining his hearing for the sound. The focus was untried and unpracticed, his attempt to use his heightened senses akin to using an unfamiliar weapon. The quiet of the forest cracked open, the flood of noise a torrent in his skull; the soft scratch of paws padding over a carpet of pine needles, the huff of deer, crunching bracken between flat teeth, the flit of wings and periodic chirps, the crackle and flutter of disturbed branches, the subtle breath of hundreds of living creatures, and the quiet steady tread of those that didn't belong. All of it poured in until Johnathan clapped his hands over his ears to cut it off.

He'd spent so much time trying to actively suppress the scents and sounds it never occurred to him that he would naturally dim them to function.

Cool hands settled on top of his hands. Vic's worried gaze filled his field of vision. "Easy, John. Breathe."

He clung to the command and sucked in a deep breath, focusing on the sound of his own breathing to shut out the cacophony of noise. Slowly, he regained his equilibrium.

"They are several miles away," he said, proud his voice remained steady.

Vic's eyebrows rose. "Far too close for comfort." His nostrils flared. "If we intend to lose them, we need to procure another conveyance."

There were trees as far as the eye could see. "Could be difficult in our current position," said Johnathan.

"We have to hit a town eventually," countered Vic, clapping a hand against Johnathan's arm. "Think you can keep up this time, my turtledove?"

"I will if you stop that right now."

This time he let Vic set the pace, the other male clearly worried he wouldn't be unable to keep up. Johnathan proved to have the greater stamina, eventually over taking, and slowing to wait for Vic. Though he feared it wasn't a renewal of his energy rather than the gradual deterioration of his companion. A fine sweat beaded Vic's brow within the hour, a far more serious tell compared to the bruising beneath his fingers. God save him from stubborn, noble vampires. He bit his tongue to keep from broaching a clearly sensitive subject to Vic. Rather, he wondered what made Vic so touchy when it came to mention of feeding. Was he worried Johnathan would judge him for the means of his survival? Or perhaps there was a level of self-loathing in Vic's refusal to acknowledge his needs, another issue Johnathan could empathize with. Better to keep his thoughts to himself. They crashed through the brush, giving little care to concealing their path. There seemed no point to subtly when it was clear their pursuers were undeterred.

Contemplating their circumstances left a bitter note in his thoughts. Johnathan had hoped for a much longer lull between life threatening encounters, if only to enjoy his present company. Worse, it bothered him how these two Agents caught up to them so quickly. He didn't believe they would be able to avoid a second conflict. Foolishly, he'd hoped they would have a respite from the Society while they dealt with Dr. Evans failed operation and the loss of so many Agents. Their encounter on the train was a true puzzle, because these Agents didn't appear to have any connection or affiliation with the Boston chapter. Who were they? When had they boarded the train and why?

He wasn't sure which of the two unsettled him more. The man, Luthor, capable of masking their presence from both Vampire and Hellhound senses while he attacked with poisoned blades. Or the woman in red, Sister Wilhem, and her strange chiming instrument filling him with dread. Johnathan didn't know either of them from Adam but couldn't shake the feeling there was a connection waiting to be discovered.

He hated floundering in ignorance, a state he found himself in far too frequently.

"Ha, ah ha!" Vic shouted, putting on a sudden burst of speed that left Johnathan scrambling after him.

Panting by the time he caught up to Vic, Johnathan found him on a spit of dirt track, winding sinuously through the trees.

"Civilization," Vic proclaimed. He spun around, his arms raised in victory.

"This is barely a foot path," Johnathan protested.

Vic flapped a hand of him. "Begone, naysayer. This is a coach road. And where there's a road, there are travelers."

Johnathan peered down what Vic generously called a 'road', where the trees appeared to swallow up the opening in either direction. Not another soul to be seen in the gathering dark. "I doubt we'll encounter anyone this time of night, so we'd best get walking."

"Walking, yes, more walking, but now we have a direction," said Vic, positively giddy. Johnathan wanted to push him into the dirt.

"Which direction shall we go? Trees." Johnathan pointed one way then the other. "Or more trees?"

Vic didn't rise to the bait, staring hard in the dark. "Neither; we are going to wait right here for the coach."

"What coach?" As the question left his lips, he caught the unmistakable grind and squeal of wheels over axel, joined by the muffled clink of tack, and a quiet equine snort. The coach was still a good distance away, but an incredulous Johnathan blinked at Vic. "How exactly are we going to procure this conveyance?"

"I'm going to politely ask if they will allow us passage," said Vic.

Johnathan made a face. "You're going to compel them." Not that he doubted Vic could, but it would be another unwelcome strain to the man's already taxed body. He kept the mutinous thought to himself.

"Of course I'm going to compel them." Vic snorted. "What sane individual would let two filthy, rough looking vagabonds into their company without supernatural persuasion?"

"Alyse," said Johnathan, running a gloved hand through his tangled hair, cringing at the crumbly sensation of dried mud. Though hesitant to follow Vic's plan, he would pay good money for a room and bath right now, if he had a cent to his name.

A fond smile tugged at Vic's mouth, lessening the stark shadows under his eyes. "Touché. Now, let's get out of the middle of the road before they spot us. They'll probably think we are bandits set to accost them."

"Close enough," mumbled Johnathan, clambering into the tangled brush lining the dirt road in clumps. The brush snagged his already ravaged clothes but provided enough cover.

Vic settled in beside him, looking far more at ease than he had a right to. A frown pinched the man's brows. "Do you still sense our pursuers?"

Johnathan closed his eyes, trying to focus on the sound of those distant chimes rather than open himself to another deluge of noise. "I think so?"

"You don't sound very convincing, John."

He opened one eye to glare at his companion. "May I remind you I am painfully new at this?" Johnathan rolled his shoulders. "They aren't in the incoming coach, if that's what you're worried about."

"I believe you, though I am curious," said Vic. "You look absolutely sure about that."

"One of the occupants is drenched in perfume," said Johnathan. The odious floral scent was nothing but a whiff, and strong enough to wither his nose hair. He pinched his nostrils closed, trying to breathe through his mouth.

A clipped laugh suspiciously close to a giggle slipped from Vic's mouth. "You'll need to hang your head out the window for the ride into town."

"Oh, do shut up," snapped Johnathan, though a smile tugged at his lips. "I'd rather cling to the roof."

"Better off wrapping a rag around your head," snickered Vic. His expression sobered with anticipation. "Not too far off. Now be quiet."

Johnathan bit back a retort, watching the blocky dark box meander along the dirt tract, weaving through ruts, and bumping over dips. Two placid horses kept a steady plodding pace, eating up the distance in painfully slow measures. Johnathan tried not to fidget beside the stock-still Vic. The coach was yet a fair distance away when the horses suddenly drew up short, dancing in place with parrying whinnies of distress.

Vic shared a look of confusion with him. The driver dismounted, attempting to calm the beasts. They listened to his soothing tones, though Johnathan could see the whites of their eyes from where he crouched in the brush. A mature feminine voice called out an inquiry from the confines of the coach.

"Stay here, I'm going to approach them," Vic whispered to him. The man was gone before Johnathan could reply.

The muscle between his shoulders twitched. Vic was more than capable of defending himself and the two unfortunate occupants of the coach weren't a danger, and yet an urge to follow pulled at him. Johnathan clenched his jaw and stayed put, knowing Vic would *not* appreciate his interference.

His fingers rapidly tapping the top of his thighs by the time Vic emerged from the cover of the trees, approaching the coach with an open smile. Johnathan could just make out the figure of the driver, who started when Vic appeared. His form quickly loosened at Vic's easy greeting. Vic might have used a touch of compulsion to smooth the way, but his natural charm helped. The driver started chatting, an easy jovial tone rolling through the quiet woods. The tightness in Johnathan's shoulders eased, Vic's success obvious when his companion leaned in through the coach window, chatting it up with the occupant. A girlish giggle emerged from the coach. Vic turned and curled his fingers, suggestively beckoning Johnathan forward. Shaking off the last of his nerves, he stood.

He barely made it ten steps when the horses reacted violently, bucking, and backing away, their heads straining at the bits in their mouths. Johnathan froze, realization creeping in as Vic helped the driver reign them in. A hot prickling sensation played along the back of his neck while Vic soothed the two mares to a calmer state. He didn't move until Vic jogged over to him.

"Something is spooking the horses," said Vic. Johnathan fought not to snap at him for stating the obvious. "But Henry and Madame Luce are more than willing to share their coach with us." He grinned. "Though you were right, John, her perfume makes the eyes water."

The good humor left his face once he noticed John's expression. "What's wrong?"

"I think." Johnathan licked his lips. "I'm spooking the horses."

Vic glanced from the horses to Johnathan. "What? No—"

Johnathan took a couple steps forward. The horses shrieked.

A contemplative look cross Vic's face. "You know, I don't think we crossed so much as a mouse during our flight from Cress Haven." They'd run to the train station just in case any leftover Society Hunters were watching the roads. And spent their time before the train's arrival casing the station for unwanted surprises. Mulling it over, Johnathan hadn't encountered another animal since his transformation. They'd spent the night in the woods, unbothered by any predators or nosy scavengers. He'd heard them from a distance, but none came close to their makeshift camp. Honestly, it was fair reasonable a herd animal might be unsettled by a demon hound in human skin.

He shifted from foot to foot, feeling unaccountably flustered. "What do we do now?"

"Hmmm." Vic tapped his chin. "Wait here." He left Johnathan, jogging back to the coach where he ducked his head inside. Whatever conversation he had with the occupant, he emerged a moment later, an unseen object in hand.

Johnathan's nose itched. He had a sneaking suspicion what Vic carried when the man approached him like one would approach a wounded animal. "Please tell me that's not what I think it is."

Vic held up a fancy crystalline bottle of dark umber liquid. "How badly do we need a ride?"

The question caught him off guard. But Johnathan knew, the familiar prick of dread creeping over him the longer they delayed. The distance between them and their mystery pursuers grew shorter every moment they wasted.

"Do it." Johnathan tried to hold his breath. There was nothing to prepare him when Vic uncapped the perfume and dumped it over his head.

CHAPTER FOUR

THE INTERIOR OF THE COACH REMAINED DIM AND CLAUSTROPHOBIC for most of the journey. Johnathan yearned for the moonlit, crisp air outside. It was difficult to gauge the passage of time within the tight quarters, compounded by the snoring Madame Luce, who dozed on despite present odorous company. Johnathan crouched across from her, the thinly padded half seat far too small for his bulk, miserable and choking on his own stink. A constant ache built in his bunched muscles. Each bump and dip in the road rattled through his skull, his jaw throbbing since he'd clenched his teeth together from the moment the coach door closed. His mood was beyond salty after Vic chose to ride up front with the driver to 'take in the fresh country air'. Desperate to be free of the coach when the rock and rumble of the ride finally ceased, Johnathan wanted to burst from the odiferous box when Vic opened the door. Luckily, cramps locked up his limbs.

"A spit of a town, but it has an inn."

Johnathan grunted in response, unfolding his length from the carriage to stretch and regain feeling in his limbs. Vic bid their ride farewell, easing them from his compulsion before they pulled away into the night, onto another destination.

Small was an understatement, their current stop over competed with

Cress Haven in terms of size and structure. The town consisted of a single road, dotted with a smattering of multi-purpose shops and a two-story inn, the tallest structure in the town. A loose cluster of houses could be seen beyond the center, while a wide river bordered the other side. A sizable dock hugged the shore, the center of the town's industry judging by the number of boats. The town likely sprung up out of necessity to support the small port, though it was a far cry from the oceanic ports of Boston. Stopping for the night amid a small-town population was not ideal with the Society on their trail, lacking the anonymity of a city or the isolation of the wilderness. Despite his misgivings, Johnathan was grateful for the reprieve. The windows of the inn held a warm glow, beckoning them inside from the damp chill of the night.

Shaking the stiffness from his shoulders, Johnathan followed Vic into the inn, closing his eyes against the sudden light. Warmth enveloped him, a damp heat of kitchen steam and enclosed bodies, that licked over his skin and weighed on his eyelids. Why had sleep continued to elude him when his body appeared to crave it? When had he last managed a true period of rest? Certainly not in that god forsaken coach, crouched down like a vagrant stowaway. Vic steered him to a corner by the stairs, well away from the lamp light since his glasses were long gone.

"Wait here," he said. Johnathan didn't argue, letting the wall support his weight. He kept his head down, observing the room through his lashes. There were a handful of patrons seated around the room, enjoying a pint and a meal. Perfume continued to assault his senses, but the sting had dulled after hours of exposure. His reek seemed contained to his section of the room. Through the noxious coat of perfume, he caught a whiff of hearty stew. His stomach rumbled. Johnathan ignored it. The tables were worn but clean. Even his corner was void of spider webs and dust, a promising sign.

The nearest chair called to him. Perhaps he could sit and rest his head for a few minutes before Vic returned. The very idea of moving from his position against the wall sent a wave of fatigue through him. The muscles of his neck and shoulders were winched tight, a mess of knots and taut tendons from his hunkered down position in the carriage and the strange anxiety at being separate from Vic in that confined space. Exhaustion didn't stifle the kick of his pulse when Vic appeared at his side, threading an arm around Johnathan's waist to lead him upstairs.

"I've had a meal sent up to the room and asked them to draw a hot bath," said Vic.

The promise of an actual bath nearly drew a moan from him, though he managed to stifle himself. "Are we staying the night, then?"

Vic nodded. "We could both use a respite. I believe we have put enough distance between ourselves and our errant pursuers." His hand shifted to the center of Johnathan's back, a gentle brush of long fingers causing his aching muscles to tingle. "And I need to secure our means of passage for the next leg of our journey, now that the train is no longer an option."

The reminder made Johnathan wince. "I'm sorry."

A frown creased Vic's brow. "Whatever for?"

Johnathan stared down at his feet as they climbed the stairs, heat creeping up the back of his neck. "They were probably tracking me."

Vic snorted. "We don't know that. The woman was too surprised by your appearance."

"You mean by that growl?" Johnathan was disgusted by his behavior there, or truthfully, shaken. It was more of a snarl than a growl, ripped from his chest at the mere mention of possible harm to Vic. The animalistic sound echoed in his memory. His hands balled into fists at his thighs.

"Mmm," Vic hummed, his fingers curling in the fabric of Johnathan's shirts. "That was something." He shook himself. "Nevertheless, we don't know what drew them to the train, and we will be well away before they find us again."

Their encounter continued to put Johnathan ill at ease. For now, there was little to do except let it simmer in the back of his thoughts, the need for a bath and food dominating all other worries. The door of their room was open, the sound of pouring water within. A young woman in uniform emerged with an empty steaming bucket, pausing at the sight of them. Her curious gaze roved over Vic and Johnathan, a blush coloring her cheeks. Her nose scrunched up when the overbearing scent of perfume hit her, swallowing a cough.

"Your bath is ready, sir," she wheezed, tucking the bucket under her arm and scurrying away.

Johnathan shook his head, already shrugging out of his coat before he was fully in the room. His vision tunneled on the steaming bathtub, and he tugged his shirt over his head with casual disregard.

"You could at least shut the door before you strip, John," Vic teased as he did so, throwing the latch. He followed in Johnathan's wake, picking up his discarded clothes with a huff. "Honestly, at least drape your clothes on a chair. I'm not your maid."

"You could have left it for a few minutes," said Johnathan, shucking his pants beside the tub without hesitation. The tub was nearly too full, water sloshing over the sides when he stepped in and sank down with an appreciative groan. The sound rolled out of him with utter abandon. Johnathan shoved himself down under the water as much as his long legs would allow. The tub was woefully inadequate for someone his size, but he managed to scrunch down so the water lapped at his sore shoulders, folding his legs against the opposite tub wall until the copper sides creaked.

Ignoring Vic's snort, Johnathan let the heat sink into him for a beat before he reached for the bar of soap on the nearby stand. He itched to scrub the perfume from his skin and hair, though rinsing the suds from his scalp would be a logistical nightmare. If he had to thrust his arse up to manage it, he would wash the cloying scent off every inch. His fingers paused, tangled in his hair. Awareness caressed the back of his neck. Johnathan glanced up through the stinging suds to find Vic watching him. That quicksilver gaze riveted on the droplets rolling down Johnathan's naked chest.

Johnathan sucked in a strained breath. A resurgence of heat made his lungs a bellows, working in time to the rising beat of his pulse. A pulse that sent blood rushing directly southward, the hot water already giving his cheeks a ruddy hue. The water concealed the rise and twitch of his cock bobbing against his leg in response to Vic's attentive gaze.

Johnathan cleared his throat and shifted in the water, wiping at the suds running into his eyes.

"That tub is barely bigger than a rain barrel," said Vic. His steps were silent, the weaving gait of cat stalking its prey. "It amazes me you wedged yourself in there." A smile curled Vic's lips. He circled the tub, passing out of sight until his breath tickled the back of Johnathan's neck. "You appear to need some assistance, my cherub."

Johnathan snorted at the teasing endearment, letting his head fall back to peer up at Vic. The man was peering down into the water, one brow raised.

"You appear to need my assistance in more ways than one," said Vic.

"Christ," Johnathan muttered, straightening. The back of his neck must be scarlet. A surge of shyness gripped him, though he didn't understand why. It wasn't like Vic hadn't seen him naked before. Except this was different, like their near intimacy in the train was different. The fresh tension in his weary muscles held a pronounced ache, stiffening all over; desire warred with uncertainty and inexperience. How could he want someone so badly and feel like a rabbit in a snare trap at the same time? Vic leaned in, his sleeves rolled up past his elbows. His bare forearms circling around Johnathan, who shivered at the gentle scrape of Vic's shirt against his neck. Cool hands pressed flat over Johnathan's chest.

"Relax," Vic whispered. "You're overthinking, my lamb."

"I can't help it," said Johnathan. "I—"

Vic stopped his words with a quick tweak of his nipple, Johnathan jerked in surprise. "Hush. Let me take care of you, John."

He opened his mouth to inquire how when Vic began kneading the tight muscles of his chest and shoulders in masterful strokes. Johnathan moaned loudly from the sensation, his head lolling against the rhythm of Vic's touch. The long-seated tension he'd carried since their flight from the train finally eased its grip on him.

"Close your eyes," said Vic.

He obeyed, grunting when water poured over his head. Vic shifted his ministrations to Johnathan's scalp, working his fingers through the tangled mane in between slow pours of warm water. The pungent perfume dissolved in the clean smell of soap, mingling with the citrus spiked odor that was uniquely Vic. Johnathan inhaled a deep breath, surreptitiously drinking in the other man's scent, drawing it into his lungs, until it permeated his being, heightening his awareness of the other man. Vic's long fingers flowed down, tracing the curve of his neck, over the planes of his chest, before they dipped beneath the water and wrapped around Johnathan's eager flesh.

His eyes fluttered, a gasp rising. Vic was already there, swallowing the sound, his velvety tongue stroking inside Johnathan's mouth, a teasing touch and go until Vic drew back to nip at his bottom lip. Johnathan gripped the sides of the tub, the copper whining in his grip while Vic worked him, drawing forth sensations Johnathan never managed to illicit during his own quick, fumbling ministrations. He'd been a lad, trying to satisfy an urge beneath a scratchy wool blanket on his cot in a crowded dormitory. Johnathan's current situation was a far cry from those clumsy motions, his back bowing as a far different tightness pervaded his lower region. Vic's hand stilled, giving him a squeeze he answered with a hiss through his teeth.

"Let me taste you," Vic whispered, his lips against Johnathan's damp temple.

Johnathan blinked, panting. It took a long moment to latch onto Vic's words through the haze of pleasure. "Taste? All right." He tilted his head to offer his neck when Vic's hands released him and shifted upward, wrapping around his waist. Johnathan didn't have time to process the intent when he went airborne. A yelp squeezed out of his throat, failing wildly before those same hands guided his descent to the bed. Johnathan bounced, shedding droplets of bathwater on the sheets. Wide eyed, he glanced at the tub across the room, a trail of splattered droplets marking his passage through the air. Vic loomed over him wearing a satisfied smirk, still fully clothed between Johnathan's legs. He went perfectly still when Vic's head lowered, strands of auburn hair tickling his thighs.

Vic blew a stream of cool air, making his stiffened cock flex before the wet heat of his mouth enveloped Johnathan, taking far more of him than he thought possible. He grasped at the damp sheets, digging his heels into the mattress for purchase. Vic pinned his hips with one hand.

Sensations boiled under his skin, a great tingling swept through his veins, while pressure built again, deep in his balls. The depth of sensation scared him, unlike anything he'd felt before, *while still human.*

A small whimper escaped his taut throat. Johnathan thrashed, tendrils of shame and disgust creeping through him, threatening to puncture the swell of pleasure rising inside him. He didn't realize Vic paused in his ministrations until he reached up to cup Johnathan's face. "Stay with me, John," Vic commanded. That quicksilver gaze snared him, offering no reprieve. "Watch me with those lovely burning eyes." The words sank their hooks into him. Johnathan couldn't breathe, watching Vic lower his head back down, his gaze fastened on the sight of Vic's tongue teasing the crown of his cock, lapping at the liquid beaded there.

"You're here with me now," Vic murmured against his skin, the vibrations of his mouth sent tingling ripples through Johnathan. "Give me your pleasure, John."

Hell couldn't pry his gaze from Vic's mouth. Watching his lips close around him, the inward pull of his cheeks when Vic drew him deep. A purr rose from the man's throat, the sensation too much for Johnathan. His senses spiraled, scents and colors crackling together in a delicious siege. A final stroke of Vic's tongue along the underside of his cockhead tipped him over a precipice. His hips jerked against Vic's hold, but that silken mouth didn't release him, taking everything until Johnathan collapsed back against the damp sheets, breathing hard. Vic gave his shaft a last long lick and crawled over the sheets to lay beside Johnathan. A hand reached over to smooth his wet hair off his forehead.

"Still with me, John?"

Dammit all. His gaze darted to Vic's wicked mouth. "I might have blacked out for a moment there."

The playful smirk on Vic's lips made his hunger rise again. "I consider that a job well down." He gave a lazy stretch, tucking an arm behind his head.

"I can't believe you threw me across the room," said Johnathan, part awed, part flustered by the act. Vic tossed him as if weighed less than a stray cat.

The smirk broke into a full grin. "The expression on your face was rather marvelous."

The room was quiet aside from Johnathan's panting breaths, slower now. The aftershocks throbbed through him, a constant fizz, hyper aware of Vic's proximity though he doubted he could reciprocate from the languid exhaustion threatening to drag him under. Vic smoothed his thumb over the crease between Johnathan's brows.

"You're not even five minutes post orgasm and already thinking too hard. What's churning in that head of yours, my pearl?"

Johnathan pursed his lips at that one. "Pearl? Honestly?" He gnawed the inside of his cheek. "This feels...imbalanced between us."

Vic made a face at him. "You don't need to measure sex with an abacus and ledger, John. There is no debt of pleasure you owe me."

Turning on his side, Johnathan studied Vic's expression, trying to find the right words to explain the worries that gnawed at him. "You know that's not what I meant."

Those silver-grey eyes watched him, glimmering in the lantern light. "Must I remind you I cannot divine your thoughts. Tell me what you mean."

This was the difficult part. Words were never easy for him, and intimacy like this was a new unfamiliar world. Johnathan pulled the words forth, halting and hoarse. "You're older. You have so much more... experience. How could I possibly measure up? I want to give you what you give to me, but I'm...afraid I can't satisfy you." Afraid to fail and offer nothing of worth.

A smile reclaimed his mouth during Johnathan's stilted explanation. "My dear idiot, you aren't the first virgin I've taken to my bed." His fingers snagged in Johnathan's hair, forcing his head back for a rough kiss. "I'm a patient man, John, and I eagerly await every attempt you wish to make."

Johnathan scanned his face. Trembling, he reached toward Vic's trousers. The other man caught his hand, lifting it up to kiss his knuckles.

"Much as I would love for this to continue, you do need rest," said Vic. "This is just beginning between us. You do not have to push yourself to catch up." He sat up, pulling the damp sheets up over Johnathan's waist. "Our lovely attendant will bring up dinner soon. Try to claim a few hours while you can. I'll wake you to eat."

Johnathan's eyelids dropped. Again, he hovered on the edge of sleep. His skin still hummed from Vic's proximity. His consciousness fought to tip over an internal cliff. At some point, Vic left to secure a means of travel for the next leg of their journey and hopefully to feed. Despite his rather hale and hearty performance earlier and his insistence he was fine, Johnathan worried for the man. The warmth and comfort of the room let him float there, in between sleep and waking, until an awareness crashed into him.

Startled, Johnathan sat up in the empty room, his heart pounding in his chest. His senses were in overdrive. Not from panic, his pulse sang with an acute alertness. His claws flexed outward, shredding the sheets beneath him. Fire licked against his ribs, a dangerous stirring. His gaze snapped around the room, searching for what pricked at his nerves. A covered bowl of stew sat on the table, the tub still full of now tepid water. Johnathan's nostrils flared. Vic's scent was present but slightly faded, a sign he hadn't been gone long.

Throwing his legs over the side of the bed, Johnathan focused on what his senses told him. Another scent teased the air, one of sweet honey, burnt vanilla, and sex. His teeth clicked together. Worse, the scent grew stronger, and a terrible suspicion took root. Johnathan scrambled out of bed, yanking on his trousers and shirt in a clumsy stumble to the door. He yanked it open before he'd finished buttoning his shirt, inhaling the thick honey-sex scent that drenched the air. There was another scent, threaded deep within the enticing smell. It whispered of sulfur and flame.

Pausing at the bottom of the stairs, Johnathan sidled along the wall, keeping his head down to avoid eye contact. He'd have to find another pair of those dreadful goggles if he had any hope of blending in. The scent was even thicker here, tangible enough to taste.

The hour was late, but the room was plenty full of patrons, drinking and carousing. Surprising for a town this size, though the adjacent dock had to operate on long hours to accommodate incoming and outgoing trade. Johnathan's gaze swept the room, moving over the grizzled visages of the men, weathered and wind burnt from hours exposed to the elements, and fastened on *her*.

She wound a sinuous path through the crowd, her trailing fingers stroking arms and shoulders. Every man she touched followed her with their gaze, a gleam of hunger in their eyes. Their gazes greedily drank in her generous curves, thinly cased in a scandalously thin gown, little more than a chemise. Her vast portions of bare skin were a rich brown, complimented by a scattering of freckles across her cheeks and nose. A wave of blue-black curls fell to her tapered waist, swaying with the 'come hither' motion of her hips. One of the men said something to make her laugh, a deep, unfiltered sound, straight from the belly. Johnathan's hackles rose. A silent snarl caught in his throat.

The woman paused, eyelids fluttering. Her gaze swept upward, catching his. Doe eyes widened; her scarlet pupils were dark enough to be mistaken for brown in the low light. She swallowed hard, giving the entrance of the inn a measuring glance before she pressed her shoulders back and sauntered over to Johnathan's corner.

"Hello, love," said the demon.

CHAPTER FIVE

HELPFULLY, JOHNATHAN FROZE. HE'D BEEN UNDER THE IMPRESSION the denizens of the Nether were a rarity 'topside' yet here was another one, staring him in the face. Good manners dictated he return the greeting.

"Um, hello," he said, cursing his awkwardness. The woman shuffled from one bare foot to the other, clasping her hands in front of her. Johnathan belatedly realized he was also barefoot. He cleared his throat, straightening. "I—"

"I'll go quietly," she blurted, leaning in to speak in a pleading murmur. "Please, don't hurt my patrons. And for what it's worth, I didn't kill anyone."

Johnathan blinked, taking a step back. "I didn't say you did."

A frown creased her brow. "You believe me? Would you vouch to your master on my behalf?"

"Master? I don't." Johnathan took a breath to keep the volume of his voice down. "I don't have a master," he finished.

The woman's eyes widened, a red gleam lighting her pupils. She ducked forward, wrapping a surprisingly strong grip around Johnathan's arm. "This would be better as a private conversation, yes?" Her sultry voice was low, a suggestive note in her question. "Do you have a room here?"

He squinted down at her, uncertain he wanted to risk another demon in close quarters. His lip curled, a low rumble rising in his chest. The woman snatched her hand back, bowing her head in submission. Johnathan's jaw dropped.

"I am so sorry," he said. "I'm not sure where that came from."

The woman appeared to be bemused by his apology. "Goodness, you must be new."

Admitting how new didn't seem in Johnathan's best interests. After their odd exchange, he agreed their conversation would be better in private. That didn't stop him from tensing when she threaded her arm through his, giving her other patrons a wave and a wink. Catcalls followed them up the stairs.

Johnathan frowned down at her. "Was that necessary?"

"Better they think you're another lay than a copper."

His frown deepened. "But I'm not a copper."

Her sharp gaze slanted up at him, but she didn't say another word until Johnathan led her to his room. The demoness stood in the center of his room, observing him and their surroundings in flitting, curious glances. Her glance lingered on the tangled sheets of the bed.

"Are you alone here?"

Johnathan debated how to answer her question. If her sense of smell was anything like his, she would have already picked up on Vic's scent. "No." He fidgeted, unwilling to give her more information without discerning her intent. "Where are my manners? I'm Johnathan." She stared at his proffered hand, as if it would turn into a serpent and strike her.

"Hesper," she said at length, forgoing the handshake. She mulled him over for several minutes and, finally, relaxed in his presence. "Now please, tell me how a Hound doesn't have a Master?"

To Hell with good manners. Johnathan sat down hard on the rumpled bed, rubbing a hand along his jaw. "It's complicated," he said. His knowledge of the Nether was incredibly lacking, a dangerous truth to admit. There was an odd familiarity to Hesper's sex and honey scent to let him roll with a theory. Demons weren't something taught at length to Prospectives but there were plenty of old wives' tales and legends about beautiful demons who led men astray into their beds. "What is a succubus doing in this sneeze of a town?"

Hesper answered with a careless shrug, the collar of her chemise drooping off her bared shoulder. "Good people here. Rough around the edges, but their hearts are open and pure."

Her answer reminded him of Vic. "What about feeding?" A traitorous blush rose to from his cheeks to his ears.

Her mouth pinched. "Since I'm not a greedy idiot, I don't take more than my patrons can give." She crossed her arms, raising a brow at his reddened face. "You are the strangest Hound I've ever met."

Johnathan laughed at her comment, rubbing the back of his neck. "Can't argue there."

Lips twitching, Hesper sighed. "Besides, the cities are crawling with black coats. Playing a dangerous game, that lot."

His ears pricked up. "Black coats? You mean the Society?" He'd shredded out of his black coat when he shed his human skin, but he wasn't about to divulge his origin to the succubus.

She nodded, failing to suppress a shudder. "You'd better steer clear yourself. I've heard plenty of rumors they are attempting to procure a Hound for themselves."

That was painfully true though it threw him that a demon in a backwater town far from Cress Haven knew of the Society's intentions when he'd been in the dark. "Heard from whom?"

"Ah, ah, I think that's enough free answers, Sir Hound," taunted the succubus, wagging a finger at him. She plopped down next to him on the bed, her skirts hiking up high to bare her thighs. The sight did positively nothing for him, though she wasn't perturbed by his lack of reaction. Peering hard into his face, she sucked on a tooth. "You truly have no master?"

"No," said Johnathan.

Hesper leaned back, tapping her fingers on top of the mattress. "The essence of the Nether still clings to you. You haven't been on this plane for long."

Not a question, though it invited an answer. Johnathan wasn't sure he wanted to share. Except Hesper didn't feel like a threat to him. Everything she said to him revealed something new and useful with every answer. He was surprised she sensed the Nether around him. "I was human three days ago."

Her lips parted. Shock rolled over her face. "You're—you're made," she whispered. "I should have guessed that by the name. Honestly, Johnathan, the Hound?" The succubus hugged herself. "Who bargained their way out of the Nether?" There was a strain of fear in her voice.

"Cernunnos," said Johnathan. The name stung his mouth when he spoke it out loud, a poignant reminder of the creature who'd stolen his humanity and nearly subsumed his will. Hesper didn't look happy to hear it either, a shudder running through her frame. He held up his hands. "We undid the bargain."

Hesper grimaced. "And you're still here." She gave him an appraising look, opening and closing her mouth. A long breath streamed out between her lips. "Pray you never end up on the Netherside, Johnathan. The elder demons never forget, and they never forgive."

That was a fate he wanted to avoid. "How does one end up on the Netherside, exactly?"

Disbelief pinched her brow, but she answered him. "Your physical body is destroyed on this plane. Your Master is destroyed." Hesper ticked off her fingers. "Or you get yourself exorcised, but most humans don't remember how to properly do that these days."

No, they wouldn't after the Society's steady campaign to reduce the Nether, Other, and Benign to nothing more than children's stories. Though Hesper confirmed what he already suspected. Cernunnos's physical body might have died, but he was alive in the Nether. "Why did you think I would take you back?"

"You really are a greenhorn, aren't you?" Hesper leaned into him. Her fingers gently pressed on his upper arm. "That's what Hounds do Johnathan. That is their purpose. The trackers and guardians of the Nether. A Hound can find a demon in any of the four realms." She sniffed. "Though you wouldn't catch any respectable demon in the company of those gilded bastards."

Johnathan wasn't certain who she referred to. Gilded didn't seem like a term to describe the fairies. "The Benign?"

Hesper harrumphed. "They aren't safe either, you know. Not for long. Those black coats are gunning for us all." Her gaze turned distant for a moment, coming back to the present with an alluring smile. "So, if you're not here to drag me back to the Nether, is there anything I can do for a fellow demon?"

She purred, shifting closer to him. "It's been so long since I've seen another." Her appearance wavered, offering a glimpse of darkened clay red skin, long black claws, and elegant curling horns rising from Hesper's mane of curls.

"That is very kind of you," said Johnathan. "And while you are quite lovely, I'm afraid I'm taken."

Hesper's brows lifted so high they disappeared beneath her hairline. "You are full of surprises, Hound." She gave a deliberate sniff, a knowing smile tilting her lips. "Oh. *Oh*. What a fortunate *gentleman*. And look at you, all blushing." She giggled.

The door opened. Vic stormed, so distracted it wasn't until he slammed the door and leaned back against it that he realized Johnathan wasn't the only one in the room. His head turned, guarded gaze observing the tableau of Johnathan and Hesper, barefoot and half-dressed on the bed.

"Well, this is unexpected," he said. Hesper's lips curled at his statement, a slight tilt of her hips causing her skirts to reveal even more warm, smooth skin in blatant invitation. Johnathan frowned at her.

"This is not what you think," said Johnathan, gesturing between himself and the succubus, though Hesper didn't help clarify matters.

Vic took a prowling step toward them. "You know what I'm thinking now?" There was a hint of humor in his tone, but Johnathan caught a sharp tang in his normally smooth citrus scent. What was that? His brows knotted.

"You haven't caught me in some uninspired tryst," said Johnathan. "No offense," he muttered to Hesper.

"Oh, none taken," she said. Yet she didn't move away from him. Her body shifted, until she was flush against his side, her curves on full display. "He is very pretty." Her fingers twined in her hair, the scent of honey and vanilla pouring off her skin.

Vic's steps faltered, his pupils dilating. "Who is your lovely friend, John?"

Johnathan finally recognized the change in Vic's scent, Hesper's scent weaving an invisible net around him. He scowled at the succubus. "Do you mind toning it down?"

Her lips drew into a pouting moue. "Sorry, can you blame me?" She tossed her hair over her shoulder, baring her neck. Vic's gaze fell to the area, an alarming flare of hunger in his eyes.

"Hesper," Johnathan snapped. But his voice broke through whatever burgeoning influence she'd been coiling around Vic. He jumped back, shaking his head hard.

The succubus pursed her lips. "Interesting. I think your pull is stronger than mine."

Vic's reaction was not so blasé. His lips drew back over his teeth. "What the hell is that creature, John?" He pointed an accusing finger at Hesper. Johnathan swore his fangs were more prominent now, though whether from hunger or anger, it didn't feel like the opportune time to bring the matter up.

"She's a succubus," Johnathan explained. Vic blinked, sputtering. Hesper snorted, delicately rearranging her body and dress to appease Johnathan. Her overpowering scent drained from the air.

"You have absolutely no tact," she said.

Regaining his composure, Vic offered a far calmer smile, though his discomfort bled through. "Hello. Pleasure." His gaze shifted to Johnathan. "May I speak to you a moment, John?"

Johnathan murmured an apology to Hesper, joining Vic on the other side of the room. The man wore a grimace, side eyeing the succubus who hadn't moved from her spot on the bed. "I leave you alone for an hour and you pick up a demon. Really, John?" Vic whispered the admonishment though Hesper likely heard every word.

"I didn't mean to, it was an accident," said Johnathan with a helpless shrug. "I sort of...sniffed her out." His cheeks reddened again.

"Yes, but why did you bring her to our room?" Vic spoke through his teeth. He appeared unsettled by his reaction to the woman, or perhaps his lack of control over his reaction, if Johnathan hazarded a guess. This was the closest he'd seen Vic to unhinged, which included their violent encounters with Evans and his men. Fighting through impalement and Deadman's blood didn't rattle Vic in the slightest but succumbing to Hesper's charms appeared to leave him unbalanced.

Moving up a step, Johnathan pressed his forehead to Vic's, the sharpness receding from his scent. "We couldn't have it out in front of the other patrons. Safer to talk up here." He reached up, gripping Vic's shoulder, the muscles tighter than a drum beneath his hold. "She thought I was here to capture her."

Vic released a breath, some of the awful tension easing at Johnathan's reply. He glanced over Johnathan's shoulder at the waiting succubus. "Forgive me, my exposure to demons is minimal and the interactions have been mixed."

The succubus lifted her hands in a complacent gesture. "If you're not here to capture me, I have no qualms with your presence." She held up a finger. "Unless you intend to claim feeding grounds. This area is taken."

Her words leeched what little color was left from Vic's face. "No, we are passing through. I've secured passage from this town to leave by first light." He moved closer to her, impatience evident in his mien, when Hesper suddenly stiffened. Johnathan couldn't discern the emotion that flickered over her features, gone in an instant, but there was a strange gleam in her gaze. Her shoulders heaved with her next breath, at odds with her apparent calm.

Hesper tapped her chin. "By coach or by boat."

While the succubus appeared to have no quarrel with them, they hadn't established any substantial trust. Who knew who her loyalties extended to, other than herself? But Vic answered without hesitation, as if conversing with an old friend. "Well, the river of course. I'd rather avoid taking John through the city. We need to shake these Society louts on our trail. I need to get him further inland as soon as possible."

Hesper's mouth tightened at mention of the Society. Johnathan glanced between them. What the hell was Vic doing? "Vic—"

"What's waiting for you there?" A sing-song quality colored her tone.

She trailed her fingers over the swell of her breasts. Her honey vanilla scent remained muted but her voice made his ears ring.

"A safe p-place," Vic stuttered. He tried to choke back the words. A fine sweat broke out across his brow.

The world throbbed against Johnathan's temples. A flashfire raced through his veins. He stood before Hesper in a blink. His hand closed around her throat, claws sinking into the tender skin of her neck. Johnathan lifted her body off the bed and slammed her against the wall. The human guise vanished, exposing her dark red skin and horns. A long thin tail lashed between her calves. Her fear tasted spoiled and sickly sweet, while she whimpered under the pressure of his hold. "Please, I'm sorry," she pleaded, "I over stepped. I'll leave. Please."

His grip tightened. "Who is *your* master, Hesper?"

She tried to shake her head; the movement stunted. Her head thudded against the wall. "It's not like that," she gasped. "I promise, it's not like that. I had to know what you were bringing here." Her gaze slid to Vic and back, a frantic edge to her words. "You don't understand. You can't trust him. His kind will ruin you."

Johnathan wanted to shake her. Even with his hand cutting off her air, she tried to set them against each other. Whatever power her scent or voice held over Vic, he was immune to it. "Stop your manipulations." The words emerged as little more than a growl, fire rising beneath the surface of his skin. Smoke streamed from his lips.

Hesper's eyes were wide as saucers in her face. "It's not a manipulation. I swear it, I—I—" Her words dissolved into incoherent babble.

Vic's fingers closed on Johnathan's wrist. "Let her go, John," he said.

Instinct screamed at Johnathan to end the threat. To dig in his claws. Hesper hadn't been a threat before, not to him, not until she tried to use her influence on Vic.

"She's terrified," said Vic. The softness of his voice that cut through the warring urges in Johnathan's mind. He snatched his hand away. The succubus sucked in air, clutching her neck.

His breath came in short gasps, the Hound close to the surface. "I'm sorry," he said. Johnathan craved fresh air, desperate to clear the foreign rage from his system, but he didn't dare leave Vic alone with this demon, no matter how defeated she appeared.

"Do not apologize to the cunning little witch." Vic huffed at the succubus. "I think it's best if we part ways, my dear."

Hesper nodded, scurrying past them. She paused at the door, glancing back at Johnathan, the bruised skin of her neck already faded. Longing and regret etched in the lines of her lovely face before she escaped. The sight of those bruises swamped him with guilt. Johnathan was a brute. This was the first hand he laid on a woman before, having trained with several female Prospectives. He'd hunted at least one lady vampire, but he hadn't intended to hurt Hesper. The violence of his reaction agitated him. If Vic hadn't interfered, he would have killed her.

"Are you with me, John?" Vic cupped his cheek, a touch to soothe the rising beast. Inside, the Hellhound laid down and showed its belly. Johnathan didn't know how to perceive that reaction.

Nodding assent, he stood mute while Vic hustled about the room, gathering the remains of Johnathan's scattered clothing. The memory of their intimacy was far too distant in the wake of the succubus's departure.

"I'm sorry," Johnathan repeated; useless words, but it was all he could think to say.

Vic took his wrist leading him to the chair rather than the bed. "You didn't even eat," he chided, pushing Johnathan down on the seat and shoved his feet into the boots.

"I can do this myself," said Johnathan. Vic batted his hands away.

"Eat. Put your gloves on," he said. "We shouldn't stay here for the remainder of the night."

That was Johnathan's fault too. Cool fingers pressed against his open mouth.

"Not another apology, John," said Vic. "Neither of us could have predicted we'd run into another demon." Vic gave an exaggerated eye roll. "One encounter in five hundred years with a demon, now they are coming out the woodwork like startled mice." He brushed his fingers along the curve of Johnathan's lip. "Don't you dare try to shoulder the blame for this."

"I didn't think," said Johnathan. "I shouldn't have brought her up here. I shouldn't have left the room."

"Liar." Vic snorted. "You constantly over think. It's one of your charms."

Johnathan bit his lip against a smile. Vic made it easy to forget the foolishness of his actions. "She didn't feel dangerous."

Vic remained silent while he finished lacing Johnathan's boots, his brows knotted in thought. For his part, Johnathan forced down the cold stew. It smelled fine, though it tasted bland on his tongue and stuck in his throat like glue. He managed half the bowl before he gave up and pulled his gloves on. The smoldering embers of his irises were exposed, but at least the claws were concealed. It was a blessing no one noticed them when he first confronted the succubus downstairs, another amateur move, worse than a newly recruited Prospective.

"I don't think she was dangerous," said Vic, rising to his feet. "Not to you." He smoothed his hands down his coat, somehow remarkably unrumpled. "There is an open storehouse dockside we can wait until dawn."

Johnathan ambled after his far more chipper companion, glancing mournfully at the tub as they exited the room. He feared it would be a dreadfully long time before he had another hot soak.

CHAPTER SIX

THE DOWNSTAIRS EMPTIED SINCE HE'D TAKEN HESPER TO THEIR ROOM. The wall lamps were dimmed to nothing, the room lit by the dying glow of coals in the hearth. Vic headed straight for the door, but Johnathan lingered, scenting the air for any trace of the succubus. What remained was faint, suggesting she'd fled the premise. His feelings concerning the female demon were a complex knot. Not a wink of trust, but he hadn't intended or wanted to dislodge her from her hunting ground. Her attitude regarding feeding seemed to align with Vic's, to do as little harm as possible. Though, if the Society did follow Johnathan and Vic to this town, better she fled before their arrival. He had the distinct impression Luthor and Sister Wilhem would destroy Hesper rather than capture her.

Johnathan fell in behind Vic, eyeing the set of his shoulders. Feeding remained a sore subject between them. There was a worrisome pallor to Vic's complexion, an unmistakable sign the man hadn't fed. He knew Vic preferred his fastidious method of needles and tubes, but surely, he would feed like any other vampire to avoid starvation? Though he itched to broach the subject, after he ruined the safety of their accommodations, he refused to stress Vic further. They walked down the quiet street, Johnathan ruminating what their encounter revealed. Hesper's manipulation exposed

Vic's fears, ones he hadn't shared with Johnathan. What could he do to gain Vic's confidence? Why hadn't he shared his worries?

Distracted, he didn't notice the faint chiming until they arrived at the dock. His gaze swept the surrounding night, failing to penetrate the pitch-black darkness between moonset and dawn. Had he imagined it? Johnathan held his breath, listening. The store house jutted up through the darkness, a shadow within a shadow. A spare structure of rough wooden beams thick as weathered bones, the walled space gaping with a deeper blackness ready to swallow them up.

Vic realized he'd fallen behind, pausing in the ominous open front of the waterfront storehouse. "John? What's wrong?"

"Do you hear that?" Johnathan whispered.

"I don't hear anything." Vic frowned.

The only sounds Johnathan heard were the river, swirling and snapping against the shore, and their uneven breaths. The air scented of nothing at all. Unnatural. Apprehension flushed through his system. Not a hint of mud or the heady undergrowth, the faint musk of animals and vegetal decay, but a void. The signature of masking.

Wind rushed at his back. Johnathan spun sideways. Years of training and enhanced reflexes took the blade in the arm rather than his spine. He staggered with a grunt of pain.

"John!"

He ignored Vic's shout, frantically searching the dark for their assailants. How did they find him so fast? Johnathan yanked the knife from his arm and tossed it into the river. Better to whittle down the Agent's supply of blades than to blindly throw it back.

Where were they? Johnathan sidled closer to Vic, trying to discern any movement in the dark. His senses fired in a chaotic flare when Luthor unmasked directly next to him. There was no time to analyze the man's worrisome level of skill. He aimed a kick for Johnathan's knee. A last second twist absorbed the bruising impact on his thigh. Luthor's dark gaze glared up at him, brimming with hate. He launched into a series of kicks and punches that kept Johnathan on the defensive, matching his supposedly superior speed.

Vic swore, a momentary distraction Johnathan couldn't afford. He risked a look. A dozen Agents surrounded them, the red clad of figure of Sister Wilhem a scarlet specter in the depths of the storehouse. The glance cost him. Luthor shoved a blade into his shoulder, scraping against bone. Johnathan shouted. He clutched the handle, failing to deflect the kick to his chest. Off balance, his arms pinwheeled to keep him on his feet, an agonizing motion. The punctured muscles in his shoulders screamed, blood soaked through his coat.

"Take them alive, Luthor," Sister Wilhem ordered, an overt threat in her voice. "I want both specimens for further examination." The words chilled Johnathan. Her cohort acknowledged her with the barest nod, but he knew from experience *alive* was a flexible definition. Johnathan tore the blade from his shoulder, flipping it in his grip to arm against the other Agent.

Another blade slid into Luthor's hand. He pressed the attack with a downward swing at Johnathan's chest. Adrenaline flooded his system. Johnathan caught the man's wrist, quickly stepping into his personal space to strike. He released his hold on Luthor's wrist and smashed the heel of his palm into the man's face. A clumsy hit, but a painful one. Luthor snarled and jumped back. Between one hit and the next, Johnathan buried the Agent's blade in his chest, a wound to match. He tugged the blade from his shoulder in a gush of blood. Luthor stared at Johnathan, bloodied teeth bared in a feral grin.

"I don't know what sort of fiend you are, but you fight like one of us." Luthor spat out a mouthful of blood. Johnathan didn't welcome the comparison. "Deadman's blood hasn't even slowed you down. Marvelous."

That wasn't a card he intended reveal, internally cursing he hadn't noticed the poison. An ineffective poison once it hit his blood, since Luthor appeared unbothered by poison or stab wound. He brushed the wound, tasting the blood off his fingertips. His dark gaze widened. "You've neutralized it," he said, a hint of chilling wonder in his voice. Johnathan tensed when that unhinged gaze focused on him.

Luthor vanished in front of him. "Shit." Johnathan dropped into a crouch, bracing himself. He was desperate to end this fight and aid Vic, though he dared not divert his attention twice.

A blade whispered against the side of his throat. Johnathan grabbed Luthor's arm, the Hunter reacting ahead of the Hound. He threw Luthor across the river. Soon as he confirmed the splash, Johnathan spun toward Vic.

There were a few Agents on the ground, in rough shape but alive. Far too many were on their feet, armed with spears and bayonets attached to rifles. They surrounded Vic, bleeding from a half a dozen cuts and unsteady on his feet. Sister Wilhem approached Vic out of his line of sight; a spider-silk thin, golden net laced between her bony fingers. Johnathan could guess the purpose of such a strange object, and he didn't want it anywhere near Vic.

The Sister's steps paused. Her milk white gaze turned to him, somehow aware of his attention. A sneer twisted her lips. "That useless idiot. Seize him," she snapped. Half the Agents shifted their attack to Johnathan, brandishing their blades. He ignored them, panic fluttering in his chest when the remaining Agents pressed forward on the vampire. A bayonet cut across Vic's cheek.

Rage strummed a chord through Johnathan's body. He seized one of the weapons thrust at his face, snapping the blade in half. A flinch ran through the cluster of Agents. They fumbled their weapons, punctuated by a click and spark. A deafening crack and flash of burnt gunpowder exploded in the dark.

"I said take them alive!" Sister Wilhem's muffled shout of protest echoed in Johnathan's ears.

Pain splintered through his sternum. Johnathan frowned at the smoking hole in his chest, where the blood pumped from the wound in time to his pulse.

"Fuck me." His legs buckled, the crackle of flame roaring through his skull. He hit the ground hard on his knees and exhaled a plume of smoke, Johnathan looked up, a high ringing pitch in his head drowned out the world. Flame licked the edge of his wandering gaze. The Agents backed away from him, confused.

Sister Wilhem watched him expectantly, her gaze lit with dark excitement. They locked gazes. Whatever she saw in Johnathan's face caused her to blanche and recede into the darkness. She vanished without warning the other men. Eyes wide, Vic staggered.

Johnathan fell forward on his hands and knees. A hoarse cry tore from his lips, his back bowed, punctuated by the snap and crack of his spine. His veins ignited. Bones burned to brittle ash, ground to dust from which new growth swelled. His body twisted into unfamiliar angles, parts of him turned inside out. Another scream ripped out of him. Bones protruded through his back in a gruesome display, receding beneath the swell of the Hound's muscles and the prickling ripple of thick black fur. His final scream ended on a mangled note; a mouth no longer capable of human sound protruded from his jaw, settling with a clack of sharp teeth. This was nothing like his first transformation, every agonizing second seared into his mind until at last he rose on all fours, staring at the gaping Agents through the Hound's burning gaze.

The Hound growled; a low threatening rumble, fire sparking between his teeth. The group took a collective step back, except for the man in the middle, anguish in his silver eyes. The Hound took a step forward, the ground charred beneath his paws. Several of the Agents fumbled with their weapons, metal and wood slipping over sweaty palms. The bitter stench of their fear drenched his tongue, stoking the rage that burned at his core, an endless white-hot blaze. It spurred him on, demanding a tribute of violence. He salivated for the taste of blood, of flesh torn beneath his teeth. The sound that rolled from his mouth was a call from the depths of the Nether, a promise of Hellfire and death. The stink of urine stained the air. The Hound sank down, powerful thighs bunching and launched him at the nearest man. His jaw closed around the man's throat, cutting off his scream. Hot blood splashed down the back of his throat. Teeth scraped bone. He tore his mouth free.

The man collapsed, a final breath gurgled through his torn throat. Blood poured from the hole into a swollen pool of dark liquid. A lull descended over the remaining men, ensnared by their terror, witnesses to the violent demise of their companion. The quiet burst in flurry of panic, the men in a mad scramble to escape, to fight, to survive. The Hound swung his massive head, the need to rend and tear unsated.

Through the tunnel of blood and fear, the Hound connected with a silver gaze. An alluring stillness in the haze of fear and frenzy. The muscles of his jaw taut with distress. Pale hands reached for him, palms up, defenseless, submissive. "John, look at me," the man whispered, his voice soothed, a calm amid the shouts of others. "Come back to me."

The name made him pause, both familiar and foreign, tugging him forward. The Hound hesitated.

Gunshot split the air. The silver eyed man clasped his arm with a hiss. The Hound tasted the trail of bitter burnt gun powder, wheeling on the shooter. A young face, a terrified face, the pistol fell from his trembling fingers.

"No, Johnathan, wait, don't," a voice gasped, swallowed by the roar of flames. The edges of his vision flared in bright red-orange hues. The world narrowed, an ashen tunnel that ended with his jaws sinking into the young man's flesh.

The Hound burned, bound to the call of claw. To rend the souls of the living. And he answered. Their fear coated his tongue, sour against the coppery taste of blood and seared meat. The Hound released his victim with one final violent yank, the body still on the ground. A howl rose from the depths of his chest. The sound broke over the remaining men, a visceral reminder their death loomed. They attempted to flee, scattering in either direction, but the Hound gave chase. He fell upon them, ran them to ground. They cursed and flailed, unable to accept their fate. Limbs scattered across the ground, the air soaked by the coppery tang of blood and foul stink of viscera. The Hound gorged, drunk on their fear and sweet, toothsome flesh. He drank down their deaths until he finally quelled the hungering rage. The inferno subsided, fur and flame yielded the man.

Johnathan's awareness returned with a vengeance, crouched on all fours at the center of a massacre. Blood drenched his hair and naked skin. The knife wounds and bullet hole in his chest were completely healed, without leaving a hint of a scar. Foul muck clung to his fingers; the ground saturated by gore. Panting, he sat back on his haunches, gaze locked on the scene around him. "Oh god," he rasped. His gorge rose, the overwhelming scent of death coated the inside of his mouth.

He'd torn them apart. Horrified, Johnathan searched for Vic, praying he'd escaped unharmed, and froze.

Vic stood in the same position he was when Johnathan fell. Blood painted his clothes in splattered patterns. An arc sprayed across his face, the heavy droplets slid down his cheek. Blood dripped from his outstretched hands, gathering in his open palms. Vic stared into the small pools, fixated. His mouth was open, a visible tremor in his jaw, while his shoulders hunched inward. His whole body vibrated with strain, pupils blown. Tentatively, his tongue flicked past his lips, slowly reaching toward the blood on his cheek.

Johnathan stifled a cry, caught in a vice of pain and fear. Vic paused. He closed his mouth with a quiet click of teeth. He didn't drop his hands, flexing his bloodied fingers. Stillness reclaimed his form, the hesitation a warning. Finally, he tore his gaze off the blood to look at Johnathan. The two stared at one another in stunned silence. Blood bloomed down the front of Vic's shirt and torn open jacket, a crimson ink stain spreading between them.

The silence stretched, bloated by the dead. Vic sucked in a shaking breath, and dropped his hands, bloody fingers clenched at his sides.

"Yell at me," he breathed. "Scream at me." A stricken look crossed his face. "I've failed you so badly."

Johnathan's throat bobbed. "Come here, please come here." He clasped the air, willing Vic to come closer, but the other man hesitated, anguish and shame warring for dominance in his expression.

"Come to me," said Johnathan, the words rough and raw. Vic finally acquiesced, stepping close enough for Johnathan to pull him the rest of the way. They crashed together, chest to chest. He wrapped his arms around Vic, heart pounding against his ribs. Dropping his face against the man's neck, desperate to breathe him in, he grasped for a tether through the horror of the moment. Beneath the clinging filth of death, he found the clean scent of citrus and musk, bruised by Vic's distress. His arms shook from the effort not to crush Vic against him.

Vic clutched at his naked back, his sob muffled by Johnathan's shoulder. They held each other, mindless of time, the filth, and the blood until the first stirrings of the morning dock crew washed over them in a burst of icy reality.

I killed them all. A hollow ache burrowed in the center of Johnathan's chest and swelled outward until the comfort of Vic's scent curled away with the morning fog.

"We need to get out of here." A numbness settled over Johnathan, and he sank into it An armor against the grisly necessities he had to commit. Snagging an empty burlap sack off from a skiff, he tied it around his waist, surveying their options. "I doubt we'll be able to wait for our ride. There's a barge preparing to push off for the day."

Vic's stared at him. "John?"

"Can't exactly leave this here either," said John, his tone neutral, void of emotion. He seized a pair of legs, dragging the dismembered body away from the center of the room through the stacks of pallets. There was no way to hide what he'd done, only delay discovery long enough for the first boats of the day to depart. Dead flesh was cold to the touch, almost waxen without the flush of vitality. He buried the shuddersome sensation deep, moving the bodies quickly. There was no sign of Sister Wilhem among the dead. Luthor might have swum ashore to rejoin the fight, but Johnathan believed he didn't. The Agent was risk adverse, a man who coated his blades in poison to strengthen his odds. If he didn't drown, he'd slink away for another day.

Vic watched him, his concern evident, but whatever he thought of Johnathan's behavior, he tucked it away to deal with their current situation. The two of them made quick work of the scene, moving the bits of pieces of the dead until only the bloody sludge remained.

One of the hanging rakes took care of the mess, The fresh dirt diminished most of the stink, a temporary mask for the fetid muck. Such a simple thing, a trick of the eye, it only took them a few minutes at most, though the sky was significantly lighter. They were rapidly losing their window to depart, sight unseen. Vic used the waxed sheet off a waiting pallet of lumber to cover the gruesome pile, the cloth settling over the bodies, muting the jut of exposed bone and ragged pieces, an illusion that would be spoiled when the blood finally seeped through.

There was nothing more to do. Johnathan nodded toward the docks.

"You move faster. Can you get us onto a boat without attracting too much attention?"

Vic seized his shoulders, trying to catch his eye. "You're too calm." Worry threaded his voice. Johnathan gently dislodged his hands.

"We need to go," Johnathan repeated. He tugged on the frayed edges of his temporary covering while he waited for Vic to act. He refused to meet Vic's stare. He could not. There was a deceptive softness to the raked dirt under his feet. He hated the give of the ground, imaging the blood oozing up through the empty footprints he left behind.

Arms circled his waist, the familiar scent of Vic a cold comfort. Johnathan closed his eyes against the blur of motion. Varying shades of light and darkness played against the back of eyelids. They skidded to a stop on one of the barges, kneeling between rows of cargo. The pallets were stacked just high enough to conceal their presence if they remained in a crouch. It wasn't ideal but it would be enough to get them away from the shore. Hopefully far enough from the small, sleepy port town before they uncovered his sin.

Johnathan slid out of Vic's hold and slumped down on the rough wooden floor of the barge. Blood and dirt had dried in tacky patches on his skin. A thick layer of rust colored grit was stuck under his fingernails.

The taste of metal lingered in his mouth; the memory of his teeth sinking into flesh rushed to the surface of his thoughts.

Johnathan scrabbled to the edge of the barge and emptied his guts into the river.

CHAPTER SEVEN

A SOUR SICK SMELL CLUNG TO JOHNATHAN AND MINGLED WITH THE foul bouquet caked on his skin. He yearned for a dousing of that wretched perfume. A quiet settled over the barge, filled with the creak of the hull and whine of the winch and harness where the team of mules dragged the barge along via the riverbank. Occasionally, the spare crew called to one another or groused around the small cabin. The quiet permeated the air and allowed Johnathan to stew in his remorse.

Vic hadn't engaged him in conversation since they left the docks, but the man didn't leave his side. Even now, he brushed against Johnathan, a subtle, vital contact to ground him. The blood on Vic's face flaked off as it dried. The stained shirt crinkled when he shifted, but he made no move to remove it or clean himself. He remained a stoic guardian, the immovable pillar the tide of Johnathan's shame and guilt crashed against. Patient and calm while Johnathan processed the trauma of their encounter.

The gradual glow of sunlight grew stronger as the day took hold. The barge maintained a placid pace on the river, broken by intermittent breaks for the mule team to rest in the infrequent patches of overhanging shade. There was little reprieve from the sun on the river. The depth of the stacks provided an indirect cover that waned through the morning, the warmth of the day added another layer of discomfort, sweat seeping through the dried caked on filth. Flies buzzed around Johnathan's head, but none landed. The insects were wary of his presence.

It was close to midday when Johnathan's choked sob broke the silence. Vic laid his head on his shoulders. "Forgive me, John."

Johnathan leaned back into the wooden boxes stacked on the pallet. "I'm positive that's my line," he said.

A crooked smile curved Vic's mouth. "I promised I would help you find another way to survive. We didn't make it a week before you were forced into another terrible position." He plucked the stiff rust-stained edge of his sleeve. "If I hadn't been half out of my mind with hunger, I might have been able to prevent it," he confessed.

Johnathan studied him. The shadows beneath Vic's eyes were deeper, hollows in his skull. He remembered that weighted moment at the docks, ensnared by the blood on his hands. Guilt etched the beautiful lines of Vic's face. Did he truly blame himself for Johnathan's actions? "What about your other kit? You told me you had a back-up. Why haven't you fed?"

"I lost my kit in the river," Vic admitted. "I told myself I could hold off until I replaced it. That was the only reason I had to risk the city." He licked his lips. "There was no other reason to go. My arrogance, my stubbornness, led to this."

"No, Vic, no," said Johnathan. He laid a hand against Vic's back, wishing he could summon the right words. Alyse was better with words. "We couldn't prepare for this." How could they? His need for rest slowed them down, and their encounter with the succubus threw Vic off balance before they reached the docks. The Society Agents caught them off guard, tracked them faster and more accurately than he'd ever seen, an inhuman pace.

He recalled the coerced information Hesper dragged out of Vic. "That safe place you mentioned? What is it?"

Vic's shoulders hunched inward. "That would be the Estate, and it might be selfish of me to bring you there," he said. The admission was lost on Johnathan since he'd never heard of it. "It's more than a sanctuary, but that's if I can convince the proprietors to take us in."

A beat of silence passed while Johnathan mulled his answer. "Why would it be selfish to bring me there?"

"The Estate is a supernatural haven. I have allies there, but it's not safe for *you*," said Vic. "Demons are rare enough to be an unquantifiable threat, and, usually, they are dangerous. They are not welcome on the grounds." He tugged at his lower lip. "But, if I can convince them that you are safe, it's our best chance for answers."

"I'm not safe," said Johnathan.

Vic inhaled through his nostrils. "Safe enough, John."

He swallowed. "What about our persistent new friends?" The extent of Sister Wilhem's resources was a worrisome mystery. If Luthor survived, and Johnathan was convinced he had, both would come after then soon as they recuperated from their loss.

Johnathan didn't believe Vic's motivations were selfish, but he worried what the other man would do if they were turned away. The Estate offered a respite and possible information. They had to try.

"They might have answers. Maybe we'll get the chance to explore the rules and pitfalls to this bond we created," said Vic.

"We have been fumbling around in the dark." Johnathan refused to hope, aware of the obstacles to overcome before they reached any level of safety. Part of him believed it would have been better for Vic if he succumbed to the Nether, but he didn't voice that out loud.

Vic reached down and grasped his hand, threading their fingers together. "I promised you I would help you walk this path and I meant it." Johnathan met his gaze, the hollow ache in his chest momentarily forgotten.

There it was, the vulnerability he craved, a tenuous thread that connected them. He lifted his hand to brush a strand of hair out of Vic's face, the sight of dried blood under his fingernails drawing him up short. His hand fell slack to his lap. Vic's expression was stark at the failed gesture. Johnathan wanted to tell him it wasn't his fault. He wasn't worth the trouble. Throat tight, mouth dry, he said nothing at all. Screams echoed in his head. Nausea gripped him, though nothing remained in his stomach to expel.

"Come back, John." Vic's voice prodded at the edges of that gaping hollow inside him. He wanted to close his eyes but dared not, afraid what grisly memories would play inside the theater of his mind. Instead, he inhaled deeply, drawing in Vic's scent for comfort, small as it was.

This was a time for truths, of inner wounds laid bare in this ephemeral moment between them.

"This wasn't like the first time," he said. "I didn't cede into the background for the beast to takeover. The Hound was me, and I was the Hound." His fingers curled into fists. "I remember everything. I felt everything." The muscles of his jaw flexed. He remembered the give of flesh between his teeth, the coppery splash of hot blood on his tongue. Death lingered, rotten and sweet in his mouth, and a secret mortified piece of him relished the taste.

A pained expression crossed Vic's face. He lifted his face to the clear sky, the brilliant blue a mockery after the violence of the night. "I am an old monster," he said. "Older than most of us get."

Johnathan frowned. This was true. Most vampires didn't survive beyond their first century of life, too hungry and arrogant for caution. Too vicious to avoid a challenge, yet the remnants of their human lives made them crave the company of others. If hunters didn't kill them, older vampires often did, unwilling to share their feeding grounds with some cocked up youngster. But Vic wasn't an anomaly. Vampires who made it past their first century were good at surviving, and there were plenty. Many of them had a notorious reputation and a bloody history in the Society archives.

"Five centuries, I've sought to control the dark half of my nature," said Vic. His expression shifted to something bleak, threaded with old guilt. "I spent a great deal of time with others of my kind. We bring out the cruelty in one another, giving in to our darkest cravings, glutting ourselves on blood. The longer we stay together, the worse we become."

Johnathan stared at him, unable to picture Vic anywhere close to cruel though he knew it was true. Sir Harry, the vampire who raised him, avoided other vampires. There were half a dozen living together only a few streets over from where he sheltered during the day. More than once, they found the broken remains of their victims within Sir Harry's hunting grounds. His guardian's cool hand would cover his eyes, but the sight was carved in his memory.

He had encountered a few groups as a Prospective. Once, his training unit had stumbled on a feeding frenzy. A trio of vampires feeding on a single victim. They drank and drank and drank, eager for every drop of blood. They tore the body apart, sucking at the marrow. So drunk on the feeding, they weren't aware they were being attacked until their heads were separated from their bodies. A group of vampires could decimate a village if left unchecked. But groups didn't last, falling to the same foils of unwanted attention and inner turmoil.

"What made you stop?"

Vic sighed. "I like humans. They are bright and vibrant. All the more because they cling so fiercely to life, fragile as it is." He clutched his elbows. "I—I want to protect them from that dreadful appetite. From me. But the hunger is always there, waiting for me to slip. I fooled myself, convinced my will was ironclad." His sad smile was full of ghosts. "Turns out I'm a monster and a liar."

There were centuries of secret sins and haunted regrets in the shadows of Vic's gaze. Johnathan wondered at his own naïveté, convinced of Vic's kind nature. He fiercely believed in Vic's control, when he knew that nobility came at a steep price. Johnathan had ignored the five hundred years of history Vic carried, weighed by the dark deeds of survival. The dogmatic human he'd been would have distanced himself from that truth, unable to handle the perceived deception. But the demon inside him understood.

He pulled Vic into his arms, kissing his temple. They were both scarred and scared of themselves, two monsters desperate to undermine their darker halves. Vic spent the last five hundred years of his life trying to find a different way to exist, to better himself for the sake of the humans he cared for, a far nobler pursuit than any man Johnathan knew. Guilt weighed on them, the guilt of a life taken, the guilt of a failure to act. It didn't matter they were being attacked, not when they possessed the strength and the power to extract themselves from the conflict.

Could they have fled without a massacre? The possibility would hang over Johnathan for a long time.

"You're not a liar," Johnathan murmured against his cheek. "We're both trying to be better." There was comfort in knowing Vic struggled so hard to hold onto his humanity. It didn't erase his feelings, but it eased the vicious guilt and shame that ate at him inside, to know he wasn't alone. "We'll walk that path together."

The tension seeped out of Vic in a stilted breath. Had he been afraid of Johnathan's rejection? An absurd notion when their conversation gave him so much insight to the vampire. The proverbial needle threaded, the discomforts of their situation took precedence. Johnathan could no longer ignore the rough wood digging into his bare backside.

"My chances with this safe house would probably improve with pants."

The chuckle was strained. "We really should find a way to look presentable," said Vic, peering through the slats of stacked cargo. "Hopefully there's another small giant among the crew so we can borrow some clothing for you."

"You'll need a new set as well," Johnathan teased. "Think you can stand donning such humble garments?"

Their banter didn't banish the hollow ache in his chest, nor had the wariness left Vic's gaze. The specter of violence lurked inside, waiting for him to drop his guard. For a moment, on the quiet river, with Vic at his side, it was better.

They waited until the barge stopped for the night. The four-man crew switched out two teams of mules throughout the day, but both teams required a few hours rest before they could resume the heavy work. This time there was no port or town, the trees thinning into stretches of farmland. The fields ran for miles, the flat landscape broken by a humble house and barn. Desperate for a shower and sustenance, the open fields and water troughs were a strangely compelling argument for leaving the barge. The craft wasn't built to accommodate passengers, made to transport cargo. A small cabin at the far end of the ship served as sleeping quarters for the crew. The barge was long but narrow. The stacks of cargo provided the only vertical break. It was an utter miracle they'd lasted the day without being spotted, but other than tending the haul mules on shore, there wasn't much reason to crawl between the cargo to ferret out stowaways.

"A quick scrub, raid a clothesline, no one's the wiser," said Vic, surveying their scant options with a calculating expression.

"I thought we were going to scavenge for supplies on the ship?" Unease prickled down Johnathan's exposed back.

Vic rolled his shoulders, shuddering at the audible crinkle from his clothes. "Honestly better if we don't. These are working men, not a lot to spare. I'd rather not take anything that will be missed and give them a reason to search for it." He started to move to the edge of the barge when Johnathan's hand clamped on his wrist.

"Don't," said Johnathan. Heat flared behind his eyes, a warning buzzed along his nerves. There was no rationale to his reaction, but he *knew* leaving the river was bad. Vic waited for him to explain. "I think...I think if you go ashore, they'll find us again." He didn't need to clarify who would find them again, though he didn't understand how he was so certain.

Vic glanced longingly at the shore but didn't dismiss Johnathan's trepidation. "I'm coming to respect your instinctual urges."

"Unless I'm the boy who cried wolf," muttered Johnathan.

"Doubtful. I wouldn't be surprised if a Hound can sense when its being tracked," said Vic. "Neither of us dispatched those two blighters. Nor do we know how they found us so fast." He nudged Johnathan's shoulder. "Besides, you *are* the wolf, not the boy."

"We still don't know why they've latched onto us." Johnathan huffed, though he had an unpleasant theory he wasn't ready to broach. "We'll have to make do with what's on hand." He raised a brow at the frown on Vic's face. "Why are you pouting?"

"This barge is so slow," Vic groaned. "It will take us twice as long to reach the Estate."

They were safe on the river, but could they remain unnoticed for an extended length of time? Johnathan considered their options, hoping the safe house would be their ultimate destination rather than a disappointment. "How long?"

"Another four days maybe?" Vic grimaced, gesturing to the dreadful state of his clothes. "We need to do something about this, Johnathan. I don't care if I must wear another burlap sack."

"What a sight that would be," Johnathan murmured. Vic scoffed. He crept across the barge to find what supplies he could. Alone, Johnathan fought to keep still. The sack he'd secured around his waist offered little modesty. The fabric was intensely uncomfortable against his privates. A dunk in the river would be paradise after spending the day covered in filth but he didn't dare move until Vic returned. His naked skin would be a pale beacon in the moonlight.

The barge was the worst mode of transport they could have chosen, limited as their options were. The bundles of cargo smelled of old wood, moldering hay, and wet animal, suggesting the barge transported a shipment of cloth. Waxed sheets protected them from the rain. A musty, stale odor billowed out when Johnathan lifted one, but it was dry, and there was enough slack to offer a spare space to hide if they pressed in tight. It would be enough to keep them from notice for four days.

A rush of air heralded Vic's return. A bundle of items spilled from his full arms. The fruits of his raiding proved abundant; a crumpled wad of clothing, a promising sack which smelled of dried meat, a bar of soap, and a spare rag.

"I'm afraid I couldn't find boots to fit those large feet," Vic apologized.

"I thought we were trying to keep the thievery to a minimum," said Johnathan.

Vic sniffed. "Nothing but necessities, my flower," he said, shoving the bar of soap at Johnathan. "Come on, we'll take turns dipping each other in the river."

Absurd though it was, that was exactly what they did. The hour was late and dark enough that anyone stumbling upon the barge would mistake them for two naked ghouls bathing in the moonlight. When Vic hauled him out of the water, Johnathan had managed to scrub most of the dried blood and muck from his skin. The soap smelt strongly of lye, but the rumpled clothes were clean.

Vic agreed the waxed sheet would provide a suitable cover. He eked out a space for them while Johnathan dried and dressed.

When Johnathan crawled in beside him, Vic was still muttering about the poor quality of his shirt. He ignored his fastidious companion and pulled a strip of dried meat from the sack to nibble on, despite his lack of appetite. He refused to let hunger muddle his thoughts.

"This is cozy," said Vic.

"You almost sound sincere," said Johnathan. He leaned back against the stacked bolts of cloth, grateful to be clothed and somewhat clean. "Hope you still enjoy my company after four days in such close quarters."

Vic's hand landed on his thigh He squeezed the muscle in a way that made Johnathan's insides tingle. "I'm sure we'll think of a way to pass the time."

CHAPTER EIGHT

A SOFTER BURN SPARKED IN JOHNATHAN'S STOMACH, THE NEED AND want a flood of sensual heat in his veins. Johnathan pulled Vic onto his lap. The space was not ideal for strenuous activity, but Vic took charge, pinning Johnathan's waist between his knees. He leaned in and brushed his lips along Johnathan's jaw, cradling his face in his hands.

This wasn't enough contact for Johnathan. He wrapped his arms around Vic, tunneling his hands through those thick auburn locks. Pressing their bodies together, Johnathan relaxed, wanting to sink in the distraction of that lush mouth.

Sightless dead eyes flashed through his mind, painted in garish tones on the backs of his closed lids. The soft drip of blood from gaping wounds echoed in his ears. Cold, slippery flesh and viscera slid beneath his fingers. He bit the inside of his cheek, the mineral taste flooded his mouth, touched with a hint of smoke. Johnathan sucked in a breath. His lust faded to a clammy chill. The enclosed darkness beneath the sheet suffocated him. Vic went still.

"Where did you go, John?" The soft-spoken question punctured his rising panic.

Vic pulled back. Cool fingers traced through the damp tear tracts on Johnathan's cheeks. Shame and nausea subsumed the pleasant heat in his gut. Bile crept up his throat, warring with the need for fresh air, but Johnathan didn't move.

"John?"

"I'm sorry," Johnathan whispered, his voice hoarse. Pressure closed around his chest, where the hollow inside him expanded in increments, threatening to swallow him from the inside out.

Vic pressed his forehead against Johnathan's, a gesture that echoed their earlier exchange, the roles reversed. "Breathe, John." His lips ghosted over Johnathan's tear-stained face. "Just breathe." Vic's hands smoothed down the back of Johnathan's neck and shoulders, each pass drawing a knot of tension from them.

"How do you do it?" Johnathan choked out the words. He gripped the back of Vic's shirt. "I can't forget their faces."

The rhythm of Vic's fingers didn't change, but there was a hitch in his breath. "You'll never forget their faces," he said. A deep sadness carried in his voice. "They're a weight that never dissipates, a shadow that grows in your wake. You simply learn to bear it."

"I killed them. Ripped them apart. Nothing but meat," whispered Johnathan. They attacked him. They attacked Vic. The Agents were intent on capturing them, Sister Wilhem bore down on Vic with her strange golden net. She'd referred to them as specimens. They'd fought for their lives, heavily outnumbered, but Johnathan knew there was a point, when the fight shifted to something else. The Agents broke and ran. Their fear saturated the air and he didn't stop. "I wanted to. I wanted to end them."

Vic's hands framed his face. "It won't be the last time you feel that urge, but you won't always answer it."

Johnathan's throat bobbed. "I can see their faces when I close my eyes. I see their fear. What I did to them."

"Guilt is good. It's vital," said Vic. "Without guilt, without remorse? We become the fiends the Society has every right to put down. But it can and will drag you into a void. You will learn to live with it."

"What if I can't?" The hollow inside his chest oozed, a band of tar that surrounded his organs. A lifetime of trauma, of violence and betrayal was something Johnathan dealt with, but this guilt, this was different.

Raw and intense, sharper than the serpent's tooth, the guilt seeped poison from that hollow place. The soothing rhythm of Vic's heartbeat stuttered beneath his fists.

"Then you won't last long," Vic murmured, the words laced with quiet grief. There was a subtle tightening in Vic's grip, as if Johnathan would slip through his fingers. It was a fair assumption.

They fell silent, the pause heavy with unspoken fears. Johnathan attempted to bury the guilt and shame, tangled his thoughts into a useless knot. Vic shifted off him, but didn't go far, nestling against Johnathan's side and clasping their hands together.

"Would you believe I didn't always possess a keen sense of fashion?"

The abrupt change in subject startled Johnathan out of his internal spiral. "What are you on about?"

Vic rested against his shoulder. The pad of his thumb stroked the back of Johnathan's hand. "I was a country noble, mind you. We were not the most forward-thinking lot. Between my humble origins and my time in the monastery, I didn't possess the knowledge or appreciation for what a carefully curated wardrobe could accomplish."

Johnathan said nothing. What was there to say? The man clearly lost his mind. His companion ignored his baffled silence and pressed on.

"That is, until I had the luck of running into a man named Francois Laroux," said Vic. Warmth seeped into his voice. "Now that man knew the power of a well-tailored waist coat. Lectured me about the subject on many occasions."

Realization ticked over. "He was your friend?"

"Oh yes, an excellent one. A brilliant mind, too. He recognized what I was not long after we began our acquaintance, but he kept it to himself for years, the blighter." Vic chuckled. "Francois was a spy for the French crown, and a good one. He moved in the circles of the wealthy for years under many aliases, but names, faces, are forgettable under the right cloth. The clothes we wear function as armor and mask. Finery and charisma gained him access to the gatherings and soirees of powerful men who never looked too closely at the man behind the brocade."

"This explains a lot about you," said Johnathan. "How did you meet him?"

Vic's mouth quirked in a self-depreciating smirk. "You could call it the end of a bad affair. I'd spent the better part of a century in the company of other vampires. They were older, cold, but they enjoyed the company of the young, their rashness and passion. I found them magnetic, glamorous, but I could feel myself slipping away. I told you; I like humans. I left with naught but the clothes on my back. I spent night after night, wandering the streets, hiding in crowded inns and taverns, slipping into the gatherings of the rich and the poor, trying to reconnect with humanity. One night, at some nobleman's soiree, after compelling the poor sod to give me a suit from his wardrobe, Francois sidled up to me with a drink in hand and told me I stuck out like a goose in a pigpen."

The comparison made Johnathan chuckle. Vic grinned. Mirth creased the corner of his eyes. "He knew I didn't belong. I could have sent him away, compelled him, scared him, but after spending so long in the company of my kind, the warmth of his skin, his steady heartbeat, even the faint whiff of body odor was a shock. It woke up something dormant inside. So, I asked him why, what made it so obvious. The expression on his face!" Vic snorted, scratching the bridge of his nose. "I think he knew I wasn't human right then, but he pulled me aside and ticked off my faults. The dreadful clash of color to my complexion to the improper ties of the vest. I'd never given much thought to clothing in my life, as a human or a vampire, but Francois took my appearance as a personal insult."

"Did he have you thrown from the party for your crimes?" Johnathan asked, curious how a friendship developed between the two.

"Quite the opposite. He took me home, dressed me from his own wardrobe. That is how the learning began," said Vic.

"Oh, you received a full-blown education from this man?"

"I did," confirmed Vic. "Francois taught me what it meant to hide in plain sight. He didn't care about my origins or what I was, but he insisted that if I intended to blend in the company of humans, I needed a better sense of fashion, of how to move with the times."

Vic's gaze was fond, though distant, caught in the memory. "He was a wit to the last. Thirty years, he charmed foreign nobles, often in my company, though I never used compulsion to ease the way. A master of his craft and not a drop of noble blood in his veins. I knew him by a dozen names during our years together and forgot most of them. But on his death bed, he told me his true name."

"Why tell you on his deathbed?" Johnathan was entranced by this piece of Vic's history.

"Because he lived a life to be forgotten. He knew I didn't age, though he never pressed me to share the secret. He never sought to become what I am. He simply asked me to remember him, to remember his name and to be its keeper," said Vic. "His own piece of immortality."

The tightness in Johnathan's chest eased. He found it strange at first, the seemingly random story of a human Vic knew centuries ago, but he recognized the intent. An offering, not only a soft distraction to the turmoil inside Johnathan, but Vic opening to him. More than a fond memory, this was a piece of who Vic was, a man who wore finery as a disguise, ached to connect with humans and wrestled with the darker aspects of his nature.

"Please, tell me more."

Vic smiled in the quiet, musty dark, warmer than sunshine.

During the day, they laid down beneath the sheet, pressed in tight against the wooden pallet akin to sardines packed in a tin. An unwelcome necessity when their theft was discovered. The small crew became more vigilant when they woke to discover their pilfered belongings, scouring the barge the next morning. That was the closest they came to discovery. Johnathan dared not breathe while the men crawled over the stacks of cargo. He feared what would happen if they were discovered, feared more blood on his hands. Vic pressed him back against the pallet, a finger over his lips.

The uneven edges of the wooden pallet dug into his back while Vic rested in his arms, a dichotomy of comfort and irritation. After his numerous injuries and mishaps, hunger took an evident toll on Vic, who craved rest to stave off the worst effects. Johnathan held him close during those long hours, grateful for the contact, the anchor that kept him from plummeting over a mental ledge.

There was no rest to be found, his mind continually looped in a ceaseless spiral, curled around the sucking pit of guilt and self-loathing. Johnathan began to suspect a consequence of his new condition cost him the welcome oblivion of sleep, though it didn't give him a pass from exhaustion. A bone deep weariness clung to him, a burial shroud of waking nightmares. Listening to the calls and activity of the crew navigating the barge along the river, Johnathan dwelled on his lost mortality, and wondered if he would carry his guilt until it collapsed into something worse, a cold apathy.

Nights were easier, simpler. Vic spun stories of his life, sharing anecdotes of the variety of beings, rich and poor, mortal and immortal, he'd encountered over the centuries he'd walked the earth. The stories soothed Johnathan's battered psyche, a reprieve to the hollow space inside him. Bright spots because they gave him a fuller picture of Vic. The man admired and loved the humans he met, forming deep friendships, and carrying their memory long after they'd turned to dust. His interactions with immortals were colored with amusement and affection, and their bonds lasted centuries.

Through his brief life, Johnathan never managed to form any such connection. After Sir Harry took him in, he never saw the children he ran with on the streets. In the Society, the Prospectives were often pitted against one another, and while they would team up on missions, there was no camaraderie. An instilled sense of rivalry kept Agents from forming true partnerships. The man he'd come to see as a mentor and secondary father had betrayed Johnathan in the worst way. The bonds he'd managed to form in Cress Haven were so new, so raw, he wasn't sure they would survive this current trial even as he sat, mollified by Vic's voice. He traced the outlines of Vic's face in the dark and committed them to memory.

The fourth day brought rain that pelted their shelter in an onslaught of noise. The ground was too wet to lie down, though the crew was too busy trying to wrangle the miserable mules to notice any unusual lumps in the coverings. Johnathan sat on the damp wood and valiantly tried to ignore the unpleasant mugginess of their shelter. His clothes were soaked by rain and sweat. Vic dozed against his shoulder; the sharpened angles of his face visible due to the influx of light where their feet breached the cloth. It exposed the deep bruising beneath his fingernails, corpse fingers. If Johnathan had met him in this state, there would have been no hiding his nature.

Worry gnawed at Johnathan. He'd admittedly seen vampires in this state before, shortly before some Prospective lopped off their head, fledglings too weakened by starvation to defend themselves. But Vic was old and nowhere near that state. Johnathan had witnessed the man's strength after a grievous injury. Rationally, he knew age lent strength, and five hundred years meant a vampire could go a long time between feedings. He knew all of this and yet he couldn't stifle the urge to wrap Vic in his arms like precious glass.

"I can feel you staring," Vic murmured, his eyes still closed.

"Would it help you to feed off me?" Johnathan blurted.

Vic's brows drew together. He cracked open one eye to peer up at Johnathan. "Lovely as that offer is, I'm not sure what your blood would do to me, sweetling."

"Maybe we should risk it," said Johnathan, too caught up in his thoughts to blush.

"I know my appearance is rather dreadful." Vic sighed. "But I assure you, I'm fine."

The statement did little to assuage his worry. Johnathan grabbed Vic's hand and stroked his thumb over his damning discolored nails. "When we were cornered at the dock, the Sister approached you with a golden net. Do you know why?"

Confusion tightened the knot between Vic's brows. "A golden net? To what purpose?" Comprehension flashed across his face. "They were after me," he said, a hitch of surprise in his voice.

"We don't know that for sure," countered Johnathan, "but they've been tracking us by unconventional means since the train. What if they intercept us before we reach the Estate?"

Vic looked up at him, a mixture of anxiety and anger in his gaze.

"What are they tracking?" The words were a murmur, his consternation reflected inward.

A memory nagged at the back of Johnathan's thoughts, of that dreadful night and all its loathsome revelations. He could almost hear Evans's words echoing through his head.

Vic stiffened beside him. "We're close."

The memory burst. "How can you tell?"

"It's a feeling, a feather stroke across the senses," said Vic. "Once you've been there, you'll be able to sense it too." He gripped the edges of the sheet and grimaced at the cold rain. "We can't wait until dark. Better make a run for it now."

There wasn't much the crew could do to them if they spotted their two stowaways now. Vic lifted the sheet high enough for Johnathan to roll out first. Fresh air was a welcome change, the heavy rain offered a grace of adjustment for his senses after days in the shrouded space. Their worry was for naught. If the crew spotted them in this mess, they deserved to be caught. The rain was so thick he could barely see his hand when he stuck it out in front of him. The torrential conditions limited their visibility and sight equally as they embarked on the shore. His clothes were soaked in minutes. He might have lost Vic in the deluge if the man hadn't clasped his hand and pulled him along.

They exited the barge without incident and waded the few feet to shore through a thigh deep stretch of the river. There was a momentary pause when they stepped back on land, waiting to see if Johnathan sensed their pursuers. Sister Wilhem and her contingent had either given up on them after their losses, or more likely, the river had disrupted their trail long enough to lose them. He doubted their luck would last long, though he hoped the weather would hinder the Society's movements as well.

Johnathan squinted through the downfall. He tried to sense what Vic described. The pounding droplets were a constant distraction. "Should we try to procure gloves? Possibly a hat?" Those pieces of Johnathan's disguise were long lost or destroyed, which meant his inhuman attributes were on full display. A feeling of exposure weighed on him. Would the mystery proprietors of the Estate recognize what he was on sight? Or were demons rare enough that they would hesitate to react?

"Trust me, it's better we don't try to hide anything about your appearance. You'll see. We'll be there soon."

Despite Vic's assurance they were close to their destination, there didn't appear to be anything for miles but more trees, the dense canopy of branches providing little relief against the rain. To Johnathan, it could have been the same damned forest they'd traipsed through days ago. The dark wet trunks blurred together, closing around him. Pine needles and branches dug into the sensitive pads of his bare feet until the cold numbed his skin. The chill ate at his stamina, each dragging step incrementally heavier. Even with Vic's guidance, the rain and cold bogged him worse than when he'd been human. They drew to a sudden stop, but Johnathan saw nothing outside the dripping branches.

"Ah, we're here," said Vic, his tone nonchalant.

Johnathan scowled and swiped a hand down his drenched face. "There's nothing here."

His companion didn't move except for his mouth. Vic gave him a tight smile. "Oh, there is. Though it appears the proprietors are still cross with me."

"The proprietors?" Johnathan swiveled around, searching through the rainy gloom for a hint of a house or person. "How can you tell they're displeased?"

"Because I can't move," said Vic, his tone absurdly calm for such a statement. Johnathan rushed to his side. He searched the ground for snares. There was nothing. Grabbing Vic's wrist was a mistake. Lightning coursed up his arm. He grunted but he didn't let go. A firm tug confirmed Vic was stuck fast. The shock faded to a dull buzz that made Johnathan snap his teeth in irritation.

"Hell and bother, what did you do to them?" The hair on the back of his neck stood on end. Johnathan's attention shifted to the figure who appeared through the trees, their features concealed by the lip of a small umbrella against the rain. There was an oddness to the air beside them, the rain fall disrupted, slowed through the patch to a near standstill.

"That one is immune to our preventatives." The voice was hollow, a discordant echo that grated on the ears.

The umbrella tipped, the person beneath it studied Johnathan. "Katherine, please see to our unwelcome guest."

The odd patch of air rippled and sped toward Johnathan. For a second, he saw the face of a woman, distorted and washed out like a reflection in a pond. The image vanished. Icy fingers sank into his skin, draining the warmth from his blood. Johnathan gasped, collapsing to his knees. His breath emerged in a chilled fog. The cold seized his lungs in his chest.

Vic swore, though he was still pinned fast. "Katherine! Wait, please, let me explain," he said.

The figure beneath the umbrella held up a hand, two fingers flicked in Johnathan's direction. The cold abated to a tolerable level, though his teeth began to chatter.

Ignoring Johnathan, the figure turned toward Vic. The umbrella tipped up, exposing the lower half of their face, revealing a delicate elfin jaw at odds with the full lush mouth. Dark red lips quirked up in a smile that promised sin. "My, my, didn't expect to see your sorry carcass for another decade." There was a throaty quality to their voice, rich and smoky.

The downpour seemed to abate when they drew closer. A decadent scent teased Johnathan, a blend of rosewater, woodsmoke, and sweet wine. Visible around the umbrella handle, their fingernails were painted a brilliant red, the color a vibrant highlight in the gloom. A direct contrast to their conservative long skirts. They stopped a few feet away, watching Vic with an air of expectation.

"This little trap you set out says otherwise," teased Vic. The tone drew Johnathan's attention. "Or were you looking to snare other vampires out here?"

A delicate snort answered him. "None of the others would have shown up without warning."

Vic blew out a huff, his lips oddly stiff from whatever spell held him fast. "My apologies for failing to do so under pursuit."

The umbrella lifted higher, a mix of amusement and scorn in their brilliant green eyes. They observed Vic's rough appearance. "I should leave you out here to rot, vampire." The harsh words were softened by their apparent humor, laced with a hint of bitterness.

"It's good to see you too, Merry," said Vic, unruffled by the threat. There was clearly a history between the two. Johnathan struggled to remain ambivalent. "You look marvelous as ever."

The newcomer laughed, a sound full of suggestion and dark promise, one that prodded at Johnathan's possessive streak, unaware he had one. He set his jaw, trying to remain still while their reunion played out, but the cold continued to drain his reserves. A full body shudder drew that sharp gaze to him.

"Well, at least you've brought a handsome piece of trouble to my door." Merry ran their tongue over their teeth. Their gaze wandered over Johnathan, arching a brow at his bare feet. The scrutiny irked him, though he couldn't understand why. He frowned and examined Merry, stare for stare. The feathery beat of their pulse, steady and sure flowed beneath their warm brown skin. Johnathan blinked.

Merry was human, though they didn't bat a lash at his unusual appearance. He'd expected Vic's mysterious proprietors to have a keen awareness of the supernatural if not be a creature themselves. Merry's perusal was a touch more personal than he expected. A hint of heat crept into his ears.

Their smile widened. "Delightful." They folded the umbrella, using the length to support themselves on the uneven terrain. "Now, let's have a look at you then," said Merry. "Katherine, hold him still for me."

Vic's calm evaporated. "Merry, wait—."

Johnathan frowned. Both Vic and Merry referred to a third person, sight unseen. Where were they? He glanced around when the cold seared him and battered at his consciousness. This was far worse than icy water or any natural cold he'd experienced in his life. It sank into the marrow of his bones. His vision wavered, eyelids fluttering as he rocked back on his heels.

"Katherine, stop. That's too much," Vic snapped, strain in his features.

Merry frowned, glancing between them. "Easy, Victor. This will only take a moment."

Their hand shot out. Painted red nails pinched Johnathan's chin, tilting his face up to meet their gaze. "Hello, lovely one," Merry purred. Their smoky, floral scent, twined around him, and Johnathan finally sensed the hidden power lurking in those green eyes. Merry might appear human to his senses but they were also something else. Weakened by the cold, he was pinned surely as Vic, while Merry peeled away his defenses, peering straight into his soul. A pale light flared deep within their pupils. The Hound rose with an internal blast of heat that beat back the cold. Johnathan jerked out of Merry's hold, his body trembling.

A feminine hiss echoed through his mind, accompanied by a faint muttering. Johnathan shook his head, trying to dislodge a voice that wasn't his own.

Merry's empty fingers twitched, their expression stunned. "What exactly have you brought to my door, Victor?" they murmured. Their gaze sharpened, tightening their grip around the umbrella handle. "Katherine?"

That diminishing cold moved through him, emerging from his chest in a shimmer of frigid air that coalesced into a woman. She whirled to stare down at him, her translucent face incredulous. The longer he watched, the more solid she became, though her appearance remained washed out, the colors leeched away to reveal an ethereal creature of gauze and gossamer. A woman without a scent, and though her cool breath fogged the air, the vital organ in her chest remained still.

The woman was dead. Judging by the state of her dated clothing, she had been dead for some time. Her accusatory gaze rounded on Vic. "You brought a demon to our door." The resonant echo of her voice sharp as cut glass.

"I can explain, please Katherine," Vic pleaded.

Katherine paced in a short circle; her hair lashed around her in an invisible wind. "Explain? Victor, you know how dangerous their kind are!"

Merry's response was less frantic, their gaze curious. "How is he here? What breed is he?"

"What does it matter?" Katherine threw up her hands.

"You don't understand," said Vic, through his teeth. There was a subtle tension in his frame that made it clear he was fighting whatever mystical hold either Katherine or Merry had on him. "There are special circumstances regarding his presence. We need information. We ask for sanctuary."

Katherine scoffed. "Demons are not welcome."

Johnathan remained slumped on the ground. Their argument was a chaotic buzz in his ears. He wanted to tell Vic to stop trying. That no matter what he told them, their minds were made up.

"You are more than welcome to stay, Victor," said Katherine. "That creature is not."

That made Johnathan flinch. Weary beyond measure, he could feel their chances slipping away, remotely aware Merry continued to observe him.

"What are you?" The tip of the umbrella gently prodded his knee. He glanced up, trying to gauge the intent behind Merry's question.

"Hound," he whispered, dragging the word from his throat. Katherine's reaction was visceral. Her disconcerting appearance was exacerbated when pieces of her faded out sight. Merry blanched and spun on Vic.

"Really, Victor? A Hellhound?" Merry gaze darted to the surrounding trees. "Where is his master?"

Vic looked miserable. "Here, I guess. I mean. It might be me?"

"*Might* be you?" Merry echoed, a tone beyond incredulity into to something bordering panic.

"That's not possible," Katherine snapped, the echo in her voice made worse by her distress.

"We aren't sure," Vic rebuked. "It's complicated. Look, he's only been a Hound for the better part of a week."

The building air of panic dispersed. The two proprietors shot each other a loaded look that made Johnathan's weary senses tingle.

Katherine threaded her fingers together. "What do you think?"

Merry pursed their lips and gave Johnathan a far more clinical perusal than before. "Are you dangerous?"

Vic sputtered. "I told you—"

"I wasn't asking you, Victor. Impeccable character that you have, your judgement here is clearly biased," said Merry.

He didn't dare look at Vic when he answered. "Yes." He continued, ignoring Vic's protests. "I don't know how to control it." He swallowed. "But I promise I will not intentionally harm either of you."

The two shared another silent exchange before Katherine gave a shrug. "See if he can get through the door."

The words meant nothing to Johnathan, but Vic perked up.

"Come on then, my troubled beauties, before you bring a swarm of demons to our door." Merry snapped their fingers, releasing the spell on Vic. The umbrella snapped back open, Merry a whirling dervish as they spun on heel and sauntered back through the trees.

Katherine shook her head in exasperation. "Such dramatics. It's good to see you, Vic, though I wish it were under less complicated circumstances." She shot Johnathan a final uncertain glance and faded from sight.

Johnathan stared after the rapidly disappearing figure, stunned by their encounter. Vic reached for him, breaching his stupor. His fingers traced the air along Johnathan's jaw, not quite touching him.

"I'm sorry I didn't warn you." Vic crouched down beside him.

Johnathan shook his head. Nothing would have prepared him for that meeting. The familiarity between Vic and Merry, however, stoked an unfamiliar emotion, prickly and uncomfortable in his own skin.

Vic sighed. "We'd better follow before they close the way out of spite." He helped Johnathan to his feet, but his hand dropped away. He headed into the gloom. Johnathan slowly followed in his wake, silence building between them.

In the days spent regaling Johnathan with stories of his past acquaintances, Vic hadn't mentioned Katherine or the peculiar Merry. He was grateful for those stories for myriad reasons, but he realized his companion was very careful not to mention one subset of companions. He itched to ask the question. There was a reason he didn't. Johnathan kept his mouth shut.

That unease was forgotten when the world pulsed, an invisible wave a of warmth ballooning around them that pushed back the heavy curtain of rain. The thick stretch of trees vanished, curving around a sizable expansive of what appeared to be an open field. Johnathan blinked when a massive structure shimmered into sight. His jaw went slack.

Nestled in the clearing, the Estate was three stories tall, a sprawling compound complete with buttresses and balconies. It was a marvel of wood, glass, and stone. The building's curving wings and towers gave it the appearance of a great beast crouched and ready to spring. The dark exterior presented an imposing front, but light burned from several windows; the front door opened wide, a beacon of safety through the chill and damp.

A low hum traced over Johnathan's skin, like when Merry grabbed him. His steps slowed, the urge to turn tail and flee rising until Vic realized he was flagging behind.

"Easy, John, let it get used to you," murmured Vic. His hand slid down Johnathan's back, a comfort that kept him in place.

What was getting used to him? Bewildered, Johnathan kept moving. He ascended the front stone stairs to the open front door, shoulders hunched by the time they reached the threshold. The welcoming scent of wood polish and lemon verbena permeated the air, the wood floor and walls beyond the door comprised of deep rich mahogany, polished to a warm glossy sheen. Intermittent glass lamps hung around the room and banished the shadows with a sunny glow.

Katherine and Merry waited a few steps inside, observing their approach with an expectant air. They paid no attention to Vic's entry, fixated on Johnathan as his feet passed over the threshold. There was a slight pressure around his shoulders, but whatever the two expected, he entered the Estate unhindered.

Merry extended their open hand. Katherine rolled her eyes and dropped a heavy silver coin into their waiting palm. "This way, gentlemen." Merry grinned.

A thick pine green carpet absorbed his footsteps. Johnathan cringed as his bare muddy feet smeared the pristine weave.

A short hall spat them out at the foot of a grand staircase, twice as wide as he was tall. An iron chandelier suspended overhead, decorated with dozens upon dozens of individual glass globes. A steady light glowed from within. Johnathan marveled at the feat of engineering, wondering how long it took to light the individual wicks. Katherine shimmered into view several steps above them. He might have passed their little test, but latent hostility lingered in her gaze.

Merry shuffled around them, ascending the first few steps. Absent the umbrella, their host was a figure swathed in layers of black gauzy skirts that clung to the curves of their body. In the warm light of the chandelier, their appearance dazzled, highlighting the golden hues in their rich brown skin. Curling brown hair reached their waist and framed the angles of their face. Their arms were folded under their breasts, flashing a healthy display of cleavage while they studied their guests.

There was an appreciative gleam in Merry's expression when they looked at Vic. Johnathan bit the inside of his cheek.

The front doors slammed shut with an air of theatrical finality, likely for their benefit. The chandelier shivered above them. A satisfied smirk tilted the corner of Katherine's mouth, making her features less severe. Johnathan's unease continued to build.

Their host's smile was one of secrets and charm, gesturing to the open staircase with a twirl of their fingers. "Welcome to the Estate."

CHAPTER NINE

MERRY LOOMED A FEW STEPS ABOVE THEM. THEY BARELY CAME TO Johnathan's shoulders but possessed a towering presence that urged him to take a step back.

"Katherine, would you prepare the workroom?" Merry didn't take their eyes off Vic. Katherine didn't bother to respond, vanishing from view. Her invisibility disturbed Johnathan. He doubted he would know she was in the room unless she wanted him to.

"Gentlemen, we have much to discuss, but I can see you are both dead on your feet, if you'll pardon the saying. Allow me to show you to your rooms to freshen up and rid yourselves of this dreadful clothing," said Merry. They glided down and took Vic's arm. Fingers curved over his forearm in a gesture more possessive than polite. "Honestly, Victor, I almost didn't recognize you in these rags. And you haven't been feeding!"

"These fine garments were the best we could do in a pinch," said Vic, looking much aggrieved at the mention of his current outfit. "As for feeding, unfortunately I lost my kit."

Merry patted his arm. "Poor Victor. Don't worry. I still have your supplies here. I'll take care of you."

"That is very generous of you," Vic replied. There was genuine warmth in his smile.

Johnathan stared at their conjoined arms and finally recognized the emotion churning in his gut. It was worse that Vic didn't look at him, too involved in his conversation with their host. Johnathan trailed behind them, his muddy feet dragged on the plush carpet, bereft and unsure how to act. He'd never been in this position before, but he was certain he did not like it.

The skin across the back of his neck tingled. Johnathan looked up to find Merry staring at him over Vic's shoulder, lips quirked in a knowing smirk. His fingers curled into fists at his side, where his claws dug into the tender skin of his palms.

The staircase led to a long hallway. The ribbed support pillars and spaced lighting were the dark throat of a giant. The walls seemed to flex and breathe under Johnathan's gaze, a gentle gust of air teased through the fine strands of hair at his temples. Vic and Merry continued their lively chat right to the first door, which Merry opened to reveal a sumptuous suite, far grander than any lodging Johnathan stayed in his life.

A large, canopied bed dominated the space, draped in gold over brown brocade. Highlights of hunter green and russet comprised the bedding and fabric, giving the room a masculine tone.

"Yes, this will do nicely," said Merry. They reached back, seizing Johnathan's wrist. "Relax your hand, dear. The room just needs to get a feel for you."

Johnathan wondered how many rooms were required to 'get used to him', but he allowed Merry to press his hand flat against the warm wood of the door. A ripple moved through the drapery and bed sheets. He swore he heard a voice, a soft imperceptible sigh before the room settled. Intrigued, he didn't immediately jerk his hand away when Merry released him, his fingers splayed over the smooth grain.

"There is a bath adjacent," said Merry. "We'll leave you to get settled. Come along, Victor."

Johnathan jerked back. Panic slid along his nerves. A protest formed and died on his lips, uncertainty tying his tongue in knots. Merry seemed somewhat aware of the dynamic between them, but Johnathan couldn't be sure. Their hold on Vic's arm could have been friendly or possessive, but it irked him either way. He teetered on the precipice of indecision. Vic said nothing but gave Johnathan an imperceptible nod.

Bowing his head, Johnathan's fingers trailed across the door, drank in the warmth of the wood. He closed it behind him and leaned his forehead against it. The scent of polish and laundered bed clothes were a welcome comfort after days beneath the musty waxed sheet on the barge.

Jealousy was a new emotion for him. He couldn't recall a time in his life it stung him so deeply, which was why it took him so long to recognize it. The other Prospectives were jealous of one another's skills or successful hunts. They vied for the attention of the high-ranking members, seeking favor, but the cutthroat nature of that competition didn't hold much appeal for Johnathan. Besides, he'd held such attentions, and look where it got him.

His relationship with Vic was so new, and while they'd shared so much in such a short amount of time there was a rift of experiences Vic held over him. That he hadn't mentioned Merry was a more than subtle hint of the nature of their past relationship, one Johnathan didn't feel was his right to prod. A whisper of doubt crept through him. How solid was their connection after Johnathan had rejected their intimacy, caught in a tangle of guilt and self-disgust?

Torn between frustration and weariness, he entered the bathroom. At the sight of the tub, his worries stuttered to a halt. He blinked, taking it in. The floor was some sort of inlaid stone, glossy as pearls, set in a semi spiral pattern around an enormous central tub. It could easily fit two or three men his size. But the crown jewel of the device were the shiny brass taps protruding from the wall.

Could it be? This isolated mansion had indoor plumbing? He'd only seen such a set up once, in the posh abode of a Boston widow with a ghoul in her attic. Though her quaint porcelain bathtub was much smaller. Johnathan gingerly turned the tap and jumped when water gushed from the central spout. The water was warm to the touch, heating the longer it poured over his hand. What better remedy for his poor confused heart than a long hot soak? Tearing his clothes off,

Johnathan scrambled into the tub. Water splashed onto the floor in his hurry to submerge his aching body.

The tub filled quickly for its size. Hot water lapped over his chest and upper arms, soothing away the last of the chill. He settled back with a sigh. His life might have gone to the pits but here he sat amidst true luxury. Johnathan spread his arms around the rim of the tub, the days of blood and grime seeped from his skin while he stared up at the ceiling. Someone had carefully rendered a dozen constellations in specks of white paint across a canvas of midnight blue. The steam rose from the bath, gathering dew on the bits of white so they sparkled in the lamp light. The effect was breath taking. The ornate woodwork, the rich fabrics, the ceiling murals, and the heated indoor plumbing, all spoke of incalculable wealth, hidden away from the world in the middle of the wilderness. Johnathan wondered how such a place could exist. Vic referred to this location as a supernatural safe house, which piqued Johnathan's curiosity to no end.

Which brought him right back to his previous train of thought. Vic had yet to come find him. He knew he was being a bit ridiculous. Merry offered Vic sustenance, something Johnathan couldn't do for him. The realization Merry was the likely donor did nothing for his sour mood or his jealousy, irrational as it was. Merry said they had the instruments Vic used on hand, another piece of evidence of their shared, possibly recent past. Not feeding from the vein. No mouths on any body parts. Though how long would the set up and procedure take? Surely Vic had to be finished by now? Or maybe they were busy catching up, natural for two people when they knew each other for many years.

Groaning, Johnathan curled his arms inward, sinking down until the water closed over his head. Underwater, the world was muted, the steady beat of his heart a calming rhythm inside his head. He concentrated on that sound, held the worry and the guilt at bay until his protesting lungs forced him to surface. Giving his head a vigorous shake, Johnathan draped his arms over his knees, letting his fingertips dangle against the surface of the bath.

Maybe he should seek out Vic. Could he be enjoying a private soak? Maybe a not so private one? Johnathan scowled at himself. Was he so quick to doubt the loyalty of his companion? Or was it so hard to believe he could hold Vic's attentions with the sensual Merry around? He didn't know their host and he'd already spun a dozen unfounded assumptions. The water was cold by the time he roused himself from his futile train of thought, the hanging towels soft against his damp skin. Not bothering to salvage his borrowed clothes from their heap on the bathroom floor, Johnathan headed for the bed. The mattress sank beneath him, partially enveloping him when he flopped down on his back. After such a long soak, he'd hoped to have calmed enough for exhaustion to claim him, but his mind kept spinning. Sleep continued to elude him, and Johnathan refused to ruminate on his circumstances for however long Vic left him there.

Sitting up, he spied a wardrobe in the corner of the room. Doubtful he'd find anything in his size, he slid it open and combed through the neatly hung shirts and trousers. His fingers stilled. They were all similar in size, and far too large for their diminutive host or Vic. Johnathan held one up against his chest, the cuffs falling just past his wrists. The entire wardrobe was sized for him.

The room needed to get a feel for him. How much had it altered itself to suit his needs? Johnathan peered around the luxurious space, wondering what level of awareness the Estate possessed, or if it existed in another realm like the Fae. Too grateful to look a gift horse in the mouth, he slid on a shirt and pants. The garments fit him better than anything he'd ever owned, the fabric silken to the touch. Though he didn't bother with the polished boots now that his feet were clean. Johnathan offered a murmured salutation to whatever force oversaw the upkeep of his room and padded barefoot to the door.

There was a small fear he'd find it locked, but it swung open on silent hinges when he turned the knob. Part of him longed to find Vic, but the familiar trail of citrus and musk wove with Merry's scent of rosewater and smoke, and he was a coward. Johnathan headed back the way toward the entrance, his unclad feet silent across the carpet. He made it to the top of the grand staircase, surveying the elegant chandelier and foyer.

"Do you always walk about like a barefoot heathen?" Katherine sat on the railing, her legs carelessly kicked the open air, feet clad in dainty slippers. Her appearance reminded Johnathan of a porcelain doll left to bleach in the sun, her youthful features frozen in time. Though his education of the supernatural wasn't as extensive as he once believed, he wondered if the Society had seen anything like her. She raised a brow at his blatant stare. "Cat got your tongue?"

"Sorry," Johnathan blurted and looked away, a familiar blush on his cheeks.

Katherine's legs stopped moving. She leaned forward, supporting her chin on her folded hands. "For a Hound, you don't seem very...demonic." She sighed. "I might owe you an apology. My opinion of demons is biased. Please, forgive my rudeness. It was not your fault, but mine."

"It's Johnathan. Johnathan Newman. I haven't had much practice being demonic," he said. And the practice he did have fueled his nightmares. The specters of his victims hovered at the back of his mind, waited for his guard to drop with blank dead eyes and torn limbs. He gave an internal shake, returning to the present. Katherine didn't notice his wandering attention.

Instead, she giggled. "A Hellhound named Johnathan?"

Johnathan managed a small smile. "Yes, it is rather anticlimactic."

"I don't remember my last name," she said, her tone wistful. "Too many years between corporeality. Memories, the details, are so hard to keep without form." She noticed his perplexed expression. "What is it?"

"I confess, I have no idea what you are," said Johnathan. Every day proved the inadequacy of his Society education.

"Oh," said Katherine. She smoothed her skirts. "I believe the most accurate terminology is Geist. I lingered on this mortal plane long enough to transcend beyond your common ghost or specter and gained a corporeal form."

"But not a poltergeist?" Johnathan leaned on the rail a few feet away from her. He didn't want to scare her off, though their encounter outside informed him the Geist was capable of bringing him down.

Katherine hummed, tapping her chin in thought. "A poltergeist gains corporeality in short bursts, just enough to move or throw objects. I am different." She held up her hand, stretching it out to him. "I can be touched."

There was a moment of hesitation, but Johnathan reached the rest of the distance and pressed his palm against hers. Icy shocks stabbed through his palm. He snatched his hand back, shaking it out.

"Sorry. I can be touched, but it's not pleasant." Katherine winced. She dropped her hands to her lap, a deep sadness in her gaze. After a moment, she perked up. "Would you like to see the workshop? Victor should still be there. We planned to give you both a moment to recuperate but Victor was very insistent he speak with Merry tonight."

Vic spoke to Merry without him? But why? That flicker of petty jealousy and unease remained, despite his efforts to bury both emotions deep. What did he want to tell Merry that he didn't want Johnathan to hear? Violence flashed through his mind, the blood saturated ground beneath him, surrounded by torn bodies. Gore dripped from his fingertips; the wet thud echoed in his ears louder than gunshot. Lifeless eyes stared up at him, the faces of the dead frozen in silent accusation...

Johnathan sucked in a breath, his hands gripped the railing so hard it creaked. A chill brushed across his shoulder. He glanced up at Katherine. Her hand hovered over him, not quite touching.

"Are you—your face went rather pale." There was a note of wary concern in her gaze. Johnathan stepped away from the railing, his fingers ached. He rubbed his stiff hands over his thighs.

"I would be grateful if could show me the way," he said.

The sumptuous design of the Estate continued through the lower hallway, this one decorated with smoother columns, recessed into the walls. There were several rooms closed off on this level as well, their contents concealed behind wide double doors. Bronze handles gleamed in the intermittent lamp light. Some doors were open, the rooms decorated in rich comfortable furnishings that bolstered the portrayal of luxury. Johnathan was out of his depth. He'd never seen such wealth in his life from a distance, never mind being in the middle of it. He kept his hands against his sides, fearing he would leave smudges on the walls or, worse, scrape them with his claws.

Katherine glided in front of him. Her skirts fell to the ground, hiding whether she floated rather than walked. Her furtive gaze darted to him.

He sighed. "What is it?"

Her posture straightened. "It's nothing." Pale fingers fidgeted in her skirts. "Is it true what Victor said? That you've only been a Hound for a week?"

Had it only been a week? He'd killed so many people in a week. Pressure squeezed his throat. He nodded, not trusting himself to speak. Guilt mantled his shoulders, a cloak that dragged behind him, weighed by a potential future of split blood. Vic brought him to the Estate for answers. To see if the beast inside him could be controlled. He never once entertained the idea Johnathan couldn't control it.

Preoccupied, he didn't immediately notice the change. The carpet beneath his bare feet gained a cool, slippery quality, a gentle prickle against his soles. He glanced down to find blades of grass poking between toes. The wooden walls of the hallway fell away, opening into a vast internal garden. The only indication they were still inside the Estate was the domed glass ceiling, high enough to mute the rain falling outside. A fragrant mix of exotic flowers surrounded him. Bright eye-watering blossoms in colors he couldn't name brushed against his shirt, streaks of golden pollen clinging to the cloth. The wondrous sight pulled him from his morose mood. He trailed his fingers over a brilliant orange bloom, the petals spread like a lady's fan.

"Bird of Paradise, though some call it the crane flower," said Katherine. A smile lit her face, the vibrant colors of the room warming her skin. "Took forever to cultivate here. They favor a more tropical climate."

"There are beautiful," he murmured. An inadequate description but the dulcet tones of Vic's voice distracted him, laced with urgency. Johnathan's hearing sharpened, tuned to their low conversation.

"—my fault, Merry. My distractions put him in that position. He's put his trust in me. I can't fail him again," said Vic.

The coiled worry in his chest frayed apart. Warmth suffused Johnathan.

"You're really in knots for this boy," Merry teased, laced with a hint of bitterness. "You always were one for hopeless causes."

"Merry, please."

"I'll consult the books, Victor, but I can't promise results," Merry responded after a beat, their tone gentled. "It's amazing his body survived the transformation. Do you know how rare that is?"

"The demon in Cress Haven managed to turn several young women before we stopped him," said Vic.

Merry made a tutting sound. "A strong enough demon could taint and transform hundreds of humans, but none of them would survive if it returned to the Nether without them. Even if the demon remained in our realm, their bodies would eventually burn up."

"Will that happen to Johnathan?" The words strangled.

There was a pause that made Johnathan's insides clench. Perhaps he wouldn't survive long enough to worry about control. How long would he have? The first victim in Cress Haven lasted nearly a year, but her body turned to ash like the rest of them when Johnathan sealed the rift. He hadn't known whether the victims were pulled into the Nether with Cerunnous or simply died.

"I don't know," Merry admitted. "I've only gotten a glimpse of him, Victor. Give me a chance to examine him."

"You're eavesdropping," Katherine whispered in his ear, the air chilled by her proximity. He half turned to her. Her lips parting at the sight of his face. "What did you hear to look so bleak?"

Johnathan shook his head and moved toward their voices. The conversation fell silent before he found them by their intwined scents. Katherine hovered at his side. In the center of the vast greenhouse sat a workstation, the surface cluttered with an array of mortars and pestles, drying herbs, fresh ground pastes and mystery liquids in glass containers. A candle burned directly beneath a glass flask suspended in a delicate apparatus of bent metal, the liquid gently bubbling away. Several bundles of dried herbs lay spread out over individual cloth wraps, a handful of clean empty bowls set out and waiting for use. Merry stood beside the table, arms folded. Vic waited in patient stillness, his face turned to Johnathan's approach.

It was evident his companion had fed. The shadows beneath Vic's eyes were gone, the angles of his face softened. He'd exchanged the rough garments for a russet suit that complimented his auburn hair and hugged his slim form. His hands were relaxed at his sides, fingernails once again a healthy pink. Whole and hale and so beautiful Johnathan's heart ached.

Quiet relief shone in Vic's eyes as he approached, but he didn't reach out to touch him. Johnathan quickly hid his hurt from the slight when Merry moved away from the table to circle him. Katherine slid onto a corner of the table, her body moving through the clutter rather than disturbing it.

"Was he this large before he transformed?" Merry peered up at Johnathan's face. "Oh, goodness, I didn't notice how his eyes flared before. I assume you concealed those on the train?"

"Yes, and I'm afraid he's always been that large," said Vic, his voice bemused. Johnathan didn't share their humor.

Merry snagged Johnathan's wrist, examining his nails. "You said he was a scion of Cernunnos?" They reached up to push his lip up over his teeth. Johnathan froze, uncomfortable at the invasive contact. "My knowledge of that particular demon is somewhat limited, but he's incredibly stabilized for someone so recently turned." A crease formed between Merry's brows. "You did close the rift, correct?"

"I did," said Johnathan. He leaned his head back to speak.

The crease deepened. "How did you anchor him to this plane?"

A soft sound escaped from Katherine. "Oh, Victor, you didn't."

Vic looked at her. "There wasn't any other way."

The Geist shook her head. "How could you be so reckless? Do you know what this could do to you? To the both of you?"

Merry glanced between the two of them. "What did I miss?" Anxiety returned to Johnathan full force.

"He's not a human, Victor! Making a blood bond with a demon." Katherine scowled. "That sort of bond flows both ways."

Johnathan shot Vic an alarmed look, but the man shook his head. "I haven't felt any different since."

"The change might not be obvious," said Merry. They stroked a hand across their throat. "Not at first."

Trepidation wormed through his bowels. Johnathan's pulse pounded in his ears. Lost to the moment, the pain when the sun crawled over the horizon, and the offer fell from Vic's lips. He'd admitted to Johnathan he didn't know what would happen, or if it would work. Had he known it would be dangerous for him as well?

"What changes—"

"Cerunnous didn't target him at random," Vic interrupted. He faced Merry, his arms folded, a withdrawn expression on his face Johnathan recognized.

His teeth ground together, a lick of flame smoldering in his veins. He kept his anger to himself, unwilling to confront Vic before their current audience.

"You mentioned there was some interference from the Society? Self-righteous bastards," sneered Merry.

"Not interference. They orchestrated the whole debacle," said Vic.

"Oh God," Katherine murmured. She pressed her hands to her face, form flickering in and out of visibility. "They failed so many times in the south, we thought they pulled back operations to reassess. How did we miss this?"

The flame sparked and caught; his anger fed by the old wound of his mentor's betrayal. "They've done this before?"

Katherine nodded. "They've been trying in earnest the past few years. We've noted over a dozen instances of failed rifts. There were a few cases of demonic transformation, but none of them survived."

Vic steepled his fingers, anger in the tightness of his jaw. "Why wasn't I told of this?"

"You left," said Merry. "There was no need for you to know."

Ignoring them, Katherine nibbled her thumb. "Why was this attempt so different?"

His anger fizzed to nothing. "Because they played the long game." The entirety of his existence boiled down to being a conditioned pawn in Doctor Evans' grand experiment. The years he'd spent under the man's tutelage, every instance of praise and punishment, his isolation and trauma were calculations, used to create a piece that could be moved into place when the conditions were right. A cultured oddity. His first assignment was so different from the other Prospectives, so much further than the others had been sent out. Coordinated for Evans to see if his machinations would yield results.

"Why are they doing this?" Johnathan looked down at his bare feet, wishing he could sink into the grass.

"We know the Society has been attempting to set events into motion for some time, but we don't have a full picture yet," said Merry. They leaned back against the table and sighed. "We need to send out a call."

Vic bristled. "Who's closest?"

Their host shot him a baleful glance. "What's wrong, Victor, not looking forward to another sentimental reunion?"

His companion didn't respond, jaw flexing.

"Alazar," said their host.

Vic's fingers twitched. The russet fabric creaked in protest. "We need to conceal Johnathan's scent."

Merry pursed their lips. "Help you control the Hound, help you study your foolishly made blood bond, help hide his scent." They ticked off the demands on their fingers. "Why should I?"

Tension charged the sudden silence. It leaked from the mask Vic wore, and the mulish expression on Merry's face. Katherine watched them, her gaze wary, but it was clear she wouldn't interfere with their quarrel.

A lover's quarrel. "We'll go," said Johnathan. His tired voice was a stone drop in the strained quiet.

"You most certainly will not," Merry snapped. They sighed in disgust, swiping a corked brown glass bottle off the table. "Don't let him leave the room without smearing this on his skin."

Vic's shoulders slumped. "Thank you, Merry."

"Don't thank me yet." Merry inhaled a deep breath through their nose. "I'll help Johnathan. Go, get out of my sight before I change my mind."

"I'll send out the call," said Katherine. She paused beside Merry to brush her hand against their arm. Their host turned their back in clear dismissal, hands braced on the tabletop.

Vic stalked away without a word, not waiting for Johnathan. He watched him go, a distance physical and mental stretched with every step.

"I'll see you off to at the stairs," said Katherine. She fell in step beside him.

Johnathan waited until they were clear of the indoor garden before he asked the question. "Why did Merry agree to help me?" Old wounds festered between Vic and their host, ones Johnathan knew he didn't have the delicacy to open.

"Merry knows what it's like to have one's autonomy taken from them," said Katherine. Johnathan wondered what that meant, but she didn't elaborate. They reached the central staircase far too soon. "Good night, Johnathan. Try to rest. The coming days are likely to be taxing."

He bowed his head to her. "Good night, Katherine."

She hid a smile behind her hand. "Such a polite demon." Her body vanished from sight.

Johnathan shook his head, not knowing what to make of the Geist. He climbed the stairs alone, wondering if he should find Vic's room. The thought of leaving this unresolved strain for the night left him miserable. The possibility of rejection was worse. Conflicted, he dragged himself into his rooms, shutting the door behind him.

Vic sat on the edge of his bed, fully clothed, his hands clasped in front of him.

Johnathan stared at him, his heart beating hard beneath his ribs. He didn't like the closed mask on Vic's face, the distance in his eyes, and he didn't know how to breach it. His hands knotted behind his back. Vic glanced up at him. The blank mask cracked.

"I'm sorry, John," he choked out. "I'm so sorry." The lines of his body were rigid. Johnathan pushed away from the door and dropped to his knees in front of him.

Leaning in, he wrapped his arms around Vic's waist. The man collapsed over Johnathan's back, holding him tight. A soft sob ruffled Johnathan's hair.

"What are you apologizing for, my beautiful idiot," he murmured into Vic's chest. A strained laugh broke the final lock in Vic's body. He pulled Johnathan up and onto the bed, shifting their bodies to lay a kiss on his temple.

"For dragging you into this mess. Binding you to me without thought to consequences. Failing to help you. Not warning you about this place. About Merry. Take your pick," said Vic. He sighed while fingers trailed up Johnathan's back, eliciting an appreciative shiver.

He was so grateful Vic touched him, he didn't immediately respond. "You have nothing to be sorry for," he said. How could Vic think he'd failed him? He'd risked and given up so much since Johnathan entered his life. His stomach churned when he thought of what he brought to their bond.

Nothing, he was nothing.

Shying away from the thought, he lifted a heavy hand, casually fiddling with the buttons of Vic's russet jacket. The sourness in his belly diffused. Warmth simmered and drifted lower. He craved contact with Vic's smooth pale skin, desperate to push back the stress and anxiety that plagued him since they fled Cress Haven. His fingers grew more insistent, working the buttons apart to slip his hand beneath; trailed his fingers over the final layer of white silk that covered Vic's abdomen. Muscles flexed beneath his touch.

Vic stroked his cheek, interest flaring in his eyes. "You're not tired?"

Johnathan shook his head. He couldn't sleep when Vic's proximity made him combust. Vic reached for him, but Johnathan grabbed his wrists. "Will you let me...explore?"

That silvered gaze turned molten. Vic's lips parted. "You have free rein."

An open invitation to touch, to taste, and experience. Johnathan grinned and rolled to straddle Vic's hips. His fingers diligently undid the fastenings of the white silk undershirt until he could push the fabric aside, baring the smooth muscles of Vic's chest. Johnathan stared down at him, entranced by this glimpse of skin. His hand traced the ridges and dips, nails grazing over rosy flat nipples. Vic shivered. The action created a flashfire up Johnathan's spine. His fingers moved upward, along Vic's collarbones. He leaned forward to follow the path with his lips, the skin under his mouth a cooler temperature than his feverish body heat, but deliciously warm. Johnathan trailed open mouth kisses up Vic's neck until their lips met, tasting and teasing one another. Vic began to sit up, hands framing Johnathan's face.

He seized Vic's wrists for the second time, pinning him back down on the bed. "No," he said, his voice rough. He tried to articulate what he needed, the need to proceed on his terms.

Vic gently nipped his bottom lip. "You lead."

Johnathan released Vic's wrists to continue his slow exploration. His hands kneaded the tight muscles of Vic's neck and shoulders, firm thighs cradled between his knees. The man shifted restlessly beneath him, his hard length brushing Johnathan's inner thigh. The two locked gazes, caught up in the breathless moment.

His hands moved to the fastenings of Vic's trousers. The tendons of Vic's neck strained as Johnathan freed his length and ran his thumb over the velvety head. A breathy groan hailed his efforts. Vic dropped his head back against the mattress, his expression a mix of pain and pleasure. His body shook while Johnathan touched, memorizing the feel of him.

He lowered himself over Vic's taut body and nuzzled his face against that smooth length. He wanted to give Vic the pleasure the man gifted to him, worried his inexperience would leave him unsatisfied.

Vic's fingers tangled into his hair. "You don't have to rush into anything you're not ready for, John," he said. That infinite patience galvanized him.

His lips parted, he took a tentative lick across the slit, tasting Vic's salty sweet essence. Tracing his lips down the length, he finally took Vic's cock into his mouth. His tongue glided on the underside, flicking along the ridges. Vic's hips bucked before he reigned in his reaction, fingers tangling in Johnathan's hair.

"You're killing me, John," Vic croaked. Johnathan paused at the words, worried he was hurting him until Vic's grip tightened. "You feel amazing."

Emboldened, he tried to emulate Vic's actions from the inn. His movements were clumsy, but Vic's reactions spurred him on, until the man's control snapped. Vic tugged at his hair until Johnathan released him. Between one breath and the next, he was flipped to his back. Vic hovered over him. Those silver eyes burned into him before Vic crushed their mouths together.

His elegant fingers thrust into Johnathan's pants and wrapped around his cock. Johnathan closed his eyes, moaning into Vic's mouth. The friction of skin and cloth rapidly brought him to an edge.

A cold sweat swept over him, piercing his ardor with icy dread. Johnathan shoved himself away. Muscles seized, his pulse ratcheted to a frenzied thrum. He couldn't breathe, lungs locked in his chest. His claws shredded the bedspread, the room a wobbling mass of shadow and light. Vic cupped Johnathan's face, his gaze marred with worry.

"John, look at me," Vic pleaded. His expression grew stark at the fear contorting Johnathan's face.

In his mind, Johnathan couldn't escape them. Faces contorted in agony, bodies piled around him. The bloody muck sucked him down.

"Talk to me," Vic whispered. His hands stroking, tugging him out of the grim and gory memories. Johnathan didn't deserve the comfort but he leaned into it. How was he any good to Vic like this? How could he survive like this?

He shook his head, the panic finally subdued by self-loathing, though he didn't push Vic away. Johnathan lay in the man's arms, soaking in those gentle touches. He wondered when Vic would grow tired of his guilt.

CHAPTER TEN

THE LULLING MOVEMENT OF VIC'S HANDS CONTINUED, SEEMINGLY content to lie there with him for hours. Shame soured what remained of his lust, left him drained.

"I'm sorry," said Johnathan. Vic stilled.

"Now who is the beautiful idiot?" He cupped Johnathan's chin, turning his face toward him. Vic's somber gaze studied his face. "Can you tell me what's wrong?"

Johnathan swallowed; his throat unbearably dry. "I don't have the words yet." This was true, his thoughts a jumbled mess of guilt and fear. Repulsed by the inherent violence of his new nature. The dead plagued him, the slick sensation of blood coated his hands every time he closed his eyes. Now, he wondered how long he was meant to last, what the blood bond would do to Vic or if his body would eventually burn up like the rest. He certainly didn't feel stable.

"When you do, I'm here." Vic pressed a kiss to the corner of his mouth. The contact drained the churning mess inside him, leeching poison from a wound. "You don't have to rush into anything physical until you are ready. I am happy just like this." The words were an antidote to his fear if Johnathan let himself accept them.

He rested his head on Vic's shoulder. The treacherous spiral of his thoughts turned to Merry. There was a history there but Johnathan wouldn't and couldn't ask, wallowing in his insecurities. The least he could do was keep them to himself instead of foisting them onto Vic. Hours dripped by, the room slowly lightening with the onset of day. Vic's body went lax, limbs loose in sleep. Johnathan pulled him closer, caged him in his arms. The smile on Vic's lips revealed his sleep wasn't deep. Tangled together, they rested in silence until the room fell dark with the oncoming night.

Vic stirred and lazily twined his fingers through Johnathan's curls. "I could stay like this forever."

There was a soft knock at the door. Vic sighed. "I'll get it. She's here for me." He gently dislodged Johnathan from his shoulder, righting his clothes as he padded across the room to the door. Johnathan quickly did the same.

Katherine waited on the other side; concern etched in the lines of her washed out face.

"My apologies; when you weren't in your room, I assumed you were here," she said, "Unfortunately, this was too important to wait."

Johnathan sat up. "What's wrong?"

"There is a contingent of Society Agents in the surrounding woods." Katherine worried her bottom lip. "Their path is too direct. I think they know we're here."

Vic stiffened. "How soon until Alazar arrives?"

"He's here. He was much closer than we realized," said Katherine. Her gaze moved to Johnathan. "Don't leave the room without donning the salve. Alazar didn't come alone." She didn't quite look Vic in the eye. "Appears to be a full family reunion tonight."

"Thank you for the warning, Katherine," said Johnathan. He noted the tight set of Vic's shoulders.

She nodded. "They're waiting downstairs. I'd hoped we could give you a longer rest, but you know how Alazar can be." She pressed a hand to Vic's shoulder. The contact loosened him. "Be careful, both of you."

Vic remained at the door after she left. Johnathan roused himself from the bed, laying a hand in the same spot as the Geist. His shoulder was still cold from the contact. "Who was she talking about?"

"I can handle them," Vic said. He glanced up at Johnathan, his expression perturbed. "I need to return to my rooms to freshen up. I left the salve on your dresser. You need to smear it along your neck like this." He mimed the movement, swiping a wide path across his neck and chest. "Wait for me?"

Johnathan nodded. Vic pressed a firm, urgent kiss to his mouth, anxiety imparting a touch of bitterness to his scent. He shut the door with a muted click behind him, a final silent ask for Johnathan to wait.

The innocuous bottled salve sat on top of the dresser. Johnathan pulled the cork. The odor made his eyes water, the initial punch was an odd woodsy musk that smelled heavily of pine and wet fur. Swallowing a cough, he smeared it on as Vic instructed, curious what he smelled like to a vampire. Hesper said the Nether still clung to him. His memory of the scent was faint, but the pungent combination of sulfur and smoke was unpleasant. What did the salve make him smell like now?

Shirt properly tucked in, he found a suitable pair of boots in the wardrobe, marveling at their precise fit. Fully dressed and partially disguised, Johnathan sat back on the bed and waited for Vic to freshen up.

The minutes crawled on. Johnathan glanced at the gilded ornate clock hanging on the wall, watching the slow march of the minute hand. After half an hour he began to worry. Katherine summons sounded urgent. He didn't think Vic would keep them waiting, whatever his feelings were.

Another ten minutes of indecision passed before Johnathan cautiously opened his door and sniffed the air. There was another scent mixed in with Vic's and the remnants of Merry, one of spice and warmth and the faintest tinge of old blood. His nostrils flared, tracking the newcomer directly to Vic's door. He paused outside the room, but heard only empty silence on the other side.

Johnathan debated whether he should return to the room and wait for Vic to debrief him after he'd spoken with the others. Part of him rebelled at hiding. What was the point of concealing his scent if he continued to act suspicious? If Vic taught him anything, the best way to conceal oneself was in plain sight.

Decided, he followed the intermingled scents. Johnathan descended the grand staircase, sliding his fingers down the polished banister. His footsteps slowed, adopting a predator's stealth. Beneath the grand chandelier, Johnathan caught another scent, a heady mix of exotic floral notes, rain, and rich dark earth. The foyer was empty, the long hallway silent except for a faint buzz he swore emitted from the hallway lamps. The new scent was strongest here, a lingering thread that led further down the hall, a spider's waiting trap. Johnathan frowned, uncertain why the comparison sprang to mind.

Troubled, he followed the trail, observing the house in avid detail. Colors and textures were sharper, more defined to his high tuned senses. The ceiling rose to a point over his head, the wood carved with intricate patterns that tugged at the corner of his eye. The subtle crunch of fibers beneath his feet. Outside, the rain had finally stopped, the usual birdsong and animal activity resuming. There came a repetitive noise, a staccato tap, tap, tap of impatient fingers.

One of the previously closed doors was now open, a spill of warm firelight reaching out into the hall, beckoning him closer. The new peculiar scent originated there. Johnathan reached the doorway, pressing a hand to the frame while his gaze swept the room.

Velvet upholstered couches and chairs surrounded a low table. An open hearth took up half the back wall, where the fire stretched twisting fingers of light across the floor.

A woman stood there, her back to him. She held a hand above the flames. The other rested against the mantle, fingertips tapping against the stone. Ebony hair spilled down her back and shoulders in a long straight sheet, gleaming in the firelight. Johnathan didn't make a sound, his silent perusal interrupted when she looked over her shoulder. Stunning was an inadequate description for her features, cast in a loving play of shadows by the flames. There was an unnatural smoothness to her brown skin, a perfection that echoed Vic, belying her nature. Her tongue darted across her lips, tinted a deep plum color, to taste the air. There was an odd allure to her that pulled at Johnathan, beckoning him closer. A whispered command to drop to his feet and worship her. To slice open his veins for her to feast. He took a step forward and rocked back, shocked she managed to hook so much influence into his mind.

Her lips curled; a fanatical light burned in her dark brown eyes. She laughed when Johnathan backed up a step, turning to the fire. The Hound within him bristled. He bit back the urge to snap his teeth. Challenging this female would be a mistake. There was something that rivaled the Morrigan, an aura of ancient forests and blood-stained teeth in the dark. She was a vampire, and she was old. Far older than Vic.

Johnathan wisely listened to his internal warning bells and left the female to her hearthside contemplations. Wondering whether his decision to come downstairs was stubborn rather than clever, he debated returning to the safety of his room before he encountered another, not so dismissive vampire.

Birdsong and the flit of unseen wings distracted him, not from outside the house but within. Johnathan kept his eyes on the female vampire until he was beyond the door, and headed deeper into the house. He emerged into the vibrant greenery of the conservatory, sucking in a breath. Sweat beaded his brow, more affected by the newcomer than he realized. Reorienting himself, he let the fresh, clean scent of the greenhouse wash over him.

A braided canopy of jewel toned greenery obscured most of the high domed ceiling, thicker than the endless local pines and firs, more vibrant than the stalwart oaks in full summer bloom. Johnathan wandered off the main path, deeper into the garden, catching faint hints of wine and smoke. Dripping vines brushed his shoulders. Blossoms in hues of violet and magenta hung in clusters, visited by birds with equally brilliant plumage, intermixed with the comparatively drab local sparrows. They chattered at his presence, flying off to the higher vines and branches when he drew too close.

He wondered how so many birds inhabited the indoor space, since there appeared to be no openings in the ceiling, a marvel of interlocked glass panels, the sky overhead a dark gray with the remains of dispersing rain clouds and oncoming night. A twilight sky, earlier than he believed. Easy to lose track of the hours between the murky rain and brightly lit interior of the Estate. He hoped to glimpse a clear night through the glass ceiling to see the stars.

"Quite the sight, isn't it? Took ages to construct." A familiar voice spoke from nearby, startling him. The influx of scents managed to hide most of Merry's scent. Johnathan had no desire to speak with his host. Setting his jaw, he pushed aside a living curtain of drooping fluted flowers, revealing the long table, most of the instruments and glass bottles cleared for a massive book, the pages yellow with age. Johnathan's gaze skirted over the text, the curved lines and symbols pricking at his nerves. There were more dried herbs spread out over the table, their light desiccated smell clouding the air.

Merry stood behind the table, working a mortar and pestle. They paused to add a sprinkle of seeds, grinding them down. "You may pull up a stool if you like," they said, not looking up from their work. Johnathan hedged, torn between curiosity and his burgeoning dislike for their host. The latter emotion, he concluded, wasn't quite fair, born out of his own speculation and doubt. Feeling foolish, he located the aforementioned stool, grateful to find a sturdy three-legged piece, and settled himself across from his host to observe their work.

The layered skirts and revealing blouse had been replaced in favor of a simple black shirt and pants, an identical outfit to Johnathan's, well-made but worn. The lip rouge was gone, though Merry's lips appeared slightly swollen. Perhaps they gnawed on their lips when they worked. There were plenty of reasons for swollen lips other than the treacherous image that came to mind.

"Where is Vic?" Johnathan kicked himself. There were a dozen other questions he wanted to lead with, but his tongue betrayed him.

Their mouth quirked up. "Likely intercepted by our new guest," said Merry. Their gaze finally slanted at him. "I'm rather surprised you're not with him. By the smell, you had a heavy hand with the salve, but considering our new arrivals, a good move."

Johnathan absently rubbed his throat. "What is this supposed to smell like to them?"

"Werewolves, though they won't find the scent pleasant either," they said.

"Oh," he replied, trying to hide his surprise.

Merry raised a brow. "I'm surprised Victor didn't explain this to you. Or were you too preoccupied for conversation? Not that I can blame him. He does have an eye for the pretty ones." They sighed, a bitterness tinging their wine and smoke scent.

He stiffened, uncertain how to proceed. This was not how he expected his encounter to go. Doubts and troubles aside, he suspected their host shared a history with Vic, this confirmed it. Merry did possess a striking appearance, and a confidence Johnathan envied. "My apologies. I didn't intend to stir up any bad memories." Johnathan bowed his head.

Merry paused and set down the pestle. They braced themselves against the table. Johnathan thought they were going to yell at him for touching on the sore subject, but their shoulders began to shake. They threw back their head in a robust laugh that startled a nearby cluster of birds to flight. Merry wiped a tear from their eye. "You are delightful."

Johnathan fidgeted, uncertain what he did that amused their host so much. Merry leaned across the table to pat his arm. "I appreciate the concern, my dear. You make it very difficult to hate the one who filled Victor's heart after me."

The signature blush flushed up through his ears. "Oh," said Johnathan. What else could he say to their blunt reveal? He'd convinced himself their history wasn't so recent. Merry's age was difficult to determine but they appeared youthful and registered as human to his senses. Merry's fingers drifted down his arm, turning over his hand to trace the lines on his palm.

"You have an interesting lifeline, my young friend," they said, tapping one of the thicker lines. "This one tells me about your relationships. Do you want to know if you have another great love in your future?"

Johnathan's hand curled away. "I don't believe in such nonsense."

Merry's nose crinkled. "A bold statement from a creature of the night." They grinned. "In this case you are right. Truthfully, I have no gift for palm reading. My talents lay elsewhere."

He rolled his eyes, torn between amusement and exasperation at his host's antics. "How long has the Estate been here?"

That knowing smile returned at his obvious subject change. "Here? A few decades, give or take. The Estate isn't a singular place. There are half a dozen similar locations spread through Europe, the Americas, even the far East."

"And now deep in the state of New York," said Johnathan.

Merry nodded. "The future great western empire, if it survives the next decade."

His eyebrows drew together. "Why the next decade?"

A painted red nail tapped his palm. Merry still cradled his hand. "Can't you feel it yet? The realms are shifting, Johnathan. A play for power is unfolding, and mankind will be the pawns."

Warning threaded through Merry's voice. Johnathan's fingers flexed. "Between whom?"

Merry suddenly straightened and seized the pestle to continue grinding. The abrupt action puzzled him until his hackles rose. There was another predator in the room.

"Hello, Alazar," said Merry. "I take it we're ready to convene?"

"I expected to find you alone, Goodkind." The bass voice poured over him. Johnathan itched to look at the source, but a lifetime of preservation against stronger, deadlier foes kept him in place. Alazar glided forward, a living shadow in a billowing black cloak. His skin was possibly a shade darker, midnight hued, and possessed the same ethereal quality as the woman he encountered earlier.

Alazar's cold black stare bore into their host, the whites of his eyes stark in his handsome face. He smoothed an absent hand over his close shaved crown, revealing long nails painted black and filed to points to enhance his fierce appearance.

"Nor was I aware we were entertaining more guests." There was a not-so-subtle challenge in that deep voice, and though Alazar clearly referred to him, he didn't spare Johnathan a glance.

Merry was unbothered. "Sanctuary doesn't require an appointment, Alazar. He accompanied Victor."

The answer clearly didn't satisfy him, but aside from flaring his nostrils, he didn't react. "Is your draught ready? We've waited long enough."

"Preparation takes time—"

"You've had plenty," snapped Alazar. "You will be ready within the hour."

Merry's mouth set into a thin line. Tension saturated the air and with so little knowledge of the circumstances, there was little he could do but observe and try not to get caught in the crossfire.

"I will be ready when I am ready," said Merry. Their sibilant tone pushed the moment over a proverbial ledge. Alazar's hand shot out, angling for their host's throat. Johnathan wrapped his fingers around the vampire's arm before it touched their host.

Incredulity flashed through that merciless black gaze. Johnathan was also surprised, but he maintained his grip on Alazar's forearm. "Attacking your host is the epitome of bad manners," he said. Apparently, he lost his sense of self preservation.

Alazar's gaze narrowed. "Who are you?" His imperious demand tempered by shock.

"Our guest." Merry recovered a measure of their composure. Calculation crossed their features. "As I told you, he came with Victor."

The pronouncement shifted Alazar's anger to haughty interest. "Strange that Victor didn't mention you." He stopped fighting Johnathan's hold. "Release me."

Johnathan bristled at the order. He waited until their host nodded before he let go. Alazar's jaw tensed at the defiant gesture, but he chose to ignore it. "How far Victor has fallen to lie down with dogs." Alazar sneered. "I suppose you will join us. Even your ilk should be aware of this matter."

Johnathan's lip curled. A low rumble rose in his chest. Merry cleared their throat. "We'll be there."

"I shall have to advise Victor to keep his mutt in check." Alazar smoothed his sleeves.

This was the first time Johnathan wanted to give in the Hound smoldering beneath his skin. Was Alazar born this arrogant, or did immortality make him a rude bastard?

"That is enough, Alazar. You might not like his presence, but Johnathan is a guest of the Estate." Merry spoke through their teeth. "Now if you will excuse me, I need to finish this draught."

The tension took on a vicious edge, Alazar's attention sharpened, a viper rearing to strike. His gaze paused on Johnathan. Whatever he saw made him withdraw with a pointed sneer. "One hour," said Alazar. He spun, robes whipping in his wake.

Merry's breath rushed out in a shudder. "I can't decide if that was brave or stupid," they said. "But thank you."

Johnathan gnawed on the inside of his cheek. He watched Merry resume their grinding, the rhythm stilted after the other man's departure. "How does that prick know Victor?"

The pestle rattled in Merry's grip. "They are old friends." Johnathan wasn't sure what to make of that, though he remembered Vic's reaction to Alazar's name.

Johnathan needed more information from their host. Merry drip fed him pieces little better than gossip. Katherine said that Alazar hadn't come alone. How many vampires were currently stalking the halls of the Estate? Why did Alazar think he should attend this meeting? What was the nature of Vic and Alazar's 'friendship'?

Merry interrupted his train of thought, tossing the pestle down with a loud thud. "What do you want to know first?"

"How do you know I want to ask you anything?" Johnathan hedged.

"Questions march across your face like soldiers on parade," said Merry. They brought out a bottle of wine from a cabinet under the table and a thin stemmed glass. The wine was a deep red, thick as fresh blood, with a sweet scent he didn't recognize.

"Pomegranate wine." Merry noted his curiosity. They dumped the contents of the mortar into the glass, the stem pinched between their fingers as they swirled the concoction together. "Alazar is not a patient man. He probably accosted Victor as soon as he arrived." Merry lifted the glass and gulped down the wine in a single go. Twin drops of red ran down the sides of their mouth.

"You don't appear to like Alazar either," said Johnathan.

Merry swiped the black of their hand across their mouth, smearing the red liquid over their chin. "It's complicated. Alazar doesn't necessarily agree with my position as caretaker of the Estate." Their wine-stained smile was full of chagrin. "But I have my reasons for being here."

They set down the empty glass with a sigh. "Would you please find Victor and bring him before the hearth within the hour?"

"I'd rather swallow hot coals than do that asshole any favors," said Johnathan. He started to get off the stool when Merry grabbed his wrist.

Their green eyes went glassy and distant. "You will have your answers, Johnathan, but remember," they warned. "All bargains have a price. One you will both pay in time." They jerked away from him. A frisson of awareness ran through him at the point of contact. Merry rubbed their temples with a winced. "I'm afraid I must ask you to leave."

Johnathan didn't need to be asked twice.

CHAPTER ELEVEN

MERRY SPOOKED HIM. THERE WAS A WEIGHT TO THEIR WORDS, THEIR host tuned to a different frequency than the rest of the world. All bargains had a price. The impending fallout loomed over Johnathan's shoulder. The birdsong seemed muted after their brief exchange. He retraced his streps through the garden, following the path from memory while he mulled over his encounter with the other vampires. Like the woman by the hearth, Alazar possessed the same magnetic draw, though he'd ruined the effect when he opened his mouth. Johnathan pondered what sort of relationship Vic could possibly have with the older vampire. Alazar clearly thought little of werewolves, though beneath his acidic insults he seemed almost spooked by Johnathan.

"Shit," he muttered. He'd stopped Alazar from attacking Merry, a strength he matched. Were werewolves weaker? Had he surprised Alazar because he interfered, or was Johnathan stronger than he thought? At least the potent salve did as intended, masking his scent. Though the charade wouldn't last long if he gave away the game with another blunder.

A door opened directly to his left. Vic pulled him into the unlit room, and closed them in. His hands landed on Johnathan's shoulders, fingers biting into the muscle before they eased. The bitter tinge in Vic's scent betrayed the worry hidden by dark.

"There you are," said Vic, his voice tight. "Why didn't you wait for me?" His hands fluttered down from Johnathan's shoulders, over his arms and chest, as if to assure Vic he was unharmed.

"Where did you go?" Johnathan submitted to the touch, bemused.

Vic huffed. "Alazar came barreling into my room. Barely had time to scrub myself."

Johnathan's amusement wilted. "You weren't dirty."

"I had to hide your scent too, John," said Vic. His hands rested against Johnathan's chest. "I'm sorry for this ruse. I worry about them seeing you—"

"Already have," said Johnathan. He bit the inside of his cheek. "How strong are werewolves?"

Vic released a strangled noise. "I dread to ask, but what happened?" Johnathan relayed the altercation between Merry and Alazar, omitting the details of his conversation with their host. He wasn't ready to bumble his way through Vic's romantic history, not certain he would ever be ready, but his curiosity piqued when it came to the older vampire.

"He didn't retaliate?" The fluttering motions of his hands resumed until Johnathan captured his wrists.

"No, but he did look surprised. Merry did impress upon him that I arrived with you." Johnathan wished he could see Vic's face. His night vision had vastly improved, but this room was so dark he could barely see the outline of the man in front of him. "Why are we having a clandestine meeting in a closet, Vic? Alazar and whoever he brought with him are waiting for us."

"It's not a closet," snapped Vic. There was a pregnant pause before he spoke. "He only brought one other, but you must be very careful John. Tamara has had encounters with the Nether before, and her hatred of demons runs deep. You must not reveal the quirks of your nature to her." The temperature of the room dropped at the implication in his words.

"I don't have that level of control," hissed Johnathan. "Should I return to my room?" Except the female vampire knew he was here. Their brief encounter was unnerving enough, he couldn't imagine what extended time in her presence would do to him.

Vic's cool breath gusted over Johnathan's face. "After you're encounter with Alazar, we can't risk your absence."

"I'll help you," Katherine chirped.

Johnathan swallowed a yelp, while Vic cursed. "Fuck, Katherine, you know I hate it when you do that."

"Language," she said in a sing-song voice. "Such uncouth speech is not meant for a lady's ears." The chill grew more pronounced, hovering in a dense patch nearby.

"Katherine," Vic growled. Johnathan's brows rose. He hadn't heard that level of exasperation from the man since they met.

"Oh, stop being so dramatic," she teased. The air shimmered as she appeared, her pale skin luminescent in the dark. It cast a faint light around her, illuminating Vic's face. She folded her arms. "You know that salve won't fool them completely. He started smoking when he got distressed."

Johnathan blinked. The last thing they needed was a display like that in front of either vampire. "How would your presence help that?"

She peered up at him. "It won't be pleasant, but the cold would make your breath naturally fog. And Alazar won't question it if I keep you close company. He doesn't like my kind either."

"He doesn't seem to like anybody," Johnathan grumbled.

"Alazar sees himself above us paltry creatures," said Katherine. She nodded to Vic. "Your presence will be another distraction. Between the two of us, Victor, we should be able to keep their attention off him."

Why would the attention of the two older vampires be so diverted by Victor? The harried expression on Vic's face made him bite his tongue.

"Fine," said Vic, "let's get this over with. It would have been better to take our chances in the woods."

Katherine grimaced. "Not with those Society Agents out there. Honestly, Victor, it can't be worse than dealing with those buffoons."

Her opinion made him cringe. Johnathan had been one of those buffoons until very recently.

"You underestimate Tamara's ire," muttered Vic.

"And you overestimate her attentiveness," Katherine retorted. She cocked her head, listening to something Johnathan couldn't hear. "Merry is almost ready. Let's not dally, shall we?"

"They can damn well wait," Vic muttered. He fussed over Johnathan, tugging, and pinching at his clothes before finger combing his hair. His fingers ran over the light growth of bristles on Johnathan's chin. It'd been a few days since he'd taken the time to shave. "This looks rather dashing on you," said Vic. Warmth stole through his agitation. "Are you sure you are up for this? Suspicions be damned, I will make excuses for you if don't want to do this."

He wanted Johnathan to know the choice was his, an invaluable sentiment. He reached for Vic's hand, holding it to his cheek. "I can do this." How could he not, when Katherine and Vic both put themselves on the line for him?

Relief flickered through Vic's face. "I wish we had prepared better but do your best to keep the Hound leashed tight tonight. They will find your appearance unusual, but with that salve, they won't recognize your nature." He caught Johnathan's chin. "Promise me you'll be careful. Leave the room if you must."

A kernel of apprehension took root in his empty stomach. "I will," he said.

"Come on, you two." Katherine hissed her impatience. "Unless you want Alazar to come looking for you."

Suitably groomed and far more apprehensive, Johnathan fell in step behind Vic as they exited the room. They headed for the firelit room he'd visited earlier. Katherine glided a few steps ahead of them, at a far enough distance so they wouldn't arrive together.

They were the last to join the party in the common room. Merry sat on the ground at the low table, their back to the hearth. Katherine hovered by the door, waiting to see where Johnathan would sit.

The well stoked fire flickered shadows over the other two *guests*. Alazar sprawled on one of the couches, one leg bent, a lazy perch for his arm. Across from him, sitting up straight with her hands clasped over her knees, was the woman who snared his mind, Tamara.

Her dark gaze lit up at their entrance. She rose to her impressive height, eye level with Johnathan, and moved forward to embrace Vic.

"Victor," she crooned. Her lilting accent enriched the sound of his name. "It's been too long." The woman brushed her lips across his cheek. Her arms enveloped him, the hold long enough to make Johnathan twitch.

"Hello, Tamara." Vic returned the gesture. He beckoned Johnathan to his side. "May I introduce you to John?"

Tamara's attention shifted to him, dark amusement in her gaze. "Greetings, little lamb." She looked him over with an appreciative eye, an obvious show for the ornament on display. "Such stunning eyes. Would you consider giving me a taste of your young paramour?" Tamara clearly didn't share the same level of disdain for werewolves Alazar held. She spoke as if they were a rare delicacy.

Johnathan stiffened, but Vic's congenial smile didn't waver. "Now, Tamara, it's never a taste. I must insist you keep your hands and your teeth to yourself, or I shall be upset." Beneath the amiable expression, a thread of steel laced Vic's voice.

The vampiress merely laughed, revealing the impressive length of her fangs and a mouthful of teeth filed to fine points. A cosmetic adjustment she must have done while still human. She playfully swatted Vic's arm, making him stagger. "You are still amusing, Victor." Her nails tapped Vic's chest. "It's why I haven't ripped your heart out."

A low snarl built in Johnathan's chest, silenced at the subtle shake of Vic's head. "We both know it would be a waste. You'd miss my charm," said Vic.

Tamara pursed her lips. "You're fortunate I find you so pretty to look at, my northern jewel."

"You wouldn't rip the wings from a butterfly," Alazar rumbled from his relaxed position on the couch. He didn't rise to greet Vic, but his expression was far calmer than earlier. "Thank you for joining us, Victor. You must introduce me to your friend later. I've found him quite... interesting."

Vic shot Johnathan a look, letting Tamara pull him down until he was halfway in her lap. With the vampires sprawled across the couches, there was no space for Johnathan. A tactic Alazar likely meant to intimidate him, but he was grateful for the excuse to keep his distance. Even if Tamara's constant contact irked him. Johnathan settled on the floor across from Merry, the thick carpet comfortable enough. From his expression, Vic longed to join Johnathan on the floor rather than keep the vicious Tamara company, but she threw her arm around him and pinned him to her side. The air around Johnathan grew frosty when Katherine sank down next to him.

Tamara pursed her lips at the Geist's presence. "So rare to see you here rather than haunting the basement, Lady Katherine."

Neither vampire had an ounce of tact, but plenty of backhanded compliments. Katherine's smile was sharper than a razor's edge. "This meeting is important, even for the addle-brained dead."

The vampire's mouth opened to retort when Alazar cleared his throat. "Let us proceed."

Though the alliance was a precarious one, they all looked to their host, who sat in a trance like state. Merry's hands rested on the table, palms up, fingers curled in repose. With their back to the fire, shadows cleaved their face. Their eyes glowed like chips of jade. "Ask your questions."

The chill that pricked his skin had nothing to do with Katherine's icy presence.

"What is the Society's next move?" Alazar's deep voice intoned.

Vic's expression closed, masking his emotions. Johnathan dug his claws into the underside of the table to keep from reacting. He realized that Alazar asked Merry directly. The events proceeding their arrival happened so fast, he'd failed to glean the nature of their host.

The Society's Chapter houses were widespread, they presented purpose to protect humanity from the dark appetites of preternatural creatures. The events of Cress Haven exposed the darker ambitions of Johnathan's former Chapter house, but Alazar's simple question hinted at something far more sinister and far reaching. The kernel of apprehension burst. Johnathan's stomach clenched.

Merry's head fell back, blank eyes wide. Their hands flipped on the tabletop, nails digging into the wooden surface as their body seized.

Power coiled through the room. Merry's head slowly dropped down, their green eyes swallowed by a white light from within.

"The Mad Man of the North's gamble has failed." A discordant voice poured from their host's mouth, reverberated throughout the room. There was a doubled quality to it, as if two people spoke at once, a man and a woman, perfectly synced with one another. Pressure pulsed against his temples. Shadows lengthened and swallowed the firelight. They crawled up the walls, living writhing creatures. Johnathan ignored them, entirely focused on that compelling voice. "The Nether remains closed, a bargain done."

"Thank the Gods for small favors," Alazar droned. "Do we know what tried to come through this time?"

Johnathan's ears rang. The name swelled on his tongue, pressed against the back of his lips. His claws cut long grooves in the wood. Better that than his palms or thigh. Bleeding in present company would be disastrous. Katherine's hand settled over his, the icy burn of her touch grounding him.

"Cernunnos," said Vic. Hearing it caused a visceral reaction, a full body shiver, but the others weren't looking at Johnathan, their focus on Vic.

Tamara raised a speculative brow. "Ah yes, weren't you staying in that territory? Another misguided attempt to pass among the living." She ran her tongue over her pointed teeth, leaving a streak of blood. "How long did this little experiment last?"

Alazar flapped a dismissive hand, ignoring her affronted hiss. "Enough, Tamara." He straightened with fresh interest. "Were you close to the incident, Victor?"

"Yes," he responded. Alazar's gaze narrowed when he failed to elaborate. The ancient vampire appeared ready to press for more information when Merry spoke.

"Cernunnos was sealed, his seeds destroyed." That emptied gaze shifted, almost imperceptibly, in Johnathan's direction. Whatever force currently rode their host had lied for him. He hadn't the faintest idea why.

"And the Mad Man of the North?" Alazar asked, his tone clipped.

"Status unknown," said the echoing voice. Alarm shot through Johnathan. His gaze flicked to Vic, who appeared equally shocked by the news. Evans was dead. Johnathan tore out his throat and watched him bleed out on the ground. How could his fate be unknown?

Alazar growled, echoing their frustrations. He pushed off the cushions to pace in front of the hearth. "These damn heretics are worse than locusts." He scowled at Vic. "Shame you couldn't nip that threat in the bud while you were there. How, exactly, were you involved?"

Vic remained stone faced. This time it was Tamara who broke their dance of tension. "Does it matter why or how he was involved, Alazar? The matter is closed. The Society is akin to one of those monsters from the Grecian myths. Cut off one head, two more grow in its place. What do the new heads pursue?"

"The Hydra," Johnathan murmured, familiar with the story. An apt comparison. The Society's threat seemed endless, a dozen unseen heads rearing to attack.

"The Scarlet Sisters continue to search for this new divine vessel. The Herald guides them to the twice blessed." Merry paused. Their breathing grew labored. Blood pooled in their mouth. "The Herald sings a song of triumph. They will soon be at our door."

Tamara stiffened. "They are coming here?"

"Even if they manage to locate the Estate through the wards, they cannot break them," said Alazar. He stroked his chin. "Do we know who they seek?"

There was a pause, two voices inhaling in tandem. "The divine touched. Twice blessed."

Alazar stepped closer. The shadows stirred in his wake, tugged at his cloak. Irritation flashed across his face. "Blessed, divine touched, yes, but who?"

"What would you do with a name? Kill them?" Vic's hands curled over his thighs, flint in his wintry gaze.

"If necessary," Alazar snarled.

Tamara shook her head, the long dark veil of her hair rippling with the motion. "That would be foolish," she purred. "A waste of power and resources. The heretics would simply turn their focus to the next potential candidate."

"You are pushing our host to their limit," warned Vic.

"That's enough, Alazar," Katherine cried out, rising to her feet. "You have enough information."

Alazar's jaw set. He fixed his attention on Merry, who swayed. Blood dribbled from the corner of their mouth. "What of the Other?"

"The heretics will ignore them," insisted Tamara. "They can't be bargained with or manipulated to do their bidding."

Alazar shook his head. "What of the Other?" he repeated.

Katherine's hands flexed, but she did not interfere. Johnathan wondered if she could or if doing so would injure Merry further.

"The influence of the Other continues to wane beneath the progress of mankind. The ground, the air, grows more poisonous to them with each passing year. Soon they will pull away from this realm completely and sever all ties to the children of Adam and Eve." The blood vessels in Merry's eyes began to burst.

"Enough," Katherine shrieked. She staggered forward, her face stricken.

Alazar glared at her and held up a hand to stall her interference. "We put down several stirrings in the south, but the Society continues to be a persistent presence. What is their intent?"

Johnathan's gaze darted around the room. Didn't they have enough information? Why did they continue to push when this force was overwhelming Merry's body?

"Unrest will continue to grow between the factions of man," said Merry. "War is a whisper in their minds. Time is short to shift the tide." Their body seized and tipped sideways. Vic caught them, settling them on the couch Alazar had vacated. Katherine rushed to Merry's side, cupping their face. The contact elicited no reaction from their host.

"It seems I've missed a great deal of the Society's activities," said Vic. He cradled Merry's head in his lap, tilting their neck so they didn't choke on their own blood.

Katherine produced a flask from her skirts, carefully dripping the contents into Merry's open mouth.

"That's what happens when you shut yourself away to live among the primitives," said Tamara, her tone drenched with disdain.

"Not all of us need to be worshipped as false idols," Vic quipped.

A cruel smile played along her lips. "There is nothing false about it. To my people I am the goddess incarnate." She smoothed her hands down her bodice to emphasize her point. "What have you sacrificed to hide among these ignorant children?"

There were differences between the two vampires though Johnathan suspected that had less to do with Vic's methodical feeding than Tamara's age. The fire painted Tamara in gilded hues, otherworldly compared to Vic's cultivated appearance. She would never blend among the citizens of Cress Haven. Whatever sacrifices Vic made, his humanity wasn't one of them.

Alazar ignored their biting banter. The flames seemed to absorb into his dark skin. He was another ancient vampire who lost the ability to blend because he was an asshole.

"We are sorely stretched to turn up our nose at allies, no matter how we feel about them." The statement likely encompassed everyone who was not Alazar. Tamara's mouth pinched into a pout. Alazar resumed pacing. "The Society has long been a nuisance to our kind, but they served their purpose, culling the population and disposing of those too impulsive to keep a low profile."

After meeting these two ancients, Johnathan knew the Society was sorely out matched. Tamara and Alazar oozed power from their skin, easily capable of wiping out the Society if they chose to. Why tolerate their presence at all?

"Yet here we are. Once again, they dabble with powers they do not understand," sneered Tamara.

"I think they understand the Nether and the Benign more than you think." Johnathan pressed his lips together the moment the words left his mouth. The older vampires had mostly ignored his presence, dismissed him as Vic's tolerated companion. The status allowed him to observe and keep a low profile. Now he'd injected himself into the conversation, bearing the scrutiny of their ancient stares. Katherine glared at him, but Vic remained calm, continuing his ministrations to the unconscious Merry. If they tried to intervene on his behalf, it would appear he had something to hide. He needed to tread through this conversational gaffe alone.

Johnathan folded his hands under the table. "The Society has spent centuries erasing all mention of the Nether and Benign from human history, reducing them to watered down stories of demons and angels while they hoarded the knowledge for their own use. I don't think they understand the reality of these beings, but they know more than enough to be dangerous." An understatement after the events in Cress Haven.

"The lamb speaks with authority." Tamara pushed her hair over her shoulder. "How does such a pretty face know such sordid details?"

"Because he used to be one of them," said Vic. Katherine went wide eyed, her jaw dropped. Alazar's gaze turned thoughtful, but the reveal delighted Tamara.

"Victor, you caught yourself a Hunter. How quaint." Her smile vanished as she regarded Johnathan. "Clearly, they've also forgotten their history. They do not comprehend the ruin they invite, vying for the power of these creatures. Their machinations have already drawn too much attention. The Benign and the Nether have begun to stir. They seek a foothold in our world, exerting their influence. Whispering in the minds of mortals to stir conflict."

"Humans believe us to be monsters." Alazar grimaced. "We've witnessed the horrors they do to one another. This country was built on spilt blood and broken backs. A wealth that thrives on the pain and suffering of slaves. Their choices splinter between the minds of this nation. That divide will continue to grow with or without interference of the realms. But the Nether and the Benign will use such a conflict to tip the scales in their favor."

"Conflict and strife drive humans to desperate measures, to bargains and concessions they would not make otherwise," said Tamara. Her expression was haunted. From Vic's brief warning, Johnathan wondered if she'd seen firsthand how the darker aspects of men opened them to demons. One man's greed allowed Cernunnos into their world.

That the Society believed they could control denizens of the Nether seemed mad, but Evans came closer to success than Johnathan *wanted* to acknowledge. They'd underestimated Cernunnos's power, but despite the high cost of life among his Agents, they came prepared with silver cages and nets, and weapons that overpowered the demon. If Vic hadn't freed Johnathan to mete his revenge, he wondered if the Society would have ultimately emerged the victor.

Johnathan's thoughts derailed when Merry began to stir. There was something strange happening to their host. Their body shifted beneath their loose-fitting clothes, thickening in some areas, and slimming in others. The curves of their breasts flattened, hips growing narrow where the bones adjusted. Muscles swelled while the angles of their face sharpened, the jaw losing its elfin delicateness in favor of a more masculine edge.

Merry's eyelids fluttered open, the transformation complete. Katherine helped them sit up, gently wiping the dried blood from the corner of their mouth. Johnathan stared in awe, though none of the vampires appeared surprised. Merry turned to Alazar, their expression glacial despite their evident exhaustion. "Did you get the answers you sought?" Their voice was a rich tenor, melodic beneath the ice.

"Adequate," Alazar grit out. "Thank you for your contributions, Merry Goodkind." The dismissal was incredibly insulting, but Merry didn't respond. They struggled to rise from the couch. Katherine slid her arm around them, but Merry winced from the cold. With Alazar and Tamara's attention no longer on him, Johnathan rose and braced Merry from the other side. Their host was now the same height. He easily took the bulk of their weight off Katherine. Merry sank against his warmth in apparent relief. Katherine sent him a grateful look, fully aware of the unfortunate effect she had on her friend.

Vic returned to his position between the two ancients but his gaze lingered on Johnathan.

"Victor, would you elaborate on your encounter with the Society in the north?" Alazar dismissed their presence now that he'd gotten what he wanted from Merry. "We need to assess the progress these heretics made. It may be time to call in our allies before this contingent arrives and makes passage difficult."

The level of banked aggression in the room was bad enough with three vampires. Johnathan would hate to see what a room full of them would do.

"John, why don't you and Katherine help our host to their rooms," said Vic. His tone held the same callous dismissal as Alazar, but there was a pleading note in his gaze. Johnathan knew Vic wanted him well away from the other two if they intended to pry any details of what happened in Cress Haven from him.

A show was a show. Johnathan turned his back on the trio with a huff. Merry struggled to hobble across the carpeted floor while Katherine fretted on their other side. Their host made it through the door on their own feet. Johnathan caught them when their legs gave out, carrying them down the hall. He couldn't shake the feeling he'd abandoned Vic, though the man was far more capable of handling those two vipers. It still bothered Johnathan how easily Vic sank beneath the aloof mask in their company.

CHAPTER TWELVE

W̲HATEVER MAGIC THEIR UNUSUAL HOST CHANNELED, IT TOOK AN immense toll on their body. They slumped into Johnathan's chest, their lids blinking heavily as they struggled to remain conscious. Their brown skin paled from the strain. Katherine kept pace beside them, dabbing at Merry's face with a dry cloth.

"You shouldn't have let them push you like that," she scolded softly.

Merry shuddered. Their teeth chattered as they tried to burrow into Johnathan's warmth. "If I failed to answer all their questions, Alazar would have forced me to do it again."

"I hate him," Katherine hissed.

Johnathan couldn't blame her. He tried to keep his arms steady, Merry's face flushed with pain at every bump, though he didn't make a sound. Between the magic and the shift that followed, their host was a wreck. "Where's your room?"

Merry shook their head. "The conservatory, bring me to the conservatory," they gasped.

Johnathan hesitated. "The garden?"

"Yes, I need—" Merry swallowed convulsively. Johnathan didn't wait for further explanation, moving fast as possible without jostling his passenger. Katherine streaked ahead of them. They arrived at the conservatory in seconds, where Johnathan eased Merry into a reclining chair near the work bench. Sweat limned their upper lip, their dark hair plastered to their forehead.

"We're here." Johnathan gave their shoulder a gentle shake to rouse them. Merry sat up with a groan, dragging themselves to the workstation in slow laborious movements. Johnathan hovered, worried their host would crash to the ground before they managed to fix whatever remedy they came here for. Where had Katherine disappeared to? He thought she meant to meet them here, but she was nowhere to be seen. "Is there anything I can get you?"

Merry fixed him with a glassy eyed stare. "Stay with me. Please. In case I keel over."

It was a simple request that made him wonder how many times Merry had to do this alone. Was Katherine not a permanent fixture of the Estate? He watched, and when their hands shook too much to manage grinding the ingredients, Johnathan gently took the pestle from them to finish.

"The same wine as before?" Merry nodded. Johnathan located the bottle and poured the wine into a fresh glass before he added the ingredients. He gave it a swirl like they'd done earlier. Merry watched him, an unreadable expression on their face when Johnathan handed them the glass.

They drank deeply; whatever the contents, the shaking subsided almost immediately. Merry set the glass down, easing back into the chair, their hands resting on their abdomen.

Their color improved by the minute. "Do you want me to go?" Johnathan asked. He itched to return to Vic, though he knew his presence would do nothing but make the other man worry. Especially if Katherine wasn't there.

"Not yet, please. Not until Katherine returns," said Merry, their voice still hoarse, exhaustion heavy on their countenance. Their head lolled to the side, meeting his gaze. "You are kind. Far kinder than I expected."

Johnathan frowned. "Expected for what?"

"For my replacement."

The sentiment didn't fill him with the same level of venom. There was something about the way the vampires treated Merry that was far too familiar. One that reminded him of a boy, the Prospective trying to prove himself. The Society didn't care about him, only how they could use him. It made Johnathan more curious about Merry's relationship with Vic than jealous.

"What was he like?" Johnathan sat down on the empty stool, scratching at the leftover husks of herbs littering the table.

A tired smile lit Merry's wan face. "Charming, beautiful." They winked at Johnathan. "An attentive lover."

He ducked his head, aware of the traitorous blush coloring his skin. "Was he patient with you?"

Merry chuckled. "I'm not certain if patient is quite the right word, but yes. He might be the most considerate lover I've ever taken, but the man had lusts and demands which he could easily sate elsewhere if I was unavailable."

The blush deepened, a worm of doubt wriggling in his gut.

"Johnathan? Now you look ill. Whatever's the matter?" Merry sat up straighter.

"It's nothing. Please don't get up," he said. The wine bottle looked awfully tempting.

Merry blinked at him. "You're blushing." They ignored his order to stay put, rising on wobbly legs. "Is Victor treating you properly?"

"What? Of course, he is. It's not that." He wanted to bury his face in his hands. Merry's expression turned thoughtful.

Pulling up another stool they sat beside Johnathan, bringing out another glass. "Wine?"

"Yes, please." Johnathan wished he were back in the common room, with the vicious duo, rather than having this conversation. He downed the contents of his glass in one swallow.

His host studied him over the rim of their own wine glass before they slapped their palm down on the table. "That's a virgin's blush." Their eyes widened. "You're a virgin?"

"No!" Though Johnathan doth protested too much, his heated exchange with Vic only a few hours ago ended in such failure his body burned from it. "Not entirely. There has been some—why are we talking about this?"

They shrugged. "You needed to." Merry stated and refilled Johnathan's wine glass. "I'd rather chat about this, numbing myself with wine, than wallow in the pain. You know, there is nothing to be ashamed of. I was a virgin well into my twenties."

His brows rose. "Really?"

Merry's mouth twisted in wry amusement. "Shockingly, it is rather difficult to find a partner comfortable with their lover shifting between sexes. Which I am rather impressed you have not asked me about yet."

Johnathan studied his claws. He hated the transformation to the Hound, but he was aware when it happened. Merry changed while unconscious. "It didn't look you had much control over it."

"An astute observation." Merry clinked their glass against his.

"That's something I understand," said Johnathan. He pressed his lips together at the unintentional slip.

Johnathan debated the wisdom of continuing this conversation. How much had Vic revealed of what happened to him before they arrived at the Estate. Did Merry know his hands were drenched in blood? The conflict must have been evident in his expression.

"Why do you think I agreed to help you?" Merry assuaged his fears. "You're safe here, Johnathan. Whatever my past with Victor, I'm committed to your cause. I believe I've found something that might help."

His head whipped up. "Do you mean it?"

"I need to rest," they said, giving his hand a pat, "but I promise we will try as soon as I've recovered."

Hope dangled on a fragile thread he dared not strain. The possibility was enough.

The moment passed. An inebriated grin lit up Merry's face. "I must admit, I am surprised you haven't gone further with him." They held up a hand. "Victor would never force you, but with all that charm it is rather interesting he hasn't, mmm, staked his claim yet."

It wasn't for lack of trying. "There are... thoughts... fears that hold me back," Johnathan admitted. The ragged hollow that plagued him remained quiet. He absently rubbed his chest. "I need to move past it," he murmured.

"He's clearly lost for you," said Merry. "Kept stealing glances at you while we were in there."

"He said he would be there when I was ready," said Johnathan.

His host poured the rest of the bottle into his glass. "If your lack of experience is what has you hesitating, sex is more instinct than you think. Maybe *you* should be the one to stake your claim." Merry grinned.

Johnathan rolled his eyes. He'd entertain that idea later, in private. "Why does magic make you shift?"

"Ouch, there's the subject change." Merry rolled their shoulders, stretching their arms over their head. "It is a payment, an exchange to use the gift I was born with, though you are the first to make that connection without explanation."

That didn't sound like much of a gift. Johnathan couldn't imagine surviving to adulthood when your body constantly remade itself. "Does it hurt?"

Merry tapped the side of their glass. "Not in the way you'd think. The Sight hurts far more, like speaking through a mouthful of broken glass."

"That's how you know about the Society's movements," said Johnathan. He wanted to ask about the twice blessed but Merry hid the information. Protecting them. The question withered on his tongue. "If there are vampires as old as Alazar and Tamara, why didn't they stop the Society sooner?"

His host snorted. "You saw what they were like in there. Congenial as feral cats, even when they share a common goal to survive. Vic is the calmest of the three, but large groups feed off one another's aggression."

Johnathan knew that, but realized he never applied it to the older vampires, who he thought would have matured past that lone predator aspect of their nature.

"The Society might be mere humans, but they are trained, they are righteous, and they are numerous," said Merry. "Gather enough ants and they can overwhelm the spider."

That was a morbid comparison. The numbers might fall in the

humans' favor, but the body count would be high. The Society knew many methods of incapacitating vampires, another point in their favor. On the battlefield they would be hard to contend with, even for an old vicious goddess like Tamara. Johnathan's lips parted.

"They know their weaknesses," he murmured.

Merry paused mid-drink. "What was that?"

"The Society knows what weakens demons," said Johnathan. "They almost succeeded in the north because they came armed with nets and cages of silver to trap a Hound. They had a weapon that nearly brought Cernunnos down."

A strained laugh spilled out of Merry's mouth. "Details I'm sure Victor is sharing with the others. Alazar will no doubt send for our extended allies." There was blatant hostility in their laugh.

"Alazar was incredibly rude to you," said Johnathan.

They drained their glass. "Most of them are like that. I might be useful, but I'm still human. Mostly," Merry amended. They held up a finger. "Victor is not like that. He sees humans differently, more than a means of food and entertainment."

Being in the same room with Alazar and Tamara made that obvious. He couldn't imagine either vampire befriending someone like Alyse or risking themselves to save the humans around them. Victor had faults and struggled with the violent urges of his nature, but at his core Johnathan believed he was a good man.

Katherine reappeared with a burst of icy air, a fistful of fresh herbs clutched in her pale hand, the vibrant stems touched with frost. She scowled at them. "I thought you were on Death's doorstep." She tossed the herbs onto the table. "Here I come back to find you chatting and drinking wine."

Merry had the grace to look contrite. "I didn't mean to worry you, Kat. Is that fresh rosemary and mint?"

"They are more effective when fresh," she said, hopping up onto the table. Her gaze wistful. "I miss wine."

Johnathan tuned them out. There was something that had been niggling at the back of his thoughts after Merry's use of the Sight. He'd been so keyed up by mention of his former mentor he nearly forgot the Scarlet Sisters.

"Who are the Scarlet Sisters?" He asked.

Merry shuddered. "Fanatics. They were not originally part of the Society, but a sect of the Catholic church that managed to maintain knowledge and worship of the Benign. They split off some time ago to form their cult. That they joined the Society in this endeavor is worrisome."

And they were coming for the Estate. How had they recuperated their forces so quickly? He could almost hear Sister Wilhem's strange chiming instrument. "What are the blessed?"

"A complicated answer, my friend," said Merry. They looked up at the glass ceiling. "I believe the vampires are done scheming by now. Go, find Victor."

An obvious evasion, there was a factor here he needed in order to piece the puzzle together. But Merry was exhausted and had given him more than enough to think about tonight. "Goodnight Merry, Katherine." He nodded to them and slipped off the stool. The wine rushed straight to his head in a pleasant buzz. Far more potent than he realized after guzzling two glasses. He managed to make it to the footpath without any embarrassing wobbles.

"Johnathan!" He stopped at Merry's voice, bracing himself on a convenient tree to look over his shoulder without falling. Their host fiddled with their empty glass, agitated. "Be careful, with Victor." Merry looked up, an unreadable expression in those tired green eyes. "His kind will ruin you."

The enjoyable buzz fizzed to a sour taste in his mouth. An echo of Hesper's warning, from someone who'd had considerably more intimate experience with Vic. He was a murderous beast who narrowly avoided Hell, how much more damage could Vic do? With a three-finger salute, Johnathan meandered toward his room to be ruined.

CHAPTER THIRTEEN

V IC WAS NOT IN HIS ROOM. JOHNATHAN GLOWERED AT THE EMPTY BED, far too sober for this disappointment. The alcohol burned out of his system by the time he made it to the stairs, and while Johnathan preferred any encounter to not be impinged by the effects of wine, a little liquid courage wouldn't be remiss. Nervous but determined. The empty rumpled blankets were a disheartening reminder of his earlier behavior. Despite Merry's assurances Vic was lost for him, there was a small voice Johnathan couldn't completely escape that wondered if Vic sought pleasure elsewhere tonight.

The thought was stupid, yet he couldn't stifle it, or the uncertainty it evoked. Johnathan headed for the connecting door to their shared bathroom, shutting it quietly despite his foul mood. Debating another luxurious soak, movement in the corner of his eye drew his gaze. He looked up to find Vic pacing across his bedroom floor. His shirt was untucked, and half unbuttoned to reveal the smooth pale skin of his throat, hair thoroughly mussed from the constant run of his hands.

The sight of him sent a flutter of need through Johnathan, kindling a low burn in his gut. Vic finally noticed him, naked relief in his expression. "John," he breathed. Vic moved toward him, hands held up in conciliatory gesture. "I'm sorry, I wasn't trying to make you feel—"

Johnathan cut him off, pulling Vic up on his toes as his mouth descended. There was nothing soft or hesitant about this kiss. Johnathan applied a punishing pressure, locking onto Vic's lips while his tongue lapped the silken seam, demanding entrance.

With a groan, Vic opened for him, gathering his hands against Johnathan's back to hold himself steady. Their tongues vied for dominance. Vic shivered when Johnathan licked along the point of a fang. Vic's hard length pressed against his hip. His earlier failings forgotten; Johnathan's hands moved to his pant fastenings. Vic's abdomen tensed at the seeking touch. He broke off the kiss, panting as he pressed his face against Johnathan's chest.

"You do not have to do this," said Vic. "I'm not going anywhere, John. Please don't rush yourself."

The words gave him pause, a balm to the worry and anxiety he'd carried with him for days. His fingers tunneled into Vic's tousled locks. He pressed his face into Vic's hair, savoring the scent of citrus and musk, shackled by it. Johnathan ruminated over Vic's assurance, waiting to see if the ghosts he carried rose to impede his lustful intentions. But they remained quiet. The hollow that had torn him apart from that terrible moment was still there, a constant scar along his soul. Johnathan wouldn't forget the dead. He couldn't forget the dead, but he refused to be swallowed by that hollow inside. Not with Vic here in his arms. This was Johnathan's choice. He was worth this moment.

Desire ignited, fire flashed up his spine so hot it edged on pain. Johnathan's grip tightened in Vic's hair, a curl of smoke escaping his nostrils. He gave a rough pull, baring the smooth column of Vic's throat and bit down.

"Fuck!" Vic shouted. The curse broke with a breathy moan. His cock jerked against Johnathan's hip, Vic's body shuddering in his hold. "Holy shit."

The sweet taste of Vic's blood flooded his mouth. He released his bite, lathing his tongue over the wound, enjoying the way the man's breath hitched. Vic's hand moved to his chest, tearing the front of his shirt in his grip. Johnathan pulled back, worried at his reaction.

Vic stared up at him, wide eyed, his swollen mouth open in apparent shock. He reached to brush the healing bite mark on his neck, a shiver coursing through him. "The hell," he gasped. He took a step back, gaping at the state of his clothes. "I've ruined my trousers."

Honestly, this wasn't how Johnathan expected him to react either. "I'm s—"

"Don't you dare apologize," Vic snarled. He grabbed Johnathan's collar, tearing the material off him in a rush. Vic pulled him off balance, following Johnathan to the floor, where their mouths tangled in a vicious dance of tongues and the scrape of teeth. There was no hesitation this time, no fear or unwelcome dread, only the heat and hardness between them. Vic pressed down on top of him, cupping Johnathan through his trousers.

Johnathan's hands were equally frantic, sliding past the waistline of Vic's pants, stroking his ass hard enough to make the vampire purr in his mouth. His hands continued their exploration, sliding along the crevice between his cheeks, eliciting another delightful shiver. Vic lifted himself up, face flushed as he stared down at Johnathan.

"Are you certain about this?" A touch of worry tempered the lust blazing in those silver eyes. Something broke open wide inside Johnathan.

He sat up, Vic's knees cradling his waist. "Yes," he said, pressing his lips to the corner of Vic's mouth. "Don't stop." He gripped the bottom of Vic's shirt, pulling it off him in one smooth motion. Heat built beneath his skin. He traced a scorching line with his lips down Vic's throat to his bare chest, grazing a nipple with his teeth.

Vic hissed. Johnathan found himself shoved back to the floor. There was another tearing sound, followed by a rush of cool air against his suddenly exposed lower half. The remains of his trousers fluttered across the room. Johnathan barely saw him move before Vic was there, braced about him, naked and beautiful.

Nervous anticipation built in his belly. Johnathan reached for him, Vic already stiff and ready once again, like silk over steel. He hissed as Johnathan's thumb ran over the slit of his cock, drawing a bead of pre-cum.

Johnathan brought it to his lips, savoring the mingling sweet and salty taste. Vic dropped his head, the direction of his mouth unmistakable, but Johnathan wanted more. The vampire huffed in surprise as Johnathan flipped him, pinning his chest with one hand.

"John?" His surprise melted when Johnathan took him into his mouth, lathing his tongue up Vic's shaft. He gripped Johnathan's shoulders, breathing in short gasps while Johnathan sucked on the head, more confident in his movements than his first attempt.

He released Vic with a soft pop. "Please tell me if I do anything wrong." Vic gave him a look of disbelief, his retort aborted as Johnathan's mouth enveloped his cock, tonguing the ridge of flesh around the head until Vic swore softly, tugging at his hair. Johnathan ignored him, taking him deeper to the back of his throat, sucking hard. He wasn't completely sure about his technique, but what he lacked in knowledge, he made up for in enthusiasm. He cupped Vic's sack, carefully stroking the sensitive skin with the tip of his claws. A litany of curses clouded the air. Vic forced him off and rolled Johnathan to his side.

"You're a fast learner," Vic wheezed. He stared at Johnathan with a contemplative expression. "Would you let me take this a step further?"

Johnathan's throat bobbed. He had a rough idea what came next, having heard more than one Prospective boast about pegging some willing woman, though he had a poor handle on the mechanics.

Vic laughed. "I can see those wheels turning, John. Don't overthink it. We can stop now, maybe draw up a bath—"

"I want it," said Johnathan, hooking a leg over Vic's waist to draw him closer. "I want all of you. Though a bath also sounds nice." Delight warmed Vic's smile before he crawled away.

"One moment," he said, disappearing in a flash of white flesh. He returned, a bottle of bath oil in hand. "This will help." He dropped to his knees. The scent of lavender teased Johnathan's nose as Vic poured several drops into his palm.

"If anything feels uncomfortable, or if you want me to stop, simply say the word," said Vic, eyeing Johnathan. "Hmm, roll onto your stomach and cup your elbows."

There was a beat of trepidation as Johnathan followed Vic's direction. He settled his forehead on his crossed forearms. His cock was pinned between his stomach and the plush carpet, long legs splayed behind him. He wasn't sure what to expect when Vic pressed a kiss to his shoulder and slid his well-oiled fingers between Johnathan's cheeks.

He startled when the pad of Vic's forefinger pressed against his puckered hole, muscles tensed. Vic shifted closer, his mouth closing on Johnathan's neck in a gentle suck to soothe his nerves. A graze of teeth made him exhale in a rush and Vic pushed the finger inside. Johnathan clutched his elbows, teetering between desire and discomfort at the invasion.

Vic's lips brushed against the shell of his ear. "Still with me, love?" He traced his tongue along the curve, nipping the lobe hard enough to draw a gasp. The hint of pain tipped him into a wave of rising pleasure. Vic moved the finger in and out in firm strokes, letting Johnathan get used to it before he teased a second one. There was a slight burn at the new addition. Vic paused, waiting for him to adjust. The moment Johnathan's muscles relaxed, Vic continued, the movements harder, more vigorous, stretching Johnathan while brushing a spot inside that made every nerve tingle. A fine tremor started in Johnathan's muscles, lost in a cascading sensation.

"Cum for me, John." Vic thrust his fingers deep, pressing against that internal spot. A white-hot lick of flame shot straight up from the base of his spine. Johnathan cried out, cumming in a sudden rush, a gush of wet warmth against his stomach. His cock throbbed in time to his thunderous pulse, both sated and not. Vic slowly slid his fingers free, shifting his body over Johnathan until he prodded against the readied entrance.

"Ready?" Vic waited, arms braced, the velvety head of his cock pressed against Johnathan's frightfully sensitive hole, while Johnathan attempted to compose his desire saturated mind. He managed little more than a nod, abandoning his hold on his elbows in favor of the floor when Vic began to push inside.

Too much, too full, Johnathan squirmed, uncertain whether he wanted to escape or take more. He made a small sound, clutching the carpet. Vic's hand gripped his waist, tilting him upward to rub against that magical place inside. The sound transformed into a moan. Johnathan bit down on his arm and pushed back.

"Christ," Vic swore. His fingers dug into Johnathan's hip.

"Don't take the lord's name in vain," said Johnathan, his voice muffled by the carpet.

Vic chuckled. He pulled back his hips, until only the tip remained inside, and thrust back in, eliciting an open-mouthed groan from Johnathan. Their rhythm set in, the slap of flesh against the flesh. A spiral of flame curled through Johnathan, flaring with each plunge of Vic's hips. He grew hard again, the carpet a sweet agony where it rubbed against his sensitized crown.

Vic suddenly hauled him up, spreading Johnathan's knees to accommodate their height difference. One arm wrapped around Johnathan's chest, while the other pulled his head back. Vic licked the pulse point at his neck. Their rhythm faltered, Vic's breathing turned ragged, a warm, uneven gush of air over Johnathan's fevered skin.

Realization dawned. He needed to bite, but Vic didn't know what Johnathan's blood would do to him. Was he afraid of Johnathan's reaction or his own?

"Do it," he whispered. That was the permission Vic needed. His teeth sank into Johnathan's flesh, his cock spasming as he came in a rush of warmth inside him.

The pain was immediate and so was the orgasm, stronger than the first. His entire body bucked at the flood of pleasure crashing through him. Johnathan's mind blanked, lost to an inward shower of sparks. His knees quivered, unable to support his weight. Vic released his bite, licking the wound to stop the bleeding. He held Johnathan up as he gently pulled out his softening member. Johnathan leaned back against him, the room quiet except for their labored breathing.

Vic had indeed ruined him.

Johnathan's throat was parched. He needed to guzzle water or another long soak in a hot bath. Probably both. His clothes were in shreds. He cringed at the mess on the floor. "We should really clean the carpet," he said. "Merry will murder us."

Vic burst out laughing. "I'll take care of it, but first a bath." He leaned down, nipping Johnathan's ear lobe. "If you aren't too sore."

The sultry whisper made his spent cock twitch. Yes, Johnathan was completely, happily, ruined.

CHAPTER FOURTEEN

JOHNATHAN LAY IN THE DARK, SOAKING IN THE AFTERGLOW. VIC SLEPT beside him, one arm and leg thrown over Johnathan. There was a delicious ache in his muscles, the scent of lavender and rose oils mingling with Vic's natural odor, and the distinctive earthy scent of sex. Nothing was different. Everything was different. The heady taste of Vic lingered on his tongue, sweeter than pomegranate wine, twice as addictive. Tentatively, he brushed his fingers over his neck, the healed over skin still sensitive from Vic's bite. A smile pulled at his lips. His reaction was on par to Vic's. There might be the beginnings of a mutual fetish there.

"I can feel you smiling," Vic teased, his voice muffled by the pillow he'd buried his face in. They crashed on the bed after another intense session in the bathtub. Johnathan was growing quite fond of the Estate bathrooms. Vic lifted his head, squinting though the shadows were still deep in the room. "You're awake? I must be losing my touch."

"I haven't slept," said Johnathan. There was a pause.

Vic rose higher on his forearms, brows drawn in a knot. "At all?"

"Not since the change." Johnathan shrugged. "I assumed it must be normal."

"It doesn't sound normal." Vic frowned. "I can go without rest for a

week, if necessary, but I'm miserable by the end. I rather enjoy sleep."
He made a face. "Not at all?"

Johnathan huffed a laugh. "I can take a lie down and close my eyes,
but I never fully drift off."

"That sounds incredible boring." He peered out the window at the
fading late afternoon sun. They'd spent hours enjoying one another while
the night bled away to morning. Johnathan let Vic sleep, content to lie
beside him, their bodies twined together.

"Come on. I want to see how Merry fares today." Vic rolled over,
stretching his arms to the ceiling while Johnathan admired his glorious
bare backside.

"That is an impressive view," he murmured. Vic grinned at him. His
heart stuttered in his chest.

"Likewise, my love," said Vic. Johnathan stared at him, a warmth
flushing from the pit of his stomach.

"I don't mind that one," he said.

Realization at Johnathan's meaning lit up Vic's face. "Then I shall be
sure to use it often." He lifted the shredded remains of Johnathan's shirt
off the floor with a fond smile. "Best grab some new clothes from the
wardrobe."

They proceeded to get dressed, sharing the bathroom to freshen up.
Vic stood on the edge of the tub to fix the increasingly wild tangle of
Johnathan's hair. It felt incredibly domestic, something Johnathan never
thought he'd have in his lifetime. He watched Vic fuss with his collar in
the mirror, the previous night's conversation with their host intruding on
his thoughts. He didn't need to know, but he wanted to, and last night
left him with a greater sense of security.

"Merry told me you used to be lovers," he blurted. Immediately, he
wished he could cram the words back into his mouth. This was not how
he wanted to broach the subject, fumbling in without preamble. Vic's
hands stilled, meeting Johnathan's awkward gaze in the mirror.

"We were," he said. "For nearly seven years." A blink for an immortal,
but Merry was human, albeit 'gifted', and while it was possibly, rather
likely, Vic had taken another to bed since then, Johnathan believed

Merry was the last significant relationship he had before...his thoughts stuttered to a halt.

This was a relationship. Johnathan hadn't allowed himself to see it in that light, mired in doubt and insecurities. Vic was more than his companion, more than his anchor, a bond stronger than both.

Vic's hand lightly brushed his jaw. "You look so unsettled. I promise, John, our relationship is long over. We've been apart longer than we were together."

He leaned into the touch. "It's not that," said Johnathan. "I trust you."

"I'll tell you anything you want to know," said Vic, brushing his lips along the curve of his cheekbone.

Johnathan bit his lip, hesitating. "How did it end?"

There was a pause while Vic composed his thoughts, his face pensive. "It wasn't an easy separation. I was the one who left. I wanted to live among humans, and Merry wanted to stay here," he said.

There was no need to know more but Johnathan was curious, and perhaps a little masochistic. "Do you regret it?"

"Do I regret how our relationship ended? Yes." Vic pursed his lips. "I cared about them, deeply. But do I regret that it ended? No. It was a wonderful experience, with many cherished memories."

Johnathan paid keen attention to the words. Vic cared for Merry, but not once had he said he loved them. And he dared not ask how Vic felt about him, when their relationship was a new bud. Instead, he thought of Merry. He hadn't forgotten their host's offer to help. Though that raised another thought Johnathan hadn't time to unpack to amid the numerous revelations he'd experienced since arrival.

"Have you told Merry about Sister Wilhem? Do you know what they meant by 'twice blessed?'"

Vic shook his head. "I told them we were evading the Society, but I didn't go into detail about what happened." He worried his lip. "Only that I had failed to help you control your new form. I'll bring it up to them."

They were nearly to the door when Vic stopped him. "You need the salve." He fetched it from the dresser.

"That would have been a blunder," said Johnathan. Nothing to spoil his post coital bliss like Tamara going for his throat.

This time, Vic smeared it over Johnathan's skin, taking the time to thoroughly rub it in. He leaned in, burying his face against Johnathan's neck. "Only a hint of smoke," he said.

"I smell like smoke?" Johnathan was curious what he smelled like to Vic.

"Smoke and heat," murmured Vic, gently nipping the underside of his jaw.

His arms slid around Vic in response, bringing their hips together. Vic groaned. "At this rate, we'll never get out of this room."

"I wouldn't be averse to that outcome," said Johnathan, nuzzling the side of Vic's face.

Vic planted his open palm over Johnathan's face. "No, there are matters to discuss. Solutions to explore. Merry is waiting."

"Merry needed to rest," insisted Johnathan, wondering if a little more pressure would send them both tumbling into bed. He began to slide his hands up the back of Vic's shirt.

"Ah, ah, no getting handsy." He caught Johnathan's wrists, nodding to the door. "Come, the daylight is waning."

"Killjoy," muttered Johnathan.

A dopey grin spread over Vic's face. "You're adorable when you're flirty."

"Does that mean we can stay?" Johnathan laughed when Vic shoved him out through the door.

The other man turned somber, linking their arms together. "Our history might be a sore point, but Merry has great insight, with and without using their gift. I'd hoped, gambled really, they would see you as I see you."

They descended the stairs, the chandelier shining bright overhead. Johnathan hadn't seen it unlit since they arrived. "How do you see me?"

"I see a good man," said Vic. He lifted Johnathan's hand to brush his lips across his knuckles.

Johnathan fell silent, pensive by the time they reached the indoor garden. Merry was at the work bench, a strange apparatus on the table. A small fire burned in a stone bowl, seemingly without fuel, while Merry fed various herbs to the flames, one piece at a time. The same ancient, worn book Johnathan glimpsed before was open beside them, the current pages faded and splattered with rust-colored stains that faintly reeked of old blood.

Merry appeared mostly recovered, though weariness lingered in the pouches beneath their eyes and the tightness around their mouth. Today, they'd donned a loose white shirt with a matching burgundy vest and trouser set that complimented the rich brown undertones of their skin. Their form hadn't changed from last night since they'd yet to perform any significant magic.

They glanced up at Vic and Johnathan's approach. "Somebody looks satisfied."

Johnathan cleared his throat. "Quite."

Vic raised a brow at him over his shoulder while Merry snickered.

"Where's Katherine?" Johnathan broke in to change the subject.

"She's gone to summon the allies," said Merry. "A Geist can travel much farther and faster than any of us. She'll be back in a day or two."

"I assume your other guests are sleeping?" Vic folded his arms.

"They've gone hunting," said Merry, peeking up at Vic. "Don't look at me like that, Victor. I'm not in the position to stop them."

Johnathan didn't want to think what damage the older vampires could do to any nearby settlements. In theory, a vampire's driving hunger waned with age, but they also grew more callous and violent and sought out the thrill of the hunt for pleasure. He swore he could hear Vic grinding his teeth.

"I'm actually glad you've pried yourselves from the bedroom," said Merry, adding a sprig to the flame. Johnathan's nose was hit with a burst of burnt sage. "The timing is ideal. I believe I have found the correct concoction for you, Johnathan."

Vic and Johnathan shared an astonished look. He knew Merry had promised to search, but he hadn't thought they would find anything so soon. Vic stepped forward, peering into the flaming bowl.

"How does it burn?" He leaned in close enough to endanger his eyebrows. Merry flicked their fingers at him.

"Well aged whiskey," Merry explained. "Seems a waste, but I didn't want to risk contaminating the ashes."

"Ashes?" Vic prodded the ancient tome with a deepening frown. "Where on Earth did you find this?"

Merry slapped his hand. "Through a trade. You're fortunate I did. This is one of the very tomes the Society attempted to snuff out." They looked at Johnathan. "Not the most comprehensive compendium regarding creatures of the Nether, but there are a few useful snippets of information."

Johnathan stayed several steps behind Vic. Perhaps it was the scent of old blood that clung to the pages, or the rather grisly illustration of a man in mid-transformation on the open page, but the book disturbed him. What other secrets about demons did those blood-spattered pages contain? What had Merry traded for something so invaluable? The sort of tome the Society would kill for. Johnathan refused to think ill of his host, not when Merry had potentially come through with something that could fix his control.

He tucked his doubts aside, circling around the far end of the table. "What are the ashes for?"

"A special draught," said Merry, pointing at Johnathan with an unrecognizable branch. "A Hound's body burns through poisons and toxins, which means it also renders most plants and herbs useless whether they are harmful or beneficial. However," they said with a flourish, feeding several leaves into the sputtering flame. "The ashes are another matter. Burnt herbs have the same effect on a Hound as fresh ones do on a man."

Johnathan made a face. "That makes no sense."

Merry pressed a fist to their hip. "Because the existence of Hellhounds is so logical."

Vic nodded. "They have a point."

He glowered, watching the flame burn itself out until a pile of damp ashes remained. Merry pulled another bottle from the cabinet beneath the table, pouring a white wine with the crisp scent of apples. The color was ruined by the addition of the ashes, turning the liquid a murky dark grey.

The draught looked incredibly unappetizing. "Why white wine?"

Merry shrugged. "It's what I had left. The flavor doesn't matter, only that we use spirits." They waggled their eyebrows at him. "Lowers the body's inhibitions."

Johnathan didn't have the heart to tell them the alcohol wore off shortly after he left. He shuffled from foot to foot. "What exactly will this do to me?"

Merry tapped their lips. "If I measured it correctly? It will give you more control of your other half." They handed the glass to Johnathan. "But first, it will force you to change."

He nearly dropped the glass. Johnathan set it down hard, the liquid sloshing ominously near the rim. "No! Are you mad?"

Vic gripped the table, his knuckles turned white. "Merry, there are two vampires who will take extreme issue with that if they return early."

"Both of you are ridiculous," said Merry. They held up a large leather pouch. "I'll set a threshold. We'll control the environment. It will be fine." They came around the table, muttering to themselves. At the entrance of the conservatory, where the carpet gave way to grass, Merry reached into the pouch. What appeared to be salt, mixed with various herbs, poured through their fingers to create a wide line.

"There," said Merry, clapping the excess off their hands. "No voyeurs, no eavesdroppers, no escapees unless I break the line. Drink up."

Johnathan panicked. "No. Not with you both here."

"Ah, ah, ah," said Merry, holding up a hand at his protests. "Did you hurt Victor the last time you transformed?"

He balked, reluctant to recall that blood-soaked encounter, but Vic shook his head. "Not so much as a nip."

Johnathan swallowed hard, still not convinced this was remotely a good idea. In the back of his mind, he could almost hear Alyse telling him not to be stupid. But what if the draught worked? Hope kept him on a razor's edge of indecision. "Merry, you shouldn't be here," he said.

They shook their head. "You won't hurt me, Johnathan. Even if this draught doesn't work."

"How can you be so sure?" Johnathan groused. He did not want to risk it, not when there was so much blood on his hands.

"Because Victor is safe," said Merry, their tone matter of fact. "You are safe. There is no threat to your lives. You will transform in a calm situation."

Vic sidled next to him. "Merry's right, John." He gave Johnathan's hand a gentle squeeze. "I will stop you."

That had to be enough. The possibility was too enticing to ignore. Johnathan raised the glass to his lips.

"Wait!" Merry shouted. Vic grabbed the glass out of Johnathan's hands to keep it from spilling. "Sorry, but it might be best to remove your clothes."

"Ah yes, wouldn't want to destroy more of your clothes," Vic quipped.

"*More?* I'm not made of money, Victor," Merry muttered.

Johnathan quickly undressed, handing his clothes to Vic. Using the table to provide some semblance of coverage, he grabbed the glass, eyeing Merry to make sure there would be no further outbursts. "Cheers."

The ash laced wine was an odd mix of bitter and sweet, tingling down his throat. He downed the draught and carefully set the glass on the table. Johnathan glanced up, meeting Vic's gaze. He tried to rein in his apprehension when the mixture hit his stomach.

"Gah," Johnathan cried out, clutching the table. The smoldering core in his chest exploded, scorching his blood, veins visibly blackening. His claws lengthened, digging deep grooves into the table before he doubled over in agony. Literal flames burst from his charred skin. This transformation was far worse than the others, one that dragged the Hound from its cage of flesh. Johnathan screamed at the rapid succession of breaking bone and tearing muscle, praying he would black out. Fire crackled through his mind. His fortunes were not that good. The Hound tore out of his skin, tottering on barely formed muscles.

The Hound fell onto his side, unable to stand, tongue lolling out of his mouth. Smoke poured up from his throat. Pain roared through his limbs. He released a canine whine, too weak to rise.

"John?" The voice tugged something deep inside. The raging blaze subsided, easing down to a manageable flame. The Hound licked his muzzle and gazed up into the most beautiful grey eyes. Vic's eyes. The connection radiated between them, a physical tether hooked directly to that fiery core within him. The Hound swung his wedge-shaped head, inhaling the scent of rosewater and ash, tinged by sweet wine.

"He's much bigger than I thought he'd be," said Merry, green eyes luminous in their face. They maintained a respectful distance, watching him with open fascination. "How do you feel, Johnathan? Can you understand me?"

Johnathan. He was Johnathan. He stared down at his paws in wonder, covered in coal black fur that absorbed the light around them. This body should have felt foreign, a shape not his own, but it was as natural as breathing. He attempted to nod, though the human gesture was odd for his canine head.

"Ha!" Merry crowed, throwing their arms in the air.

Vic knelt on the grass, grey eyes overly bright. "Are you still in pain?" There was a strain in his voice. He held up his hands, beckoning Johnathan closer. His palms were smeared with red, blood embedded under his fingernails. Johnathan wiggled closer, nudging his head against Vic's chest. The weight knocked him right over, but he landed with a laugh. Vic buried his face in Johnathan's fur.

"You're surprisingly soft," said Vic.

"I'm afraid I must interrupt," said Merry. "You should try to change back, Johnathan, before the draught cycles through your system."

A fresh spiral of panic set in. He'd been so focused on the prospect of control, he'd forgotten the morbid caveat of his transformation.

Vic shared his concern. "I've only seen Hounds regain their human form after taking a life." Johnathan scrabbled out of his hold, muscles tensing. How could they have been so stupid?

Merry folded their arms, exasperated. "Honestly, you two." They rolled their eyes. "Victor, I cannot help him without trying other methods. Why don't you help things along and give him some encouragement?"

Vic scowled. "I doubt positive affirmation will help in this matter."

Their host stared at him until he threw up his hands. "Fine," he snapped, turning to Johnathan. "Come on, John. You can do this. Come back to me."

Johnathan focused on Vic's words, trying to find the man inside the beast. He closed his eyes, Vic's encouragement droned through his skull, a soft murmur that pulled him down. He sank deep, deeper, into the mass of smoke and flame at the core of his being.

The ground beneath his paws squelched. Something dripped from his muzzle. A coppery scent tinted the air, filled his mouth, and coated his tongue. Overflowing, it spilled over, drenching his fur, the copper scent growing stronger until he gagged on it. Johnathan's eyes opened. The sightless dead stared up at him from the ground.

He froze trapped in the living nightmare, covered in blood. Not blood, there was no blood here. But Johnathan couldn't escape the stench of it. The feel of it, matting his fur, soaking the grass under his paws. He tucked his snout between his paws, trying to claw it off.

"Johnathan!" The illusion broke. Vic's strong fingers seized his jaw, prying it open to pour a bitter mixture down his throat. Johnathan didn't fight him, even as the liquid made him convulse. His guts turned inside out. He howled, a broken, ragged sound as the Hound began to recede. The reversal was possibly more painful. Johnathan tore at the ground, his body a twisted amalgamation of bones and joints. The sight must have been hideous, but Vic stayed beside him, urging him to continue. He locked onto that voice, clinging to it with everything he had. With a final violent snap, the Hound was locked beneath the skin.

Johnathan curled on the ground, a sweaty, feverish mess. Every muscle twinged with a watery ache, as if he'd emerged from a long illness, weak as a kitten. Vic pulled Johnathan's head onto his lap, while Merry produced a blanket to drape over him.

"I need to break the threshold soon, Victor," Merry whispered, rubbing a hand down Johnathan's back. They looked shaken by what they'd seen. "Alazar is sniffing at the other side."

Alazar was there? When had he returned? How long had Johnathan been in the grip of the Hound? He shuddered, trying to force his quivering muscles to move. His legs refused to cooperate.

"He can't even stand," snapped Vic, visibly shaken. His hands remained gentle, pushing Johnathan's damp hair out of his face. "He couldn't change back without that second draught."

Merry grabbed his wrist. "But it worked. Which means it will work again. We can use this to help him control it." They glanced down at Johnathan, their expression apologetic. "Though I didn't expect it to be so painful for you."

He nodded in reply, too weary to speak.

"Alazar can't see him like this," Vic hissed. "He reeks of the Nether." Transforming made him smell more like the Nether? Johnathan was vaguely mortified. His sense of smell was currently muffled, as if he breathed through a cotton rag.

Merry grabbed another vial off the table, wiping the salve over Johnathan's neck and shoulders. The familiar woodsy smell was faint to his dulled nose. Vic coughed.

"Fetch his clothes," Merry ordered. "Take him through the back left hall. That should circle back to your rooms. I'll get the sage burning."

Johnathan was a dead weight. It took both their efforts to maneuver him into his trousers. Vic didn't bother with the shirt. He draped it over his shoulder and lifted Johnathan in his arms.

"Well, isn't this familiar," he teased. Johnathan appreciated the levity, though he loathed that he was once again being carried like a fainting damsel. To give himself a fair shake, he had just broken and reformed his whole body. Twice.

Their host cleared the table, shutting the book and tucking it away before they lit a bundle of sage. The burning herb stung Johnathan's healing nose. "A good long soak will do him wonders, Victor. Use the peppermint oil."

Johnathan barely registered the journey back to their rooms, a blur of green and brown. Vic set him gently on the bed, still rumpled from the previous night. He lay there, floating on a wave of weariness, until Vic carried him to the bath. The hot water eased the deep-seated ache, the sharp bite of peppermint reviving his energy. Vic sat on the edge of the tub, pants rolled up, bare legs dangling in the water. He watched Johnathan with an air of concern.

It hit him then, the full weight of what they had accomplished. Johnathan had transformed without taking a life. They needed two draughts to do so, but they'd done it. He laughed, his voice hoarse and cracked, the burn of relief pricking at his eyes.

"I did it," Johnathan whispered. There was a world of possibility wrapped in that simple affirmation. A path forward in his new existence that wouldn't break his soul, worth the pain. Merry assured him it would be easier next time, and the next, until, hopefully, there was no need for the draught to change back and forth.

Vic nodded, solemn. "Yes, you did." He shifted closer along the edge of the tub, laying his hand on Johnathan's shoulders. "How do you feel?"

He considered the question, mentally assessing himself. Muscles were still sore, but excitement welled up inside him, singing through his veins. The bath gave him a fresh burst of energy that begged to be expended. Johnathan slid a hand up Vic's thigh.

"Take me to bed."

Vic needed no further invitation.

CHAPTER FIFTEEN

VIC SLAMMED HIS FIST ON THE TABLE. A MORTAR JUMPED FROM THE table and fell to the grass with a dull thud. "Absolutely not," he snapped.

"You're being stubborn." Merry pinched the bridge of their nose. "We have to take advantage of the time we have before more of your allies arrive, Victor."

"The risk is too great," insisted Vic. "Yesterday was too close."

Merry sighed, reaching across the table for his wrists. "You're right, which is why you are going to hate this next suggestion."

Johnathan watched the two of them go at it from his seat on the stool. They'd been arguing for the past twenty minutes, treading back and forth over the same talking points. Merry urged Johnathan to practice with the draught, impressing the importance of their limited time before others arrived at the Estate. Vic didn't like the idea when Alazar and Tamara roamed the house.

Johnathan was torn on the matter. Shredding his body so soon after his last trial wasn't a palatable idea, but the idea of gaining control sooner rather than later was a siren's lure. The air to Johnathan's right turned frigid.

"Katherine! You're back." He smiled when the Geist materialized next to him. She blinked at him, startled.

"You knew I was here." She frowned.

"Of course," said Johnathan, confused. "I knew by the cold."

Her eyes widened. She leaned in, careful not to brush against him. "You felt that?"

Johnathan laughed. "How could I not? Every time it's like someone dumped a bucket of snow over my head." He held up a hand. "Not that I mind your company. It is quite pleasant."

"You are out of your mind," Vic sputtered, intruding on their conversation.

"We can't wait for them to hunt, Victor. The best way to keep him safe is to keep them distracted. Use that overbearing charm of yours and catch up on old times," said Merry.

"You saw him. I had to pry open his jaws to administer that second draught. Do you know how strong he is? He would crush you," Vic retorted.

Katherine's brow wrinkled at their exchange. "I take it Merry's hypothetical draught was a success?"

Johnathan shrugged. "Sort of. I didn't kill anyone."

A smirk tugged at her lips. "That's good. I'm sure Merry appreciated you not getting blood all over their lab."

He ran a hand over his face. "Vic has a point. I couldn't change back without the second draught, and I wasn't exactly in my right mind to drink it myself."

Concern creased Katherine's face. "What happened?"

Johnathan looked at her, debating if he should share that bloody dark secret with her and Merry. Would they think him evil? Vic called him a good man, but blood trailed through his thoughts. He hadn't known either of them for long, but he found their opinion mattered to him. "I don't know," he said. "I don't want to hurt Merry."

Katherine smiled. In life, she must have been breathtaking. She swept her fingertips along his brow, her icy touch a soft bite on his skin. "You won't." She turned to the arguing pair. "Distract the others, Victor. I'll keep the Hound in line."

Vic blanched. "You're formidable, Katherine, I agree, but how do you intend to do so?"

Merry slapped their forehead. "Of course. I thought he was overreacting."

"I did too, until he felt my arrival," said Katherine.

Vic blinked, his argument brought up short.

"You're that sensitive to the cold?" Merry pinched their chin in thought.

"It really hurts you," Vic murmured. "Why didn't you say anything, John? I thought you just found it unpleasant."

"I thought she did that to everyone," said Johnathan. Why did Vic look so guilty? "It didn't kill me."

"I don't think it will," Katherine agreed. "Your body reacted when it became too much."

Vic's expression turned mutinous. "I don't like this. There are too many variables that could go wrong."

Johnathan stood up and pulled Vic into the surrounding greenery. "I'll be okay," he said, brushing his thumb across Vic's bottom lip.

"I hate that you have to go through this pain," whispered Vic. "I would take it for you, if I could." There was a vulnerability in his gaze.

I will gladly suffer every day if I can stay by your side. He kissed the corner of Vic's mouth, wishing he had the courage to say the words aloud. "Merry is right. The more practice, the better. I want to do this."

Vic breathed deep through his nose, tugging Johnathan down into a fierce kiss. He nipped his lip before releasing him. "I'll make it up to you later."

"Promises, promises," teased Johnathan.

"You two are gross," Merry whined. Katherine smacked their arm.

Johnathan could feel the reluctance in Vic's body as he pulled away. He glared at Merry over Johnathan's shoulder. "Lay a threshold. Don't release it for anyone but me."

"If you don't get out there, I will hex you," said Merry.

"You don't know how to do hexes," said Vic.

"I'll learn," snapped Merry.

Katherine took Vic's hand, leading him away. "We'll take care of him, Victor. I promise."

"You, I trust," muttered Vic.

"I heard that, you fang-faced charlatan," Merry yelled after them. Their shoulders heaved by the time Katherine returned alone.

Johnathan hoped they weren't foolhardy to send Vic away. Katherine leaned across the table from Merry, shaking her head.

"Why do you still let him get to you like that? You don't even have the excuse of great make up sex-" She clapped a hand over her mouth.

Merry regained their composure with a snort. "You didn't let the cat out of the bag, Kat. He knows."

"Still not details I want to discuss," Johnathan chimed in. He wasn't even upset, pondering whether he should incite a light argument with Vic later.

"Sorry, John." Katherine laid her hands on the counter. "How shall we proceed?"

The humor drained from the group.

"I know what I said to Vic, but, are you sure you want to do this?" Merry bit their lip. "I wouldn't argue for putting you through this unless I truly believed it would help."

Johnathan stared at the two draughts Merry had prepared for the day. "The pain isn't what I'm worried about."

Merry swallowed. "I know. I didn't expect you to react like that when you tried to change back."

"How bad was it?" Katherine slid her hand next to Johnathan's without touching, the gesture comforting.

"He tried to claw his face off," said Merry, biting their thumb. "What did you feel in the moment, John? We might be able to help you through it if we know what we're dealing with."

An opening to tell them everything if he dared. Tell them of the men he tore apart with tooth and claw. The ghosts haunted him with visions of blood and death. Katherine and Merry believed he was different than other demons, but was he?

"I was blocked. Trapped," he lied, biting the inside of his cheek until he tasted blood. His claws dug into his palms.

"We'll help you find the way out," said Katherine. Her kindness made him feel worse.

Merry pushed the first draught toward him. "Kat, cover your eyes. Johnathan, please leave your clothes in a neatly folded pile in the basket."

"Oh goodness," said Katherine. She politely covered her eyes.

"No peeking," said Merry.

"I would never." Katherine sounded scandalized.

Johnathan undressed in a daze, doing as Merry instructed. He picked up the draught, turning the small vial over in his fingers. Bracing himself, he popped the cork and swallowed the bittersweet ash and wine.

The first wave made him cry out. He fell to the grass, clutching his stomach where the fire ate away at him. Bones cracked and snapped, sharp angles digging against the underside of his skin. Johnathan hugged the ground and screamed. The world filled with fire.

The change rampaged through his body, breaking him into new angles, until the Hound squeezed out of his skin. He lay on the ground, fighting for breath, a steady plume of smoke rising out of his mouth.

Katherine's hands covered her mouth, her expression horrified.

"Johnathan?" Merry gripped the table. Their eyes were wide, features pinched.

He snuffled, unable to summon the energy to move his body.

Katherine crouched at his side, her hands curled against her chest. "That was nothing like a werewolf," she gasped. Her hand shook when she reached for him, brushing her icy fingers along his jaw. The stinging touch roused him somewhat. Johnathan shook his head, slowly rolling into a crouch. "Was he like this yesterday?"

"No," said Merry, their fingers spread over their lips. They held the second vial in their hand, absently tapping it on the counter. "This feels wrong. What if we're burning through his body?"

Their words buzzed in Johnathan's muddled mind. They were important. He needed to focus on them. A fog shrouded his senses, making him long for the clarity of pain. Without conscious thought, he leaned into the cold hovering beside him.

Katherine yelped, the Hound burrowing his head against her chest. Ice bit at his nerves, searing away the cotton that clung to him. Johnathan sneezed and peddled back. His snout tingled. The grass was on fire.

"What just happened?" Katherine stared at the burning grass in shock.

Merry stomped it out. "A demon set my garden on fire," they said. They crouched in front of Johnathan, mindless of the teeth inches away. "I think he used the cold to revive himself. You in there, John?"

They must have really believed in the effects of that draught to get this close to him without Vic in the room. He huffed, blowing Merry's hair out of their face.

"Are you ready to change back?"

The suggestion made him want to throw up. A soft whine escaped from deep in his chest, the canine sound of his fear. A tear tracked down Merry's cheek.

"There's no rush, John," they said. Hesitantly they stroked a hand down his neck. The touch didn't illicit the same sense of safety Vic gave him, but he didn't shy away from the comfort. "Rest awhile. We'll try when you've recovered a bit."

Johnathan settled down on the grass, grateful for the respite. He let his body rest, listening to the low conversation between Katherine and Merry.

"I don't like this, Merry," Katherine whispered. "I've seen hundreds of shifters transform. It's not supposed to be this painful."

"He's not a born or turned shifter, Kat. He's a made Hellhound. The gifts of demons are not pleasant or gentle," said Merry. "I never thought I'd see you pity one of them."

Katherine's cold fingers trailed over his fur, a balm to the constant smoldering fire inside him. Johnathan sighed under her touch. "No one deserves this," she said.

There was a long pause. His mind drifted in the welcome silence.

"How long until the allies arrive?" Merry remained nearby.

"Close to a week," said Katherine. "Even Beatrice said she'd come."

"Christ, an alpha will definitely scent him," said Merry.

"She doesn't know the scent of the Nether. She'd just know something's off," Katherine insisted. She continued to pet him, leaving trails of frost along his back. "That contingent of Agents is getting close. Do you think they're tracking him?"

"No," said Merry. "Not him."

"You're the only divine touched here," whispered Katherine.

"Don't tell the others," Merry said, a wobble in their voice. "You know how Alazar will react."

"I won't let them take you," said Katherine, her voice sharp.

Merry sighed. "Hush, Kat. He needs to rest." The only sound was the soft rasp of Katherine's hand through his fur. Johnathan turned over their conversation while his body recovered an ounce of strength. He wondered what meeting an actual werewolf would be like. He'd never tangled with one as a Prospective, but the Society knew they existed. Their very nature kept them out of densely populated cities. They weren't considered a great threat, much more natural hunters that fed off game animals rather than innocent humans. Johnathan once believed the myth they were weak to silver, until he learned the truth. Silver for Nether, Iron for Other, Gold for Benign...

He opened his eyes, lifting his head. Merry dozed with their head down on a free corner of the worktable. Katherine's hand paused. "You're awake."

He hadn't gone to sleep, but she didn't need to know that. Merry stirred. They perked up when they noticed Johnathan sitting up.

"Ready to change back?"

He wasn't, but he needed to. Johnathan needed a human mouth. He unhinged his jaw, tipping his head for the second draught.

"That is a lot of teeth," said Merry.

"Give it," said Katherine. They handed over the vial without argument. The Geist maneuvered around him, eventually managing to pour the liquid down his throat.

Johnathan writhed beneath the change, unable to hold himself up after the final awful crack and shift of his spine. He lay panting on the ground, the taste of metal in his mouth.

"Was that easier in the slightest?" Merry looked him over, their expression pained.

He grimaced, unable to answer the question. "How does one become divine touched?"

They blanched. "You were asleep."

"I don't sleep." Johnathan shrugged.

"Definitely a demon's gift," muttered Katherine.

"I won't say anything to Alazar," said Johnathan. He'd rather spit in the older vampire's face.

"I know." Merry sighed. "I told you I was born this way, Johnathan. A 'blessing' from birth."

He frowned. "Only humans are divine touched? What about creatures?"

Merry shook their head. "Demons, the divine? They can only influence the children of Adam and Eve. Most creatures are off shoots of the Fae."

What was he missing? "Even turned humans?"

"Transformation of the soul," said Katherine. She pressed her hand to her chest. "My death irrevocably broke my connection to the human realm. I exist, but I no longer answer the call of my bloodline."

Johnathan mulled over the information. "You can't be blessed by the Nether *and* the Benign, right?"

Merry scratched their neck. "Somewhere a philosophy scholar's head has exploded. Would you like your pants?"

He glanced at Katherine, who studiously peered up at the glass ceiling. Night had fallen while he rested from the change, the starry night sky a sparkling net over the dome. He needed to move, groaning at the ache in his joints. Every movement sent needles of pain shooting through his limbs. He donned his pants in a series of grunts, his fingers shaking with effort when he fastened them closed.

"Maybe we should let you rest a day or two," said Merry.

Would rest do anything for him or just prolong the process? "The allies are coming. The Society is searching. There is no rest for the wicked," said Johnathan.

"You're not wicked," said Katherine.

"But I am damned." Abandoning his shirt and shoes, he hobbled from the room. Neither Katherine nor Merry stopped him. He took the same back hallway Vic carried him through last night, stopping at frequent intervals to rest against the wall. The ache in his body was worse than before. Maybe Merry was right. Forcing the change would shorten his lifespan.

He would rather endure this than slaughter humans, innocent or not. How long before the guilt faded? Before he didn't care whose blood he spilt, men, women, children. Vampires killed to feed. What did he kill for other than blood lust?

Self-preservation, an internal voice protested. He'd killed to protect Vic. A weak argument when Vic could have fled the scene without taking a life.

Johnathan didn't want to kill. He wanted to be a good man.

He couldn't gauge how long it took him to make it back to his room. Vic wasn't there. He collapsed on the lush carpet beside the bed, unable to summon the strength to climb onto the mattress. Pain rolled through his bones. Johnathan ignored it, wishing he could crawl into the tub, though he feared he might drown in this state.

He roused to Vic's cry.

Vic lifted him, cradling him close until the bed slid under him. Johnathan coughed, his throat dry as sun bleached bone. For a moment, he thought Katherine was there, stroking his face with icy fingers.

"You're burning up," Vic whispered. It was his touch on Johnathan's feverish skin.

A derisive laugh hacked free from his throat. "I don't think I was built to last."

"Don't you dare die on me, Johnathan Newman," Vic hissed. He raised his wrist to his mouth, biting down.

Fear seized him, battered against the ache in his body. "Stop." He tried to push Vic away, unwilling to deepen the other man's debt. A drop of blood slid along his lips, the sweetness spreading over his tongue like dissolving sugar. Citrus and musk surrounded him, weakening his resolve. Blood gushed into his mouth, trickling down his throat. The reaction was rote memory, the muscles of his throat swallowed the offering down. Johnathan shoved Vic away from him. He clutched his chest. The fire in his core sputtered to life. It flared and seared the ache in his bones to an ashen numbness.

"I told you not to," he shouted, heedless if the other vampires heard him. His vision blurred, moisture gathering in his lashes.

Vic flinched back as if Johnathan had slapped him. The shock on his face made Johnathan feel every inch the monster.

"Don't ask me to watch you die," said Vic. His fingers curled over his thighs. The wound at his wrist had healed, leaving behind the stain.

"I wasn't going to die," said Johnathan.

Vic tensed. "You were hot enough to combust. I thought your blood would start boiling. How could they leave you like this?"

"They didn't," he said. "I left."

Another verbal slap. Vic flinched. "Why didn't you send them for me?"

"I made it back to the room," he mumbled. He rubbed his face, his body tender despite the infusion of Vic's blood.

"Johnathan." Vic reached for him. His hand hovered as if he waited for another blow. Johnathan kept his hands limp in his lap, unable to look him in the eye.

"I'm going back tomorrow," he said.

"No!" Vic seized his shoulders, his grip careful despite the tension in his fingers. "Please, this is too dangerous."

"I have too." The words tumbled out of him. "I can't live like this."

Vic pulled him close, arms shaking when they wrapped around Johnathan's back. "We will find another way."

What if the next transformation was worse? Would Vic give him more blood? Deepening their bond, adding to the unseen debt of their bargain. "I'm not worth the price." Vic's grip tightened. Johnathan hadn't meant to say the words out loud, but they'd slipped from him.

"What? Shut up. What are you talking about?" He pulled back, true anger flashing in his gaze. "Explain, dammit."

Johnathan clenched his jaw. He didn't want to talk about this. Not after the intimacy they'd shared, moments of pure bliss, sullied by how much he loathed himself. He licked his lips, tasting the honeyed sweetness of Vic's blood. "I'm not a good man. I'm barely a man. Why did you risk yourself to save me? I'm not worth it."

Vic grabbed his face. Anger warred with anguish in his eyes. "How could you say that John?" He caught the tear on Johnathan's cheek with his thumb. "Brave and strong and so beautifully kind after this world has taken so much from you. You were human and you dazzled me. I would have cut off a limb to save you then. I will freely tear my heart from my chest to save you now. Your worth is immeasurable."

The hollow in his chest throbbed, the swollen tangle of his guilt and pain burst, spilling down in face in steaming tears, a festering wound freely bleeding out the buildup of bile and pus until it ran clean. Vic held him through it, stroking his hands along Johnathan back while he murmured in his ear. It took him a while to focus on those soft words, but eventually he caught them.

"Stay with me, love. Please stay."

"I will," said Johnathan. He captured Vic's mouth in a slow sensuous tease of lips and tongue.

Vic brushed the errant curls out of Johnathan's face. "Thank you," he whispered, "for finding the words."

Remorse crept over him for his display, but Vic pinched his chin. "This is bravery, Johnathan." He pulled Johnathan down with him onto the bed, their limbs entangled, pressed chest to chest. Vic's hold filled him with a sweet ache, which Johnathan clung to through the long hours of the night.

CHAPTER SIXTEEN

SILVER FOR NETHER, IRON FOR OTHER, GOLD FOR BENIGN...

Johnathan stroked Vic's back, the other man relaxed in slumber beside him. He'd stood over a precipice last night, and Vic had pulled him back. His gaze traced over the smooth lines of Vic's face, drinking in his features: from the slender prow of his nose, those long red gold lashes, to the curve of his jaw. At some point, he stripped off his shirt to enjoy the contact of skin to skin.

There was a lightness in his chest. The sucking hollow was not completely gone, but Johnathan sensed the difference. Vic's words echoed through his thoughts, burying the guilt deep. Johnathan would always carry it, but guilt was good. It would keep him human, same as the man in his arms.

He pressed a kiss to Vic's throat, trailing a path of intent down his chest, until he hovered over the fastening of his trousers.

"Well, don't stop now," Vic drawled. Johnathan grinned. "That grin will be my undoing. Come here, let me—"

Johnathan sank his teeth into Vic's exposed hip.

"Fuck!" Vic's cock kicked against his chest. "Ah, ah, wait, John! Fuck!" Wet warmth spread beneath the fabric. Vic lay back, panting, his fingers threaded in Johnathan's hair.

Johnathan nuzzled the rapidly healing bite. "I will never tire of that reaction."

"My wardrobe will quickly tire of that reaction," Vic griped, but there was a smile on his face that warmed Johnathan to his marrow.

He traced a finger along Vic's hip bone, his thoughts returning to that nagging phrase. "Vic, were you divine touched when you were human?"

Vic lifted his head to frown at him. "What brought this up?"

"Something Katherine told me." If it was true that transformation severed the connection to the divine, then it shouldn't matter, but Johnathan couldn't stop mulling it over, worrying at it like a sore tooth.

"I don't think so." Vic pursed his lips. "I didn't possess any other worldly gifts, unless charming every lad and maiden within the township to my bed counts as a blessing."

"That sounds like a different sort of blessing," Johnathan teased. He tapped his thumb against Vic's hip. "Do you know what sort of blessings the divine touched possessed?"

"Seer sight is one," said Vic, his tone thoughtful. "There are reasons Merry chose seclusion aside from the side effects of their gift."

From the way Alazar exploited Merry's gift, he could imagine what other people would the Seer to do. "Why would the Society want someone who was divine touched? How would it give them access to the Benign?" The Nether slithered through rifts using the faults and sins of man. Demons were driven by the need to consume, and an unending hunger that would devour everything in its path. The Other moved freely between the realms but adhered to a system of rules and customs. Their weakness was the easiest of the three to exploit. The Benign were a mystery, what humans believed to be angels, but that did not mean they were kind.

"Likely how they gain a foothold," said Vic. His fingers massaged Johnathan's scalp. "The Nether use bargains, the Benign require permission." He trailed off, going still. "Maybe they use the divine touched as vessels."

Did the Benign control their hosts like demons controlled their creations? Cerunnous subsumed Johnathan's will for a few minutes, and he thought his entire being would be snuffed out. What would a divine creature do to the body it possessed? How would a human survive that influx of power? He imagined it would be a similar fate to what happened to humans tainted by demons. Their bodies would simply burn up. But what if they found an immortal vessel?

Johnathan sat up. "What other gifts? What constitutes a divine blessing?"

"All sorts of things I imagine," said Vic. "Never growing sick, healing others, maybe personal wealth. Any number of small miracles."

"None that applied to you?" Johnathan pressed.

Vic's brow creased in confusion. "No, I told you, I was ordinary. A second son, a huge disappointment, sent off to be a man of the cloth. I was barely out of my mid-twenties when the plague hit. My human life ended with little fanfare."

He wasn't sure about that. Vic told him how the vampire killed most of the occupants of the monastery. The vampire must have chosen him for his will to live, crawling from his sick bed to escape. If divine touched were blessed from birth, the blessing would have revealed itself before then. Being turned rather than killed could be misconstrued as a divine gift, but it didn't seem likely. Johnathan couldn't let the theory go. "I wonder what you were like as a human."

"Not so different than I am now," said Vic. "Reckless, ignorant in the ways of the world. A great deal more arrogant than I had any right to be. Though I did maintain my charm. My mother used to say I could convince a saint to sin. I could never tell if she was denouncing me or bragging."

That pulled a smile from Johnathan. "Surprised you didn't talk your father out of sending you to a monastery."

Vic snorted. "I didn't want to."

Johnathan blinked in surprise. "Why not? A monk leads a harsh life."

"But it was away from my father, who hated me, and filled with lovely, lonely men. Heaven on earth compared to my father's home. He almost tossed me to the military," said Vic.

"So really, you talked your father into sending you to the monastery." Johnathan laughed. Would a silver tongue be considered a divine gift?

There were plenty of charismatic humans in the world. It appeared Vic lived his human life as an ordinary man. If he hadn't been turned, he would have died to the plague, returned to dust. Johnathan sighed and pressed his face against Vic's side. "I think I should return to the garden."

Vic sucked in a breath. "Johnathan, please, don't take that draught again. At least let your body heal for a couple days if you're that determined to risk yourself."

"I want to talk to them. There's a puzzle here, and I'm missing something," he said. He glanced up to find Vic staring up at the ceiling, his face unreadable. "What's wrong?"

"It doesn't make sense," said Vic. "They are targeting me, aren't they?"

In the violent end of that night, he'd nearly forgotten how Sister Wilhem approached Vic with a golden net. She'd been tracking them without fail, since their initial encounter on the train. Johnathan swore he could almost hear the faint chiming of her strange instrument here in the room, as if the Sister waited for them in every shadowed corner. He'd been slowly piecing the connection together, forming a troublesome conclusion. Yes, what he'd learned of the Divine Touched didn't mesh with Sister Wilhem's pursuit.

"Come with me," Johnathan pleaded. "They might know something." He secretly hoped Katherine and Merry would scoff at his theories, explain them away. That is what he wanted. He needed to put this fear to rest.

"Fine, make me get out of bed when we could laze the day away," Vic grumbled, but he rolled off the bed, tugging on a shirt while Johnathan did the same. He smeared a fresh coat of salve on Johnathan's throat. A cautionary measure since they took the back hall back to the conservatory to avoid the other vampires. Johnathan thought they were over cautious when neither Tamara nor Alazar rose before noon.

The indoor garden was quiet, the birdsong muted despite the early hour. Merry sat at the workbench, pouring over the ancient book on the Nether, their fingers stained with ink. They looked up at their approach, their wary gaze giving him the once over.

"Hello John," they said. "I wasn't sure we'd see you today." He noticed there were no prepared draughts on the bench. Would Merry let him try again if he asked?

A patch of cold air informed him of Katherine's arrival. "John! How are you feeling? We were worried when you staggered out of here."

"I'm fine," he said, holding up a hand to halt further conversation. "Yesterday, you told me a person was divine touched from birth. Is it always obvious? Or are some blessings subtle?"

Katherine and Merry shared a look. The Geist grabbed the pouch of salt, setting the barriers while Merry dug through the drawers beneath the table. They emerged with a plain wooden box and a pair of brown leather gloves. Merry set the box on the table and leaned on it with their elbow.

Vic clasped his hands in front of him. "I assume you don't want your other guests to overhear this conversation?"

"They are more restless than you believe," said Katherine, her gaze on Merry.

Their host looked up. "Blessings are never subtle," said Merry. "The divine touched are rare for a reason."

"They rarely survive to old age," said Katherine.

Johnathan frowned. "Why?"

Merry's mouth closed in a tight line. It was Katherine who answered. "Persecution. Humans rarely trust that which is different."

Johnathan knew that truth far too well. "Even if their gifts were beneficial to others?" He could understand a seer being feared. People were quick to shift the blame of their choices to the one who warned them. But what about healers? Or those who could make crops grow?

"Humans aren't the only ones who feared them," said Katherine. "Most creatures would kill them on sight."

Vic fidgeted. Merry noticed, their gaze met his. "Or they turn them," said Merry.

"It would have the same result," insisted Katherine. "The connection to the Benign would be severed."

Johnathan frowned at her. "Wait, it's a direct connection to the Benign or their realm?"

She folded her arms. "From what I've seen and heard, a blessing is like a bridge with a door at the end. If a Benign were to transgress into this world, they would need to knock first."

"What would happen to the human who answered?"

"It wouldn't be pleasant," said Merry. They twisted the leather gloves. "Where are you going with this line of questioning?"

"John, this doesn't make sense," said Vic. "There is nothing about me that stood out. I wasn't blessed."

"Even if you were," said Katherine, "it wouldn't matter now."

Merry pursed their lips. They donned the gloves.

Johnathan rubbed his face. There was an answer that seemed obvious to him. "Would the Benign bless an immortal?"

"No. They would no longer be considered a child of Eve," said Katherine.

"And there's no way to reform that connection?"

Katherine paused. Her lips parted, mulling over his question.

"Victor."

Johnathan tensed. There was something in Merry's tone that made his hackles rise. He looked at their host. The box was open. Merry's gloved hand lifted a small object from within.

"Catch." They threw it toward Vic, who caught it on reflex.

Vic cried out, clutching his wrist. The lump of gold slipped through his fingers, landing in the grass. Johnathan surged forward, his thoughts blanking until ice encircled his waist.

"Calm down," Katherine ordered. "You must calm down."

"Easy, John, I'm okay." Vic spoke at his ear.

His claws were inches from Merry's throat. Their host swallowed, wide green eyes locked on the sharp tips. Vic was wedged between them, his injured hand tucked against Johnathan's chest.

"There was no intent to hurt him," they said quietly. "This was a test."

Johnathan sucked in a breath and jerked his hand away. "I'm sorry," he gasped, shocked by his reaction. Katherine released him. Vic stepped away, staring down at his wounded hand. It hadn't healed.

Merry offered a frayed smile. "This was partially my fault. I forgot your instincts."

"Hounds are very protective," said Katherine. She bit her lip, glancing at Vic. "Did you suspect?"

Vic shook his head. "How is this possible? I've handled gold before." He looked up at them, his expression lost. "This shouldn't be possible."

"You're right," said Merry. "But you're not the only impossible one in this room."

Johnathan's stomach dropped. This was exactly what he didn't want to hear. "This is our price."

"Oh my God," said Katherine. "You think the blood bond did this?" She searched their faces. "No. That can't be. It would connect Victor to the Nether, not the Benign."

"It's a connection that can be used," said Johnathan. "A reformed path over a broken bridge."

Vic sat down hard. "Shit."

"They're coming here for you," said Merry.

Katherine stared at them. "Well, we can't let that happen."

"I should tell Alazar." Vic's throat worked.

"No!" the three of them shouted in tandem.

"They would destroy you," said Merry.

Vic's gaze hardened. "No, they wouldn't." He sighed. "We have to tell them. The Society will be here any day."

"Yes, and they will be caught between the defenses of the Estate and the arrival of our allies," said Katherine. "You might have faith in your past relationship with them, Victor, but Alazar is ruthless. If Tamara caught onto your ruse, she would destroy Johnathan in an instant. Don't risk it."

"They are not all cruelty and rage," said Victor.

"Then tell them when the others arrive," said Merry. "Don't put yourself at their mercy alone."

Johnathan slid beside him, gently turning over Vic's hand. An angry welt remained, the skin of his palm still inflamed. "What do we do until then?"

"The Society is closing in," said Katherine. "They'll find this place sooner rather than later."

"We strengthen the wards," said Merry. "They might find us, but I'll be damned if they get in."

Vic leaned against him, his gaze shattered. "I didn't want to believe they were after me," he admitted, his tone apologetic. "I guessed, but I didn't want to believe."

He ached to comfort him. Neither of them could have seen this outcome. How could they when they'd stumbled blindly into the thick of this mess? He bent over Vic's injured hand, pressing a careful kiss to the raw skin. The scent of old metal pricked at his nose. His tongue darted out. Vic jumped.

"You licked me?" A hint of bemusement breaking through his bleak expression. "That's so—" He sucked in a breath as the burn vanished.

There was a beat of silence. Johnathan looked up to find Merry and Katherine staring at them with a mixture of fascination and fear. The implications sat heavy in the air between them, but no one said a word. It wasn't until Vic expressed his desire to return to their room that he pulled their host aside.

"Make the draughts," said Johnathan. There was a web closing around them, their actions crippled by the secrets they were forced to keep. Johnathan wouldn't let the Society or the Benign take Vic. He had to find a way to control the Hound, even if he needed to break himself a hundred times to do it.

CHAPTER SEVENTEEN

JOHNATHAN'S RESOLVE DID NOT SIT WELL WITH VIC. THEY'D ARGUED extensively, spinning in a familiar circle, but in the end, it was Johnathan's choice. Not a victory, when each forced transformation left him weaker than the last. Deepening the conflict, he'd refused to take more of Vic's blood. His body did heal, the process slow and painful but it did heal. Despite his disapproval, Vic held Johnathan through those long hours, while shudders wracked his body. Each morning, he begged Johnathan to stop, his mouth closing in a tight white line when he refused.

For three days, Johnathan walked down to the garden alone, submitting himself to be ripped apart. Merry and Katherine kept watch, but Vic could not. It was more than a need to distract their comrades. He could tell how shaken Vic was by the revelation, sensed his rising guilt in every agonized look and hesitant touch. Their roles had reversed, and Johnathan didn't know how to fix it.

This *was* his choice; one Vic would not take from him no matter how much he wanted to. Johnathan wanted to believe it was the right one. He didn't want to be a killer. He wanted control of the Hound, to fight. To protect. The draught did what it was meant to, but Johnathan didn't have a better grasp on the change than the first time.

This latest transformation was the worst. The cool grass kissed his naked skin, covered in sweat. A high-pitched bell rang between his ears. He couldn't hear anything else. He stared blankly at Katherine's panicked face, numb to the touch of her hands. The taste of metal filled his mouth.

Johnathan vomited a stream of blood onto the grass. He collapsed on his side, staring at his arm, splayed out in front of him. The veins beneath his skin were charred black. They'd been black since yesterday.

His eyelids were so heavy. Vic hovered over him; the angles of his face sharpened by his distress. Johnathan hadn't noticed him arrive. Another long blink. The cotton sheets were abrasive against his raw skin. When had Vic taken him to bed? He didn't remember the journey. Familiar sweetness hit his tongue. He sighed, accepting the offering, unable to refuse. Vic's mouth closed over his, releasing a gush of blood down his throat. Johnathan didn't have the chance to shove him back. Vic released him, wiping his mouth with the back of his hand. A red smear trailed off his lips. His grey eyes darkened with fury.

"I can't watch you do this," he spat. "I begged you to reconsider. I'm done." He slid off the bed, tension in every line of his body. Vic clawed at his scalp. "Why are you doing this to yourself? Do you hate yourself that much? Do you hate me?"

The question broke through Johnathan's shock. "No. God, no." He reached for Vic's wrist, but the other man pulled away. His hand fell. "This is not about worth. I don't hate you."

Vic's face crumpled. "Then why?"

"I want to protect those I love," whispered Johnathan. They stared at one another after Johnathan's inadvertent confession. Vic leapt on him, slamming him back on the bed.

"Find another way," he snarled in Johnathan's face.

Entranced, he stared up at Vic. His fury was beautiful. His hands shackled Johnathan's wrists, pinning them above his head in a gentle cuff of living iron. Vic's shoulders heaved, his hair mussed, lips bruised from their blood kiss.

Johnathan surged up, capturing Vic's mouth in a clash of wills. Vic's teeth snapped, biting his lips, before his tongue soothed the sting. He hooked his leg around Vic's waist and rolled them over until Johnathan hovered above him. Their hips pressed together, heat and hardness and the insistent throb that demanded more. Vic sat up, refusing to yield to Johnathan's position, anger lingering in each biting kiss. He yanked Johnathan's arms behind his back, bending his head to bite a trail down his chest. Johnathan ground his hips against Vic's, groaning at the spiral of pleasure and pain.

Vic effortlessly shifted his body, forcing Johnathan's legs apart to accommodate his shoulders as he continued that hot stinging trail. He released Johnathan's wrists, lifting him up by his waist. His legs bent until his ass was exposed. Teeth nipped the sensitive skin of Johnathan's inner thigh, before Vic's head dropped lower, tongue flicking over his puckered hole.

That wicked tongue pierced him. Johnathan cried out, his limbs locked in Vic's hold as his tongue worked. He thrashed, sensation boiling up inside him. An orgasm hovered close when Vic replaced his tongue with fingers, hard thrusts that demanded Johnathan open for him.

"Please," Johnathan begged. He yearned for more, straddling the edge. A feral snarl tore out of Vic's chest. He tore at his clothes with one hand, fingers still buried inside Johnathan, until he freed his cock. His fingers pulled free. The absence was brief as Vic yanked Johnathan's hips forward to plunge inside, setting a brutal pace of slapping flesh that left them gulping air.

Johnathan finally tipped over the edge with a wordless yell. His cock spasmed, spilling over his stomach. Vic lifted his head, the tendons of his neck tight as he came, filling Johnathan with liquid heat.

They stared at one another, panting hard, Vic still mostly dressed. Johnathan's muscles quivered. A line of fading bites decorated his chest, while his cum pooled on his stomach.

"I'll find another way," said Johnathan.

The two of them were resting in blissed out exhaustion when the room shook. A rumbling sound, deep as a church bell, rippled through the walls. Johnathan sat up, watching the walls shiver, dread crawling up his throat. He jumped when it started again, the terrible sound crashing through his head, full of warning. Vic bolted upright, wide awake, his sleep mussed hair stuck in a dozen different directions. His knuckles went white clutching the remains of their bed sheets.

A momentarily silence fell, the calm before the crash of thunder. "What was that?" Johnathan whispered, though he had a fair idea. Vic's hand released the sheet, seeking Johnathan's hand.

"A knock at the door." His jaw clenched. "I believe Sister Wilhem has caught up to us."

The room quaked. Johnathan released Vic and scrambled from the bed. "We need to get down there." Vic fixed his clothes while Johnathan grabbed whatever came first from the wardrobe. He would have bolted from the room if Vic hadn't grabbed him, smearing the salve across the back of this neck. The tumbled together into the hall. Another assault shook the building. The lamps began to drop from the walls, broken glass scattered across the carpet.

The front door of the Estate was wide open, the door bucking on its hinges. Outside, the others stood in a staggered line. Merry stood between the vampires. A set of scales hung from their outstretched hand. Katherine stood a step behind Merry, her hands fisted at her sides. Alazar's robes flapped behind him like crow wings.

Having spent most of his time in the indoor garden, Johnathan hadn't seen the physical barrier that surrounded the Estate. He knew it was there, a faint crackling wall that occasionally brushed his senses, invisible to the eye, but now he could see it, a massive shimmer of rising heat. The next strike was a stone thrown onto a still pond; the surface tension broken in a violent wave that fought to regain its equilibrium.

Outside the barrier waited a small army, far more men than they'd encountered at the docks. The familiar black coats of the Society surrounded a handful of Scarlet Sisters, the luminous face of Sister Wilhem at their center. He didn't see Luthor among the black coats, but that didn't mean the Agent wasn't there, masking his presence. Sister Wilhem detached from the group, gliding toward them. Her movements possessed languid grace, giving her an ethereal aura. A slight wind whipped the fine strands of her hair away from her thin face. The chiming device hovered between her hands, radiating golden light. Her face pinched with concentration when the device pulsed, glowing bright. The light slammed against the barrier, seeking a way through. Johnathan jumped when the impact tolled through the Estate, but the barrier held.

"It appears we are at an impasse, Sister." Merry raised the scales. The plates were evenly balanced, a physical representation of their opposing forces. The Society couldn't get in, nor could the vampires leave. Johnathan believed they held the superior position, but Sister Wilhem's smile left him feel anything but secure.

"Not for long," she said. The barrier distorted her voice, the sound filtered through a great distance through she couldn't have been more than ten feet from them. The device revved up for another pulse.

Merry shook their head. "The Herald is an impressive machine, but the power of these grounds is far older and malleable than anything you can throw at it."

The Sister's brow lifted, a secretive smile on her lips. "Anything? A dangerous word 'anything', full of arrogance." Her pale white eyes shifted to look at Johnathan and Vic. "Empires have fallen for less."

Tamara took a step closer to the crackling barrier, her long black hair pinned up in a coiled braid that emphasized the graceful curve of her neck. "Truer words were never spoken," she sneered. "You seem intent on chasing your fall to the ground. Tell me, what will you do, Sister, when your gods turn on you?"

Wilhem's cool gaze assessed the vampiress. "We seek no false gods, fiend," she said. "Only the benevolence of the Benign."

"Benevolence?" Tamara cackled, baring her chiseled teeth. The closest Agents took a step back. "You are stupid, pitiful fool." Her laugh faded, a cold rage emanating from her face. Sister Wilhem possessed a waifish fanatical energy, but Tamara was a natural disaster, a tempest. She was the one contained by the barrier. "You will find no angels here," she hissed.

The threat fell on deaf ears, an eerie smile on the Sister's face. "On the contrary, our fortunes have improved. The Herald has led us to not one but two potential hosts. Once we capture them." Her milk white gaze shifted to Merry. "We will only need to persuade them."

Merry stumbled back a step, the scales shivering in their hand. Katherine caught them, the air clouding with frost around her. Johnathan fought the same urge to retreat. A growl stuck in his throat, a threat he clamped down on in Tamara and Alazar's proximity. Though he couldn't help shifting his body in front of Vic as if to shield him from the Sister's gaze. The action seemed to summon her attention. That milky gaze shot straight through him. Sister Wilhem's smile was saccharine.

A whiff of honey and sex snagged Johnathan's attention, distracting him from the confrontation. He startled, searching the crowd of black coats for that familiar scent. Was he imagining things? How could *she* be here?

"We will get through your barrier," said Sister Wilhem, a hint of menace in her gentle tone. "Today, tomorrow, it is only a matter of time."

"We have plenty of time," said Alazar. "Shall we see who outlasts the other?"

The Sister smiled in reply. "See you soon."

That was enough for Merry. They raised the scale high above their head with a shout. The rippling air solidified. The Society's army vanished behind the deceptive display of the quiet forest.

Their host collapsed to their knees, the scales clattering to the ground. Merry groaned, the sound rising an octave as their body began to shift. Flesh rippled and smoothed into feminine curves. Katherine crouched next to them, helping Merry to their feet. Johnathan took a step away from Vic's side, still searching for that out of place scent when Alazar whirled around.

"Which one of you is it?" He bore down on them. His dark gaze fastened on Johnathan. "Is it you? You're the unknown element."

Johnathan attempted to back-peddle, but Alazar was faster. A fist seized the front of Johnathan's shirt, yanking him off his feet. He had maybe an inch on the imposing ancient, their strength matched, but the accusation caught him off guard. He dug in his heels to keep his balance.

Vic was there in an instant. He grabbed Alazar's wrist. "You will release him now." He bared his teeth. Alazar didn't budge.

Tamara loomed behind Vic, her arms sliding over his chest in a possessive hold. "Not so hasty. Are you certain you haven't brought a poison bloom with you?"

Johnathan wanted to tear her face off, wrestling against his anger as he realized the full scope of their folly. Collectively, they'd sought to keep the attention of the two vampires off Johnathan to hide his true nature, but Merry never clarified who the Society tracked. Neither had Sister Wilhem, shifting suspicion with the direction of her mad gaze. He'd managed to become a target. Fire flared in his chest, demanding an outlet. Johnathan gripped Alazar's fist and began to squeeze.

"That heretic looked right at you and your little paramour, Victor," said Tamara, her voice silky smooth. "I've known you a long time, and while your charms are impressive, I would not call them blessed."

The irony of her statement was not lost on Johnathan. The Hound stirred at the promise of violence. A familiar burn flared through his veins. He clenched his teeth, trying to reign it in. Alazar's bones cracked in his grip. The vampire swore and shoved him away. He turned to their host, still recovering on the ground. "What have you allowed into our sanctuary?" The glare he shot Johnathan was pure venom. "We should kill him now, before those zealots get their hands on him."

Vic snapped his head back. He caught Tamara by surprise. She released him with a snarl, clutching her face. He planted his hand on Alazar's chest and shoved him. Spreading his arms, he dropped into a crouch, pressing Johnathan back toward the Estate entrance.

"You will not touch him," Vic shouted. Rage grated his voice raw.

Alazar met his anger head on, baring his teeth, stark white against his dark skin. "You'd choose that mutt over your family, Victor? Perhaps we should offer you up instead."

Tamara straightened her nose with an audible crack. "Don't be crass, Alazar. Victor is passionate. He can keep his little pet." Her gaze slid to Katherine and Merry, huddled on the ground during their confrontation. "You forget, the Society has their eyes on him and the freak." Merry flinched at the words but Tamara pressed on. "That little heretic intends to shove an angel into their vessel. We cannot let this happen. Better to destroy all three of them than risk it." Her expression was almost wistful.

Johnathan braced himself for a fight. The earth trembled beneath their feet.

"Try it and the ground will swallow you," Merry rasped, peering at Tamara through the curtain of their hair, their expression carefully leashed. "Nobody is being expelled from these grounds."

The vampiress ran her tongue along her pointed teeth. "We do not know the full power of this Herald. Are you so certain they won't breech your precious sanctuary?"

"No," said Merry. They pushed their hair off their face. "The Sister was correct in one aspect. There are no guarantees in this world." They glanced at Alazar, still brimming with barely suppressed violence. "The others will be here soon. You will need me if we are to open a path through our foes."

Alazar's jaw clenched. He turned and stormed to the open door. Tamara chuckled, sauntering after him. Their host stared at the departing vampires. Their facade cracked, unmasked hatred burning in their gaze. It was the first time Johnathan had seen that expression on Merry's face, though he wasn't surprised. Katherine helped Merry to their feet, her gaze locked on the illusion.

Though the two vampires were no longer in immediate proximity, Vic remained tense and braced for conflict.

"I've miscalculated, badly," he confessed.

Denial was on Johnathan's lips, though matters were complicated. Piling Alazar and Tamara's suspicion on him may have been a tactical move on the Sister's part, though he didn't think she grasped the dynamics of their group enough to manipulate them. What concerned him more was the longing in her pale gaze, her stare covetous at the sight of Vic. If her strange device managed to break through the barrier, she would go right for him.

Their host sighed. "Yes. Though now that the Sister knows there are two of us, she may switch to an easier target."

Vic slumped. "Now I've put us both in danger. How have I walked this Earth for centuries without a single run in with the Society" His voice rose as he ranted. "And now I can't escape the bastards."

"Victor, that is not your fault," said Katherine, though Merry didn't chime in. Johnathan couldn't blame them when they were the most vulnerable.

Johnathan placed a hand on his shoulder. Vic leaned into him. "I should have told Alazar about me."

"That remains inadvisable, my friend." Merry adjusted their robes to cover their curves. "This Herald they yield is something I've never seen before. I've never felt power like that, but it almost seemed—."

"Divine," said Johnathan.

Merry hugged themselves. "Go inside, Victor. I will strengthen the barrier while those two argue their next course of action. Katherine, I need you to scout the area. I'd hoped our summons would beat them here, but our luck has run out."

"I'll find a path through," she said. Her body dispersed.

Vic looked like he wanted to say more, but his mouth snapped shut with a click of teeth. He stared out into the false serenity of the forest, expression contemplative.

"Don't leave the grounds," Merry warned. "For all our sakes."

He feared Vic would do just that, in some misguided attempt to lead danger away from them. Johnathan slid his hand down, twining their fingers together. He gently pulled. Vic deflated somewhat, falling in step beside him as they headed inside.

Johnathan glanced over his shoulder to where Merry stood, a lone figure against the towering forest, their smoky rosewater scent tinged bitter with the tang of fear.

CHAPTER EIGHTEEN

THE ESTATE WAS STRANGELY QUIET AFTER THEIR STANDOFF WITH THE older vampires. Johnathan expected Alazar to confront them immediately, but both he and Tamara made themselves scarce, skulking off to whatever room they occupied to plot and scheme their next move. He didn't take their reprieve for granted, hustling Vic back to the relative safety of their quarters.

A pall hung over them, heavy with the knowledge that though they could not see the black-clad army, it waited for them beyond the barrier. Johnathan sat behind Vic on their shared bed in his room, cradling him between his legs. Vic leaned back against his chest. His companion had been lost to silent contemplation for some time.

"I miss the days when I only knew about vampires," said Johnathan. Vic huffed and pulled Johnathan's arms around him. "It was simpler when it was just you and something that wanted to eat you. Now we have demons and angels in the mix, vying for influence. I know what the Nether wants, but the Benign?"

"I doubt it's good," said Vic. "I don't know if the Nether and Benign are meant to be opposites or if they parallel each other." He shook his head, muscles tight from his frustration. "There have been so many little coincidences, bleeding into each other. This feels like a grand scheme, John. A divine joke, and we are the punchline."

Johnathan frowned, uncertain what he was driving at. "What coincidence? You had no idea who I was, or what would happen in Cress Haven. You certainly didn't know that you were blessed."

Vic fidgeted in his arms. "What if that is how I saved you?" He swallowed hard. "The Morrigan might have known and said nothing. The Fae don't freely give information."

There was a kernel of truth in that theory. The Morrigan was a strange incomprehensible being who'd helped them immeasurably, at the cost of Johnathan's long-kept secrets. The local Fae were familiar with Vic, to the point where they teased him. If Vic was blessed, it seemed like something the Fae would have leveraged in their games. Or maybe there were rules, like their inability to lie, that kept them from revealing that piece of information, a code of conduct between the realms. But there was an overriding peculiarity, a sense of grand manipulation though Johnathan couldn't figure out who or what might be putting pieces into play.

Tainted by the Nether, blessed by the Benign, their lives intricately woven together by the blood bond Vic used to save his life. A bond they'd created with no knowledge or a guarantee it would take. A risk Vic took after the Morrigan's cryptic hints.

"I need to talk to Alazar. It's too dangerous to let them suspect you." Vic let his head loll onto Johnathan's shoulders. From that angle, Johnathan could see the shadows had crept back beneath his eyes. He suspected Vic hadn't fed since their first night at the Estate. Johnathan was partially responsible for that. Vic had forced down his throat more than once to heal him. When they weren't fully occupied with each other, Vic was contending with the older vampires.

"How can you stand him? Either of them? They are ancient, selfish, and cruel."

"Alazar is brusque and a complete ass, but when the chips are down, his loyalty will surprise you," said Vic. "He cares enough about his race to corral us together when necessary, and strong enough to force most of us in line."

Johnathan's brow arched. This was a generous description of the recalcitrant vampire. "How long have you known him?"

"A long time, John." He reached over his head, twisting his fingers in Johnathan's hair. "Remember when I told you I once lived with other vampires?"

"Those two? Really?"

Vic smiled. "Really. Believe it or not, Alazar kept me alive through my first century, when I was arrogant and stupid and knew I was superior to those milksop humans."

"I thought older vampires had no tolerance for newborns," said Johnathan.

"I might have been young and stupid, but I had my charms," said Vic, a teasing purr in his voice.

"How long did you live together?"

"Over a century," said Vic. "But I mourned the loss of my humanity in a way they didn't. I lost that sense of superiority the longer I stayed with them, yearned to love, and be loved, with the ferocity that humans have for one another." He wove his fingers with Johnathan's, kissing the back of his hand. "Alazar once told me he was too old for the foils of passion."

Johnathan snorted. "What about Tamara?"

Vic sighed. "She wasn't always like this. We carry sorrow and pain like anyone else, John, but immortality twists those emotions into something colder and darker." He patted Johnathan's leg, easing himself off the bed. "This might take me a few hours."

"I don't like you going to meet them alone as it is. I don't think I can stay here that long and do nothing," said Johnathan.

"Maybe check on Merry," said Vic. "I've never seen them so angry with Alazar before."

The reminder made him wince. Johnathan hadn't intended to leave Merry out there alone and wobbly from their forced shift. He recognized that sort of rage, something he'd felt himself, staring at his former mentor from the confines of a silver cage.

"Don't let Alazar push you into agreeing to anything stupid," said Johnathan.

Vic waved him off. "He hasn't managed yet in the five centuries of our friendship." Johnathan watched him leave, worry pricking his nerves. He had to trust Vic knew what he was doing. There was a long history between the vampires, one that made Johnathan more than a little jealous. He wondered, provided they survived the next fortnight, if Vic would tire of his presence after a century. Would his body last that long? Would he eventually age and wither away? It was hard to think in terms of years, let alone centuries, when danger hung over them, a reaper's scythe to fall at any time.

There was nothing for it but to don a pair of boots and search for their host.

Contrary to form, Merry was not at their workbench. Johnathan wandered through the lush greenery, hoping to catch a glimpse of their host crouched over a patch of herbs. Their scent permeated the conservatory, soaked into the very ground, and still quite fresh but after searching every nook, Merry was nowhere to be found.

Itching to return to Vic's side, Johnathan tried to walk off his nerves, surprised to find the front door cracked open. Had Merry forgotten to shut it when coming inside? That seemed out of character for their host. He poked his head out, staring out into the forest, keenly aware the Society lurked within the lie. Johnathan started to retreat inside when he caught the unmistakable scent of sex and honey. He whipped around, searching the dark.

Was she on the other side of the barrier? Johnathan self-consciously lifted his nose, inhaling deeply. The scent abruptly thickened and clogged his nose. He sneezed. Where was she? Squinting into the shadows until his head ached, he scowled. Did he believe the wayward succubus was a threat? No. But he didn't know why she was here, or frankly how when Society Agents crawled through the woods. He had to track her. Hesitating, he stared out into Merry's illusion. If he couldn't see the Agents, they couldn't see him, and yet, he swore he could see feel Sister Wilhem's gaze on him.

Feeling ridiculous, Johnathan tiptoed in the shadows along the side of the mansion, following the succubus's thickening scent. He'd circled a quarter of the property when a faint rustle of branches made him pause.

"Hesper?" A squeak made him look up. The succubus perched on a narrow branch, her crimson eyes huge in her face. She'd forgone her human disguise, demonic features on full display, from the curling horns to the thin tail draped over her arm like a skirt train.

"I don't think that branch is going to hold you—"

The crack drowned out his words. Hesper yelped, tumbling off the broken branch. Johnathan caught her and gently lowered her to her feet.

"So gallant," she sputtered, awkwardly patting his arm.

Johnathan stared down at her. There was a twitch developing in his right eye. "What are you doing here? No." He held up a finger. "Scratch that, how are you here?"

Hesper glanced over her shoulder; her expression mildly confused. "Oh, you mean how did I get through the barrier?"

"Yes, the barrier," Johnathan hissed.

She held up her hands in a placating gesture. "Easy, big guy. I'm still shaken from the fall. Give me a second—"

"Now," he snapped.

"Um, ah, well, I walked through?" Her face scrunched up. The succubus was a terrible liar.

Johnathan rubbed his temples. "Try again."

Hesper bit her lip. Not a sexy gesture, her upper teeth denting her bottom lip. "I snuck through when the other one went out," she blurted. "That's the truth, I swear."

His brows drew together. "What other one?" Did she mean Katherine? He didn't think the Geist would create an opening in the barrier large enough for the succubus to slip through.

"The one that stank of divine magic," said Hesper. "They scuttled out here, all kitted up for the cloak and dagger act. When they stepped through, so did I. But don't worry, they didn't see me." She grinned.

Was she talking about Merry? Why would Merry go through the barrier? They were one of Sister Wilhem's targets. "How did they not see you?"

"Like this," said Hesper. She took a step back. Her body blended seamlessly into the shadows. If Johnathan concentrated on her directly, he could make out the outline of her form, but she was nearly as invisible as Katherine. She moved forward and shimmered back into view. "Yeah?" Another step in, step out. "Impressive right?"

Johnathan hated to admit it, but it was. "Is that something all succubi can do?"

Incredulity scrawled across her face. "I'm not skilled at it but all demons shade walk. You-you just did it, Hound," she said.

"What?" Johnathan glanced back at the shadowy passage he'd picked along the wall. "No. Wouldn't I feel it?"

Hesper placed a hand against his chest and pushed. He stumbled back a step, surprised by the strength in her slender limbs. "Yup, shade walking."

Johnathan glanced down, unnerved by the sight of his body blending into the dark. A small jump expunged him from the shadows.

"I keep forgetting how new you are to this, Hound," said the succubus.

"Johnathan, not Hound, Johnathan," he said. He scowled. "Why are you here, Hesper?"

She shrugged at the question, her tail lashing around her legs. "I know our last encounter ended on a sour note," she said.

"An understatement," he muttered. He'd nearly strangled her.

"And I'm sorry for that," she said. "Your lover scared me. I reacted badly."

"Because he's a vampire?" Maybe there was bad blood between the different predators.

Hesper shot him a look. "Are you playing dumb or are you truly a simpleton?"

"I should have strangled you," he growled. Johnathan slumped back against the house. "You knew he was divine touched?"

She blinked at him in disbelief. "How did you not know, Hound? That blessing practically oozes out of his skin."

He twisted his hands in his lap. "I didn't know. Why did he scare you?"

Hesper worried her lip. "He shouldn't exist." She shuddered. "I don't know how those blinding bastards managed it."

Apprehension crawled along his spine. Johnathan swallowed. "Most divine touched are humans. What happens when a divine touched gives permission?"

The succubus snorted. "They try their best to pick strong ones. It's not like a demon lord. They know better. It takes a sliver of essence to taint a human. They might break a few, but some will survive. A few will be strong enough for their lineage to take hold. Angels, though." She spat on the ground. "They're stupid. They cram all that divine energy into a pulpy human body and—"

She clapped her hands together. Johnathan jumped. Hesper shook her head. "Some might last a while, but it always ends the same." She lazily scratched the back of her neck.

"They always die?"

She nodded. "That's why he scares me, Hound." She leaned closer, her crimson eyes glowing in the dark. "Do you know what the Benign would do if they got their hands on a custom-made immortal vessel like that? We'd be fucked."

The thought of an angel cramming itself into Vic was horrifying in a way Johnathan couldn't fully comprehend. "That bad?"

"There's a balance," said Hesper. "We're always looking for a way to tip the scales, but let's be honest. No one really wants that."

Johnathan snorted. "I beg to differ." Cerunnous was persistent in his goal to the end.

"Sure, the higher ranks might put on a good show, but they respect the balance. They might bend the rules, but they don't break them. Every bargain has an out. An immortal vessel is a scale tipper, Hound." She glanced at him.

He went still. "Why are you here, Hesper?" Did she intend to kill Vic? Fire stirred in his gut at the thought. He would tear out her throat.

She drew in a deep breath. "Because I saw you at the docks."

He'd thought the mention of his bloody actions would stir the guilt and shame, but his thoughts were consumed by the threat in front of him.

"I saw you after," she said, fiddling with her tail. "I saw him after." Her eyes glistened, overly bright. "How he was with you." There was open longing in her face.

Johnathan released a shuddering breath, the fire receding. "You followed us?"

"Yes," she admitted, her voice small.

"What did you intend to do?" They were surrounded by Society Agents who would kill her if they caught her. If the current inhabitants of the Estate caught her, they'd kill her. Johnathan didn't understand why she'd risked herself.

"Help you," she said, without guile.

She'd already helped more than she knew. "I can't bring you inside," he said, knocking the back of his hand against the house. He didn't think she would make it past the threshold, even if Hesper was mostly harmless.

"I'll be fine out here," she said. She twirled her tail, creating a soft whistling sound as it spun through the air. "Don't tell them I'm out here."

Johnathan raised a brow. "I won't lie to Vic. Why don't you want me to tell him you're here? That's not very trustworthy."

She stuck her tongue out at him, the end forked. "If you want to tell your lover about your clandestine meeting with a succubus in the dark, that is your prerogative, Hound. I meant the others hiding in there like mice in a burrow."

"Obviously. Half of them don't know what I am," said Johnathan.

"That is a dangerous gambit," said Hesper. Her nose wrinkled. "Is that why you smell like wet dog?"

He chuckled. "I barely notice it now."

"That is a clever trick," Hesper admitted. She hesitated before finally sinking down next to him. "How does a Hound spend his day in a house full of secrets?"

"Oh, we're being conversational now?" Johnathan tilted his head back to look at her.

She made a face. "This is the longest I've spoken to another demon in decades. Humor me."

He hadn't thought of that, how lonely her existence must be. Hesper had to conceal her true nature from everyone. Johnathan considered himself terrible at social interaction and he'd managed to procure a small circle of confidants. Though he supposed he couldn't be too terrible if Hesper sought out his company. "This is the longest I've spoken to a demon ever," he said.

Her lips twitched. "Such a smart arse for a pup."

A small smile lifted the corner of his mouth. "I've been trying to control my shift," he confessed.

Her brows crept up into her riot of curls. "You've been having trouble?" She held up a hand. "Right, you were made." Her fingers fluttered. "Any luck?"

"It's not going well," said Johnathan. "Each time seems worse."

Hesper frowned. "How are you triggering the change?"

"The proprietor, our host, has been preparing a draught of burnt herbs—"

She grabbed his arm, pushing up his sleeve to reveal the blackened veins at his wrist, still fading despite the infusion of Vic's blood. Hesper made a scandalized sound and smacked him in the back of the head. "You've been poisoning yourself to transform? Do you have a death wish?"

"Ow." Johnathan rubbed his head. She'd nailed him. "I'm not poisoning myself! The herbs don't work without burning them."

"Because they are poisonous," Hesper snapped. "Did you ask what herbs they were using? Look at this," she shook his wrist. "That poison is so potent, you're overheating to compensate." She reared back. "How many times have you taken it?"

Johnathan's shoulders sank. "A dozen times or so."

She gaped at him. "You should be dead. Couldn't you tell it was poison?"

He rubbed a finger along his blackened veins. "I didn't know." He didn't think Merry knew either, though they'd seen the result. Did they truly not know the potency of the draught, or was Johnathan hoping for their ignorance? "They took it from a book."

"Of course they did." Hesper's mouth twisted in disgust. "Humans get all sorts of ideas from their books."

"This one was older, with information on the Nether," said Johnathan, feeling defensive.

Hesper rolled her eyes. "Any information humans managed to procure about the Nether would not be beneficial to demons, Hound."

"Please, it's Johnathan," he said.

Hesper sighed. "Johnathan, why did you feel the need to use a draught to begin with?"

"You saw me at the docks," he said. "I can't transform without mortal danger, and I can't change back without taking a life."

The succubus stared at him. "Who told you that great lie?"

Johnathan froze. It was the truth he'd gained through trial and error. The one he'd seen through his interactions with the other Hellhounds in Cress Haven. A truth he'd believed because he knew no different. And no one had told him otherwise. "But I killed them all. I couldn't stop," he whispered.

"Why would you?" Hesper nudged her shoulder against his arm. "You and your master were still in danger. Would you stop a hunt mid-lunge?"

"But I didn't have to kill them," said Johnathan.

"How do you think this works, Johnathan? Growl and snap until they back off?" She shook her head. "Hellhounds are lethal enforcers. If there is a threat, they will eliminate it with prejudice."

"I don't want to murder every human I encounter," he retorted.

Hesper gently flicked his forehead. "Why would you hurt someone if they're not attacking you? That would be a waste. Have you hurt anyone that wasn't directly threatening you before?"

The revelation shook him. He opened his mouth to answer her when he caught the scent of smoke and rosewater. Johnathan straightened, trying to pinpoint its direction.

"What is it? You look spooked," said Hesper. He slid his hand over her mouth, holding a finger to his lips. She nodded, the two of them waiting in silence when the barrier shivered near the front of the house. Johnathan pulled himself and Hesper deeper into the shadows and ran alongside the house. They faded into the dark as the distortion grew more pronounced. The ripple bulged inward, finally peeling around a cloaked figure. Smoke, wine, and rosewater. Johnathan grew more conflicted by the second, watching Merry glance around to see if their entrance was noticed. They failed to spot the two demons hiding in the shadows.

Johnathan waited for their next move. They didn't head for the front entrance, circling the building toward where he and the succubus hid. Johnathan pulled Hesper against him, holding his breath when Merry passed a few feet in front of them. Their steps slowed, looking out into the trees. After an impossibly long moment, Merry's steps resumed, until they disappeared around the back. He suspected there was another entrance to the conservatory.

He released Hesper, letting out his breath in a rush.

"That was far too close," whispered Hesper.

"I told you it wasn't safe," he said. Not for any of them. Why had Merry traversed the barrier after they were so adamant that Vic not do so? He wanted to give their host the benefit of the doubt. Perhaps their allies had arrived and Merry had gone to meet them. Except Johnathan couldn't shake the feeling that wasn't who their host paid a visit.

CHAPTER NINETEEN

JOHNATHAN KNEW HE'D BEEN OUT HERE TOO LONG. HE EXTRICATED himself from the shadows, wondering what to do with the succubus. Leaving her out here, trapped behind the barrier, didn't seem like the best idea.

She patted his arm. "Go," said Hesper. "I'll find my way out like I found my way in."

He hesitated. "There are a lot of Agents out there," he said.

"Worried about me, Johnathan?" She grinned at him. "I'm not helpless."

"I didn't mean to imply you were," he said.

"That's why I like you," she said with a wink. "We shall see each other again. Be careful, Hound. Don't let the secrets of this house bury you."

He mulled over her words, heading back toward the front so he wouldn't cross paths with Merry. Should he tell Vic what he saw? That would mean explaining why he was out here. He'd been telling Hesper the truth when he told her he wouldn't lie to Vic though he wondered how Vic would react to news of her presence inside the barrier. If Hesper managed to sneak in, how long before Sister Wilhem found a crack to slip through? He knew it would be better to speak to Vic before he accused Merry of anything. It was possible he'd misread the situation.

Was Vic still in a meeting with Alazar? Thinking it might be best to wait for Vic's return in their room, he headed for the stairs. The muscles of his stomach tightened. It appeared Hesper wouldn't be his only late-night encounter.

Tamara sat on the banister, her legs dangling over the side. Johnathan's steps slowed as he approached her, though she didn't seem ready to ambush him. He was surprised to find her here and not holed up arguing with the other two. She stared at the floor, paying him no mind, her expression lost in thought. Without the perpetual mocking sneer on her lips, Johnathan could see the beauty he'd glimpsed before. It was easy to believe she'd been worshipped as a goddess.

A tear slid down her face. She wiped it absently, her gaze lifting to watch his approach. Johnathan bowed his head, intending to leave her to her vigil.

"The wolves are closing in, my lamb," she said, her voice filled with a hidden sorrow behind the blank mask of her perfect face. "The Sister rushes headlong into the arms of death."

Johnathan hesitated. Vic admitted he didn't possess much knowledge of the divine, but Tamara spoke with the certainty of first-hand knowledge. "Are the Benign worse than the Nether?"

Tamara lifted her legs and lay down, lounging on the narrow, slanted beam. She propped a fist beneath her cheek, blowing her hair out of her eyes. "Both are equally terrible in their way. The Nether is a bottomless stomach. It eats and eats and eats, until everything is pure chaos. But the Benign demands order, obedience, control. Dominion over all. And what it can't absorb it destroys." Tamara lifted her hand toward the ceiling, examining her nails.

"Humans are messy creatures," Johnathan murmured. They worshipped, hated, loved, and despaired, often in quick succession. Human nature was imperfect. The Benign would lay them to waste, striving for an order that could not be reached.

She nodded. "I knew you were smart, lamb. Victor says everything and nothing when he speaks of you, but I can see the truth in his eyes." A genuine smile curved her lush mouth. "I haven't seen worship like that in centuries."

His ears tingled at her observation. Johnathan moved closer, leaning on the railing not far from her. "You said you *were* worshipped as a goddess. What happened to your devoted?"

"Perhaps too smart," she murmured. Her dark gaze fixed on him. "My poor, sweet children. To them, I was Coatlicue incarnate, a goddess of life and death, draped in serpents. They offered their bleeding hearts on stone altars, for my power and protection. I watched over them for centuries before the angels began to whisper in their ears. My children heard the voice of the divine, demanding their love. Demanding their obedience. It asked them to open the way, bestowing blessings on those favored individuals." Her lips parted. "Marvelous gifts, and each bore a heavy price."

Blessings or bargains, the payment was often worse than both. Johnathan gnawed the inside of his cheek. "I take it these blessings weren't arbitrary?"

Tamara snorted. "No indeed. They were seeds, carefully nurtured and coaxed until the priests found the crack to its realm. My children called it Quetzalcoatl, the creator. The great lie." A hard bitterness flashed across her gaze. "They welcomed the feathered serpent with open arms, and invited it right in. That was when the priests found out that not all vessels were created equal."

A sick feeling twisted his gut. "They couldn't contain it." Hesper told him as much.

Tamara's example was as visceral as the succubus's had been, smacking her fist into her open palm. "Like over ripe fruit," she said. "Some of the blessed would last longer, and even in a mortal body, their strength is a terrible sight to behold. That winged serpent decimated my children. Chewed through them until there was no one left to sacrifice themselves."

The Nether needed an anchor, the Benign needed a vessel. "What happened when it ran out of suitable bodies?"

Tamara shrugged. "It faded back to its realm, after I finished with it." She folded her hands over her stomach, crossing her ankles on the precarious width of the banister.

"Perhaps they learned from their mistakes," said Johnathan, though he was loathe to voice the idea out loud.

"We are lucky it is impossible for them to make an immortal vessel," said Tamara. "The Benign would tear down the world."

The implications weighed on Johnathan when he finally returned to their rooms. It was no wonder the Scarlet Sisters were so focused on Vic; he was the key to success. And the worst for their world.

The hour was late when Vic finally arrived back at their rooms, exhausted but relieved. "Well, that could have gone better." He dropped backward onto the bed.

Johnathan frowned. "Did you tell him you were their target?"

"Yes, he was quite adamant it was impossible. He believed me after the coin." He held up a hand, revealing a slowly fading circular burn mark. "He wants input from our allies before he decides what to do with me."

"That sounds ominous," Johnathan muttered. "How long do you think before the others arrive?"

The Society would notice if more creatures descended on the Estate. There would be a blood bath unless they had a way to sneak the others inside. Not that the Society would wait for reinforcements to show up before they made a move. "They'll keep trying to break through."

"Agreed, though Merry insists the barrier will hold," said Vic, his expression pinched with uncertainty. Johnathan crawled over the bed, lying on his stomach beside him.

"You need to feed soon," he said, stroking his fingers down the side of Vic's face and neck, who turned into his touch.

"You're worse than a mother hen, harping on me to eat more." He sighed. "Before our unwelcome friends arrived, Merry had arranged for a donation at the nearest town. I'm not sure I'll manage to retrieve it before it spoils," said Vic.

"Didn't Merry give you blood our first night here?"

Vic nodded. "Yes, but asking for more would be taking advantage. Our relationship is not what it used to be. I don't want to erode what goodwill remains between us."

Johnathan hesitated. "I wanted to ask for your input about something." He relayed his conversation with Hesper and how he'd seen Merry come through the barrier. Vic listened, worry and outrage warring for dominance.

"I can't believe that succubus weaseled her way through," muttered Vic. His gaze slanted at Johnathan. "Do you believe her, about that draught being poison?"

"I don't think Merry was intentionally trying to poison me, Vic, but why were they coming through the barrier?"

"They might be helping Katherine find a way to sneak our incoming guests through the Society's forces," said Vic. "I'm not making excuses for them, John, I've just known Merry a long time. They won't betray us."

"You've known everyone a long time, old man," said Johnathan.

Vic chuckled, nestling further into Johnathan's arms. After hours of verbal sparring with Alazar, he looked exhausted.

"You know, you could feed from me," said Johnathan. It wasn't the first time he'd offered, and the act of offering to Vic was a far cry from the experience of his youth. He'd spent years as a lure for Sir Harry, the vampire who comprised the entirety of his world for so many years. When he'd failed to reel in a meal, he provided sustenance. Johnathan once believed he loved Sir Harry, the man who'd been both father and fiend. But their relationship had been skewed, a one-sided take, take, take. If his life had gone differently, without the intervention of Evans, eventually Sir Harry would have taken everything.

There was a give and take between Johnathan and Vic. He wanted to give this to Vic, to banish the shadows that clung to his face. "You've bitten me plenty of times. Let me help you."

Vic's gaze snapped to his face. He was shocked to see the pain in those grey eyes. "No," he murmured. He rolled over, cupping Johnathan's face. "No, John. No." Vic pressed his forehead against his, breath fanning over his cheeks. "It's not the same."

There was a beat of silence, filled with unspoken questions and wanting words. Johnathan wanted to ask why Vic refused to do so, but didn't want to press the issue, not when it seemed to hurt him. Instead he tugged the man's hips closer, lifting his face to gently nip at Vic's full bottom lip. "Then let me sustain you in other ways." Vic smiled against his mouth.

CHAPTER TWENTY

THE ALLIES BEGAN TO ARRIVE TWO DAYS LATER. THE HOURS PASSED AT a glacial pace, barring the stolen, heated moments when Johnathan or Vic pulled the other aside for distraction. More often, they were separated while Vic contended with the older vampires. Despite their illuminating stairwell conversation, Johnathan stayed away from Tamara, though for a very practical reason.

The Hound was close to the surface. After his encounter with Hesper, he paid careful attention to his reactions. Though he hadn't managed to successfully turn at will, there was a climbing tension in the Estate, and the hovering possibility of attack left Johnathan a hair's breadth from bursting out of his skin. A persistent muscle twitch took up residence between his shoulders, while a rumbling growl hovered in his throat. Occasionally, smoke curled from his nostrils. Vic ordered him to keep well away from the other vampires in his current state. Johnathan couldn't help but agree, though he now found himself at loose ends. With the Society camped outside and the arrival of their allies imminent, Merry and Katherine made themselves scarce, wrapped up in preparations and planning.

Johnathan began a careful exploration of the grounds and the interior of the Estate, peeking into the previously closed off rooms. None of them held a candle to the beauty of the indoor garden, but there was a well-kept ballroom, the marble floor polished to a luminous sheen, and a chandelier larger than the one in the foyer, waiting to be lit.

When he wasn't exploring, he tried to meditate. Control over his dark impulses was more important than ever; he wondered how long their secret would last when the Estate filled with creatures.

During their stolen moments, Vic revealed many of their allies weren't vampires. The Society often concentrated their efforts on vampires due to their cunning nature and dangerous strength, but they hunted whatever creatures sought to feed on humans. Johnathan hadn't encountered many during his time in the Boston chapter, because most either stayed out of the densely populated cities or kept a far lower profile than more arrogant predators. The anticipation of meeting so many dangerous creatures piled on his inward tension.

Meditation wasn't happening right now. His nerves were too frayed to sit for any length of time. He'd been on edge since morning.

Keeping away from Alazar and Tamara's critical eye, Johnathan exited the house, strolling along the exterior perimeter of the Estate. To his relief, or chagrin, Hesper had managed to slip back through the barrier. She'd been gone for at least a day, her sex and honey scent nearly gone. He lifted his nose to scent the air, seeing if he could pick up foe and friend alike through the barrier, though he couldn't determine much other than a faint, charred scent, like the air after a lightning storm.

Since the barrier masked their scents, it meant the first allies caught him by surprise, appearing in a sudden ripple of air. Johnathan froze when the wolves approached, their movements far more deliberate and bolder than any wild animal.

They were also enormous, nearly twice the size of actual wolves. The lead wolf paused, body shuddering in the beginning of stages of transformation. Johnathan watched, fascinated by the gray fur receding to pale skin. The muscles thickened and filled as the wolf's thinner legs shifted to human. There was no gut-wrenching crack of bone or tearing flesh, the transition from animal to human so smooth Johnathan immediately envied them. The shift was over in seconds.

A naked woman crouched in the wolf's stead. Johnathan glimpsed her light amber eyes, a richer, more natural color than his own, and her claw tipped hands, when his sense of propriety smacked him between the eyes. His gaze shot upward.

"Terribly sorry, miss, that was incredibly bad manners," he sputtered. Despite his embarrassment, understanding finally clicked into place. Johnathan never understood why Alazar and Tamara accepted his inhuman appearance so easily, until he saw the werewolves. He jumped when a cold nose pressed against his throat, the unmistakable brush of a female and very naked body against him. He looked down into those puzzled amber eyes, set above a slightly crooked nose, likely broken more than once. A disarming sprinkle of freckles dusted her cheeks.

"You don't smell like a wolf," she said in a throaty whisper. Alarm shot through his mind. He'd remembered to smear on the salve before he left the room. Was her sense of smell that much stronger than the vampires? What did he smell like to her? He was on the verge of a full-blown panic when her eyebrows rose in speculation. "But you do smell like Victor."

Johnathan blushed harder.

The man in question cleared his throat somewhere behind him, likely informed of the arrival of their guests by Merry or Katherine. "Welcome, Beatrice, I see you've met Johnathan."

He caught Vic's bemused expression. The naked woman gave him a final sniff before settling back on her heels. She accepted the robe Vic held out for her, though her pack stayed in wolf form as they headed inside.

"Do you know everyone?" Johnathan blurted.

Vic gave a hapless shrug. "The older you are, the smaller the immortal community, my love. You'll see."

There was such certainty in his words, Johnathan couldn't help but grin. He still had trouble wrapping his mind around concepts of forever and immortality, but Vic would be there to guide him through the turbulent period of acceptance. Because Johnathan would not let the Society have him.

More allies began to trickle in over the next few days. Several vampires, most as old as Vic or older. Werewolves weren't the only creatures. A gray skinned gentleman in a suit and stove pipe hat arrived late at night. His skin was cool to the touch when Johnathan shook his hand, fingernails ragged and torn, but the most unsettling aspect of his nature was the smile.

Johnathan leaned to Vic when the smiling gentleman was well out of ear shot. "You invited a ghoul?"

"Not in a position to be choosy, John," Vic muttered out of the corner of his mouth.

The halls of the Estate soon brimmed with all manner of creatures. He had no idea how Merry and Katherine managed to slip so many through the Society's forces unseen, but he admired their skill. His suspicions seemed laughable now. He wished he could find their hosts so he could apologize for doubting them. Unfortunately, the flood of guests meant their hosts were constantly engaged. Most of them were barely civil at the best of times

Johnathan spent more time outside or wandering the more remote spaces of the Estate, trying to avoid the constant spats. He was engaged in that exact activity when Vic found him, wandering the basement.

"Why does a sanctuary need holding cells?" Johnathan squinted at the thick bars. Vic slid to a stop beside him.

"A number of unsavory reasons," said Vic. He slipped his hand in Johnathan's. No matter how stressed or busy, Vic found moments for contact. Johnathan clung to those small touches to make it through the long hours, eager for the moment they came together at the end of the day, in locked lips and intertwined limbs. "Our gracious host informs me there will a gathering tonight in the ballroom. I know you haven't been one to socialize, but I would like to introduce you to a few old friends."

Johnathan chewed the inside of his lip. The idea of being around so many keen noses left him more than a little uneasy. "I am certain that is a terrible idea. The salve didn't work on the werewolves."

"I may have a solution for that," said Vic with a grin, retrieving a small vial of bath oil from his pocket. Memories of what they used the variety of oils for were enough to elicit a faint blush, but Johnathan took a step back.

"You are not dumping that on my head," he protested. He could pick up the heady scent of peppermint through the stopper. The entire vial would be overpowering to him and every immortal in the Estate.

Vic laughed. "We won't go that extreme. However, it should confuse your scent enough without trying to hide it like the salve." He uncorked the vial, dabbing a healthy amount on his own wrist. "And you won't be the only one wearing it." The peppermint would confuse both their scents, a rather devious method of ensuring no one tried too hard to discern Johnathan's unique origins.

Hesitation continued to spin in his gut. The slow crawl of tension he'd experienced since dawn felt like it was coming to a head. Apprehension clouded his head, making it difficult to think. He didn't believe in ill omens, but there was a strange flavor to the air, the ozone taste of storms. "Is it important to you that I attend?"

Vic went quiet, rubbing the oil into the skin of his wrists. "You are important to me. I would love the opportunity to show you off," he said. "If you think it's a bad idea, I won't force you, John."

The words were more than enough to sway him, though there was another practical excuse to attend. Merry would be there. Johnathan itched to talk to them about the draught and what herbs they used. He wondered if Merry would tell him the origins of the book.

"I'll go," said Johnathan. Though Vic's answering smile made the heat pool deep in his belly, his dread continued to build.

When Johnathan last saw the ballroom, the massive chandelier sported a thin layer of dust. Well kept, but rarely used, the fixtures were polished mirror bright. The chandelier had been cleaned for the occasion, boasting close to a thousand individual globes of light. Johnathan couldn't imagine how long it took to light the monstrosity. More lit fixtures lined the walls. The massive room was lit up bright as a summer day. On the far wall, a long table held lines of empty wine glasses, enough for everyone in the room.

The attending creatures matched the luminous interior, equally colorful in vibrant silk dresses and brilliantly colored vests. The werewolf

Beatrice wore a deep orange gown that complimented her curvy frame, surrounded by a contingent of hirsute men in perfectly tailored suits. This was the first time Johnathan saw her pack in human form. He'd gotten used to them wandering the halls and grounds as wolves. Even Alazar wore something other than his robes, dressed in form fitting slacks and a creamy dress shirt, the loose material billowing around his muscular frame.

Tamara was resplendent in a creation fit for a feral goddess. Gauzy silk streamers twined around her thighs like living serpents, while numerous copper chains covered her breasts, leaving her back bare. Copper cuffs covered her wrists and ankles, the outfit completed by her bare feet, toenails painted to match the color of her cuffs.

The one who held Johnathan's attention, though, was the man beside him. Their wardrobes had provided evening wear for both. The sight of Vic made him want to drag him to bed to mess up that sinfully neat cravat. Judging by the heat in Vic's gaze, Johnathan cleaned up well enough.

He was grateful for the distraction of a splendid partner. The ballroom was massive, but it seemed stuffed to the rafters by the sizable personalities and powers in attendance. Vic's hand remained at the small of his back, as if he sensed Johnathan's urge to bolt. He steered them through a dozen immortals until they stopped beside a familiar dainty looking female.

"Hello, Katherine." Victor grinned.

Her outfit was the same she wore every day, but her translucent smile was dazzling. She held out her hand with a flourish, which Johnathan took without hesitation. Her icy skin was wonderful in the overly warm room. He brushed his lips over her knuckles. The contact stung, but her giggle made it worth it.

"Can you believe how many answered the summons? Even Wardlow crawled out of his burrow," said Katherine, nodding to the ghoul in the grey suit.

"It's been some time since we sent out a call," said Vic. "You know they enjoy the chance to dress up and socialize without needing to hide."

"Speaking of, you both look so handsome." She flicked her fingers along Johnathan's suit. "I think this is the first time I've seen you properly dressed, John. Clothes suit you."

"That they do," Vic agreed, pinching his chin. "Though, no clothes also suit him."

"Very true," said Katherine, sagely. "Very true."

"You're both incorrigible," muttered Johnathan.

Vic snickered, threading Katherine's arm through the crook of his elbow. "Picked up anything interesting?"

Katherine's good humor dimmed. "Bits and pieces. We knew the Society had been busy, but there have been a few surprises." Her soulful eyes flashed. "Your name came up a few times, Victor. Word spreads fast when you tangle with a demon."

Johnathan failed to hide his flinch. Katherine patted his shoulder.

"One we successfully thwarted," said Vic, his mouth a grim line.

The Geist shook her head. "You know how they are, worse than gossiping housewives." She leaned in, mouthing the words rather than risk speaking to them out loud. *"The werewolves said he smells like fire."*

Vic gave her a tight smile. "They've been discreet thus far. Could you keep an ear out for any other rumors in case we need to make a swift exit?"

"Of course," said Katherine. She carefully laid her hand over Vic's clothed arm. "Did you really spill your status to Alazar?"

"I'm afraid so," Vic murmured. Johnathan remained silent. They had danced around this subject and the wisdom of staying put within the Estate since that night. Despite the constant strain on his nerves, Johnathan argued in favor of staying from a vantage point of known terrain. He'd spent the last few days exploring the hallways and walkways of the acreage. If Merry's barrier fell, he would lure and incapacitate the Sister's invasion force in the maze of the Estate. Vic, however, continued to lean toward self-sacrifice. Without Johnathan's protest, he wondered if his companion would have forged ahead on his own.

Their host made their entrance at last, carrying two bottles of wine. "Good evening, my charming guests. Grab a glass to prepare for the toast."

Johnathan frowned, leaning in closer to Vic's ear. "Do they mean everyone to partake?" He wasn't certain all the guests could imbibe wine.

It was Katherine who answered him. "Yes, this isn't a toast but a ceremony," she said. "A share of power to strengthen the barriers of our sanctuary against those who threaten us." She handed Johnathan an empty glass, chilled by her touch.

"Pomegranate wine," said Vic. "Masks the taste of the herbs. Even the finickiest of appetites can stomach a small glass."

"I still find mine a little bitter," muttered Katherine. He was shocked the Geist could imbibe at all.

"How do you drink? Half the time you're incorporeal," he said.

Katherine sniffed. "I just need to maintain it long enough for the herbs to take effect."

Merry waltzed through the room in a dove gray silk shirt that accented their curves. Their slacks hugged the rounded shape of their thighs, drawing many appreciative gazes to the sway of their hips. Their wild curls were tamed in a tight knot at the back of their head, giving their face an almost severe appearance. They stopped throughout the room, welcoming their allies, taking each glass in hand to add a mix of wine and herbs. Merry greeted Tamara with cool politeness, Alazar with barely a word, before they moved on to Johnathan and his companions.

"Good evening, Katherine," said Merry, not quite brushing their lips across her cheek.

"Hello, Merry. You look radiant tonight." Katherine took a glass, her portion of wine much smaller than most since she needed to maintain a body to savor it.

"Flattery and praise are my great weaknesses, as you know." Merry winked. They filled Vic's glass next. "You look rather ravishing yourself, Victor."

"A good suit is its own armor," said Vic.

Merry rolled their eyes. "Honestly, who taught you to put such stock in fashion?"

Johnathan's lips twitched, glancing sidelong at his companion. Merry took his glass, fiddling with the herbs before adding a healthy swig of pomegranate wine. Taking the glass back, he paused, keenly aware of Katherine's astute hearing.

"Are there any side effects I should know?" He whispered the question, hoping it sounded like first time nerves rather than anything suspicious.

Their host patted his arm. "It's a simple ceremony, Johnathan. A quick gulp and done. I promise, you'll feel nothing you haven't felt before." Merry smiled and moved onto the next cluster of guests.

A frisson threaded through Johnathan's nerves. He stared down at the glass of wine, thicker than the usual reds, deep and dark as fresh blood.

"What's wrong?" Vic murmured.

He wasn't sure. Johnathan was saved from trying to answer as Merry stepped to the center of the room.

"It has been long since we have gathered in our sacred places," said Merry. "Many of you have come from a great distance to meet the rising threat before us." The audience remained quiet while they spoke. "Tonight, we gather against the coming storm. The oldest of foes stirs once again; their influence over man increases every day. And now the Society, once dismissed as a human nuisance, seeks to give the Nether and the Benign a foot hold in this world."

"Do we know why that is?" Beatrice asked, her blunt tone cut through the room. "What is their goal?"

"We have not been able to attain that information yet," said Alazar.

"Feels like we've been concentrating more on preventing their plans than their endgame," Johnathan whispered to her.

Katherine glanced at him. "Seems fair backward, doesn't it? How can we stop them without knowing what they're about?"

She had a point. Merry, however, would not be derailed. "We may not know their end goals, but we do know the danger they pose. There will be time to uncover the full extent of their schemes once we solve our current dilemma." They raised their glass of wine above their heads. "Tonight, you'll share your strength with this sanctuary, so that we may keep our enemies at bay. Tonight, we gather to act against those who would hunt us. Drink."

Their host drained their glass. The others followed suit. Vic and Katherine drank their portions down. Johnathan lifted the glass to his lips. An errant thought occurring to him as the thick, sweet wine hit his tongue.

Merry's smile hadn't reached their eyes.

Pain lanced through him. The glass fell from his hand, shattering on the polished floor. Johnathan clutched his stomach, the faint taste of ash at the back of his throat. He met Katherine and Vic's horrified gaze before his legs buckled out from under him. His body crashed down, broken glass cutting into his hands and knees. A negligible pain when his spine tore upright through his skin, a crack loud enough to shiver the chandelier. The reactions of the others were muddled, bursts of screams, outrage, and scattering footsteps, fleeing the Hound that burst from the man. The strained beat of his heart overrode everything else, thundering between his ears until the transformation ran its course.

He hadn't taken the draught in days. The change was faster than last time, possibly under a minute, and his body experienced every agonizing second. This transformation didn't devastate his body, healed from previous administrations. Johnathan rose, his hind legs watery but firm. His mind was frightfully clear, but it still took him a moment too long to register the incoming threat. Lithe arms wrapped around his neck.

In his human form, Tamara might have snapped his neck. But this form, weak from the change and the poison in the draught, still bore a terrible strength. And unlike his previous transformations in the conservatory, there was a present threat. Johnathan twisted, sinking his teeth into the ancient vampire's arm. He jerked his head, pulling her off his back where he pinned her to the floor, a paw on her chest, claws digging into her skin. Instinct overrode his human judgement as his jaw closed over her throat. She was a threat to be eliminated. He bit down.

"John, no!" He froze at Vic's shout. Awareness of his surroundings snapped to the fore. The guests had scrambled away from him, their expressions an almost comical tableau of shock, fear, and hatred. Many were crouched in defensive positions. The werewolf Beatrice stalked at the edge of the crowd, gnashing her teeth.

Vic strained to reach him, pinned to the floor by Alazar and another vampire. Alazar gripped him by the hair and pulled his head back.

"You brought a demon to our sanctuary?" Alazar hissed. Vic bared his teeth. A snarl ripped from Johnathan's throat. Smoke curled from his nostrils. The vampire in his jaws tensed, limbs quivering with barely leashed violence. The moment Johnathan released her, she would retaliate.

Katherine was caught between helping Vic or Johnathan, holding up her hands. "Alazar, stop this."

"Please, you don't understand," Vic pleaded. His knees skidded on the floor as he tried to gain leverage. He pried at Alazar's hold, but the other vampire was much older, and Vic was not at peak strength. "Let me talk to him. Please."

There wasn't an ounce of mercy on Alazar's severe face. Fear splintered the need to destroy the female in his jaws, the older vampire looked ready to tear Vic's head off.

Alazar released Vic with a gasp, his body seizing. Katherine stood behind him, her semi corporeal hand inside the vampire's chest. "I said stop this. Let him explain," she said, her calm voice seeped in ice. Alazar's lips were already tinged blue. Katherine looked to Vic, her gaze tinged by sadness. "Can you talk Johnathan down?"

He didn't need to. Johnathan was aware of the precarity of their current situation. He also knew Tamara would kill them both if he released her. Could he risk it? He looked at the other guests, gauging how many would attack him should he kill the vampiress. His gaze settled on Merry. Their jaw clenched, a flash of regret in their green eyes, gone in an instant. Their host had exposed him, though he didn't know why.

His attention tore away from their treacherous host when Vic crawled toward him. The fear in his eyes tore at Johnathan's heart. Not fear of him, but for him. Both knew this would not end well.

"You have to let her go, John," said Vic. There was no denying that voice.

Johnathan dropped her and braced himself. Tamara scrambled to her feet with a sibilant hiss. Her face twisted in a mask of disgust. "A demon,

Victor? Really?" She bared her pointed teeth. "You've betrayed us all." She seethed, hands curled against her sides.

"Tamara, wait—" Vic reached for her, but she was already moving. Her fist drove up toward Johnathan's jaw, and he let it. The impact made him skid back a step, a blossom of fiery pain that numbed and faded in seconds. She might have made a second attack if Vic hadn't put himself between them.

"He is not our enemy," Vic roared. He'd dropped into a defensive position, ready to fight for Johnathan with his life. "Merry, why—"

"You brought the Society to our door," another vampire interrupted. "A demon into our sanctuary."

The werewolf's patience snapped. Beatrice transformed, shredding her brilliant orange gown. A single barking call signaled the rest of her pack to follow suit, the ballroom littered with strips of finery. The wolves circled Vic. Johnathan stepped to his side, smoke pouring from his mouth. In the sharp relief of the lit room, he looked every inch the hell spawn.

"Beatrice, this does not have to end in violence," Katherine begged, resignation in her voice.

"Yes, it does," sneered Tamara. The vampiress flanked the wolves, but there was a pause, as if waiting for permission. Johnathan glanced at their host, standing passive amid the immortals.

"Take them down," said Merry. Their voice rolled through the room like the slam of a judge's gavel. Vic flinched.

"Try not to kill anyone. Believe it or not, these are our allies," Vic muttered to him. Johnathan wanted to call him mad, since the others clearly intended to snuff them out, but he didn't want to kill them either.

Chaos erupted, a flurry of furred bodies and snarling vampires. Johnathan slammed into Beatrice before she could tackle Vic. She staggered, attempting to shake off the blow. The rest of her pack closed in. A rumble rose in his chest. The demonic sound startled a couple of wolves. Johnathan became a whirling dervish, using his size and strength to drive some back or knock them away. He tried to avoid the use of his teeth, his instincts singing for split blood. But the man was in control and despite his lethal form, he managed to keep bloodshed to a minimum.

Katherine helped them where she could, driving several foes to the ground with an aura of ice. Her aid might have given them an upper hand when she gasped and vanished. Johnathan didn't have time to wonder what happened to her with the werewolves piling on him.

Vic engaged Tamara. Though the other vampire was older he appeared to be holding his own. A situation that was about to shift when Alazar flanked him. Johnathan downed the last wolf and charged Alazar. Bloodlust rode him hard. The vampire spun to meet him at the last moment, clawing at Johnathan's sides, attempting to gain purchase in the sleek fur. Alazar hit the floor with a shout, his usual sneer replaced by a touch of fear.

Johnathan wanted to tear his throat out. He balanced on the edge, his control frayed to breaking. Vic told him not to kill anyone. They were still under threat, surrounded by danger, but he knew if he tore Alazar's head from his body, it would be the end for Vic. Johnathan backed off the vampire's chest.

Alazar's dark eyes flashed with disbelief. There wasn't time to congratulate himself on not murdering the arrogant bastard. The pack swarmed Johnathan, finally catching on to the fact he'd abstained from killing them. Their teeth nipped at his flank, at his shoulder, tore at the muscles. Another vampire rushed in. They were about to be overwhelmed. Johnathan looked over to find Vic on his knees, hands restrained behind his back by the smiling ghoul. Blood smeared his face from where Tamara slashed him, the wounds already closed. She appeared in front of Johnathan, the vengeful goddess. The wolves corralled him. There was nowhere for Johnathan to go to avoid the hammer of her fists but down. His paws lost purchase on the polished floor.

His apparent collapse emboldened the other guests. Blows assaulted him, but they weren't enough to knock him out. Katherine reappeared at the edge of the group, her expression immeasurably sad. Her body flickered forward, closer in a blink. The other creatures fell back at her approach. She leaned over his prone form; her hand extended to him.

Johnathan didn't want her to touch him. He desperately needed her to touch him. A soft whine escaped him. He needed her to knock him out. Her gaze snapped to his face, conflicted. It was a mercy when she finally drove her hand through his chest. The cold sapped his strength. The brush of her fingers sent him tumbling into darkness.

CHAPTER TWENTY-ONE

JOHNATHAN OPENED HIS EYES, STUNNED TO BE ALIVE. HIS BODY WAS A dull mess of pain. At some point he'd regained his human form. Rough stone abraded his bare back. He turned his head, regretting it at the jolt of pain, though he recognized where he was.

They'd thrown him into the basement. He wasn't alone, though it wasn't the company he expected. Katherine and Alazar kept vigil outside his cell.

Aware of his nudity, but unable to sit up, he covered himself with his hands. Even that small lift was a struggle for his aching arms. He wondered how long he'd been knocked out, an odd sensation after not sleeping for weeks. There were no dreams, and the missing chunk of time between the fiasco in the ballroom to waking in the cell left him unsettled.

Johnathan licked his lips, desperate for a drink of water, though he doubted Alazar would acquiesce to give him anything. "Where's Vic?" He refused to believe the man was anything other than alive.

"Trying to convince the others to let you live," Katherine answered. She clasped her hands in front of her gauzy skirts, her jaw clenched. Johnathan wondered if she was angry with him or Alazar. He said nothing to her statement. There was nothing to say. He'd spent days among these creatures without incident, but he'd seen the loathing in their faces.

"You'll say nothing to defend yourself, demon?" Alazar's tone lacked its usual venom. He stood with his arms folded, wearing his uniform robes.

The idea was laughable. Johnathan couldn't sway centuries of hatred. "Don't kill him," he rasped. He didn't expect to survive the day. The night? There were no windows in the basement level. Another thought occurred to him. "Did the ritual work? Is the barrier strengthened?"

Katherine stepped closer. "It did. Not that it matters—"

"They're gone. The Scarlet Sister cleared out her army," said Alazar. Johnathan's skin prickled in the chill air. There was no way Sister Wilhem would give up. An overarching sense of manipulation rankled him. As Vic would say, this was a grand joke.

His jaw clenched. Would Alazar believe him if he told them of their host's betrayal? He'd given Merry the benefit of the doubt despite the nagging details. Vic believed Merry would never betray him, and in truth, they hadn't. Had Merry come to see him while he lay in this cell, unconscious? What did they promise Sister Wilhem?

Katherine watched him. "Awfully convenient, isn't it?"

"It's bloody impossible," snapped Alazar. "Those heretics would never leave without their prize."

Johnathan's head lolled to the side to peer at the vampire. "Two possible prizes." There it was, a possible explanation, plausible if their host was that great a coward. Alazar's nostrils flared.

"Our illustrious host is overseeing the proceedings," he informed Johnathan. "They are calling for mercy."

That was a surprise. His mercy? Or Vic's? What game was Merry playing?

Alazar interrupted his thoughts. "In the millennia I've walked this earth, I've encountered a few demons. Never seen one that tempered their violence." His imperious stare seemed to press Johnathan into the stones. The vampire spun away, black robes flapping behind him as he ascended the stairs.

Johnathan turned his head to look at Katherine. "Has he always been that dramatic?"

"He was born royalty," she said, settling on the floor outside his cell in a spread of skirts.

"I suppose that makes sense then." Johnathan shifted his bulk, trying to ease the pinch of his muscles, keenly aware of Katherine's proximity. "I don't suppose you brought a pair of trousers with you?"

A tearing sound drew his attention. Katherine ripped a sizable portion from the bottom of her skirt, passing the cloth to him through the bars. "Sorry it's cold."

"I'm surprised you are able to do that," he said.

"The skirts are real," she said. "I have to concentrate to take them with me when I vanish."

An icy rag was better than nothing. Johnathan sat up with a groan, draping the cloth around his privates. He sat with his hands on his knees, observing his guard.

"Did you know what Merry had planned?"

Katherine's face crumpled. She shook her head. "No, John, I swear I didn't." There was a spark of anger in her gaze.

"What happened to you?" Johnathan tried to bend his neck, wincing at the pain. "You vanished mid-fight."

Her anger flared. "I was dispersed. It took me time to rebuild my body," she said. "I made it back in time to put you down."

"Thank you," said Johnathan. If she hadn't knocked him out, he would probably be dead. They sat in silence, before the weight of it became too much for him to bear.

"You hate demons, too." It wasn't a question. He remembered the distant conversation between her and Merry while Johnathan rested on the grass.

"I don't hate you," she said softly.

He nodded, grateful she'd stayed with him. "But you do hate them."

Katherine smoothed the remains of her skirts over her bared calves. "Did Victor tell you how I died?"

Johnathan shook his head. "Not if it was your story to tell."

She smiled. "He always had impeccable manners," she said. Her dark gaze caught him. "I died in the arms of the man I loved. He happened to be the demon that killed me."

Her words dropped through him like a stone. "Was he like me?"

"A Hound? No." she shook her head. "I don't think the gathered assembly understands how rare and unusual Hellhounds are outside the Nether." A dozen questions sprang to Johnathan's lips. Katherine sighed. "He was an incubus. The feeders are the ones you're most likely to find topside. They slip through the cracks, able to maintain an anchor in our world through draining human essence."

"They don't have to kill for that," said Johnathan. Hesper survived without killing. He wished he had a chance to speak with the succubus more, wondering if she'd managed to slip away before the Society retreated.

"And he didn't. He was so careful with me," said Katherine, her expression bitter. "We are such jealous creatures. I thought I could sustain him alone. But humans are not made to mix with the Nether or the Benign."

A lesson Johnathan knew too well. "What happened to him?"

A terrible expression crossed her face. "It destroyed him," she whispered. "He tried to reverse it, feeding his energy into my corpse until he lost his hold on our realm. I watched him fade, trapped between life and death, unable to tell him to stop." Her dark gaze glinted with unshed tears. "Demons love as fiercely as humans, but they are also ruled by instincts they cannot avoid."

Johnathan wanted to deny he would ever hurt Vic, difficult when Johnathan's very presence might get them both executed by the allies he'd hoped would help them. He did know Vic's death would destroy him. "I don't want to hurt Vic," Johnathan confessed.

"You won't," said Katherine. "Hounds are not like feeders. They are the servants, the trackers, and the guardians of the Nether. Beings that other demons fear."

Their companionable silence resumed, though the dread impending death spun through his head. He craved distraction. "Do you know how they will kill me?" He suspected the Geist would play his executioner as well, since her touch was so effective against him.

Katherine's brow rose. "So certain of your demise. You have more allies than you know."

He'd considered Merry an ally. Their betrayal stung more than anything else. "What do you think will be the outcome?"

Her eyes flashed. "They won't kill you, but they won't let you stay."

His thoughts turned over. "Would they let Vic stay if I left?"

Her jaw clenched. "Yes, but he won't."

No, he wouldn't. And with the Society's mysterious retreat, a very troubling possibility emerged. Footsteps sounded on the stairs, derailing their conversation. Johnathan's relief was palpable when Vic appeared, looking a bit haggard around the edges, but alive. He carried a bundle of clothes in his arms, his expression resigned as he came to stop outside Johnathan's cell.

Johnathan managed to stand, gathering the cloth around his privates for modesty's sake. "What is their decision?"

A quiet rage burned in Vic's gaze. "We're being banished."

Once Johnathan dressed himself, he and Vic were escorted to the edge of the barrier by Katherine. The grand hallways of the Estate held a brittle allure to Johnathan, suspiciously empty as they headed for the front entrance. Their host was notably absent, but to his surprise, Alazar waited for them at the edge of the property, where the barrier continued to reflect the empty woods. Johnathan wondered if the reports of the Society's retreat had been exaggerated, leaving them to walk into an ambush. Apprehension stirred the Hound's instincts but the smoldering core inside him was quiet, exhausted by the events of the previous day.

Vic spent nearly six hours arguing for their lives. Frustratingly, he wouldn't share the details of that debate with Johnathan, not yet, but it clearly weighed on him. How many of Vic's supposed allies, beings he'd known for centuries, called for his death? Johnathan wished he could bear the hurt for him.

Alazar greeted them with a curt nod. "I wish you would stay, Victor.

What you told me seems much more plausible today than it did yesterday."

Johnathan could hear Vic's teeth grinding. "Watch your back, Alazar."

The other vampire's gaze slid to Johnathan. "You've given me much to think about. So I will give you fair warning. Tamara left our sanctuary early this morning. She does not yet know the verdict we reached here today, but she may hunt you when she does." He bowed his head.

Johnathan wasn't sure how to respond. He didn't like Alazar, and was certain the vampire hated him, but he'd taken the time to see them off. "Thank you for the warning."

The vampire headed back to the house, pausing to clap Vic on the shoulder. Only Katherine remained, her expression troubled.

"This doesn't feel right," she said. She glared at the house. "You are the one who needs sanctuary. How could they be so stupid?"

Vic leaned in to kiss her cheek. "They need you in there. You're the most level-headed of the lot. Make them work together, Katherine. The threat is still growing."

She nodded, turning to Johnathan. "Guard him well, John."

"Be careful, Katherine," he said. He hadn't known the Geist long, but he hoped to see her again. Johnathan cast the Estate one final bittersweet glance, taking Vic's hand. Stepping through the barrier was akin to walking through a waterfall, leaving a tingling buzz on his skin.

No ambush waited from them. The emptied woods were alive with the sounds of animals going about their business.

"There's a town about five miles upriver," said Vic. "We'll head there first before we secure transportation."

Where would they go? It wouldn't be long before Sister Wilhem and her henchman, Luthor, picked up on their trail once more. Johnathan stifled the line of questioning. Guilt dragged on him, though he knew he didn't bear the full responsibility for the shift of their fortunes. There was no time to discuss Merry's heel turn since he'd been separated from Vic during their 'trial'. They were still too close to the Estate for Johnathan's comfort, though he wondered if Merry observed their departure.

The silence between them was loaded with unspoken questions and a sour tension that made Johnathan restless. He wanted to soothe the hurt and sadness in Vic's gaze, humbled by the knowledge that Vic had once again chosen him.

"We could continue upriver. Try a passenger vessel this time," he said. Vic squeezed his fingers but said nothing. Johnathan ducked his head, gaze fixed on the bracken strewn ground. They'd only been in the Estate for a couple weeks, but the trees outside were considerably bare, hinting at the oncoming winter. After several minutes of that unbearable silence, Johnathan decided he'd settle for awkward conversation over nothing.

"Rather astonished Alazar came to send us off," he said.

"He voted to spare your life." Vic's mouth tightened to a thin line. The conversational gulf widened.

Johnathan tried again. "Hopefully Katherine will be able to keep them—"

Vic stopped, gripping Johnathan's wrists, thumbs pressing lightly into his palms. "I can't do this right now, John. Give me time."

A petulant part of him wanted to push the conversation, but he couldn't ignore the request. Guilt sank its hooks into his skin, tugging at him. He followed behind Vic in sullen silence until the township came into view. A far cry from the constant bustle of a proper city, this was one of the largest settlements they'd managed to visit yet, complete with a central hub of multiple avenues, with lit street lamps to push against the oncoming dark. The far side of quaint, it was just busy enough that two gentlemen traipsing out of the woods didn't garner too much notice. Though they were overdressed compared to most of the citizens they passed by, particularly Vic in his disheveled evening wear.

Ignoring the town's sizable hotel, Vic led the way into the more industry-oriented side of town. The plain buildings rose on either side of them, constructed sentinels that eventually gave way to a modest neighborhood of row houses, most of the apartments already dark, their tenants sleeping for work that started at dawn. Their location puzzled Johnathan, but his mouth remained shut. Intent, Vic approached one of the apartments, removing a hitherto unknown key that he used to unlock the door.

He didn't bother with a light source, slumping into a chair not far from the door. Johnathan could see well enough not to bother but habit led him to fumble through the apartment's miniscule kitchen until he produced a pair of fat candles and a match box. The sallow flames crackled through a layer of dust, doing little to illuminate the dark room, but the light was a small human comfort. He placed one of the candles on the table beside the brooding vampire and knelt on the floor. Touching their foreheads together was becoming a ritual gesture between them. Johnathan inhaled Vic's scent, needing to assure himself after their separation.

The contact lessened the strain in Vic's features. They stayed like that, soaking in one another's presence, until Vic released a shaky sigh.

"Talk to me, John."

The first words out of his mouth were the wrong words. "I'm sorry I got us banished."

Vic reared back just enough to smack his head into Johnathan's. "Idiot."

"Ow," said Johnathan. He began to pull away when Vic grabbed him, holding him still for a kiss that kindled the fiery core in his chest. The candle cracked and spat. Legs still weak, Johnathan tipped off balance, held up by Vic's embrace.

It was Vic who broke the kiss first. "You didn't get us banished. I took you to the Estate for answers. To find hope." A broken laugh spilled from his swollen lips. "What a mess we're in."

Johnathan ran his thumb along Vic's jaw. "We found some answers," he said. The next words made him hesitate, not because he didn't think Vic wouldn't believe him, but because there were still holes in his theory. "Merry drugged my wine."

"I know," said Vic, anger flickering in his grey gaze. "They told me they did."

The audacity of it left Johnathan flabbergasted. "Why? Why do any of this?"

His companion ran a hand through his hair. "I don't know. None of this fits the person I knew." He gestured to the apartment. "They provided this, a safe space to recuperate."

That made him uneasy. Did Vic really know the person Merry had become? They spent seven years together, but fear and anger changed a person. It ate away at the good pieces, until their edges were unrecognizable. Merry had a lot of rage. He doubted Vic realized how much his former paramour carried in their heart.

Johnathan found it odd that Merry didn't seem to know about Francoise or the spy's impact on Vic's life. Or a dozen other small things Vic shared with him. He'd already admitted to Johnathan there was never real love between them. Why had Merry provided this apartment when they'd been instrumental in evicting Johnathan from their sanctuary?

Whatever Merry's true motivations, they no longer had the protections of the Estate. "Where will we go?"

There was a shuttered expression on Vic's face. "I don't know," he said. His allies had turned on him. His sanctuary was lost. There was a target on his back. His features were sharpened by anger and hunger. He wiped his face. "There's a parcel of supplies waiting for me at the post office. I'll head there in the morning, see if anything can be salvaged."

That would be one less problem hanging over them. The rest they would figure out, together. "Why don't you get some rest? I'll see to it no one bursts through the door." Johnathan didn't trust a single gift from their former treacherous host.

Lack of blood and the exertion of the fight left Vic more than ready for rest. He collapsed on the bed in a cloud of dust, too tired to care about the state of his clothes. Johnathan watched him sleep, his senses tuned for the slightest change in the air. The hours stretched long through the night.

During the late hours, long before dawn, Johnathan straightened, catching a scent of honey and sex, gone before he could get a lock on it. He opened the door, searching for the succubus's outline in the shadows, but her scent had vanished. Convinced he'd imagined it, he settled back into Vic's vacated chair, watching the candle wick burn.

CHAPTER TWENTY-TWO

THE PACING BEGAN BEFORE THE SUN ROSE. VIC TOSSED OFTEN IN HIS sleep. Eyelids darting, his body tensed in the grip of some nightmare or another. Once he woke with a start, gasping while his frantic gaze sought out Johnathan.

He'd joined Vic in the bed shortly after, soothing the worst of whatever plagued his partner's dreams by holding him close. There was an acrid touch to Vic's scent that worried Johnathan, a sour note in normally delectable citrus and musk. It was something he'd belatedly registered when they left the Estate, Vic lost in the troubling spiral of his thoughts. Though Johnathan didn't know how to help Vic through this morass of twisted emotions, he could hold him while he slept, safe and secure in Johnathan's arms.

Those moments, in the quiet pauses between his sleeping partner's breaths, Johnathan allowed himself to accept the depth of feeling he had for Vic. How deeply he'd come to love him. It wasn't an epiphany, but it still shook him. Their recent brush with death made Johnathan wish he could rewind time to the moment on the train, laughing and teasing one another. Before Sister Wilhem invaded their lives.

Vic woke close to dawn, unable to stay still in Johnathan's hold. He rolled from the bed, pacing the narrow space, twitching at small noises.

Johnathan recognized those signs, having seen them often in with the vampire who raised him, and the ones he later hunted.

"Maybe I should retrieve your parcel alone," said Johnathan. He'd meant to lead with a suggestion, but tact was never his strong point. The skin around Vic's eyes pinched tight. He glanced about their humble lodgings, gaze never settling. If he'd been seated, his legs would be jogging in place. He could tell the vampire wanted to deny the wisdom of such a statement, but Vic knew himself better than that.

His shoulders slumped in resignation. "If it's spoiled, I may need you to accompany me later until I locate a donor," he admitted.

"I could distract you," Johnathan offered, with a suggestive waggle of his eyebrows. He managed to elicit a smile from Vic, but the man shook his head.

"Delightful as that offer is, I'm afraid I must decline, my love," he said, though he wouldn't explain why. Johnathan worried he'd done something to cause a rift between them but when Vic finally sat in the chair, he could see the lines of strain etched on his face.

"You're worse off than I expected," said Johnathan. "What did I miss?"

Vic hesitated. "I didn't stop resisting after Katherine knocked you out." He cleared his throat. "To my detriment."

He'd been injured worse than what Vic witnessed, badly if his reluctance to talk about it was anything to go by.

Johnathan didn't want to leave Vic at all, but the post would open soon, and the sooner he grabbed the kit the better. "I won't be long."

In the light of day, the warehouses they'd passed bustled with activity, the packing, storing, and shipping of goods to their new destinations. This was an in-between town, the stop over to larger grander destination, but the streets were neatly lined. Many of the new buildings still possessed the sap rich scent of cut lumber. The aroma of food made Johnathan's stomach growl, realizing he hadn't eaten more than a scant heel of stale bread before he left his cell. They both needed to attain nourishment today, shore themselves up for whatever trials lay ahead.

A stroke of good fortune meant a quiet morning at the post. Johnathan gave Vic's name to the clerk, tucking the brown parcel under his arm. The errand took him less than half an hour. He headed back toward their lodgings at a steady jog.

Rosewater and smoke caressed his senses. Johnathan skidded to a halt in the middle of the packing houses. It couldn't be. Why would Merry follow them here? He thought he might have imagined it if not for the hooded figure darting away at the edge of his vision. Johnathan gave chase before his sense of logic caught up to him.

Merry's presence meant nothing good. His steps slowed, the scent leading him to the ominous darkened entrance of a warehouse. Since his experiences with similar establishments were less than stellar, he decided to avoid prancing into an obvious trap. He began to back away until Merry's familiar voice snared him.

"You truly are too intelligent for your own good," said Merry. Their voice did not come from the interior of the doorway. Johnathan turned, startled to find them directly behind him. Merry held up their hand, blowing a silvery powder into his face.

Johnathan staggered back, his lungs seizing. The parcel fell to the ground. He clutched at his throat, choking as if he'd swallowed a thousand tiny blades. Blood bubbled to his lips in a pinkish foam. He collapsed to his knees on the ground, unable to pull air into his lungs. The smoldering core in his chest flickered, unable to form a spark. Merry watched his struggle with a detached gaze.

When it was clear he was incapable of retaliating, Merry withdrew a length of silver chain from the folds of their dress. It hurt to look at it, the metal overly bright to his gaze. Johnathan wanted to flee, to scream, or give voice to a thousand curses, choking on blood and spittle as Merry wrapped the chain around his wrists. The silver seared his exposed flesh, burning through his clothes.

"Your kind don't have many weaknesses," said Merry, their tone conversational as they circled Johnathan, looping the chain around his bare neck. He gagged, his bound hands pulling the chain taut when he tried to scrabble at the horrid collar. "You'll eject the silver powder from your lungs eventually, but to fulfill my part of the arrangement, I need to incapacitate you as long as possible."

Panic drove him up to his knees. He retched a mouthful of silverspecked blood, hatred boiling in his gaze. Merry's gaze flickered, a flash of regret and pain, but they scooped up the broken parcel from the ground, wagging it in Johnathan's face. "I will ensure Vic receives this."

Johnathan couldn't respond, jerking against his restraints. Merry bit their lip, their resolve wavering.

"You aren't the only one who loves Victor," they whispered, clutching their fist to their chest. "I gave him years of my life. My affections, my time, *my blood*, but it wasn't enough to keep him by my side. I wasn't enough." Tears welled in their eyes. "We are never enough for them. No matter how unique, how *blessed*." They spat the word. "No matter how much we give. No matter how much we sacrifice. I am nothing but a tool they use to power their sanctuary. To read their futures. But the Benign are worse than any callous immortal."

A frantic energy entered their gaze. "The Society will take one of us. I cannot endure their torture, John, I won't. I won't become their vessel." They crouched down in front of him, slipping a vial into their bloodied fingers. "But they can't have Vic either." They pressed a kiss to Johnathan's forehead. "I'm sorry," Merry sobbed, a broken sound lost on unsympathetic ears.

Johnathan was alone, drowning in silver, bound in burning chains. In the distance, he heard the high-pitched chiming of the Herald.

CHAPTER TWENTY-THREE

JOHNATHAN THRASHED ON THE GROUND. THOUGH THE BUILDINGS around him crawled with humans at work, Merry managed to lure him to a remote corner. No one came at the sound of his struggles. He lay on his side, a steady stream of blood pouring from his mouth as the silver powder expelled itself from his lungs. The Society was coming for Vic.

Resolve weakened by hunger, he feared what Vic would do to stop himself from tipping over that ledge. Would the sight of blood make him freeze up again? His struggles renewed, a helpless anger welling inside him. The vial slid through his numb fingers, rolling away. The silver branded his skin, a poisonous unending slice across his raw nerves.

Time trickled to a standstill. Seeped in agony, he didn't know if he lay there for minutes or hours, aside from the shift of daylight overhead. The scent of honey and sex teased his ravaged nose. Relief surged through him. Hesper had found him.

Her brown feet padded across the dirt as she approached him. They paused at the puddle of silver-laced blood. That honeyed scent wafted over him as she ruffled her skirts, bending over him.

Hesper hissed. The silver burned her fingers, but she kept picking at the chain until she dislodged it from around his neck. Johnathan groaned when she unwound it from his wrists, cut deep from his struggles. The last piece peeled away from his ruined flesh. She tossed the chain away, her somber red gaze peering down at him.

"Come on, Johnathan, push it out of your system."

She kept vigil over him during those perilous long moments it took for his body to start healing.

Johnathan swallowed painfully; his throat still shredded by the silver powder. "You came for me," he rasped.

Hesper nibbled on her lip. "I'm sorry it took so long. I was enjoying the company of a very robust gentleman," she confessed.

Johnathan rolled to his side, searching the area for any trace of his betrayer. "Did you see Merry?"

"I missed them," she said, her demeanor contrite. "What will you do, Hound? The Scarlet Sister has taken your vampire."

He closed his eyes. His mind screamed at him for action but his body needed a few minutes to recover. "You saw?"

Hesper shivered. "There were so many of them, Johnathan. The Scarlet Sister possessed the Herald. It rang through the streets, the chime of victory."

Frowning, he gingerly rubbed his throat. "How do you know what a Herald is? Isn't it one of the Society's machines?" He only knew the term from Merry's Sight-spun visions.

The succubus shook her head, hugging her knees. "It's not a machine, it's a Favor, bestowed by the Benign to their chosen followers. If the Benign are exerting that much influence over this realm, nowhere and no one is safe." Her eyes were haunted. "They dragged him into the streets in a golden net, burning his beautiful skin. They will use the Herald to break him."

The implications swept through him. Johnathan snatched the cursed vial off the ground and stumbled to his feet.

"Where are you going?" Hesper hiked up her skirts, trotting after him.

"I have to stop them," said Johnathan, his tone curt. He paused, unable to ignore good manners. "Thank you for your aid." There were dozens of questions he wanted to ask her, but panic sang in his veins. He needed to get to Vic.

Hesper grabbed his wrists, slowing him down a step. "Whoa, what do you mean you have to stop them? You're a single demon. Not even a Hound can withstand an embodied Benign. We need to run."

"I won't run." Johnathan gently extricated himself from her grip. "I love him."

Pain filled her gaze. "Then you'll die," she said. "Is this worth dying forth?"

"Madam, I assure you it is," said Johnathan, resuming his run to the apartment.

"But he's your anchor," she sputtered, keeping pace at his side.

Was this a taboo among demons he wasn't aware of? Johnathan didn't care. His pulse tripped when he saw the broken door. He knew what he would find, and it still filled him with rage. He burst into the empty apartment, Vic's scent tangled with a multitude of others, faded enough to indicate Johnathan had been out of commission for hours. He needed to pick up their trail, but the rigors of the last few days had taken their toll.

The vial was still clenched in his fist. Merry's final bittersweet gift. He put his anger for the treacherous seer aside, popping the cork with his thumb.

Hesper's nose wrinkled. "Tell me that is not the poison draught," she hissed.

"My senses are better as a Hound. I need to transform," he said.

She seized his shoulders, giving him a shake. "Are you mad? You can't shade walk in broad daylight! A Hellhound racing through the streets will have every hunter on the eastern seaboard breathing down your neck."

Not that it mattered since there was a strong possibility he wouldn't survive this encounter. "Take care, Hesper." He lifted the vial to his mouth, when her hand closed over the top.

"I can't let you do this alone," she said, her voice soft. Her nostrils flared. "I think...I think between the two of us, we can shade walk until we're close. But I'm not a fighter."

The succubus was already shaking in fear, but still willing to put herself on the line to help him. "Whatever aid you can give, I am grateful," said Johnathan, and meant it. She was the last person he'd expected to see at the ninth hour, but he wouldn't turn her help away. He downed the contents of the vial, bitter ash and wine blooming on his tongue.

The change wasn't any less painful, but somehow smoother, easier. Maybe his body had become more practiced in reshaping itself each time he became the Hound. Using the draught left him with the usual woozy sensation. Slightly unsteady, Johnathan shook himself, looking at the succubus expectantly.

Hesper appeared somewhat horrified by the means of his transformation, sniffing at the empty vial. "You've got to stop using this shit, Hound." She shook her head and slid onto his back.

Johnathan barely registered her weight, though he was surprised by her comfort with his form. She lay down along the length of his spine, careful of his healing wounds when she wrapped her arms around his neck.

"Shade walking during the day is different from night. You might find it disorienting," she said. "When I pull, follow me."

A tugging sensation throbbed through his bones. He heard her exhale and the world shifted. If was as if they'd entered another plane. Sounds were distorted, wavering nonsensical echoes impossible to decipher. The world around them shared a similar dissonance, as if he viewed everything through warped glass. There weren't enough shadows to hide them so Hesper had created her own null space.

His sense of smell, however, functioned perfectly. Johnathan locked onto Vic's fading scent. He would find his lover. With the succubus clinging to his back, he took off, running full tilt to whatever fate awaited him.

The scent trail led him out of the town proper, the denser clusters of buildings giving way to farmland, notable structures more isolated among the fields and fallow. The coppery taint of blood threaded Vic's scent, punctuated by sweet floral notes that made Johnathan's lips curl in a silent snarl.

If they'd used the golden net, his wounds wouldn't heal quickly without help. Johnathan poured on more speed. Fire flickered through his muscles, a welcome flame, fed by the molten center inside him. His claws tore into the ground, leaving sizzling grooves that would no doubt bewilder any passerby. Hesper hummed against his neck, an unrecognizable song though the chord sank into his bones, seeming to soothe the lingering ache of his transformation. There was a familiarity to her song, though he couldn't fathom where he'd heard it before.

Vic's scent thickened, tangled with half a dozen others, sweat, gunpowder, leather, coupled by the burnt air odor of lightning and an oddly potent metal. The only structure for miles was single farm, a low humble house accompanied by a handful of sheds, coops, and a large barn, easily big enough to hide a small contingent of Society Agents. The doors were firmly closed but this was the unmistakable end of the trail.

Johnathan's steps slowed as he drew close, debating how he would enter the building when the succubus gave his neck a pat. Hesper slid off him, snapping the world into sharp focus. The sun was still high in the sky, the air a chill lick against his steaming coat. Hesper grasped the large barn doors, her face scrunched in concentration to avoid setting off any squealing hinges. She eased them open wide enough for a Hellhound to enter.

"Try not to die," she whispered. Hesper gave Johnathan a final nod and sank into the natural shadows within the barn. Nudging the width of his shoulders through the open down, Johnathan braced himself.

It was not enough. Blood tinged the air, it pressed against his senses, a whisper of retribution. A half a dozen Agents circled a central trio, a much smaller number than Johnathan anticipated fighting, but when he focused on the center of the room, his control frayed to nothing against a wave of blind rage.

The Scarlet Sister held the Herald aloft, the soft chiming a mocking accompaniment to the grim tableau. Vic hung from a chain draped over one of the ceiling rafters, clothes soaked in blood despite the lack of open wounds on his stark white skin. The insidious Luthor stood nearby, a bloodied gold chain wrapped around his gloved knuckles.

"One word, and this stops," Sister Wilhem crooned, "The Divine Kushiel waits for you beyond the veil. Let him in and your pain will end."

The name sent a shot of dread through Johnathan. It held a faint ring of familiarity, as if engrained in his mind.

Vic raised his head to glare at her, his face white from blood loss. "Why do you want this? They will kill all of you."

Wilhem sighed. "Do you not see the destructive path of humanity, fiend? Wars? Famine? Disease? Even now, conflict stirs in the belly of this country. It draws the Nether and the Benign ever closer." The Herald pulsed in her grip. "A convergence is coming, a joining of the realms. And we've helped it along."

He stared at her in disbelief. "That would kill everyone."

"Not everyone," said Wilhem, tilting her head. "Not their chosen. But this is necessary, a new world order for humanity." A fanatical light gleamed in her eyes. "You shall be the catalyst for our vision. Not with the brute force of demons, but the mercy of angels." Her smile was serene.

"No," said Vic.

Her smile faded a touch, her gaze cold. "Then we shall continue to convince you," she said, her tone reasonable. She nodded to Luthor.

The Agent pressed the gold to Vic's face. His reaction wasn't immediate. The muscles of his neck strained when the metal began to burn him.

Johnathan's snarl startled the other Agents. They spun to meet him, weapons raised.

A potent mix of hope and fear shone in Vic's face, his grey eyes beacons in his gaunt face.

Luthor's expression was one of anticipation, but the Sister appeared irritated by his appearance.

"It appears our agreement has fallen through," she said. "Do not let the beast interfere."

Her order spurred the others into action. The Agents attacked in tandem. Johnathan launched at the nearest man. The thunderous boom of their close-range pistols temporarily deafened Johnathan, accompanied by the sting of bullets glancing off his flank. It failed to slow him down. He tore out the first Agent's throat without a flare of remorse. Johnathan felt nothing as he methodically tore through the Sister's minions. These men were a threat, and he would eliminate them with prejudice. Later, if he survived, perhaps he would mourn the waste of their lives.

The Society certainly wouldn't.

The final Agent fell in a quivering mass, bleeding out from the ragged wound in his shoulder. Smoke poured out of Johnathan's mouth as approached the trio. Luthor turned slightly, face lit with excitement.

"Johnathan, stop!" Vic cried out

He froze, the warning enforced by the buzz of his instincts. Luthor hissed, slicing a hidden silver blade across Vic's face in retaliation. The wound closed in seconds. A growl rumbled in Johnathan's chest, but he didn't move, waiting for Luthor to give him an opening.

The Sister burst out laughing. "Oh, but this is a marvelous development. We didn't think it was possible to combine our efforts."

Vic's head snapped up, his gaze flickering between Johnathan and the Sister in panic. "Keep your filthy hands off of him." He gasped the words, yanking on his restraints.

Sister Wilhem raised the Herald. "I can sense the link between you. Somehow you are this demon's master. This must be the blessing of Kushiel."

"Kushiel," said Vic, with a hint of recognition.

The Sister drew closer, lifting a hand to stroke the side of Vic's face. "Do you not understand the boon you have been given, my dear vessel? Twice, you have caught their eye. Twice, you've been blessed. A Hellhound that will guard you until death. He will stay by your side while Kushiel rides your body, ending every threat until we achieve our dream."

Horror dawned across Vic's face. He slumped in the chains. A tear slid down his cheek. Wilhem's words broke something inside him. Johnathan circled the group, needing to tear her throat out.

In the short course of their relationship, Vic never once made him feel as if there were a master and servant dynamic between them.

Cernunnos demanded dominance, subsuming the will of the Hellhounds he made. A command that sank hooks into him, unable to deny the call of the arch demon.

Would Kushiel be able to enact his will over Johnathan if Vic let him in? Sister Wilhem believed Kushiel would wield him like a mindless tool.

The golden weapons were taking their toll on Vic. He could see the vulnerability in the face of the man he loved. A weakness that could be exploited. The Herald's chiming pitched higher, an insistent whine that grated on his ears.

Sister Wilhem gasped, her expression radiant. "Kushiel comes." The taste of storms thickened the air around them.

Hesper's warning rang in his mind. He had to free Vic before the Benign appeared. Johnathan believed Vic would resist the angel, he had to, because if Vic gave permission, they would all die. The Hound's form gave him a combat advantage, but he cursed the loss of his voice. Silently he begged Vic to hold on. They had saved one another's lives. The heat between them, the connection, was one they forged through trial and pain. Their relationship was more than a blessing or a manipulation of the divine, and he would do everything in his power to prove it.

Johnathan took a step forward, a rumble of sound rolling from his chest. Luthor stalked toward him. The silver knife was a burr to his senses, but he knew he had to go through the Agent to get to Vic. The chiming increased, a discordant sound that made his back teeth ache. The Sister spread her arms, the Herald hovering without support in front of her.

His frustration mounted. Vic was despondent, seemingly unaware of the approaching Benign. Johnathan feared the Sister would manipulate him in such a state, but could not take his attention from Luthor. The Agent vanished, reappearing on Johnathan's flank with an arcing slash of the silver knife. A burning line of pain opened across his hind leg. Johnathan snarled, falling into a whirling, deadly dance. The Hound's superior strength and size were undermined by the Agent's agility. Luthor left a dozen cuts before Johnathan managed to graze him with his teeth.

Unable to get the upper hand, he tried to break away to save Vic.

Luthor sank the blade deep in his back. Johnathan's howl of pain made Vic look up, snapping out of the malaise. The Agent yanked the blade free, preparing to strike again.

"John." He yanked at his chains, the metal straining. If he hadn't given permission, why did the Benign draw closer? Or did the Sister believe she could still break Vic?

Wilhem stepped closer, guiding the Herald to Vic, who shied away from it, wide eyed. "Let him in," said the Sister.

The air beside them shimmered. Hesper appeared, wide eyed and frantic. She seized the Herald and smashed it on the floor. The chiming faltered, the pressure destabilizing. Sister Wilhem screamed her denial.

"Kill them, John!" The succubus went for Vic's chains, adding enough strength to break them. Luthor sneered, pulling back his arm, a blade pinched between his fingers. Johnathan recognized the tilt of his wrist, a throw he'd practiced many times. He snapped forward, clamping on the man's wrist in a bone crushing hold. Luthor yelped, dropping the silver blade as he scrabbled at Johnathan's jaw. Hesper freed Vic's other arm, supporting his weight when his legs buckled.

"No. NO!" Sister Wilhem cried. "Don't leave, Kushiel. Come! I invite you in."

The four of them froze. Even Luthor, his pained expression incredulous. Hesper blanched, frantically dragging Vic away from the Sister.

The pressure of the air increased, an electric crackle that strummed along every single nerve. Johnathan released the Agent from his bite, but Luthor didn't retaliate, cradling his mauled wrist as he backed toward the entrance.

The air moved, an unseen presence writhing around Sister Wilhem. Her body jerked, a blissful expression on her face as it slowly sank into her skin. Her pale milk eyes clouded, tinged a startling blue by the being riding her body. It looked about the room. A sneer curled her lips at the sight of Hesper holding Vic.

"*That is mine.*" The voice that poured out of Sister Wilhem's mouth was horrid. The call of the horn that sounded the end of the world. The screams of a thousand souls awaiting judgement. Johnathan whined, wishing he could clap his hands over his ears. He clawed at the dirt floor.

The Benign turned at the sound. *"Hound,"* it hissed. A drop of blood slid from the Sister's nose. Johnathan recognized that symptom. Divine energy took a toll on the body, and this was its purest unfiltered form. *Like overripe fruit.*

He charged her. The Sister back handed him. The blow sent him flying, but it was the punch of Divine energy behind it that knocked his senses off kilter. Johnathan lost his grip on his form. The transition took him suddenly, a strangely painless shift, considering the agony that wracked his body. Human and naked, he landed in a roll. Johnathan scrambled to his hands and knees, staring in horror at the Sister.

Wilhem took a step toward him, the whites of her eyes turning red where her blood vessels burst. The Benign stopped, frowning down at its hands where bloody bruises bloomed beneath the Sister's pale skin. It turned to look at Vic.

"We are patient," said the Benign. *"We will see you again."*

The Sister exploded in a burst of blood and gore. Vic and Hesper dropped to the ground to avoid the worst.

"That was nothing like overripe fruit," Johnathan wheezed. His stomach rolled. Flecks of Sister Wilhem covered his face and chest. "That was disgusting." He sat down hard in the dirt. Luthor could have shanked him then and there, but the Agent appeared to have fled.

"Told you. Pop." Hesper helped Vic over to him, easing the vampire to the ground. There was a fragile quality to Vic's expression.

"Don't you dare," said Johnathan. Vic flinched.

He looked away, unable to look Johnathan in the eye. "What she said—"

"I am not your blessing," Johnathan snapped. "That is not what connects us."

The wounded look in those grey eyes nearly undid him. "How can you be so sure?" Vic whispered. "Maybe it's my fault you were targeted in the first place. Maybe this has been a long scheme by the Benign."

"Would you shut up," said Hesper. "You two are clearly miserable for each other. Don't let that babbling heretic convince you otherwise." She crouched in front of them, hugging her knees. "You proved me wrong, John. Good job staying alive."

Vic shifted closer to him, wincing at the raw wounds left from the gold. "Do you know what's the worst? I wanted to say yes. I don't even know why. It was as if a part of me wanted to please Kushiel."

Johnathan gently took his hand, threading their fingers together. "But you didn't. And you won't."

"How can you be so sure?" Vic didn't pull away, but fear clung to him.

"Because I trust you, and I know you're strong enough to resist them," said Johnathan.

Vic swallowed. "I hope you are right."

"I am." He pulled Vic toward him, resting his check against the top of his head. "If it was a choice between you and the world, I'd burn it all down. I would do anything to ease your grief because that is how intricately you're entwined with my soul. I would destroy anything that threatened you, not because it's a threat, but because I love you and I put your life above mine."

Vic sucked in a breath, tightening his fingers around Johnathan's. "I fear I lost my heart to you in Cress Haven, the moment you put me in a head lock."

Johnathan grinned, titling Vic's face to crash their lips together. He lost himself in the silk and fire sensations, the scent of citrus and musk vital as air. He'd completely forgotten they had an audience until he heard Hesper's faint sputter.

They broke apart to find the succubus fanning herself. "Woo," she exhaled. "No, sorry, carry on."

Vic burst out laughing, leaning into Johnathan's embrace. There was still a touch of wariness in his eyes, and Johnathan knew the subject continued to bother him. He refused to let the Scarlet Sister's manipulations stain their relationship like she was currently staining his skin.

"God, I need a bath," he groaned.

"And clothes," remarked Vic. "Our wardrobe budget will be atrocious."

They glanced at the grisly scene in the barn, spattered by the remains of Sister Wilhem. The Benign's promise to see them again hung over them with a pall of uncertainty. Merry had thoroughly betrayed them, turning most of Vic's allies against him. They had no idea how many other Agents were out there, seeding bargains for the Nether and hunting vessels for the Benign. There was some truth in Wilhem's words, echoed by Merry's visions. The realms were stirring and they would bring disaster with them. Johnathan didn't know how they could stop such a vast force. He didn't know where they'd begin.

Johnathan sighed. "Where do we go now?"

Hesper cleared her throat, drawing their attention. "There's someone I could take you to." She fidgeted with her skirts. "They could possibly help you hide your essence from any future Favors like the Herald."

They exchanged a look. "It's as good a direction as any," said Vic. "I admit I would appreciate a way to stop those fanatics from finding us so easily. But first." He patted his ragged coat, producing a stained but intact brown parcel. "We rest, restore, and recuperate."

Jonathan stared at the parcel in his hands. "Did Merry bring that to you?"

"Yes," said Vic, a touch of bitterness in his tone. "They apologized for their role in our expulsion. The Society arrived a minute after they left."

Hesper frowned at them. "Do you mean the Seer? Benign touched like you?"

"Yes, our former host," sneered Johnathan. "They cut a deal with Wilhem to isolate Vic in exchange for their safety."

She pursed her lips. "I don't think the Society kept their end of the bargain. I saw them, your Merry, being bound and carted away by the Sister's men."

Vic paled. The news struck Johnathan with a conflict of emotion. He wanted Merry to pay for their betrayal, but if the Scarlet Sisters got their hands on another Benign touched, one with far less pain tolerance than Vic, then the Benign would shake their world sooner rather than later.

Even if Merry's body didn't last long.

"I still need a bath first," said Johnathan. Vic snorted, tucking Johnathan's arm against him.

The future was grim and full of peril, and they would face it together.

EPILOGUE

THE DORMITORY WAS SILENT THIS LATE AT NIGHT, THE PROSPECTIVES taking a well-earned rest after a day of hard training. Alyse longed to join them, the call of her pallet a siren's song as she crept through the empty halls, taking care where she placed her booted feet. A whine of wood might get her caught, another demerit she didn't need impeding her efforts.

The day she watched the train carrying Johnathan and Vic into dangers unknown, she'd boarded the next one heading to Boston. Alyse had a scholar's mind, but her body had a farmer's hardness. Tools she'd applied to her task. The greatest detriment to their success in Cress Haven, the error that nearly killed them all, was their ignorance. If Vic and Johnathan intended to learn more about the otherworldly forces interfering in their lives, Alyse considered it her duty to do the same for the human component.

What she'd learned in the weeks she'd infiltrated this place was enough to curdle her blood, but she knew there was something more, a vital piece of information she needed to save her boys.

She thought of Vic and Johnathan every day, praying they hadn't done anything too stupid without her. With what she'd learned tonight, she the front door of the dormitory opened on silent hinges; she'd greased them herself the second night she was here. It was impossible to conduct secretive business if the door screamed her presence. Cool night air soothed her heated face, a welcome relief from the stuffy interior. The Society's Boston facility was nestled away from the main bustle two streets over, bordered by a spit of thick wooded land that muffled the constant flow of noise. It gave the sensation of being isolated while heavily integrated into the lifeblood of the harbor city.

Alyse headed for the spit of trees, heart pounding in her chest. She knew Vic might argue the wisdom of her current alliance, rightfully so, but there was a secret part of her eager to see her new ally again, for more reasons than she cared to examine. The core of the matter was that she was deep in enemy territory, and she needed all the help she could get.

The plot of trees wasn't wide. During the day, they could glimpse the adjacent neighborhood through the widely spaced trunks. At night, the air was different, the sounds of civilization falling away to something wild and untamed, though Alyse didn't know if that was an effect of the night or the one who waited for her. The caress of night lifted the fine hair on the back of her arms. A whisper of sound murmured in the breeze that brushed her skin. The wind picked up, rushing through the tree trunks in a mourning howl, the baying of hounds on the hunt.

The wind died with a soft sigh. Alyse looked up. A figure stood amidst the pale trunks; a veil draped from the elegant antlers that rose from their brow. Alyse released her breath.

"Hello, Morrigan," she called softly.

"Good evening, my brave one," said the Fae.

Alyse shored her courage. It had brought her this far. "I need a favor."

Thank you for reading! Did you enjoy? Please add your review because nothing helps an author more and encourages readers to take a chance on a book than a review.

And don't miss more in the Midnight Guardians series coming soon!

Until then read more paranormal romance like FLIPPING, by City Owl Author, R. Lee Fryar. Turn the page for a sneak peek!

You can also sign up for the City Owl Press newsletter to receive notice of all book releases!

SNEAK PEEK OF FLIPPING

By R. Lee Fryar

The old lady who thought she owned our house was dead. They were burying her this morning. I watched the funeral from our front porch, cup of coffee in one hand, a warm biscuit in the other.

Alice, dressed in her graveyard best, slipped through the door and glided out next to me, glancing at my coffee cup with detached interest. "How nice of the house to keep that for you."

"It was." I smiled down at the rosebud cup with its delicate gold-leaf handle. It was one of the few things Ms. Martingale owned that might've belonged to this place, back when it was a grand Greek Revival mansion, dripping with Southern antebellum charm and wisteria vines. The morning she died, the entire service, cups, plates, and creamer pitcher, appeared in the butler's pantry for me, brand spanking new. The faint aroma of death already surrounded it like it surrounded everything we ghosts owned in the house.

"I thought you were going with Robert," Alice said. "For spiritual support."

Ah, yes, nothing like a hot guilt trip with breakfast.

"I went to my own funeral. That was one too many." I leaned against the graying column, careful not to slip into it, and stared out at the falling rain.

"You're his mentor. You're supposed to give him the benefit of your experience."

Crimson anger flooded the edges of my essence. "He used to be married. That's plenty of experience." She wasn't going to let this go, but I didn't want to watch Robert turn ten shades of purple if I talked about love, loss, and my "experience."

"Charley, he's not been dead that long—"

"He's eighty-five years old, Alice, a grown man. He fucked up. He's got to deal with it."

She pursed her lips in prudish disapproval. Although greatly faded since the day of her death, her sharp blue eyes could still cut me open. "You might've at least made a showing if you cared." None of us were in the best of moods, not with the recent upheaval in our afterlives.

"Levi went with him. It's better that way. He always knows what to say."

I set my plate on the stone balustrade. The house left it sitting, reminding me there were starving ghosts that would love to have it. They would too. The house baked the best biscuits. But guilt seeped through me, thick and slow as sorghum, turning me puce and taking my appetite with it. I cared. I cared a lot. Dammit, I'd warned the old coot, I had! The dead had no business getting involved with the living. It could only end in grief, and hadn't he, like all of us, had enough grief for a lifetime? If I'd told him once, I'd told him a thousand times, even as he mooned about after the old woman like a love-sick puppy. He chose not to listen. He'd howled for days after they took her body away. No amount of ashes-to-ashes, dust-to-dust consolation would fix things. She'd gone on. Most people do.

It takes a certain kind of personality to be a ghost—a strong resistance to change, a desire for things to remain familiar, an uncompromising soul and... All right, so maybe ghosts are just stubborn or scared out of our pea-picking minds of what lies beyond the grave. That was how it happened for me. I'd died, quite literally with my pants down around my ankles in a quiet alley, and when I came to myself, a door opened in the air in front of me. Now, I'm not saying I saw smoke seeping around the hinges or anything, but it sure wasn't the pearly gates. Nothing lay beyond, only a gray mist. I dithered. Should I go through, take my chances with the door? Or should I stay with the person I'd known my whole life—my corpse? My life had sucked, but at least I knew what to expect. So I stayed. We'd all stayed for one reason or another. Charley Dalton didn't need a better reason than anyone else.

Robert was the youngest ghost. I was forty-five years dead, in my prime—it would be my golden death-day in a month in fact. He was my responsibility. It fell on me to show him how to manage those turbulent years of early ghosthood, where every day was like the next. The monotony could overwhelm a person and make him question his choice. But he seemed like such a sensible man—an investment banker, married, wife deceased, a passel of grandkids, stoic, unassuming—the last kind of man I'd expect to do something stupid like fall in love.

What that ghost needed was a swift kick in his transparent ass. Too late now.

I glanced at the ancient For Sale sign turned over in the grass, marking the end of an age better than any tombstone.

Alice's gaze followed mine. "See anyone we don't know?"

"No," I said.

She drifted closer to me, accompanied by waves of ancient rose fragrance lingering about her like a burial shroud. "Some grandson. He inherits everything and doesn't even bother to go to the funeral."

"Some grandson." I tried and mostly succeeded in not going white around the edges. I wasn't about to admit I'd come out here less to watch the funeral and more to see if I could catch a glimpse of the bulldozer about to ruin our happily-ever-afterlife.

I stuck my hands in the pockets of my faded pants. "Robert will be a sponge when he gets back. I'll have to run him through the wringer with the rest of the sheets."

She frowned. "He needs to get over her, and soon."

"He will."

"Let's hope. We'll all be haunting overtime if that man tries to move in," Alice said. "You aren't old enough to remember when Ms. Martingale and her husband first got here—it was a complete disaster."

"*That's* not going to happen. More than likely, he'll grab his pictures, ransack her jewelry box for those pearls she used to wear, and run. I don't see him wanting to live here."

"He might though, for sentimental reasons."

"The last time he visited he was, what, five? What kind of attachment can he possibly have to—"

Alice straightened, gazing out at the cemetery. "There he is."

I went bright white with anticipation, but it was only Robert, gliding away from the red smear of dirt, all that remained of his love. Levi accompanied him, so transparent I could barely make him out in the rain.

"I'll get Jeff," Alice said. She turned and glided back through the door.

I followed, not without a grimace as I pushed through the heavy oak panels. Alice and Jeff, both aged ghosts, found it easy enough. Levi, the oldest, popped in and out of walls all day long like they weren't there. But for me, going through something solid manifested as a pricking in my essence, a ripping, tearing sensation that left me a bit tattered around the edges. I always came together on the other side as whole as I went in. But I'd yet to lose a moment's hesitation before walking through an object.

The empty house echoed with the sad drip of a roof leak, plunk-plunk-plunking into a bucket in the laundry room. The washed-out light of the rainy day filled the house, turning the silent grandfather clock and faded woodwork a uniform tone of ghost gray. It had been years since I contemplated the house the way the living would see it, years since I'd acknowledged the lie.

The real house—our house—was beyond beautiful. Live oak paneling shone with a golden glow. A banister of the same flanked the grand staircase rising to the second floor. The grandfather clock, polished glass, ticked away eternity by the minutes. Everything around the spiritual architecture could crumble away, but the place we called home would always be perfect. Everything that dies becomes perfect over time—people, food, houses. Provided nobody fucks with them.

I drifted down the long hallway and into my kitchen.

Under the shabby veneer of aged appliances, worn Formica countertops, cheap maple cabinets, and stained linoleum smelling of rancid milk and sour mop water was the most amazing room in the house, at least in my opinion. Soapstone tile floors gleamed, black and shining. Countertops of polished cherry wood glistened with many coats of beeswax. A massive double-basin stone sink with an arched copper faucet easily accommodated the giant stock pot I used for steaming clams. A bank of open windows with shining glass panes admitted the light breeze of a past summer day, a stark contrast to the rain now beating against the single dingy window behind its faded curtain. On the long oak trestle table, the house prepared brunch, popping up plates and silverware like mushrooms through the tablecloth. Buttery biscuits, a hot pot of coffee, fresh milk in a pitcher, and a silver platter of cream cheese danishes appeared.

Shit. Robert must really be feeling bad. Violet with guilt, I took my seat as Robert and Levi came in by the back door.

Robert slouched into the kitchen. A rag followed, busily mopping up after him.

Levi, being far more transparent, didn't even drip. "Hurrah, breakfast!" He sailed to the table, grabbed a biscuit, and started gobbling.

"Well, don't wait for the jelly or anything," I said.

"Mmph, doesn't need jelly," he said, spewing crumbs. "S'delicious, Charley."

I smiled. I appreciated the compliment, particularly since I expected a proper scolding once Levi shed his veneer of a nine-year-old perpetual eating machine and assumed the mantle of ghost-in-charge.

Alice glided in, followed by Jeff, breathtakingly handsome as usual in his military uniform. I'd have loved him in a heartbeat, back when I had one. Just my luck to die and get my first crush on a straight man. It had taken me years to get over it and start thinking of him as a friend.

Robert slumped in his seat with a wet squelch. He eyed the danishes and then set one on his plate.

"So how was it?" Alice asked.

"Nice," Levi said, and downed a giant gulp of milk. "That preacher did the service, the one Robert knocked the teapot over on, remember? And Ms. Edie brought a bunch of gardenias for the grave. They smelled like soap."

"Are you okay, Robert?" Jeff sat down to his cup of coffee and a fresh biscuit, swimming in sorghum.

"No, I'm not okay," Robert said. "I don't understand. She said she'd stay for me." He flung down his fork in a red fury. "She said she loved me. Why did she lie?"

Alice looked at me like I could help.

I stared at the pristine white tablecloth, at a loss for what to say. *Sorry, Robert, the lady did what ladies do, which is what they want. Maybe you weren't everything to her that you thought you were.* I had zero bedside manner when it came to this kind of thing.

"Staying—well, staying is a hard choice, Robert," I said. "Ms. Martingale believed in heaven. At the end, she might've felt a duty to go on. Promises made to a dead man might not mean much when faced with the prospect of seeing her husband again." Personally, I had no family I ever wanted to see again, but Robert would understand. He'd loved his wife, and—

He went the most alarming shade of charcoal.

Fuckkkkkk me. In some ways, it was nice we ghosts wore our emotions as color in our souls, but it also meant a man got a crystal-clear message when he'd screwed up. Charcoal meant despair. Complete, abject despair.

"Perfect." His voice dripped with misery. "She'll go to heaven and tell my wife what we've been doing."

"Good job, Charley," Alice sneered.

"Look, I'm just trying to make a point—she's gone to a better place, and—"

"There's no such thing as heaven." Jeff set his fork down with an audible clink. "Or hell. And if there was, we aren't going to find out. We're ghosts. The morality of the living does not concern us—"

Alice flashed an irritated orange. "Way to go, Jeff. You always know how to make a ghost feel better by completely discounting their religion—"

"Religion is nothing more than the foolish shroud of morality draped over the solid corpse of human ignorance—"

"Shut up, all of you," Levi said. He rose and set his small, ancient hand on Robert's shoulder. "Whatever happened happened. It's over, and we'll go on. It doesn't matter. She's dead now."

Robert relaxed. The gray in his essence faded to a sad, resigned blue.

Levi was right. Ms. Martingale was dead. Robert could love her forever now, no problem. The living were the problem.

"Right now, we can't be angry with each other. We've got to stick together and take care of the house," Levi said. "We don't know when this man is coming. It could be today, it could be tomorrow, or it could be a week from now. We've got one chance to get this house for ourselves. Let's not waste it."

"Here, here," Alice said, raising her coffee cup.

"First things first, I want everyone to keep their eyes peeled for anything out of the ordinary. We know he used to own a sports car. We can watch for it. Jeff, you've got the side street. Alice, watch the upstairs window at the end of the hall. Robert, you take the gardens and the back street behind Ms. Edie's. I'll patrol the neighborhood. Charley, I want you in the front room."

"I have cooking to do," I reminded him.

Levi ignored me. "When one of us spots him, alert the others and send Alice to find me. The rest of you, stick to what you do best."

"I'm not best at anything," Robert muttered.

"You can come out of the closet throwing clothes at him," Levi suggested. "Alice will short out some of the light switches and make the overheads flicker. That's always good for a scare. Jeff can do his ghost moan."

"Really?" Jeff rolled his eyes.

"Better you than Charley. When he does it, it sounds like someone sat on George Washington."

"Or ran the rocker over his tail." Alice snorted her coffee.

"What do you want me to do?" I asked. "Since you say I moan like the cat—should I throw spaghetti at them and see if it sticks?"

Levi fixed me with his perfectly clear eyes. He was so old and see-through that his emotions, like the rain, went right through him. The barest hint of ruby shone in his pupils.

"I want you to push a clock over on him when he walks by it," he said. "I want you to kick him out of bed if he's in it. I want you to pull the chair out from under him if he sits. Whatever it takes to get rid of him, you've got to do it. You're the strongest ghost here, Charley. If he's going to be scared of us—really and truly terrified—it's going to be your job to make sure he is. Understand?"

I understood. This was my chance to redeem myself after Robert. In life, with my own family, wrongs were never forgiven or forgotten. In the afterlife, I could make amends.

"You can count on me," I said. "He won't be able to see me, right? I mean—he's not a kid anymore. He'd outgrow the ability, wouldn't he?"

Levi turned to Jeff. "What do you think? You're the expert on whether living people actually see us or just imagine they do."

Jeff studiously applied himself to his biscuit, avoiding Robert's troubled face. "Ms. Martingale possessed some extrasensory perception. That kind of thing is hereditary, at least to a degree. But she couldn't see Robert any more than she could see the rest of us. I expect her grandson will be the same. He might sense our presence, or feel we are watching him, or believe there are hostile spirits living here—"

"Yeah," Levi said with a gap-toothed grin. "Very hostile spirits. Run him off, and we're good. The house will go up for sale again, and nobody ever buys a haunted house. Everything will be fine."

With that, he dove into the eggs, bacon, and sausage gravy appearing like a grand finale on the table.

Don't stop now. Keep reading with your copy of FLIPPING, by City Owl Author, R. Lee Fryar.

And find more from Kristin Jacques at www.kristinjacques.com

Want even more paranormal romance? Try FLIPPING, by City Owl Author, R. Lee Fryar, and find more from Kristin Jacques at www.kristinjacques.com

---

Charley Dalton died a homeless man. He's *not* about to be a homeless ghost.

When Charley's haunted house passes into the hands of psychic house flipper, Austin Sparks, Charley promises himself and the ghosts he lives with that he'll haunt overtime to get rid of the threat. Once people start pulling up carpets and tearing down walls, a haunted house is doomed.

Charley devises a plan to scare Austin off for good. But Austin Sparks doesn't scare easily. Worse, he's sexy as hell, and soon Charley has a bigger problem than failed plans. He's got the hots for the enemy.

But forbidden romance isn't part of a ghost's happily-ever-afterlife.

ACKNOWLEDGMENTS

Writing is often times a lonely business, but with luck you have friends who will listen to the ranting and raving. Thank you, Lucy and Nicole, for listening to many rants, the inordinate amount of butt stuff, and the memes.

Thank you to MB for being my support New Englander.

Thank you to the City Owl fam for enduring many panicked emails and exclamation points. A huge thank you to Charissa who believed in my series and characters and Danielle who took up the banner. I am so happy to be part of this pub family.

ABOUT THE AUTHOR

KRISTIN JACQUES is an award-winning author of speculative fiction for teens and adults. She currently lives in small town Connecticut with her partner, sons, and two gremlins who think they are cats. When not writing, she's usually chasing her boys around or catching some excellent b-horror movies. She is currently working on projects full of magic, mystery, and delight.

www.kristinjacques.com

 facebook.com/krazydiamondwrites

twitter.com/Krazydiamond07

instagram.com/krazydiamond_writes

bookbub.com/profile/kristin-jacques

ABOUT THE PUBLISHER

City Owl Press is a cutting edge indie publishing company, bringing the world of romance and speculative fiction to discerning readers.

Escape Your World. Get Lost in Ours!

www.cityowlpress.com

 facebook.com/YourCityOwlPress

twitter.com/cityowlpress

instagram.com/cityowlbooks

pinterest.com/cityowlpress